My name is Greg Lane and I am 49 years old. I have been married for 23 years and have 5 children. I grew up in a small southern town in Georgia and have lived in the South my whole life. When I finished high school, I went to Auburn University and graduated with a business degree. I have been an entrepreneur my whole life and lived in many southern towns, finally settling in Auburn, AL to raise my family. My father was in the Vietnam War and used to tell me many different stories about what he did and hearing those during my childhood made me want to become a writer. I chose to write this book because of how inspiring his stories were. I hope all of you enjoy reading it as much as I did writing it. Thank you and God bless!

TABLE OF CONTENTS

CHAPTER 1

CAPTURED! After eight years of difficult, even death defying missions, Jake and Henderson were captured for nothing more than a traffic stop in Yazd, a city in the middle of Iran. They were two of the most wanted American agents that had helped revolutionize the Middle East. Jake and Henderson were the two most important CIA agents that the United States had. They had helped rebels throughout the Middle East with the use of weapons and had gained crucial intelligence throughout the area. These countries governments had finally gotten profiles and names for the two Americans and had gotten word that both Jake and Henderson were in Iran, trying to help a small group of rebels start a revolution. Even though Jake and Henderson had taken all precautions, they could not get away from forty soldiers pointing AK – 47's at their head.

They had no choice but to surrender and now the both of them were hanging with their wrist shackled from the ceiling of dark Iranian prison cell, awaiting their execution. Though they were two of the best agents the CIA had ever had, the United States intelligence community had no idea that they existed. Only Jon Higgins, their handler, who was second in command to Tom Claiborne, head of the CIA, knew of their existence. Claiborne also knew, but would never acknowledge their existence. He would not take the fall for their shortcomings and made sure that Higgins was aware of this. Unfortunately, Higgins would be the only person who could get their freedom.

"Hey Henderson," Jake yelled, the first time he had called his friend by his name in eight years "What's worse, hanging from your wrist awaiting your death, or hell week at our old Frat house."

"Don't know" Henderson startled that his name was called "But at least we know the outcome for our fate this time around."

Jake Garland and Eric Henderson had met within a week of getting on campus at Auburn University. They were suite mates and quickly became friends. Jake was from Montgomery, an only child, coming from a divorced household, whose mother worked days as a maid and nights at a diner to make ends meet. Jake's father had abandoned him and his family when Jake was only two years old. No one had heard from him and most presumed Jake's father had taken up with another woman and moved away to another state. Even though Jake had not grown up with a father, he still had discipline from his mother. Jake's mother saw a potential in him at a very young age and made sure that Jake studied hard all throughout school. It had paid off and Jake had graduated the top in his class and had earned a full scholarship to Auburn University. Even though he had no money, Auburn would pay him his scholarship, plus $500 a month just to come to the school. He wanted to be close to his mother so he accepted and enrolled in the summer of '95.

Eric Henderson, or Henderson, on the other hand, came from a small town called Summerville. It was 20 miles south of Huntsville, AL. He was the fourth of six children, having three brother and two sisters. His parents were still married, with his dad owning Henderson Oil, a chain of 16 convenient stores throughout northern Alabama and southern Tennessee. There was plenty of work for Henderson to do when he was young, and he did not need the financial aid that Jake had used to get into Auburn. Henderson had grown up an Auburn fan and had wanted to go there his whole life. He had made very good grades, but did not warrant a scholarship, but with his Dad's donations to Auburn, he had no problem getting in and he was accepted and enrolled in the summer of '95 as well.

The two hit it off very well and Henderson talked Jake into going through rush. Jake never had time to join any clubs or any types of organizations in high school, because he was either studying or working an odd job. He never had a girlfriend, but was a good looking guy. Jake was 6' 2", athletic, with a muscular build and golden blonde hair, blue eyes and had a personality that could win over a hostile crowd. He was a born leader and coming to college would allow him to see his leadership role. Henderson was 6' and also athletic. He had brown hair and brown eyes. He was not a natural leader like Jake, but was not a push over at all. He was able to convince Jake that joining a fraternity was the best thing that either could do in college for having friends, and most importantly meeting girls.

So both took the plunge and became pledges of Pi Kappa Alpha. Neither one of them new what they had in store for them when joining the order but one thing was for sure, it only strengthened their friendship. Jakes leadership role took over and he was voted president of his pledge class. After five months of pledge ship, hell week started- a week when anything goes. The pledges could not sleep and ate nothing but leftovers. They had to do whatever a brother asked from them, but finally after the week was over; they were initiated into the order and were brothers for life. Even though Jake and Henderson were not blood related, they felt like brothers and would back each other up at all cost. They had a bond that would be hard to break and would help them excel in their near future.

Both decided that computer science was their destination and decided that would be their major. Since home computers were so new in the mid 90's, it excited both of them and they wanted to be a part of this new development. One day during the fall of their sophomore year, a member of the Justice Department was doing interviews and having students take IQ test. This interested Jake so he took it and he had Henderson take it as well. After finishing the test and interview, they went on their way and over time completely forgot about the exams.

Later that year, in December of '96, Jake received a phone call from his aunt. She told him that his mother had been killed in an automobile wreck and that he needed to come home to make the funeral arrangements for her. This was the only family he had ever known. He loved his mother. She had given him everything she had and had encouraged him to follow his dreams to school. Jake was in total shock. He had just talked to her the other day and could not wait to come home for Christmas. Now, he would have to have Christmas alone. Henderson was there for him. He went to Montgomery with Jake and helped with all the arrangements. After the funeral, Henderson invited Jake to come to his home in Summerville for Christmas. Jake accepted the invitation and kept his grief to himself. He knew that his mother would want him to be strong and this was not the time for him to feel sorry for himself. This would lead him to change how he looked at life and also made him fearless. He knew Henderson was the only family he had and he made sure Henderson knew how much he appreciated him.

Jake and Henderson decided to stay for the summer of '97 and get an early start on the junior year. In August of that year, they came back to their fraternity house where they both lived. They notice their door was opened and thought that one of the brothers of the house had entered and played a prank on them, but instead there were two men in dark suits that wanted to talk to Jake. Henderson was asked to leave, but Jake did not want to be alone with to complete strangers who had broken into his room.

"Whatever needs to be said or done, Henderson will stay" Jake exclaimed.

"Jake Garland, we are head hunters for the FBI and have been watching you for over six months. You scored a perfect score on our FBI IQ test and had an outstanding interview. We know that you have not finished college, but we have a way that you can earn your degree and start with us by September. Are you interested in coming into our program?"

Jake had been taken for a back. Since his mother's death, he really had no idea what kind of profession he wanted to do. He liked computers, but he did want to add more adventure into his life.

"Guys, you break into my room and give me credentials, tell me what I want to hear, but what kind of work would I do? I really do not even like the government and have never had any interest in working for them. I see myself as an outdoor guy anyway and do not want to be trying to catch some criminal writing bad checks and things. Thanks for stopping by, but I am not interested. I want to finish school and enjoy the last two years."

The two men in suits remained quiet. They did not answer Jake, but instead they handed him a card. The card read that they would be staying at the local Best Western for the next couple of days. If Jake would change his mind, he should stop by and talk. Jake thought that it was odd for them to hand out a card for a response, but was polite and told them thanks. He informed them that they should just go back to Washington and he would not be stopping by. The two men nodded their heads and left his room.

Henderson had been lying on the couch and saw the whole thing transpired. He finally spoke up and said, "What the hell was that? You are twenty years old. Do they think you are just going to go to the FBI and change the world or something? I say the hell with them. Let's get out of here and go hang out."

Jake agreed with him and they left his room and went to a local establishment that did not check ID's. They hung out for a few hours drinking a couple of beers and shooting some pool.

"Man, I am not worried about this government stuff; I am just worried about the next party at the house and trying to hook up with some chick." Jake said as he drunk another sip out of his twenty ounce beer mug. Henderson agreed. They were two young guys that could only think of girls and having a few parties. The Justice Department was the least of their worries.

The next morning Jake got out of bed, having not slept a bit. He tried, but could not the two men in suits he had met the day before out of his mind. He questioned himself wondering if he wanted to work for the FBI. After blowing the two men in suits off the day before, he now began to have second thoughts. He wondered if they were right and if he would indeed be good at what they talked about. He began to think back at the test he took and could not believe that he tested off the charts. He thought back to his mother, who had pushed him to do his best and to find his talent. He wondered if this would be his talent. He knew that the only way that he would find out if he actually accepted what the two men presented to him. He was excited, but he did not want to go into this new adventure by himself. He wanted his good friend Henderson to come along with him and join the FBI if he did. Jake had always been able to convince Henderson to join him in his fraternity pranks, but he knew that this was something completely different than a prank.

Jake walked into Henderson's room and said, "Hey Henderson, get up."

Henderson, who liked to sleep late, answered with his eyes shut, "What's up Jake? You look tired, did you get any sleep?"

Jake replied "I been thinking all night. As you know, my mother is dead; I do not have a girl friend. I love Auburn, but really do not know if there is a life for me in computers. I may give this FBI thing a try."

"Really?" Henderson answered, but looked puzzled at what Jake had said.

"Yeah," Jake answered with a serious look on his face. "But I am not going to do it if you don't do it with me."

"Are you serious, Jake?" Henderson answered with a smile on his face, thinking that Jake was kidding. "You want me to do this thing too? Those FBI guys did not even want to talk to me. They could care less about me."

"Henderson," Jake answered. "The only way that I go to the FBI is if you go with me. I will make sure that they understand that. If it does not work out we will have our degrees and can get started doing something else. Hell, I like adventure. This may be more than just wearing a dark suit and catching illegal gambling. It might even be fun."

"I tell you what, Jake," Henderson responded. "If you can convince them to take me, then I am in."

Now all Jake had to do was convince the FBI that if they wanted him, they would have to take Henderson. He would not go it alone.

That afternoon Jake and Henderson drove over to the Best Western. Jake told Henderson to stay in the car and he would go up and talk to the two men. He knocked on the door and it opened to one of the guys in the suit. He told Jake that he was expecting him and that his partner had already left to go back to Washington to set everything up.

"You do not even know that I want to be a part of the FBI," Jake said.

The man simply stood their staring a Jake trying to intimidate him, but Jake did not back down. After a minute the man said, "I knew you would be a good one. You did not blink and you looked me straight in the eye. If you can continue to do that you will be a huge addition to our organization. I have been in this business a long time and know that is why you came to see me. Isn't that right Jake Garland?"

"Before I agree to be a part of this organization I have one request. Henderson, my best friend who has become a brother to me, has to come along as well."

The man in the suit replied, "As I said before, I have been in this organization for a long time, 17 years to be exact and I take every scenario into play. I figured that you would ask that question and sent my partner back early yesterday. We had started on your paperwork, but when we saw your bond with Henderson in your room yesterday, we figured that it was best to get started on two orders instead of one. It will be done. I have gotten confirmation that you and Henderson will start Sept 1. I already have your plane tickets printed and they are in this envelope."

He handed Jake a manila envelope and continued, "Your itinerary is also inside this envelope. It will tell the two of you where we are meeting and also what time. Remember, do not be late."

The agent shut the door and in just a short instance, Jake and Henderson had made a life changing decision. They would leave their comfortable lives at Auburn and move to Washington to be FBI agents. The two of them were anxious, but exited and had no idea what would be in store for them.

It was now the summer of '99, and Jake and Henderson had no idea that they would be going such an intense training and for so long. They had been in northern Virginia now for two years and had yet been told what the FBI had in store for them. Both though, had now chiseled into two fine specimens, who were experts with a gun and also hand to hand combat. They were twenty-two years old, but were older than they looked. They were drilled with training over the last two years and they seemed to be trained better than most field agents. The only thing that they lacked was field experience. They knew that was coming, but another type of training was right around the corner.

One afternoon after a five mile run, both Jake and Henderson walked into their room at the training facility. There was a man in their room waiting for them. His name was Jon Higgins. Higgins was a gray haired man in his mid to late forties. He was a retired green beret, who had done some intelligence work during the first Iraq War. He left the Green Berets and had done some field work for the FBI. He later left the FBI and began working for the CIA, where he had moved up the chain of command at a rapid pace. He had level 5 clearances, which was the highest for any classified material. He was ruthless with his enemies and did not trust anyone. People knew never to cross him for fear that their days would be numbered in the agency. Many people believed his ruthlessness had to do with his late wife. She had died of cancer early in his career, and it left him bitter. He never remarried. Though he was respected, he was feared even more and people knew not to get in his way.

Higgins had just started a new project and he was looking for new prospects. Because he had worked with the FBI, he still had contacts that kept him abreast of new recruits and their achievements. He was looking for two young guys who had impeccable working behavior and also an unblemished record. His main objective was for the two new recruits to only do things he wanted them to do and answer only to him. He was informed of the progress that Jake and Henderson had accomplished and the two seemed to be exactly what he wanted. Higgins had come to their room to see if they had any interest in what he had to offer.

"Young men," Higgins said with a deep voice. "I have been looking over your training records for the last two years. You both have put together an unbelievable resume. Jake, you have the highest marks in fire arms and hand to hand combat that I have ever read in a file. Henderson, you are second only to Jake for the past two years. Both of your testing has been off the charts. Well enough of the flattery. My name is Jon Higgins. I work in intelligence and am looking for two young men who would like to join me in a new venture. Would you guys be interested in hearing what it might entail?"

The two looked puzzled. They had been in training for the last two years, yet have not been given any assignments, and now it looks as if there career is being completely shifted in another direction. Jake and Henderson were told early in their training that things would change at any time and for them to be ready for it. Both of them being young and naive were eager for a change, for some action.

"As you know, Mr. Higgins, sir" Jake answered, "We work as a team, the two of us. We have been talking lately that we are ready for field action. What kind of work would we be doing?"

Higgins handed them a vanilla envelope. "Everything is in there. I will be in touch."

Jake and Henderson were indeed intrigued. They had been training for two long years. Even though they were young, they knew that they were ready for action, for adventure.

"What is in the envelope?" Henderson asked.

Jake opened it expecting a lot of detail notes and directions, but it was just two words: Eagle and Mustang, two names that they would become accustomed to over the next 10 years.

"What the hell does this mean?" they both yelled.

They could not believe this. This only made what Higgins had said, even more intriguing. When was he going to contact them? They knew that they were eager to hear more of the new project he had talked about. They wanted to be a part of it.

Two weeks had gone by and no word from Higgins. Jake and Henderson had not forgotten about the meeting with Higgins, but figured he did not want them to be involved with the project. The phone rang around midnight one night.

Jake answered the phone and he heard, "Eagle and Mustang, meet at 1350 Boulevard Way at 14:00 hours."

The phone went silent and a dial tone was heard on the other end.

"Hey Henderson, wake up."

Henderson moved a little and grunted. Jake knew he was awake so he asked Henderson, "I think we have a meeting with this guy Higgins tomorrow at two o'clock. Do you want to do check it out?" Jake asked.

"I guess," Henderson grunted, "at least we will talk with him and find out a little more about it. Now let me go back to sleep."

Henderson rolled over and fell back to sleep, but Jake was too excited to sleep. He stayed up the rest of the night wondering what Higgins had in store for them.

The two of them arrived a little before two just to get the lay of the land. Actually, it wasn't much to get the lay of. They arrived at a beautiful white brick home. It looked to be a very big home and it was located beside other big homes. This must be where Higgins lives, Jake thought.

"I guess this guy Higgins just wants us to come over and talk a little," Henderson said.

"Who knows," Jake answered, "Let's go in and see what he wants."

They walked up to the house and knocked on the big oak door. An older lady, who looked to be in her 70's opened the door.

"Can I help you boys?" she asked.

"Yes mam," Jake replied. "Eagle and Mustang are here. I hope this is the right place."

"Oh yes, I have been expecting you. Come in. Make yourselves comfortable. Would you two nice boys want some tea?" She asked.

"Yes, mam," they both replied as they went over to the sofa to sit down.

Right before they were about to sit down, Higgins appeared. "Are you guys ready to change your whole aspect in training and go into a totally different direction?" Higgins asked.

"We don't know," Jake answered. "That is why we are here. Could you please tell us what you want us to do?"

"It is quite simple, really," Higgins answered. "As you know I work in intelligence, basically I am an operative for the CIA. I could tell you about my credentials, but the two of you would not be here if that is what you are interested in. Instead, I am going to get right to the point. We have a different war to fight now. The days of the Cold War are behind us and Russia is more our ally than our enemy. There is a different enemy that we have to fight and that enemy is not one country anymore.

We all know about the army, the navy, etc., but we need to try and start a different type of war. As you both know, terrorism is our biggest threat to our national security. We may never fight another country, but we will have to contend with insurgents, who live all over the world. I am now the commander of a new army. We will help other insurgents on our side to defeat these terrorists that may one day come over here to hurt us. I am looking for two young men, like you, to help our country train our allies so that they can defeat these terrorists.

Higgins continued, "The two of you will have to give up your names and be known only as Eagle and Mustang. You will not live here in the U.S., but be stationed all throughout the world. Your contact and handler will be me. I will be known simply as Buckeye. Never refer to me by name or yourselves by name. This is very important. If your identity is ever revealed, it could cost you your life. Yes, this is a dangerous world and you will face many dangerous missions, but there is great reward for you in the end."

"How long are we talking about?" Henderson asked.

"What is the reward?" Jake wondered aloud.

"There is no time table set for these missions to end," Higgins answered. "Your reward will be more than you will ever realize. Now do you guys want to be a part of this new army and help fight and destroy the enemy that wants to destroy you; Yes or no?"

"Yes," they both answered. "When do we start?"

The elderly lady came back into the room. She had two glasses of tea and laid them both on a table in front of Jake and Henderson.

"Drink your tea," Higgins said, "and I will let you know when the training starts when you finish."

They both finished off the tea and were eager to hear when they would start. Jake looked over at Henderson and saw that he had passed out. Before Jake could say anything, he passed out on top of Henderson. The training had just begun.

CHAPTER 2

Higgins had many contacts all over the world, but his most important contacts were located in the Middle East. As a young man, Higgins helped the Afghan army in the late 80's. He helped them train for combat which enabled them to win their war against the Russians. He later moved all over the Middle East and got permission to set up a small training camp in Saudi Arabia. He set up a camp in the mid 90's and it was established to train recruits in the ways and culture of the Middle East. Higgins knew that the only way to be successful as a spy was to be able to mix right in. This camp helped to train many of Higgins recruits in spying, combat, and most importantly how to adapt to the land. He had trained many, but was still looking for the two agents who could help change the world. Jake and Henderson seem to fit the bill by his standards.

"Wake up; it is time to get started." Higgins shouted at the two new recruits.

They had been drugged with a very powerful sleeping pill that had put both of them out for almost 24 hours.

"Where are we?" they asked.

"You will know soon enough, but right now put these clothes on and meet me in that tent over there. You guys need to get some food in you and I will tell you what you will be doing for the next two years."

Jake and Henderson were definitely ready to start whatever assignment that lay ahead of them. They changed their clothes and went into a tent where they met Higgins.

"Well, what do you have in store for us?" they asked him.

"I will put it to you like this," Higgins said. "You are in Saudi Arabia at our training facility for anti-terrorist activity. You will be here for the next two years under my supervision. This will be the most intense operation that you will ever go through, mentally and physically. By the time the training is over the two of you will be expert sharpshooters, you will be trained in taekwondo, a hand to hand combat, you will learn many different languages, and you will be able to adapt to different cultures. The thing I mentioned is the most important. The faster you learn to adapt to your environment, the longer you will live. There is no turning back, gentlemen. You will only answer to me and as I said earlier, forget your names and identities. Jake, you are Mustang and Henderson, you are Eagle. Never give your names to anyone. That could be your downfall. Do you understand?"

Higgins was a no nonsense person who wanted things to go his way. He demanded respect and earned every bit of it.

Over the next two years of training, Jake and Henderson learned more than they thought they could ever learn about espionage. Higgins had a team of trainers that were the best in the world at what they did. He came and went from the camp, but kept up on all of his recruits. He especially followed the progress of his two youngest recruits, Jake and Henderson. He knew that they were ready for assignments and new that the two would do his bidding for him and do it without ever being caught. If anything leaked out about what they were up to, he knew his camp would be shut down and all his plans would be squashed. He was very reluctant to put recruits out in field, but knew that his two prize recruits could do the job.

Higgins came to his two recruits and said, "Mustang and Eagle, it is time, your time. You both are ready and will be a team. Always guard you backs. The more you trust each other, the longer you will stay alive. Remember, you will only answer to me, Buckeye. You will get your information through different channels. There will be codes that only you know how to decipher. When you get them, you will know what to do. I have faith in both of you. Good luck."

That was the end of their training. They had lasted four two long years and it was finally over. They were ready to go. Their adventure started in the summer of 2001. Jake and Henderson both loved each other like brothers. They were always on the same page and trusted each other with their lives. They had assignments that took them throughout the most dangerous place in the Middle East. They helped set up all kinds of plots to eliminate terrorist all over these dangerous areas. They knew what they did helped the United States government, but sadly no one would ever know what they were doing. Neither had been home in eight years and in the summer of '09 they got a message from Higgins. This was unusual, even though he was their handler; he had never sent a message like this before. After decoding it, all signs pointed that it was a legit message.

It read, "Go to Yazd, Iran. You will meet a contact. The contact will tell you what to do. After completion, you will come home: Buckeye."

This seemed like any other mission that they had been on before, but this one was a little different, there was a completion at the end of the mission. Jake and Henderson would get to come back home, back to Alabama. Both of them were 30 years old now and were ready for a short break and the thought of going home made this mission the most important that they had ever done.

Jake and Henderson were in the back of an old pickup truck on a dirt road to Yazd, Iran. All of a sudden, an explosive rocket came out of nowhere and blew up right in front of the pickup truck. Jake and Henderson had been in similar situations before, but this was different. Someone knew they were coming. The enemy was prepared and had blocked off all escape routes. Jake and Henderson were trapped and could not go anywhere. A tank camp up from behind them and an army of about forty men armed with ak-47s told them to get out of the truck.   Jake and Henderson were finally caught. After eight years of espionage, they were caught by the Iranian army. The Iranian government had been tipped off that these two were going to be in this area. They jumped at the chance to capture two of the most notorious American infidels. Jake and Henderson knew their fate, and it would be death.

By this time Higgins had moved up the chain of command and had become second in command in the CIA. He had heard of his two prize soldiers getting caught in Iran and knew that the United States government would not recognize them as captives. He wanted to get them out of there, but had to persuade the head of the CIA, John Claiborne, to help him. Mustang and Eagle were classified and Higgins had set up this classified operation so that only he and the director knew about them and what they had been doing.

"Director Claiborne," Higgins said as he walked into the director's office and shut the door. "It has come to my attention that two of our foot soldiers have been captured in enemy territory and have been sentenced to death."

Claiborne looked up, knowing why Higgins was in his office. He responded, "Well, what do you suggest that we do?"

Higgins had been in contact with channels in the Iranian government and knew that they would only free his two agents on one condition; the United States had to release 50 known terrorist that Israel had captured only a few days before, ironically with the help of Mustang and Eagle. He informed the director of this and Claiborne looked up from his desk and shook his head.

He looked right into Higgins eyes and said, "The price is too steep. I say we stay put. I am not going down with this one. Do what you have to do, but know this, there will be consequences for these actions of getting caught. They knew what would happen to them when they came into this operation. I am sorry that they were captured, but that is all the remorse that I will give concerning this unfortunate event. Remember, I will cover your butt concerning this, but not these two boys. They are now finished in my book."

Higgins could not release anyone. He knew that Jake and Henderson had put in eight unbelievable years and he felt the United States owed it to them to save their lives, but he knew the United States policy and they would not release any terrorist. Higgins had to come up with a different task, but he did not have much time. He had told Jake and Henderson that if they were captured, they could die. Higgins hands were tied, but he did have one other way.

"Unlock them and get them out of here." Jake and Henderson heard an Arabic voice say. They had no idea where they were going.

"Put these over their eyes and put the bags over their heads."

This was a scary moment for both Jake and Henderson. They did not know what was going on. They had been tortured, starved, deprived of sleep. They were very weak and could barely walk. "Grab onto this and walk this way," a voice said.

Jake and Henderson grabbed onto a long wooden pool and walked quickly. Their legs were shackled and hands were tied together. They could not see where they were going, but the voice led them into the back of a truck. They were pushed into the truck and the truck sped away.

The time went slowly and it seemed like an eternity, but finally the truck stopped. They were pushed out of the truck. When they stepped out, they had no idea what their fate was going to be. They heard the truck speed away, but still could not see what was going on. A few minutes later, they heard a helicopter sound. It was coming closer. They heard it land on the ground.

"There isn't much time. Get in," a voice said to them.

Jake and Henderson had no idea what was going on, but the voices sounded American so they did what they were told. "Get those bags off their heads and the blindfolds off. Cut the ropes off their hands. We'll get those leg shackles off when we get back to base."

When the blindfolds came off, they looked around and were felt like they were in shock. "We thought we were going to die today," they both exclaimed.

"Not today," the soldier behind the voice said. "You boys are going home."

It took a few days after they were released, but they finally made it back to the States. This was the first time that they had been on their home soil in ten years. A lot had changed and they wondered what was to come of them. Why were they freed and where do they go from here, they thought. Jake and Henderson received a note from the military pilot when they were leaving the plane. The note read, "Come to the Langley. I will speak to you there: Buckeye."

It took a few days, but they made it to Langley, the location of CIA headquarters. Once the arrived there was a soldier there to meet them. He had them follow him and he took them down a few flights of stairs and into a room. The room was all white with a table and three chairs. There was also a mirror in the room. The soldier told them to wait and he walked out of the room.

Jake and Henderson entered the room and sat down. They waited for awhile and finally the door opened. It was Higgins.

"You boys alright?" he asked them.

Jake did not know what to say. It had been a long time sense he had seen his mentor. He wanted to get out of his chair and give him a hug, but knew that the best thing for him to do was to sit still and stay quiet. Henderson followed Jake's lead and also remained quiet.

Higgins asked the two the same question, but this time Jake and Henderson answered back that they were fine.

"You guys did a lot of good things for me, but unfortunately for you, you guys screwed up in the end. You got caught. I had to give up a lot to get you guys back. I felt responsible for you, but unfortunately, my butt is on the line. I will not go into detail about what transpired for your return. I can only tell you that your time is up with the agency. Your file will be deleted. You two are now civilians. I did tell you that you would be rewarded when this was over, and your reward is your life. Good day and God bless."

Higgins got up and left the room.

"That's it. That's all. This is crazy!" Jake yelled. "We put in ten years and that's all we get. I've got nothing. You've got nothing, Henderson. We completely change our identities for the last ten years and our government tells they do not owe us anything. What are we going to do?"

"I tell you what I am going to do," Henderson said. "I am going home. I haven't seen my parents, brothers, or sisters in ten years. I am tired of this life. We are still young and have plenty of years left. Higgins was right about one thing, our reward is our life."

Jake was not finished. He said to Henderson, "I love you man, but I cannot believe that you are not pissed off. This is all I know. What the hell am I going to do? I have no home, I have nowhere to go."

Jake was angry. He wanted someone's ass for being told that his duty was over. Right then, the soldier came back and said "Let's go. Follow me."

He took them to the front door of the Pentagon and led them outside. The soldier looked at them and said "Have a nice day."

It was over. Just like that. Ten years of servitude to the government to make America safer and it was over.

"Henderson," Jake said. "You have been a brother to me and I love you for that. You go home and see your parents. I am going to stay here for a while and see if I can talk to someone who knows something. I will come down and see you in a couple of weeks."

"Are you sure you going to be okay" Henderson ask.

"Yeah, I will be fine. I will see you in two weeks."

Jake grabbed Henderson, gave him a hug and walked away. Henderson had a feeling that he may never see Jake again, but yelled out, "You will come down in two weeks."

Jake turned around and said, "I will see you in two weeks."

CHAPTER 3

East Africa, located in the northeast corner of Africa, had become a very powerful country overnight. It was a country that was bordered by Sudan to the in the west, Ethiopia in the south, Eritrea in the north, and the Red Sea to its east. It was a young country, formed ten years earlier, being a buffer zone to two countries, Sudan and Ethiopia, who had been in conflict against each other for over the last ten years.

Sudan and Ethiopia got into a disagreement over land and ports that were located beside the Red Sea. The disagreement became larger and it lead to troops being sent to each other's borders and eventually a war ensued between the two countries. The conflict lasted for almost a decade until the United States and United Nations stepped in to end the bloodshed. Neither country wanted to surrender, feeling that a defeat would be demoralizing to their people. The United States stepped in and drew up a treaty, but neither country could agree on it. The United State pressured both to sign it, ending the long conflict. Because neither side could agree on the land and ports, the treaty that the two governments signed, took away the land and ports in question from both countries and a small country was formed that became known as East Africa.

This agreement angered both Sudan's and Ethiopia's governments, but it did not matter because the United States backed the new country. The United States needed an ally in the region and basically established a new country for this purpose. Unfortunately for the United States, it only seemed to breed more hatred toward the super power from other countries around the world. The United States needed more allies, with all the danger in the world and felt that it had a trusted friend in the newly formed, American backed East Africa.

Ten years passed since the country was formed and it was now the year 2019. The United States, the peacemaker earlier in the century, was hated even more throughout the world, especially in the Middle East and Africa. The Iraq war ended a few years earlier, longer than ever expected, and this event fueled the hatred that had spawned over most countries in the region. Many new terrorist cells had formed and were causing higher deaths and destruction throughout the world than ever before. Their main targets were toward the American military and also toward American civilians. There seemed like there was no end in sight.

Not only were the American people worried about their safety, they were now worried about energy consumption. The demand outweighed the supply, not only in the United States, but throughout the world as well. The price of oil had sky rocketed and year after year gas prices continued to rise. It became such an issue that it finally caused the biggest energy crisis the world had ever seen. Prices for gasoline went well over twenty dollars a gallon and the world's economy was at a standstill because of this. There seemed to be no end in sight for oil prices. Unfortunately, other technology had not become a substitute and oil still remained the standard and number one source of energy. It had now become a scarce commodity.

Everything seemed to change in the spring. A discovery of epic proportions was found in the northern region of East Africa. The discovery was oil and it was the largest the world had ever seen since oil was discovered in the Middle East in the early 1900's. The discovery was in its early stages, but many experts believed it could help change the fate of the world. It was predicted that the discovery could help solve the energy crisis, bring gas prices down, and revamp many economies around the world, especially the United States.

There was one problem with the discovery in East Africa; the government was run by one man, Mahmud Osman Kier, who at one time was backed by the United States government. He was put in place by the United States government ten years earlier and welcomed the United States with opened arms. He was a peaceful ruler for the first eight years, but something changed and over the last two years, he had become power hungry and had led his country with an iron fist. Early in his tenure, he had relied on the United States as an ally, but had recently turned his back on them and cut off all ties.

Mahmud Osman Kier was born in the Sudan, but had moved away at a very young age. His father was a diplomat for the Sudanese government and became an ambassador to Great Britain. Because of this, Kier's father was able to give his family more than what most Sudanese men could. He sent his children to the best private schools that England had to offer, he gave them the best clothes to wear and he always had food on the table for them to eat. Kier's father pushed his children toward the western culture for he saw no future for them in his native land. He saw the prosperity in the West and he tried to instill in his children to embrace the West, hoping that they would never go back to their homeland.

Mahmud Osman Kier excelled in his early years and earned a scholarship to Oxford, in England. After four years, he graduated and moved to the United States, deciding to attend Harvard and received a master's degree in African studies. The next three years would shape his direction the rest of his life. It was now the mid 90's, and Kier got to see firsthand how prosperous America was. He studied about Africa and Sudan and realized how little his country had. He envisioned one day of going back to his homeland, uniting it and bringing it prosperity as well. He knew it was a dream, but he also knew that sometimes dreams came true.

Kier embraced the Western culture and felt that he could take this culture back to Sudan. He wanted to help his country and as soon as he finished his education in the States, Kier left for Sudan. He came back to his country in the late 90's, as a young, naïve man, who vowed to make a difference in his new home. He would make a difference, but the difference would be for a new country that would be formed in the near future, because there was no hope for his homeland.

Kier had now entered his mid twenties and had entered his new country, hoping to make an immediate impact. He saw the turmoil and poverty Sudan was suffering from. There was no order or law and villages were run by the local militia. Each militia ruled the villages by fear, using rape and murder to keep the villagers in order. Kier saw his countrymen suffering from lack of leadership and went to them, preaching freedom and hoping to help them.

Kier disliked the Sudanese government and vowed to the people that he would help change their lives for the better. He had traveled throughout the country trying to bring hope and peace to anyone that would listen. Five years passed since he had arrived and he knew his purpose was to bring unity and prosperity to his country. It would not be easy and there would be many obstacles standing in his way, but Kier would not let this slow him down.

He became the leader of a small uprising in the region and formed his own militia. He controlled the eastern region of Sudan. This was a very important part of Sudan because the port to the Red Sea was located in the region. He controlled the imports and exports that went in and out of the country. The port's importance grew over the years and Sudan's economy rose at an enormous rate. Kier's importance grew as business grew.

Ethiopia noticed the importance of the port and the growth of Sudan's economy. They wanted control of the port. They assembled troops and sent them to take over the region. Sudan did not want this to happen and they sent their own troops, but in an unexpected move, Kier refused their help. He had been able to build his own militia and he also had an ace in his bag of tricks. He turned to the military assistance of the United States for assistance against the Ethiopian military forces.

This infuriated the government of Sudan as they responded by sending troops to take back control of the port. Unfortunately, for Sudan, the United States military had already flocked to the region. A huge battle between them ensued. The Sudanese army was no match to the biggest military in the world and the battle was over within days.

Meanwhile, Ethiopia continued toward the port, but Kier and his militia stopped them before they got there. American troops turned their attention to Ethiopia's military and they completely dismantled it in matter of a few weeks. For his courageous actions, Kier became an instant hero and popularity grew throughout the region.

Because of the conflict, the region was not safe between Sudan and Ethiopia. There was a feeling that another attack could be imminent. The State Department, feeling heat from the rest of the world, needed a truce in the region and worked with both countries on a treaty. Against the wishes of both Sudan and Ethiopia, the United States and United Nations established a new country called East Africa. It would be a buffer between the two feuding countries with Kier becoming the leader of the new country. He had gone to the region to bring peace to Sudan, but gave up on the idea and focused his efforts on East Africa. He did not think that Sudan had much hope, but he saw the potential of East Africa and took on the responsibility.

The United States did not have any allies in the region outside of Israel, but with the establishment of East Africa, a new ally in a very tumultuous part of the world was formed. No one would have thought that that the newly formed country that was established by the United States would have played a major role in the world in the near future, but something would make this country a major force in the world.

During the first few years of East Africa's existence, the United States trained a small military force of East Africans. The military was small, but was backed by the American military, which was not too shabby. Because East Africa was surrounded by the United States' enemies, they were able to build an unbreakable border. It was a huge fence that was built by the United States and took over two years to build. Some experts compared it to the Great Wall of China, but it was built to keep the enemy out, not to keep anyone in the country. It was a safe country and the people were free to come and go as they pleased. This helped the people of East Africa to enjoy a freedom that most people in the region never had experienced. That experience was peace and the people were ever grateful to their leader, Kier.

During the war, later called the East African Revolutionary War, a cleric served under Kier by the name, Qatar. He had been the lead advisor to the leader of the Sudanese government. Unfortunately for him, his services were belittled by the current administration and he knew that his days were numbered. He went to Kier offering support and strategy and was a key for their victory and separation from Sudan. Qatar pledged his allegiance to Kier and Kier rewarded him by anointing him supreme leader of the East African military, even though it was relatively small with only five hundred troops. They would work side by side for the next decade.

No other country dared to take on the small military of East Africa, for fear that the United States would unleash its' fury on anyone who dared to harm its only ally in the region. East Africa enjoyed the freedom from any attack from outside its wall and also inside its wall. The people were rewarded with ten years of peace and this allowed it to prosper and grow economically. In only ten years it went from a tumultuous, third world region, to an economically strong and peaceful country. Industry boomed, and the people enjoyed their lives.

The people of East Africa were of Sudanese and Ethiopian backgrounds. They had never enjoyed freedom and prosperity that East Africa would attain. The people were used to tyranny and poverty and Kier had a challenge on his hand. During his time as leader of the region he had brought some prosperity to them, but freedom was entirely a different state of mind for them. He knew the only way to accomplish this was to change the landscape of the new nation. He went to the United States for even more help.

He had convinced the people of East Africa that he looked after their well being and had their interest at heart. He was loved by his countrymen and the people believed everything that he told them. Not only did he feel loved by his people, but on the other hand, he felt that he was also a target for his enemies. Because Kier feared for his safety, he was able to convince the people of East Africa and the United States government that he needed protection.

He had a huge lavish palace built where he would live and establish his government. It was built in New Helen, the capital city of East Africa and it took two years to complete. It was one of the largest of its kind, but more importantly, it was built for his safety. He was overwhelmed by it, proclaimed that the palace would be for all the people of East Africa. He allowed the people to tour it, much like the White House in Washington.

He continued to allow the United State access into his country. He accepted more aid from them and in turn allowed the United States to bring into his country new businesses and commerce. This would better his young country, helping to bring it into the 21st century. Over time East Africa had new roads, electricity, running water, and even new homes. There were still some small villages that had not enjoyed the transformation, but all in all, especially in the two biggest cities of East Africa, New Helen and Turin, which was the second largest city in the country, enjoyed a better way of life.

East Africa became a booming country and an industrial superpower of which the continent of Africa had never seen. The country prospered like no other country in the region. He continued to have great relations with the American government. Kier had them continue to send aide to his country. Years passed and he allowed the U.S. to send their best engineers over to the East Africa to look for any raw materials that would help not only his country, but the United States as well.

During their time in they were in East Africa, the engineers came across an unimaginable find. While mining for coal, they discovered a strange activity in the northern part of the country. When they began to drill they could not believe what they had found. The discovery that they had uncovered, led the largest oil reserves that had ever been discovered in the modern age.

Unfortunately the discovery was the beginning to the end of the ten year friendship the U.S. had with East Africa. During the next few months after the oil was found, things seemed too changed for the worse very quickly in East Africa. The engineers that had helped with the discovery had mysteriously disappeared. When authorities for the United States came over to investigate, they were not let into the country. When the State Department asked for an explanation, they did not get a response.

Kier, who had been a friend to the United States, had inexplicitly changed his views toward America. For no apparent reason, he cut off all ties to the U.S. and became a recluse. He retired to his palace and quit making live appearances outside of the palace. He only addressed the people of East Africa and the United States with video that was taped days before. Because he was such a recluse, no one knew what had come over him. They figured his change had to be because of the oil and all the power it possessed. Overnight, peace and freedom, which the people of East Africa had experience for the last decade, were replaced with tyranny and death all over again. Two weeks after the engineers' disappearance, the United States received a memo from Kier that they were no longer an ally, but an enemy to him and that they would not have any chance to receive oil from him.

Earlier in the decade, every African and Middle Eastern country had vowed together to keep all Westerners out of its borders. It was centered toward United States, but East Africa had refrained from that vow and continued to keep the United States as a close ally. But all that changed in only a matter of weeks and East Africa joined the pledge against the powerful country located in the West.

The young country which America had formed and protected, join the vow with all the other countries and also went one step further. Feeling that the vow would not be enough to keep the U. S. out of its country, Kier went to the United Nations and explained to the whole world their situation. They agreed with him and it did not take long for the United Nations to pass an act that it would be criminal if the United States tried to force their way into back into East Africa, especially for the oil. Every country, except Israel, backed the United Nations and they would declare war if the U.S. entered East Africa again. The United States government did not like what they were forced to do, but the administration felt pressure at home as well, by its people to stay away from East Africa. The people were tired of conflict and it seemed that they could care less about the energy crisis, especially if it meant more losses to their military. When the United States finally gave in and left East Africa, gas prices escalated and there was no end in sight. However, a small agency within the United States had something else in mind.

CHAPTER 4

It was seven o'clock in the morning when the phone rang, waking Jake up from a deep sleep. Jake knew that it had to be another creditor that he owed money to. He did not want to answer the phone, but did answer, acting half asleep.

"Hello, who is this and what do you want," he mumbled, hoping the person on the other end would feel sorry for him for calling so early in the morning.

They did not and replied, "This is your power company, we are reminding you that your final notice is up and your power will be turned off today. You have until three o'clock this afternoon to pay the bill."

"Thanks," Jake said getting irritated. "I will get your payment to you." Jake hung up the phone, knowing that he would not make any kind of payment to them.

It had been ten years since he walked out of the Pentagon and was told that his file had been deleted. He had yet to recover. He left his best friend, the only family he knew, and never looked back. He had become depressed by civilian life. He had been at a crossroads and could not shake it. He knew he wanted to be back in the action, but his government did not want him. He could not handle that and became a drifter. He went from city to city, doing off jobs, hoping to find a meaning to his life.

Jake now lived in Colorado and had a job where he trained horses. It was not his lifelong dream, but it something that helped pay the bills. He had been in little bit of a rut lately. The power bill wasn't the only bill that was late. There were others that were late as well. Jake was tired of always living week to week with a paycheck, but had no real desire to go out and try to do anything else. He was now forty years old and felt his age. He had quit working out and had gained a few extra pounds and his waistline had added a few inches. He had grown his hair out, added a mustache and beard. He drank more than a few beers at night. He had gone from one of the most feared men in the Middle East, to a fat, lazy slob, who had no direction in his life.

Jake had no one to blame, but himself. He had no family, no friends, and had gained plenty of enemies over the years. He needed to move around because he had alienated everyone he had come into contact with. He felt he was mistreated and lost all trust for anyone. He didn't care to go back to his state of Alabama, let alone to Montgomery. He did not even want to go to Summerville to see his friend Henderson, whom he had once called his brother. He hadn't tried to contact Henderson and had no idea if Henderson had tried to contact him. He often wondered what Henderson's life was like, but did not care to make the time to find out. All and all, Jake Garland had become a bitter, selfish man with no direction for his future in life.

Since Jake owed plenty of bills and business had dried up, he felt he had worn out his welcome and decided that he needed to be on the move again. He packed up what little he owned and got in the car and just started to drive. This would be his fifth move in as many years, and he had no idea where he was going. Jake could not understand what he had done in his life that was so wrong. Trouble just seemed to follow him and he could only wish that life was simpler for him. Over the last ten years he had lived in eleven different towns all throughout the United States.

He could not keep a job, owed a lot of bills, and had no friends. Nothing seemed to go his way.

Jake blamed his disappointing life on his mentor, Jon Higgins. It had been ten years and he tried to block the memory of Higgins out of his mind, but when anything bad happened to him, Higgins' name would pop back into his head. He had let the memory of Higgins control him and this made Jake a loaner. He felt betrayed by his government and it had taken over his life. He wanted a second chance, but he had gotten ten years older and he was out of shape. It did not matter. He was going over all the things that had not gone his way lost himself as he drove on the highway. He forgot to check his speed when he looked up into his rear view mirror; he saw blue lights and knew that was not good news for him.

"Pull over," a voice said out of a microphone.

Those were two words Jake did not want to hear. He knew he was busted. He had let his tags expire and had no identification. He had skipped out couple of years ago on a warrant that he had gotten in Utah for a mishap between him and a convenience store owner. He had escaped the law until today. He knew he was going to jail, but he decided to take a chance and run from the police. Unfortunately, his old Nissan Sentra did not have the speed or gas to outrun the police. Jake could not believe his misfortune as his car ran out of gas and he had to pull over to the side of the road.

"Get out of the car with your hands up!" the police officer shouted through his microphone.

Jake knew he had no chance to run and decided that maybe prison was the best place for him. He got out of the car and was immediately for some reason policeman took him down to the ground without warning. He then put hand cuffs on him and threw him in the back of his police car. Jake yelled at the policeman that he had done nothing wrong, but the policeman remained silent and got into the car and began to drive down the highway.

On the ride to the police station, Jake began to think about all the good times that he had experienced. He thought about the time Henderson and he helped the rebels in Syria defend a territory against the Syrian army. He remembered how he rescued Henderson from a gunman in a small village in Iraq. There were so many different adventures that he had gone on, he had lost count. Those were the times that Jake longed for. Jake felt those days were in his past and now he was going to prison for a very long time. He began to feel sorry for himself and felt that maybe prison was the best place for him. His life had not gone in the right direction since he was forced to leave the agency and felt at that at least he would have a roof over his head and food to eat in jail. He just shut his eyes and just hoped that whatever was in front of him, would be over in a hurry.

Jake had no idea what town or even what state he was in, but he knew the bars on his cell were real and that he had no money to get himself out. He had been in jail now for a week waiting on his court date. He was told his court date was over a month away. Jake knew that he would go crazy if he stayed in the small cell for that long. He needed a way to get out of this predicament. He just did not know anyone who could help him.

One morning Jake woke up to his usual breakfast, running eggs and burnt sausage, with a small glass of dirty water. He took a bit of his eggs and he looked up to see the guard looking at him in a strange way.

"Hey, you got a visitor," the guard yelled at Jake.

"What do you mean I have a visitor? I do not know anyone that would come to see me," he said to the guard.

"I could care less who it is. I just know that there is someone here to see you so get your ass up and come with me," the guard grunted out as he unlocked the cell door.

Jake walked out of the cell and wondered who would come to see him in jail. Jake had pissed off everyone that would even care for his existence. He could not think of anyone who would be here to see him. He followed the guard through a doorway and he led him into an interrogation room. Jake could not understand why they had gone into the interrogation room, but since he had never had a visitor before, just figured that visitation took place in this room. He walked in and was told to sit in a chair that was located in the corner. The guard handcuffed him to a bar on the wall so that he could not move around.

"Listen, buddy," he said to the guard. "You know that I am not going anywhere, so is this really necessary?"

The guard looked at him and said that it was standard procedure and to just deal with it. The guard then turned around and left the room turning the light and shutting the door behind him. After sitting in the dark room for what seem like forever, a bright light was turned on and appeared in front of Jake's face.

"Turn that crap off. I can't see anything!" Jake yelled into the light.

"That's the point," a voice that Jake had never heard of before, yelled back at him. "Now shut up and listen to me."

Jake had been through a lot of dangerous missions in his life and it took a lot to get him worried. He had fought and escaped death in the Middle East, been kicked around by his government, and practically lived on nothing for the past ten years, but now he was locked to a rod iron bar in a dark room with a bright light in his face. The voice that he heard startled him. He felt defenseless and he did not know what to do. He decided that the best thing for him to do was to do exactly what the voice said for him to do. He remained quiet so that he could hear what the voice had to say; hoping that nothing bad would happen to him.

"We have been watching you for a while, now" the voice answered.

Jake wondered who would want to watch him and asked, "What do you want from me? I have nothing."

"You underestimate yourself," the voice answered. "You are exactly what we are looking for."

The light in Jake's eyes turned off and he now sat in a dark room again. All of sudden he could not keep his eyes opened and he passed out.

Jake woke up on a cot behind bars. Jake thought he had been dreaming, but then he noticed that he was in a different cell. Where am I, Jake thought? He got up and walked over to look out of the window in his new cell. He knew that he was not in the same jail that he had been in for the last month. H saw nothing but a wooded area. He walked over to the cell door and yelled, "Is anyone here?" No one came to the door. Jake went back and sat on his cot. He could only wonder where he was and what was in store for him.

"He is finally awake. What do you want to do with him now?" Simeon asked his superior.

"You will need to get him into shape," his superior answered. "We do not have a lot of time. I am going in to talk to him. I want to see where he is at, mentally."

Simeon's superior was simply known by the name H. He was a mysterious man in his early fifties. He knew that there was not much time so they had to start quickly with the plan.

H walked toward the cell and began going over what he was going to say to Jake. He needed Jake to cooperate with him and do what he said without complaints. H walked to the cell and opened the door. He entered the cell and said,

"Jake, my name is H. I know you have a lot of questions for me, but I am not the one to ask. Just do what you are told for the next month and you may or may not have your questions answered. Do I make myself clear?"

Jake was not one that would allow someone he did not know to make demands on him. He did indeed have a lot of questions and demanded to know what was going on. H stood still and held his ground and took the verbal abuse from Jake.

"You can sit in here as long as you want or you can do what you are told and make life easier on yourself. What will it be?" H said as Jake continued to verbally attack H.

Jake gave H the finger and told him to figure it out.

"Have it your way, I know you will come around. Call for me when you are ready." H left the cell area and returned to the room where Simeon was. He made a phone call and told the person on the other line what had transpired and both agreed that Jake would come around within a few days.

Two days passed and Jake was still sitting in his cell. He had not received any food or water during this time and he had lost a lot of energy and was just plain thirsty. He finally yelled out of his cell, "Somebody get H. I am ready to listen to what he has to say."

A few minutes later H appeared and asked, "Are you ready to listen?"

"I do not know," Jake responded. "I really would like to know what is going on."

With that answer H turned his back on Jake and started to walk away.

"Alright, alright," Jake said. "Wait a minute. I am thirsty and hungry, I am a little delirious. Give me something to eat and drink and I will listen to what you have to say. Just give me a minute to think. A lot has happened over the last few days."

H nodded and said, "I will get you some food and water. When you are finished, my partner Simeon will come in and take you to get a shower. We will meet after that." H left the cell.

After he had a shower, Jake was escorted by Simeon, to a room, with a bed and a window. It wasn't much bigger than the cell, but at least he had a room with a view and a soft place to sleep. He was told to get dressed and to wait there until further notice. After about ten minutes Simeon came back and said for Jake to come with him. Simeon led him to another room and told him to go in and wait. Jake went into the room and sat down.

Jake looked out of the window. He saw a lot of trees and knew that he was surrounded by a wooded area. His room was small and was located in a small building on the property. He could not tell if the area was surrounded by a fence, but he could see what seemed to be an obstacle racing course outside. Jake knew that he was in for something that he had not experienced in awhile and that was hard work.

The door swung open and H appeared. "How is the room?"

"A little small, but it beats the cell I have been in for the last couple of days," Jake responded.

"Good. I want to reiterate that I cannot answer any questions that you might have, but I can tell you want I want from you. You can take it or not."

Jake had a lot of questions to ask, but was tired and did not want to go back in the cell. "I am all ears." Jake answered.

H started by saying, "I have been watching you for a while, Jake."

Jake did not know what to think of the man that sat in front of him. H did look straight into Jake's eyes and he always felt that a man was more trustworthy if they looked you square in one's eyes. He did not know H, but he felt that he was probably going to tell him the truth.

"I need for you to get your body into great physical shape," H continued. "There is not much time to do it. There will be very physical and mental test for you to accomplish over the next month. Again, do not ask me why, but I can only tell you that you have a month to accomplish these goals. You can take the deal or I will send you back to jail and let the system take care of your mishaps, plus, I will add a few more on your record. Do you understand?"

Jake nodded. He knew exactly what H meant and he did not want to go back to jail for any amount of time. This seemed like fun and Jake needed to get in shape. It was just for a month and he had nowhere to go at this time.

"I will try it out. When do I start?" Jake asked.

"As I said, we don't have much time. Your training started ten minutes ago. The first thing that we need to do is to get you into shape, physically," H said.

Simeon walked into the room. He was a very large man. Simeon was a very big man, around 6'6", and weighed a muscular 250 lbs.

"You've met already, but haven't been introduced. This is Simeon," H said. "He will be in charge of getting you into the best shape possible. The two of you will get started immediately. As I have stated before, there is just not much time. I will be watching your progress from a far. I will be back with you in one month. Do not disappoint me."

H left the room. Simeon looked down at Jake, who was sitting on his bed. He told him to get up off the bed and to come with him.

"Simeon, what kind of operation is this," Jake asked. "So far I have been locked up without food or water for two days, not been given any info on where I am and what I am doing. Now here I am in front of a huge individual who is supposed to get me into shape in a month. Can you let me know something?"

Simeon looked over at Jake with a snarl. He did not like for anyone to ask him questions. He was a man of few words and did not like questions. "I will tell you one thing," Simeon said. "You will be going through hell for the next 30 days. That hell starts today."

The training was separated into two fifteen day periods. The first fifteen days were going to be physical. Jake would run until he passed out. When he got up in the morning, he would run again. Jake was not in good shape, but ten years ago he was the most fit person on earth, or so he thought. Even though he was ten years older, he knew how to return to his form of the past. Simeon was there to take him through every obstacle.

Jake was able to shed fifteen pounds and regain some of his muscle. Finally, those fifteen days of hell were over and the second part of the training began. This training period was even harder and more physical challenge than the first. The training only increased with the runs lasting longer and the workouts doubling. All the training that Jake did completely changed his physical appearance. Just a month earlier he felt he had nothing to live for; no meaning in his life, but the training he had endured over the last thirty days had completely change his outlook on life. Though he had no idea what he was in for or why he was at the training facility, he felt good about himself again and he was ready for any challenge. The thirty days were finally over and Simeon, who was very demanding to Jake and had never given him a compliment, looked at him and nodded, acknowledge to him that he had done a good job.

During the whole month of the physical training that Jake endured, Simeon did not speak much to Jake. He had only trained him. Simeon had done that for a reason. He needed to know that Jake was going to be dedicated to his task at hand and that he was up to the challenge. Simeon had trained many different people and only two had passed his test. Jake was the second one, the first one was the reason Jake was here.

Because Jake had accomplished all he had done, Simeon felt that Jake had earned some respect from. He felt it was time to let Jake know a little about himself. He had been working for H for the last five years. Simeon told Jake that he too was running from the law as well. H had rescued him from a terrible past life. Simeon did not go into details about his past and Jake did not ask. Simeon told Jake that he had been brought in for training five years ago and passed with flying colors. H offered and Simeon accepted a post on H's team to be the only trainer. Simeon did not want to share too much information. He did not know what H would do with Jake. He had not been informed if Jake was going to be put on the team. Simeon did not tell Jake much more about the operation. He would leave that up to H.

"Jake," Simeon said as they walked outside of the small building where Jake had been staying for the last month, "you have passed my test with flying colors. I have been impressed with the way you were able to get into shape quickly and feel that you will get to move on with this organization. If you decide to stay with us, always know that I will get your back."

Jake told Simeon that he had brought back an enthusiasm to him that he had lost. He thanked Simeon. Simeon nodded and walked away leaving Jake beside the entrance of the complex.

As Jake waited for whatever was in front of him, he began to think of what Simeon had said. He really did not know what his purpose was or why he had gone through the training of the past month, but he finally knew that he was part of an organization again. It had been ten years, but he was finally exited about his future.

A black sedan with tented windows pulled up beside Jake. "Get in, there isn't much time." Jake jumped in the car and was greeted by H. "Your month of training went great. I can tell. You look fit and in shape. How are you holding up?"

"I feel great," Jake answered. "I am in the best shape of my life. I had been lying around for the last ten years with no direction, getting lazy and fat, but this month was intense. It showed me that I can still accomplish goals that I set out for myself. The only problem with this is that I have no idea what is ahead of me. Not that I am complaining, but I would like some answers."

H began to drive. He knew that Jake needed an explanation and could tell that Jake seemed a little frustrated. H knew Jake needed answers, so he decided that he would go ahead and tell Jake what he needed him to know. He first wanted to give some background on himself and felt Jake deserved to know everything.

"We have a long drive so I know you have the time to hear what I have to say," H said.

"I am all ears," Jake responded.

H kept his hand on the wheel as he drove the black sedan. He kept looking straight ahead and told Jake his story, "I entered the agency in the mid 80's and have been a part of this ever since. I began as a field agent and moved myself up through the ranks. In the early 90's I went to Iraq to help field a rebel alliance against Saddam Hussein during the first Iraq War. Unfortunately that flopped, but I learned many lessons from that debacle. I decided to not try to train an army for a revolution, but to agents in a different way. This was referred to in the United States as terrorism. I referred to it as a means to an end.

I was pulled out of the region by my handler, because they felt that what I was doing was not the way the standards that the United States wanted. The United States did not like my methods, but it worked. I did not understand their reasoning at the time, and still don't to this day. While I was there, I met a lot of contacts in the Middle East that I still have today. When I came back to the United States, I was put to work in cubical, but I did not like my desk job. I wanted to be a part of the action that was going on throughout the world. I did not want to leave the agency, so to occupy my time I invented a test to help determine a way to screen recruits that wanted to come into the agency. There were many tests the agency had come out with, but this one was the best of its kind. Each recruit was given a written test and if they did not achieve a certain grade, they were not allowed to continue being in the agency."

Jake interrupted H, to point out that he had taken a similar test in college.

"I am getting to that," H said as he continued to drive the car. "That is where you come in, Jake."

"As I said, I developed this test," H continued without worrying about Jake's interruption. "The agency picked out certain areas to conduct this test. Eastern Alabama was one of the areas that came up on our radar so we sent agents down there to conduct the test. Naturally, Auburn University was the site that we chose. You were not handpicked to take it, but you did indeed take it and scored very high on it. Actually, you scored the highest on the test than anyone ever before you and after you."

Jake seemed pleased that he had scored high on the test that H was talking about, but it was twenty years ago since he took it. He wanted to know what motive H had by telling him this information. H did not answer the question and continued to drive the car down the road. He told Jake to sit back, relax, and rest his eyes. They would be on the road for a little while longer.

Before Jake shut his eyes to get some sleep as they drove, he asked, "Why are you telling me all of this. I have been out of the business for ten years and was told that my file was deleted. How do you know all this?"

"I am getting to that," H said as if perturbed by the question. "Listen, Jake, I will get to all of this in time, but right now we have more training to do. I told you some things, but before I go on, you need to drink this."

H handed Jake a bottle of water. Jake held it in his hand, not knowing why H had done that.

H continued, "I am now taking you to another facility. This facility is top secret. We will arrive in a couple of hours. Make sure your drink all of the water. It will put you to sleep."

Jake was hesitant at first, but H reassured him by saying, "Trust me, you will need to sleep."

Jake did not know if he should trust H, but he wanted to know more and enjoyed the training he had received over the last month. He thought, what the hell, and turned it up and finished the bottle and shortly after that Jake fell fast asleep.

CHAPTER 5

"Damn, it's cold out here today," Jake yelled over to Henderson, who he saw blowing on his hands to stay warm. "Are you cold too?"

"Nah," he said as he continued to blow on his hands. "Put this on," he said as he handed Jake the usual, a turban for his head and the classic Bisht, an Arabic robe worn by every man in Iran.

"Nights are just cold in Iran. I know we have been in this area for awhile, but I still miss the summer nights in Alabama," Jake said as he put on the robe that Henderson had given him. "You just can't beat those warm summer nights, sitting on the porch, sipping on some lemonade. I miss those days,"

It was an unusually cold summer night in Iran. It had been that way for some time and both Jake and Henderson were getting tired of it. They had been on the trail of a terrorist for about a month and had gone behind enemy lines to catch him. Their contact had told them that the man they were after was in the town of Yazd a town located in the center of Iran. The contact was supposed to have a meeting with them in the eastern part of the town. Jake and Henderson were staying outside of the town and were going to get in a truck and ride into Yazd the following day.

They rarely slept before their missions, especially Jake. He was too pumped up and needed to stay on target. "I do not care how many times we do this," Jake said to Henderson. "It never gets old. I stay exited and cannot sleep."

Henderson looked over to Jake and said, "I know, I can always tell. You may not be able to sleep, but I am going to get some shut eye. Get me up in a couple of hours." Henderson rolled over and shut his eyes. Jake could not wait to get moving and stayed up thinking about the mission they were about to go on.

The next morning the truck arrived on time and both Jake and Henderson got into to the back of the truck. They began to drive to the city of Yazd, and it seemed like everything was going fine until they heard some gun fire. A bomb exploded in front of them. The truck came to a complete stop.

"What the hell is going on?" Henderson screamed to Jake.

"I do not know, but with hearing that explosion I know that it does not look good for us." Jake replied.

Jake and Henderson had been invincible for the last ten years. They knew it was over and just hoped that they could survive. An Iranian soldier yelled inside to the two Americans who were not visible, but the soldier knew they were in the back of the truck. He demanded that they get out of the truck, with their hands raised. The two of them obeyed and came out of the back of the truck without saying a word.

"Where were you two going?" The soldier demanded.

"We are just out on a joy ride, trying to check out the scenery," Jake answered with a smile.

The officer did not like the answer and got his M16 and struck Jake in the back of the head. Jake went down in pain. He looked up at the soldier and began to black out. He was knocked out cold.

"Wake up, Jake!" Simeon yelled as he stood above him.

"What, where am I?" Jake asked as he was still half asleep.

"Don't worry about where we are. We need to get started right away. We have a lot to do and little time to do it."

Jake was surprised to see Simeon and said to him, "I thought I would not see you again."

"Nah, I will be with you as long as you stay with us. I know a lot of things that I need to teach you. I need you to learn and listen and grasp whatever I teach you in a hurry."

Jake looked around, but did not recognize where he was. He knew that Simeon needed him and he was ready to go. "Let's get started," Jake said to Simeon with a smile.

Simeon knew he was under the gun to get Jake to finish his training. He knew that there was not much time, so he was going to get started as soon as possible. "You must trust me for this to work. You will be going through a completely different training that you have experience so far. Do you want to continue?"

Jake knew that he wanted to continue. He wanted more answers out of H and knew the only way to get those answers was to continue the training that he had started. He felt great and wondered what else there was for him to do.

"Let's get to it."

This would be the last of the training that Jake would get from Simeon. It would only last a week and Simeon started immediately with Jake. Jake trusted Simeon and knew that this was part of the training. Simeon did not let Jake sleep and put him through the worst kind of torture. He treated Jake like a prisoner, trying to get information out of him. Jake had been under this type of training almost twenty years before, but never this intense. Jake was electrocuted, was beaten with a rubber hose, you name it, Jake endured it. Simeon began to torture Jake, but it did not faze him and Jake wanted more. He wanted to prove to Simeon that he could take anything that he threw at him.

Finally, the week was over and the torture training was done. Simeon was exhausted and Jake was half dead. Simeon took Jake to a small shack that was on the property where they had been training, and laid him down on a small cot so that Jake could rest and recover. He could only give Jake twenty four hours to sleep, for Simeon knew there was not much time before they had to be ready to go into action. Simeon knew that their mission would start as soon as the twenty four hours were over.

* * *

"Wake up you disgusting piece of scum," yelled the Iranian officer as he kicked at Jake lying on the floor of a small cell. "Who is your contact and what were you sent to do."

The Iranian continued to kick Jake as he lay on the floor. Jake had never been in this situation, never been captured, but he had trained for this situation. He and Henderson knew that if they were caught, that they would be tortured and possibly killed. Jake looked around and did not see his friend. He felt a huge shock go through his entire body right. Electrodes had been attached all over his body and the pain continued.

"Who is your contact!" yelled the officer.

Jake did not say anything. He knew that his chance of survival was for him to keep quiet. The longer he held out and did not say anything the longer they would keep him around. He just needed to stay quiet and come up with a plan to get himself out of this situation and be hopeful that Henderson was still alive as well. Another shock went through his body and Jake grimaced in pain.

"We will kill you, do you know that," the Iranian soldier yelled to him. "Who is your contact?"

Again, Jake looked up and said nothing. The third shock was so strong and lasted so long that Jake could not take it. He passed out from the pain.

* * *

"Hey man, how are you feeling?" Simeon asked as he saw Jake opening his eyes. "Like old times," Jake said as he rubbed his eyes to help him wake up. "I am a little sore, but other than that I am ready to go."

Simeon had never seen anyone take the punishment he had dished out to Jake. This had made him more impressed with Jake. He was not about to give him another compliment, but he knew that Jake would be ready for whatever lay ahead.

"H should be here any minute," Simeon said as he looked out the window of the shack. "When he gets here, we need to get into his car. Remember, don't ask any questions."

Jake knew very little as to where he was going, and what he was going to do. He stood up and the pain that he had experienced had yet to leave his body. He knew that the pain would eventually go away, but not as quickly as it once had in the past. Jake knew that he could deal with it and he wanted to show H and Simeon that he was prepared for anything that was ahead of him.

"I am hurting a little, but I will get over it," Jake said to Simeon. "I am ready to do whatever you need me to do."

Simeon was still looking out of the window. He nodded to Jake and saw the black sedan pull up. "H is here," Simeon said. "Let's go." Simeon and Jake left the small shack and got into the car.

Jake had been with H and Simeon for almost a month and a half. During this time, Jake had been put through a gut wrenching training, and off the wall torture. It had brought back memories of his training that he gone through twenty years before. Even though he had gone through all of it, he still did not have any answers to his question. He had asked H what his purpose was, but had gotten little information from H.

"H," Jake asked as he was riding in the front seat of the sedan. "I have done everything you asked of me. Can you give me some answers to my purpose?"

H, who seemed very mysterious to Jake, but also very much in command of what goes on around him, answered Jake by saying "Look out the window, what do you see?"

Jake looked out the window and saw the same thing that he saw every day. Nothing important, he thought, but he still answered H.

"I see just a plain ole sunny day." Jake said with a smart remark.

"I am not being funny." H said angrily. "Do you like what you see outside?"

Jake knew that H was not joking around. "Yeah, I do. I like sunny days."

"Well, I do to" H responded, "and with your help, we will continue to have sunny, rainy, windy, hell even snowy days for a long time to come."

Jake did not know exactly what H was trying to say. He asked H, "What do you mean?"

H was not about to give him any answers so he said to Jake, "We have a long car ride ahead of us, so just sit back and enjoy the view. You need to get some sleep, Jake. I know that you are tired. I will wake you up when we get to our destination."

The problem for Jake was he wanted to know where he was going and what the job would be. Even though it was against his nature, he did what he was told and shut his eyes and fell asleep.

* * *

"This will all be over soon," the voice said as Jake lay on the ground. "I know you have to start talking sometime. We have already killed your buddy and we will soon kill you." Jake looked up, but he could hardly hold his eyes open. He had been tortured now for the last ten hours. He was weak and had no answer. He would rather die than give out any information. He loved Henderson and he held out all hope that he was still alive. He had been trained not to give in to anyone and that his enemy would tell him anything to make him talk.

Jake looked up and saw his enemy in front of him. He said in a very weak voice "Kill me, then."

"You will have your wish," the soldier yelled back at him.

The gun was raised and the barrel was put on the back Jake's head. Jake could hear the trigger being pulled and knew that this would be his end. The door to the cell swung open and an Iranian officer entered.

"Stop, do not shoot him," the officer yelled. "We need him alive."

The gun was put down and Jake's life had been spared. He was carried into another cell and hung up by his arms. Jake looked over and saw his friend, Henderson, and thanked God that he was still alive. Jake looked back at one of the guards and smiled. He knew that they had been doing everything they could to get him to talk, but he had remained quiet. The guard did not like the smirk on Jake's face and walked over and hit him with the back of his gun. Jake did not even have a chance to feel the pain and was knocked out by the force to the back of his head.

* * *

"Get up, Jake. We are here." Simeon said with his deep voice, shaking Jake to wake him up.

They had driven all night to an old airport in the southern part of Georgia. Jake had dozed off and slept for the majority of the trip. He was still sore from the training he had endured, but knew that pain that he was experiencing served some sort of purpose. He just hoped that he would learn what the purpose was and soon.

"All right, all right, hold your horses, I'm up," Jake said as he opened his eyes. "Where are we?"

"Look around," Simeon answered. "I know it is early, but we are in South Georgia. H is over in that small shack over there. He is laying out the plans of what is in store for us."

Jake was ready for some action and he and Simeon headed toward the shack. Jake opened the door of the shack and saw all kinds of guns and different kind of weapons. He had not seen these types of weapons in a long time.

"Are you ready for some target practice," Simeon asked Jake.

"I was pretty good back in the day, but hell yeah," Jake answered. They both grabbed a couple of guns and headed out to an open field to practice shooting.

Jake was a top shot at one time and showed Simeon that he had not lost his touch. "It is like riding a bike," Jake said to Simeon.

"You don't forget." Simeon had become a big admirer of Jake. He had put him through a touch month and a half and Jake had passed easily. He knew that Jake knew much more than he did and knew that he could now start to learn from Jake.

"Jake," Simeon said "If you haven't seen already, H is a very private and secretive person. I would like to tell you what is going on, but I just do not know. I do what I am told, but I want you to trust me. Will you trust me, Jake?"

Jake knew he wanted Simeon's trust. He could tell that Simeon needed Jake to trust him as well. He knew that he would need Simeon to be by his side for whatever may come before them in the near future.

"Simeon, if you haven't seen it already, I trust you." They shook hands and continued target practice.

After finishing shooting most of the day, they both walked back to the shack where H was setting up shop. "Simeon, can you excuse Jake and I for a minute, I need to talk to him in private."

Simeon nodded and walked outside the shack. H wanted Jake to sit down because he needed to talk to him about some things. Jake felt that he finally was going to share what was going on and he was right.

H begun by saying, "As you know, I worked for the CIA for a long time. I talked about my early days and about the test that I came up with. As you know Jake, you have the second highest score that I have ever seen. I know about your past, Jake, about what happen to you in Iran.

Jake was eager to listen. He came in the shack and sat down at the table. The table had papers scattered all over it. He tried to look to see what they were and what they said, but H told him he would get to that. First, H needed to tell Jake why he was chosen and what he was chosen for.

"Jake," H said "I will not beat around the bush. If you do not know already, I know about your past. I know Jon Higgins."

Jake had not heard that name in ten years. He had felt that Jon Higgins had betrayed him and blamed most of his problems on him.

"You knew him?" Jake answered nonchalantly, trying not to show the hatred that he had for Jon Higgins.

"Yes, I knew him. He and I worked side by side for fifteen years. We started working together around the same time that you came into the agency. I was always in the background and Higgins was the front man. I told him that you would be a star for us and I was right. You never surprised me. I watched in the background as you flourished and became our top field agent. I know that you did not work alone. You and Henderson were a fantastic duo, but it was you who pulled most of the weight. I am not taking anything away from what Henderson did, because he helped our cause just as much as you, but you were the best."

Jake sat there, listening to every word H had to say. He liked the compliments, but he wanted H to get to the point.

"Something happened in Iran. You two had been invisible for ten years and out of nowhere, you were captured. Your case files have been classified for ever since you were dismissed, but I got my hands on them and here they are." H handed a huge file to Jake. "I will give you a few minutes to review them."

Jake opened his file. He looked it over, bringing back memories of what he and Henderson did. "I do not need to read over my life again. I know what I did. Plus I thought that my file was deleted."

H looked at Jake and said, "They were not deleted. You were told that so that you would forget about Iran and leave it alone. You will not find anything in there that you do not know already, but there is something that has been puzzling me for a long time. First, the only people that had access to you and your file were Higgins and I. We knew where you were at all times. We communicated with your contacts and knew that they were airtight. Secondly, this seemed to work great for over one hundred missions that you accomplished, but for some reason, one mission what we did, failed. For your failure, you were brought back to the U.S. and sent away like you had done nothing for this country."

This was the first time that Jake thought that his last mission could have been compromised. He had racked his brain trying to find out what he had done wrong, but now he realized that someone might have turned him in.

"Do you have factual evidence backing this up?" Jake asked H.

"I dug deep into what had happened and could not figure it out. Evidence pointed back to our agency, but I was stopped dead in my tracks every time I got close to it. Unfortunately, I ran out of time and had to move on."

"What do you mean ran out of time?" he asked H.

He looked at Jake, knowing he needed to tell him everything, said "I am no longer in the CIA. I have been excused of my duties. I was locked out of files and my contact in the agency told me to keep a low profile. I cannot contact any of my old contacts because I am being watched. That is why I decided to bring you in on what this is. There is a lot more to it, and I do not have the time to tell you everything yet, but I need to move on about you and your past and move to what we need to do now."

Jake was startled. All this was over whelming him. He wanted to know more about his past, but now was interested in what his purpose was. "Obviously you need me for something."

H did indeed need Jake. He needed someone who could fly under the radar and be undetected. H knew that Jake still had what it took to get the job done and also Jake was the only one who could help.

CHAPTER 6

Gas prices were over twenty dollars a gallon at the pump and prices were continuing to rise with no end in sight. The United States economy had been strong, but because of the high gas prices, the economy was going into a recession. Many people were losing their jobs and there was no hope that the economy would change. When the news hit about the discovery, all things seem to change for the good. Unfortunately, the United States became an unwelcomed enemy and what seemed like a miracle, turned into a disaster.

The State Department knew it had to do something. The Iraq war had ended just a year earlier, lasting almost twenty years, and the American people were not desperate enough to have another conflict. The President was up for re-election. He read the polls on a daily basis and the polls showed him that another war would ultimately end his political career. He knew that his re-election depended on bring gas prices down and East Africa was his ticket to a second term. The President needed help with a very sticky situation and would contact the CIA for a plan to keep him in office.

* * *

Higgins had been in command of the Middle East and East African region for fifteen years. He considered H his protégé and had him by his side to learn everything that the region had to offer. Higgins had been around the CIA for years and was considered one of its top agents. He was a brilliant man and his specialty was dealing with Middle Eastern affairs. In a bold move, Higgins turned his attention to a smaller and less hostile environment, Eastern Africa. He turned over his Middle East affairs and concentrated a lot of energy toward Eastern Africa. During this time, he helped with the revolution of East Africa and he was the man responsible for establishing the new country and the United States as allies.

Higgins made East Africa his top priority. He was able to establish a friendship with their new leadership, during the civil war. He supplied Mahmud Osman Kier and his militia with weapons and materials that help them win the war. Because of the relationship he had established with Kier, this allowed the United States to become an ally to East Africa.

During the next five years Higgins became reclusive, especially towards H. H had become the head of Middle Eastern affairs, but still needed Higgins input on many different occasions. Higgins had higher clearance than H and made H come to him for access to any file. H had stumble on a few case files and had approached Higgins concerning these issues. Higgins explanations were that the files were classified and that H had to have higher clearance to access them. Higgins assured H that he would work on having him promoted to a higher clearance, but that day never came.

H had enough of Higgins's excuses and went over his boss's head to report him, but by the time an investigation got under way, Higgins had suddenly disappeared and the files in questioned were missing. H began to search for his mentor over the next five years, but Higgins looked to have just fallen of the face of the earth. He was well connected throughout the world and could easily adapt to any environment. The agency did not want to believe that Higgins was a "rogue" agent and their excuse was that Higgins had a mental break down and the high pressure of espionage got to him. H could not accept that excuse that his superiors gave him and he felt that Higgins was on the run.

Higgins disappearance only made H more confident that his formal mentor had not been totally honest about his work. H immediately began looking back at all the different case files that Higgins had been working on and he came across a lot of shady activity. Unfortunately for H, there was not enough evidence that could pin point the activity toward Higgins. Though it was a setback, it did not discourage him from continuing his quest to prove that Higgins was indeed a "rogue" agent.

He would take other evidence to his superiors, only to have his superiors never take it seriously. He would be told that Jon Higgins was a loyal and devoted employee and that he had an unblemished record. They had heard of his nonsense about Higgins and did not want to be bothered about him anymore. They felt that Higgins had enough of the pressure and stress of the agency and he decided to leave on his own terms. H was advised by his superiors to forget about the disappearance and move on to something else. He would not allow himself to forget about it and move on. He knew that if he could not convince his superiors that Higgins was not an honest agent, he would then have to make it his mission to hunt down his old boss and prove them wrong.

H took over Higgins' affairs in the agency. He was given more authority than he had and decided to use this new found authority to his advantage. He created a small, but sophisticated agency and had a training facility built so that he could properly train new agents that he wanted to join him. He would handpick these agents and put them through a very tough physical and mental test. H knew that things were changing in the world and that his agents would have to be more mentally and physically sound than ever before. He ran off many wannabes that could not cut it. The training was not for the faint of heart.

H made sure that the agency would be a small outfit and would be known as Code Seven. He would recruit an agent and would only train one agent at a time. The agent would train for up to two years and when H felt that they were ready he would send them on very difficult missions. That was his vision, but the problem was finding the right agent. He needed someone he could trust to help him with this project.

Simeon had come onto the agency with a checkered past, but this did not bother H. He had met him on several different occasions and had grown to like him. H trusted Simeon. H was very detailed oriented and liked that Simeon would do exactly what was told of him. H was the leader and he made sure that that Simeon knew it. H would put Simeon through a series of tests, both physical and mental, before he let Simeon become a part of Code Seven. Simeon accomplished every feat and when he was finished, H had a new job for him; Simeon would become the trainer of any future recruits that H would bring into Code Seven.

After two years of training, Simeon had learned the basics of Code Seven from H. He turned the reins over to Simeon, allowing him to oversee all training from a distance. H knew that Simeon would be a disciplined trainer; H knew how valuable he would be and never wanted to put him in the field. H made sure that Simeon knew he might be relied on to go out into the field at any moment and that he need to be prepared for this task. Simeon wanted to be the field trainer and he was the best trainer that H could ever hope for. They had a good working relationship that would continue for the next five years.

Finding a prospect was never an easy task for H. He wanted the best agent, a super agent, and he wanted the agent to be above all the rest. He decided that there would be two criteria that an agent must pass before he or she would become part of his agency. The first part was one must pass the field training exam by Simeon and must pass the mental test given by H. The field training was a very difficult task. The second part was a very grueling mental test that H would give after the field test was completed.

Unfortunately, over the next year, no one had ever passed the field test given by Simeon that allowed them to get to the second part training, the test that was given by H. H and Simeon felt as if they would never find anyone to become part of Code Seven, but it would not be long until they would find their "super agent" that H longed for.

Sasha Prince was a young, but very determined to accomplish great things. She was self sufficient and very strong willed. She was well educated, having graduated with honors from MIT. She was a math genius and had majored in statistics. She was in incredible shape, having won the Boston Marathon in record time. She had entered and won many triathlons. She loved to win at everything she did. Losing was not an option, neither was quitting. She had been raised by a steel worker in a small town right outside Pittsburg. Her mother had died of breast cancer when Sasha was only 12, and her father died right after Sasha graduated from college. She had been raised to always want more and that is what she strived for. She took a job as a stock broker, but became bored and felt that it was not the challenge she was looking for. Sasha quit, trying to find a higher calling in life and felt that she had found that calling in the CIA. She got an interview and was quickly hired into the agency.

It did not take long for her to catch H's eye. Not only was she a fast learner, but she was a very beautiful woman. She was able to move through the agency at rapid pace and had risen quickly through the ranks in only a few years. H had struggled with trying to find the perfect agent, but he knew he did not have to look much further than Sasha. He knew that he would have to come to her with a plan and lure her into Code Seven.

H decided to have Simeon spy on her. He needed to know where she went, what she liked, and who she knew. Code 7 was a very secretive operation and he did not want to bring anyone into the outfit that he did not know anything about. Simeon spied on her for over three months. He had set up surveillance on her and he knew every small detail on her. He knew what she liked to eat, when she went to sleep, who she talked to on the phone, what time she went to work. Basically, Simeon knew Sasha like the back of his hand. He took the information he had gathered over the three months to H. H and Simeon discussed Sasha and they agreed that she would be the one that they wanted in Code 7.

One morning, on the way to work, Sasha stopped off at the local coffee shop to get a cup of coffee. She did this everyday and Simeon was there watching her. He had put an envelope in a newspaper that she always would buy. He waited inside the coffee shop to make sure she got the right newspaper. Once she picked the newspaper up, he slipped out the back so that he would not be noticed. Sasha ordered her coffee and opened the newspaper. The envelope fell out and simply said, 'Read Me, Sasha Prince.' She looked around to see if she notice anyone unfamiliar, but nothing seemed out of the ordinary. She did not want to read it in the coffee shop. Sasha wanted to read it at her office where she felt more secure. She hurried her coffee and left to go to her office.

Sasha was very anxious to read what was in the envelope. Once she got into her office, she locked her door and opened it, nervously, not knowing what it might read. There was just an address and a time on one sheet of paper: 'Boulevard A, 22:00, Tonight. Come alone.' She had no idea what it meant, and would struggle at work the whole day. She thought about the coffee shop and all the people that she had seen there, but she still had no idea who had put that envelope in her newspaper. She could not concentrate at work and began to since some paranoia of who was watching her and why. She looked around at her work, but knew that no one she worked with was the one that left her the envelope.

She would go and meet at the destination, but did not like the fact that she had to go alone. Sasha knew that she could protect herself, but she did not know what she would be walking into. She decided to get to the address early and scout out the area. She arrived an hour early and watched from a distance, but notice that there was nothing was going on at the address. When ten o'clock arrived, Sasha got out of her car and began to walk toward the address. After a she had taken a few steps, someone came up behind her. She was startled and wanted to turn around, but was told to stay still and not to move.

"Do not be afraid, but come with me," the person said as he instructed her to move toward a car that pulled in front of them. "There is someone that I want you to meet."

Sasha did not like what was going on. She felt over powered and wanted to leave, but she was still intrigued agreed to follow him to the car. The door opened and she was told to get inside. When she sat down, the inside light turned on and a man sat in front of her.

"Sasha, my name is H. I do not beat around the bush. I am direct and to the point. I have had my eyes on you for awhile now and know who you work for. I work for the same agency that you do. That is why I have called you here. I have a small operation that is new and classified. My operation is called Code 7. It consists of me and my trainer, Simeon, the man who just escorted you to my car. You will only answer to me and any mission you might go on would be classified. I cannot go into any more details, but to say that it takes someone special to be a part of this small, but important organization. Many agents have failed at this task. I have read your file and seen you work. I see in you same traits that I see in myself, and that is the desire for greatness. I know that you will have what it takes to be a part of my organization and help change the world. My question to you is, do you want to be a part of history and join me and my team at Code 7?"

Sasha had never turned down a challenge. She had joined the CIA to help change the world. She had moved up in the agency, but not as quickly as she had hoped. Sasha wanted to be part of something special and could see that H was sincere in what he wanted to accomplish.

"I will not offer you this again," H said. "I need an answer before you leave tonight."

Sasha replied, "I always felt that I had a higher calling for something. I have been looking for that challenge my whole life. I know that this is what that challenge is. Yes, H, I will be a part of Code 7."

H was very happy with her decision, but did not crack a smile. He leaned over in his seat a grabbed a file. "Read over this information and meet me at 6:00 tomorrow morning. The address is inside as well."

Sasha got out of the car and H drove away. She did not know what the future held, but felt very secure about it.

The next morning did not come quickly enough for Sasha. She wanted to get an early start and she arrived an hour early. H, who always arrived before anyone, was already there with Simeon.

"Glad to see your enthusiasm," he said. "I know that you have met, but let me be the first to introduce you to the big fella. This is Simeon. You will be working with him for a while. Get to know him. Trust him. He will be your only liaison to the outside world as long as you are with Code 7." H was all business all the time and said, "Enough with the pleasantries, now let's get to work."

Over the next year, Sasha would train very long and hard. She would go through many different physical tests that she would pass with ease. She became a great marks woman. Her work ethic was unquestioned. She accomplished every goal that was thrown at her. She felt she was ready. Simeon agreed. He had tried to train others, but they had failed to accomplish half of what Sasha had accomplished. Simeon knew that Sasha was something special and finally felt that it was time for H to give her his test. H had designed a test for Code 7 to be a very grueling test. No one had taken it, until Sasha. H was please with himself for picking Sasha to be a part of his team. He had expected her to over achieve and she accomplish everything that was put in front of her. She was not out of the woods because she had to continue Code 7's training.

The test had moved from the physical aspect to the mental aspect. H knew that the test would challenge Sasha more mentally than she was tested physically. H knew if she passed the mental aspect of the test, she would be able to start the missions that he wanted to do immediately.

Sasha was physically ready, but now came the interesting scenario that H wanted to see if she could handle the mental aspect of the job. H wanted her to think quickly and outside the box. He knew when she would go on missions; she would be alone and would not have him around to tell her what to do. He knew that she was smart, but he needed to test her intelligence. Sasha walked into H's office and asked him what her first assignment would be.

"What do you mean," questioned H. "You have no assignments within this agency anymore."

"What are you saying," Sasha asked with a puzzled look on her face.

"We do not need you," H responded. "We decided to go a different direction. Here is your stuff. Get out."

Sasha could not believe what she was hearing. She had worked her butt off for a year, had given her all, and thought she had passed everything that was required from her. Now she was told to leave. She did not want H to see her lose her cool. She decided to remain calm and ask him a few questions.

"Are you shutting down Code Seven? This organization is very small. Unless I do not know something, this organization has just the two of you in it now." Sasha was referring to H and Simeon.

"Listen, I am sorry it did not work out. You need to leave. There is nothing more that I can do for you." H did not even look up to see her reaction. Sasha just stood there in silence. She was not going to just walk away. She had put too much time into the project and wanted more answers as to why she was not needed anymore. She had figured H out and knew that he would not give her any, but decided to just stand there in complete silence until he said something else.

After about thirty minutes of standing and H not acknowledging her presence, Sasha decided to sit down and read a magazine in H's office. H knew now she was not leaving and his plan was working. He had no intention of letting her go. He wanted her to keep her cool and she had. Now he needed her to finish the challenge.

"Here is your assignment on the table. You have got twenty-four hours to accomplish what is in there. Don't come back if you cannot finish this within the amount of time."

He still never looked up. Sasha was not dumb and figured out that H was testing her, and knew that she had passed part of it. She grabbed the file and left H's office.

Sasha had been training for this opportunity for over a year and would finish what she had started. She opened the file and read the instructions. The instructions read for her to get into a classified area in CIA headquarters and to take a file that was called SO10 and get it out of the building. She could not be seen entering of leaving the area. She was given a code clearance and a different security badge so that no one would know that she had entered in the building. She had been given a map and the location of the file, but was told that all files in this location were heavily guarded and that if she were caught, she would be on her on without any help from H. Sasha knew that she did not have a lot of time, but it did not matter. She would figure out a way and left to start on her task immediately.

Sasha returned within the allotted time that H had given her with SO10 file. H did not ask how she had gotten the file, but was pleased she had. Sasha proved that she was ready to be a part of Code 7 and H knew it. He felt that he had finally found his super agent. She was beautiful, intelligent, and now very cunning in what she could do. She was also trained as a top marksman and she also was trained in hand to hand combat. H knew it was time to put her out in the field and she would start immediately.

H was working at his desk when Sasha came into his office. He looked up and said to Sasha, "great job, you have passed my test and you are now part of Code 7."

"Thank you," she answered. "I have worked hard. I am ready to start. I never looked at the SO10 file, but is that my assignment now?"

"Yes it is," H answered. "I have been studying this case file for four and a half years. This was the missing piece. I will brief you on the story, so you might want to take a seat."

H told Sasha about his old boss, Higgins and told her how he and Higgins worked side by side for fifteen years. He talked to her about how Higgins had focused so much of his energy in western Africa and how Higgins would not allow him to look at any of the files concerning this area. H told her about Higgins sudden disappearance. He told her that he believed that there was more to it than just a disappearance. Things just did not add up in his opinion. He felt that Higgins was not burned out and was up to something else, but could not prove it.

H knew the file had a lot of classified information concerning Higgins activities and he wanted to review it. He hoped it would share some light on anything new concerning his old boss. He needed Sasha to help him locate Higgins and he had a plan concerning how to find him. He had information that Higgins had relocated to Honduras and needed Sasha to go and see if Higgins was there. He knew that he could prove that Higgins was evil and needed Sasha to go down to Honduras to monitor Higgins and report all her findings to H.

They had finished their discussion and Simeon walked in and interrupted H and Sasha. "There is something very important on television that both of you need to take a look at." H grabbed the remote and turned on the television and they all watched the news broadcast the story of the huge oil discovery in East Africa. H decided that he might be best to put Higgins on hold and monitor this situation instead. He knew that the East Africa was an American ally, one of the few the United States had, and he wanted to see what role, if any he would have in this situation.

Over the next two weeks in East Africa, the United States embassy was taken hostage, all U.S. businesses were over taken over by the East African military and all communication between the East African government and the State Department of the United States was dissolved. H wondered what had happened. H knew that United States had a strong ally in the East Africa, but overnight, after the world changing oil discovery, the friendship was suddenly over.

H decided to completely change the direction of his agency. He knew his government wanted answers. He knew the United States could not send in their military into the region of they could face a World War. The United States was already thought of as the evil empire by the world and new that the United Nation would not stand for any kind of threat toward East Africa. The United States government needed secrecy and needed H and his new agency. They came to him for a plan and he had exactly the plan they needed, and that plan was Sasha.

CHAPTER 7

Jake, H, and Simeon were heading to another secret location to finish his training. "Jake," H said. "I have always felt responsible for you, ever since you were dismissed from the agency. I have followed your life intensively and watched how you moved all over the country. I know that you never found your calling again and I can see disappointment it in your eyes. This business, the spy business, is in your blood. You need it just as much as it needs you. I need you to forget about what happened ten years ago and move on. I need you to join us and become part of something again."

The CIA had left a bitter taste in Jake's mouth. He did not want anything to do with the agency anymore or anyone that was a part of the agency.

"Stop the car," Jake said. "I want to get out."

H looked backed and asked, "why the change of heart?"

"It is not you," Jake said. "You and Simeon have been good to me. I owe my new found resilience to the both of you. I just do not want to put myself back into the situation as I was in ten years ago. I felt that I gave my life to this country and it just chewed me up and spit me out. I do not want that to happen to me again."

H slowed the car to a halt. He looked back at Jake and said, "We are not the CIA, Jake. We are not backed by the U.S. I feel the same as you. My country gave up on me like it did to you, but we still have a duty and responsibility. I have an agent out there that I need for you to go get. If you do not help me, I have no one else to turn to. Jake, you were made for these missions. Do not turn your back on me. I need you."

H never opened up to anyone, but wanted to show Jake his sincerity to his project. H felt rejected. He had experience the same rejection that Jake had over the last ten years. He understood Jake's feelings, but on the other hand he wanted to rectify the situation for himself and for Jake. Jake had opened the door of the car. His head told him to get out and walk away. His heart told him to stay.

"H," Jake said "I appreciate you rescuing me and getting me into shape, but I do not owe you anything. I owe nothing to this country. The United States has taken everything from me. If I do take on this mission, I don't do it for anyone but, myself."

H nodded and agreed to those terms. Jake shut the door and H put the car back into drive and drove to the destination.

H continued to talk to Jake about the upcoming mission. "We are constantly on the move. We know that we are being tracked by the CIA, but right now we have yet to be caught. We need to stay under the radar because I started Code 7 for a reason and a purpose and we are yet to accomplish it. Getting caught is not an option."

H knew that there was not a lot of time left before the CIA would catch up to him and his activities.

"What exactly happened?" Jake asked. "I have bits and pieces to the story, but you have not given me the whole story." Jake was getting a little impatient, but as always, he kept his emotions in check.

H looked back at Jake and said, "We will be there shortly and I will tell you more of the story. Just enjoy the ride."

After a couple of hours they arrived at their location. Jake woke up from his nap in the car and saw a small shack in the middle of nowhere. He opened the door and go out of the car. He grabbed his bag and headed to the shack. H and Simeon were already inside. Jake opened the door to the shack and saw them sitting at a small table.

"Welcome," H said. "Take a seat, there are some things we need to go over."

Jake grabbed a small chair and sat down. He was eager to hear what H had to say. H looked at Jake and made sure that what he was about to tell him would not leave the shack. Jake nodded.

H started by saying, "As I stated earlier, Higgins and I had a great working relationship. The relationship seemed to sour after you and Henderson were captured. He became a recluse. Higgins had a higher clearance level than I did, and he used this against me. He made sure I stayed busy doing simple projects. The projects were task that younger agents would be required to do when they joined the agency. He wanted me to be preoccupied with other things so that I would not keep tabs on his activities. Looking back now I admit that I should have watched his every move. We had worked so long together that I never worried about anything that he did. When I questioned him for the task I did, he assured me that it was necessary to do the little things. He always told me that it would lead to something. It never did and I never put two and two together, until files that I was looking into came up on a hunch, came up missing. I questioned Higgins about these files, but he had no answer for me. He told me to not worry about the files and also not to report it, because he would take care of it.

I started checking into this more closely, but again, I found nothing that would implicate him. Finally, I approached him over a file concerning East Africa and activity that was going over there. This made him uneasy. He did not like all the questions and scolded me. He had never acted like that before. This made me angry and we had a huge argument. We had to be restrained because we almost came to hitting each other. We were separated and we both went home to sleep on it. I felt horrible about what had happened and waited for him the next day, but he never came into his office. No one has seen or heard from Higgins since. People in the agency said that our argument drove him over the edge and into early retirement. Others say that the stress of the job got to him and he will never come back to the agency. I felt differently and believed that he was doing something illegal and knew that he was going to get caught. The best way for someone to not get caught is to disappear."

"What do you mean?" Jake asked. "Why do you feel that he just did not want to quit. I have been in the business before. I have seen others quit and never been heard from again. Do you have any proof?"

"This is the proof I have," H answered laying a folder on the table. Jake grabbed the folder and opened it up.

"What am I supposed to look for?" Jake asked while he looked through a few pictures and documents.

"If you look closely you will see what I mean," H answered. "These pictures are only a few months old; they are of Higgins, look here. He is a few years older than the last time you saw him, but this is him, right her."

H was pointing his finger at a figure in the picture. Jake did see what H was pointing at and did notice it was Higgins. That was the first time Jake had seen Higgins in ten years. He felt Higgins did him an injustice, walking away from him and not caring about him their last meeting. He had wished that Higgins was dead, but that was not the case. He still wanted to know what H's point was by showing him Higgins. He looked back up at H and said, "So what, that might be Higgins, but what does it prove?"

"My sole purpose was to track him down and bring him to justice. No one believed that he was a rogue agent. I looked into his activities and found many things that did not add up. I started Code 7 for the sole purpose of capturing him. If you can remember, he was always a very smart and cunning man. It was difficult, but I was able to track him down. Through a series of contacts and a lot of time, I was able to get some proof of his activities. These pictures are the proof that he is still working, but I don't know how old these pictures are and I also don't know what he is up to. I was lead to believe that he was located in Honduras and I had trained an agent to hunt him down. Code 7 was set to go to after him, but our government stepped in and completely switch my intentions. I was not happy, but I had to put Higgins on hold and turn my attention to East Africa. I know that you have been out of pocket for a while, so I ask you if you are familiar with this situation."

"I have been out of pocket with what is going on with the world since I was relieved of my duties. I am all ears."

H told him the story of East Africa and of the oil discovery. Jake never listened to the news, and could not believe that he had been in such a bubble over the last ten years that he had not heard of any of this information. H educated him on Kier and East Africa over the next hour.

Jake interrupted the story and asked, "How could he justify kicking the United States out of his country? Did he give any real reason for this?"

H answered by saying "Yes he did. He said that the U.S. came in and took advantage of every opportunity. He also said that our country's main goal was to take over his newly formed government and to eventually take over the entire region."

"Did he have any proof that this is what we were do or just make up these things to get other countries on his side," Jake asked.

"Who knows where he got his information," H answered. "He was able to get other countries to come to his aid. Also, the United Nations stepped in and told the U.S. not to have anymore contact with East Africa or there would be major consequences."

"There was an immense amount of pressure put on the administration not to do anything concerning the oil discovery. Kier made it clear he did not want any communication between himself and our administration and the people of our country was all for it. They would not stand for another invasion on another country and I believe that Kier knew we would do nothing. He has been right so far. The White House, because of pressure it was getting from the U.N. and the American people, decided that they would stop all communication toward East Africa.

On the other hand, the CIA could not stand still and allow this to happen. The agency had to know what had made Kier break of all ties toward us. At the time that this occurred, I was still part of the CIA, but had started the secret agency Code 7. Even though the agency operates as secretly as possible, it still needed an agency that no one knew about. That is why they came to me. Only two people, Tom Claiborne, who is the Director, and his top associate knew of Code 7's existence. They felt that my agency was small and could fly under the radar undetected. I was focused on Higgins at the time, but I changed gears in a hurry. I sent my one agent to East Africa to get me information and intel on what was going on over there."

H continued by saying, "I was told by the CIA that this was a top secret mission. No one in the administration knew about it and if anything went wrong many people's careers were on the line. The CIA would not recognize my agency and would not help me with any extraction. My agent had been trained extensively in these matters and we both were very confident that nothing would go wrong. We would get in, get the information we needed, and get out. We strategized over our plan for over three months and finally the time came and we went in.

Simeon flew our agent into enemy territory and the agent parachuted in. Communication worked very well and we kept the lines open for three weeks. The agent had gotten to the capital city undetected and said that there were some disturbing activity, but suddenly something went wrong and our communication was cut off. That was two months ago and I have heard nothing since then."

He continued, "Unfortunately, the agreement I had with my operatives with the CIA, would be for me to shut down immediately. That was not acceptable for us to do. We could not allow Code 7 to shut down and leave our only agent in East Africa. Because we did not shut down our operation, we have been on the run looking over our shoulders, making sure we are always one step ahead of them. This endeavor was not what we imagined, but I will say that I don't know if the agent is dead or alive, but I will not stay here and do nothing about it. Even though all my communication has been shut down, we will continue to do what we can do to save the agent."

"Why not go to the administration for help," Jake asked.

"The U.S. administration would deny any involvement," H snapped back quickly as if Jake had not been listening. "First of all the administration told all parts of the State Department to stay out of East Africa. This incident could cost the administration re-election. With the pressure from the American people and worldwide pressure, the last thing this administration wants is a scandal, especially one over there."

"Listen, Jake," H said as he looked him straight in the eyes, feeling that Jake might have second thoughts, "I had nowhere else to turn. I had no other agents I could go after, because we would have been located and shut down. I went after you, knowing that your file was destroyed in everyone's eyes except mine and that you would not be monitored. You would be the last person that my superiors would expect me to contact, of even acknowledge knowing.

I know that I have not been as honest with you as I should have been and I understand if you do not want to go further with us, but I want you to understand something. As much as we need you to be a part of us, you need us as well. This life is what you were trained to do a long time ago, and I know this is what you were put here on earth to do still. Are you with me?"

Jake knew that H was right. He had wasted the last ten years of his life bouncing around from one place to the other, blaming others for his problems. Now he had a chance to get back the only life he had love and longed for. This lifestyle was in his blood and enjoy being back in it. He had missed the action so long that he did not care who he worked for. He just wanted to get back into the game.

"Do you feel that I have had enough training," Jake asked. "You know I am not as young as I used to be."

H started to laugh a little and answered, "You are right, you are not as young as you used to be, but you were the best field agent I ever saw." He then changed his tone and got serious, "You did things that I can't train you to do. You let your instincts take over and that is why you will be so successful. That is the Jake that I remembered. Not the one that was in unbelievable shape, but the one that did things that no one could explain."

Jake knew that he did not have a lot of time to decide if he was in or out and H needed an answer immediately. He still blamed not only Higgins, but also the U.S. government for throwing him to the curb. He had never been compensated for the ten years he had put in earlier and wanted to make sure that he would be taken care of. He also did not want to get caught by anyone remotely part of the government and knew they had to keep moving. He knew what he wanted to do but still had a few things he wanted to ask first before he made his decision.

Jake asked H, "If I do this, what's in it for me? The last time I was on a mission, I got nothing out of it. I was captured and almost killed. When I got home, I was told that I was no longer needed and that all my service was not appreciated. I received no compensation and my life went into a tailspin. Now I have nothing to my name, except the clothes on my back. Basically, I want to know what I get in return, if I do rescue your agent."

H knew that he could not pay Jake anything, but had a better opportunity. "First of all, if you join in and be a part of this, it will not be for the money. I will say that if you can get back without incident and rescue my agent, I know that Code 7 will become part of the CIA again. I can assure you that you will be welcomed back as part of the family and we can look for Higgins together. I believe he holds the key to your capture ten years ago and we can track him down together and bring him to justice."

Jake had never cared about material things and money was never his reason to get into the CIA in the first place. He just wanted to hear what H had for him. He liked the aspect of revenge and bringing down the guy who got him kicked out of the agency in the first place. The last ten years he had no life and knew that he was getting a second chance to start over. He lived for the action and was ready to start immediately.

"I'll do it," he said. "I am ready right now, when do we leave?"

H smiled. He knew that Jake was the right man for the job and knew that he would join even thought he did have to twist his arm a little. "We will leave in the morning," H said after hearing the good news. "By the way, there is one more thing that I need to warn you about. This could be your first and last mission. There is anarchy and chaos in the region and this is very dangerous job. You could lose your life and if you have anything you would like to get off your shoulders, tonight could be your last night."

Jake had plenty of problems that he had caused over the years, but knew there was not enough time to clear them up by morning. He just looked at H and said, "There is nothing that comes to mind."

"I guess I need to make myself a little clearer," H responded. "Don't forget that I have been keeping my eye on you for a long time now. I know about you and your friend, Henderson and how you have not spoken with him for quite some time."

Jake was startled. He had thought of Henderson often, but had made no contact with him for a long time.

"What about Henderson?" Jake asked. H continued what he was saying. "Do not ask me how I know this, but he lives a few miles from here. Here are the directions and my keys. Again, we leave first thing in the morning, so do what you want with that information. I will talk to you in the morning." H walked away and headed off to get some sleep.

Jake relished the fact that he had a chance to see Henderson again, and it did not take long for him to decide to see his friend. He took up the offer from H and decided to go see Henderson.

CHAPTER 8

Eric Henderson loved growing up in the Deep South. He had grown up an Alabama boy, and he always missed his home while he working for the CIA. He did not like the fact of how he was dismissed from the agency, but he put it behind him and he was exited to go home and be with his family again. He never really liked the fast pace and death defying missions he went on. He was glad that he helped make the world a safer place for his country, but he was also glad to let someone else take his place.

Henderson and Jake had completely different personalities, and because of that reason, they had become very good friends. He always felt Jake was part of his family and could not understand why Jake had disappeared from his life. Henderson made several attempts to locate him, but to no avail. He did not want to give up on his friend, but he just accepted the fact that Jake did not want to be contacted.

After Henderson returned home, he decided that he would enter into his father's business. He worked for a few years with his father and his brothers running convenient stores, but got bored and wanted to move on to do something else. He had always enjoyed teaching people and wanted to pursue that as a career. He applied and was accepted to become a 6th grade science teacher for his home town middle school in Summerville, Alabama. Even though he never really excelled in school, he really excelled at teaching. He became the most popular teacher in the county and got many awards during his tenure.

While living in his hometown, Henderson met a beautiful young woman. They began to date each other and married a year later. He was finally happy. He had moved on, putting the last ten years of espionage behind him. He was able to block his memory, never telling anyone, even his wife, of the perils he had been through over the last ten years. He was not ashamed of what he had had done, actually he was proud of the death defying missions he had accomplished; he did not want to have to relive those moments again.

He became an excellent teacher and was given many different job offers. He loved living in Alabama, but an opportunity presented itself to him and he had to take it. This was a more prestigious job working at one of the top private schools in America. It also tripled his salary. He packed his bags and moved himself and his wife to Savannah, Georgia.

Savannah was a wonderful city. It still was in the Deep South like he loved and was a bigger city than where he lived. He also believed Savannah would give him a better opportunity than he had. Because of the pay raise it allowed Henderson and his wife to start a family and soon after moving, his wife got pregnant. He was ecstatic and everything in his life was good. He really enjoyed working in Savannah and later became head of the science department for all Savannah public schools.

Henderson and his wife had their first child and he became a father. Life could never get any better than what he was experiencing, but later it did. His wife had a second child and Henderson was living the American Dream. He never imagined this could be possible as he hung on for dear life in Iran prison, but he now had a wonderful family, had a big house, and was an important part of the Savannah school system. Ten years had passed and Henderson was still great health and felt that his life was perfect. He felt that he had put his earlier life finally behind him, but his past came back to him one evening.

Jake had not talked to or seen Henderson in a very long time. He was nervous, and knew that this may be his last chance to see his lifelong friend. Actually he thought, this was the only true friend he had ever had. They had been through many different experiences throughout their lives. Even though Jake had not seen his friend since they left CIA headquarters together, he never quit thinking of him. He wondered what Henderson would think of him, if he would acknowledge him.

He had driven to Henderson's house which was an old Victorian style two story brick home. It was located in a secluded neighborhood that had children of all ages, riding bikes and playing tag on the street and in their yards. Jake could not believe that his friend lived like this. He had a hard time imagining either of them settling down and now after ten years Henderson was a family man, settled down in a small and quaint neighborhood. This just blew Jake's mind.

Jake sat in the car as he parked across the street from Henderson's house to watch the surroundings of the neighborhood. He saw a small bike parked outside his friend's house, with small toys scattered throughout the yard. Jake had waited long enough and he finally got out of his car and made his way to Henderson's front door.

He walked up the path, through a white picket fence toward the steps that led to the front porch. He noticed a swinging chair that was connected to the ceiling of the porch and just imagined what Henderson thought about, when he swung there at night. He finally had enough courage to knock on the door. He did not knock hard, just hard enough to make him feel good about coming by. He hoped that no one heard him or that no one was home and he started to walk away, but the door opened and a little voice asked, "Who are you?"

Jake turned around and saw a little girl that was probably six years old. He knew that she was Henderson's daughter because she was the spitting image of him. Jake smiled at the little girl and answered, "I am an old friend of your daddy. Is he home?"

"Yes sir, he is," the little girl said. "Wait here a minute and I will run and get him."

While Jake waited for his friend, all kind of thoughts went through Jake's head. He wondered if Henderson was mad at him for disappearing and not contacting him for the last ten years. He did not know if Henderson would even want to talk to him. Jake wanted to leave, but instead of leaving, wondered off the porch into the front yard. He hid behind an old oak tree just to see who came to the door.

Henderson came to the door and looked out. "Sweetie, are you sure someone is here," he asked his daughter.

"Yes sir," she said. "There was a man here a minute ago. I told him to wait and that I would be right back."

"Well I don't see anyone, maybe he went around back," Henderson said as he opened the front door and walked off the porch. He walked around back, but did not see anyone. Whoever was here must have left and in a hurry, he thought as he walked back to the front of his house.

Henderson was about to go up his stairs to his porch, but felt that there was someone in his yard. He looked around his yard and only saw the big oak tree, but still he yelled out, "Is there anyone in my yard."

He heard someone reply, "Hey, Eagle, you got a minute."

Henderson was startled. He had not heard that name in a long time and thought he would never hear it again. He turned around slowing, wondering who it was that knew his old code name. "Who's there, show yourself," he yelled out.

Jake, who was still hiding behind the big oak tree, came around the tree with a big grin on his face. "It has been a long time, my friend," Jake said to a very startled Henderson.

Henderson had not seen Jake in over a decade and now his long lost friend just showed up on his doorstep. All kind of things raced through Henderson's head and even though he had waited over ten years to see his friend, he had a loss for words. He had always wondered if he was ever going to see Jake again. He was very happy that his friend had finally come to see him again.

"I thought I would never see you again," Henderson said looking straight into Jake's eyes. "Where have you been for the past ten years and how in the world did you track me down?"

Jake knew that Henderson had a lot of questions for him, but he did not have a lot of time to answer them. He did, however, have a few hours and just hoped Henderson would allow him to explain some things to him. "I know you have a million questions, and obviously I have no right to embark on you and bring you my problems, but I wanted to see you again. You were always like a brother to me and I felt that I owed you plenty of explanations. I will leave you alone if you want me to, but I hoped that you will give me a couple of hours to talk to you."

Henderson had never told his family the truth about his past, but now his past had just walked up on his doorstep. "One thing I know," Henderson said, "is that you don't owe me anything or any explanations. We had a good run. I have put what we did ten years ago behind me. Again, what's done is done. I'm just glad that you are alive and well. Oh, by the way, what are you doing here?"

Jake was indeed alive and well. He had been through a lot since he walked away from his friend. A lot of things had changed since the day they had last seen each other. Jake was about to go on his first mission with Code 7 and did not know if he was coming back alive. The only person he wanted to see before that happened was his friend, but at this very moment he really did not what to say.

He looked at Henderson and said, "It's been a long time my friend, too long. I am sorry that I just showed up without contacting you. I know it's not right for me to come in and bother you and your family. I just wanted to thank you for being there for me all those years. You did want I wanted to do and helped me achieve my goals. You were a true friend and I thank you for that. I will let you get back to your family. It was good to see you again."

Jake turned to leave, but Henderson snapped back, "Jake, I haven't seen you for over decade; you show up on my doorstep, tell me thanks for being a friend, and now you just want to walk away. You at least owe me a dinner and some sort of an explanation. I will get my wife to cook up something and we will talk a little bit. You at least owe me that."

Jake knew that Henderson had a point and he was hungry. He decided that he had a few hours to burn and really wanted to catch up. "What's she cookin'," he asked, letting his southern accent come out for the first time in awhile.

Henderson knew his friend would stay around for awhile and he grinned and said, "Don't worry about it. She is a good cook, so come on inside and stay awhile."

Jake followed Henderson into the house. Henderson called out to his children to come down and meet an old friend. Jake saw two a little girl and a little boy running down the stairs. "Hey guys," he said to his children, "this is Mr. Jake. He is an old college friend of daddy's."

The little girl smile at Jake and said, "I have already met him."

Jake smiled back at the little girl. He could not believe that Henderson was a father to two children. Henderson's wife came out of the kitchen. She was a beautiful woman. Jake could see the love in her eyes that she had for Henderson.

"Well, who do we have here?" she asked in a soft southern voice.

"Honey, do you remember me telling you about my best friend from college."

"Yes I do," she answered.

"Well, he was passing through town and stopped by to say hello. I have not seen him in a while and thought you wouldn't mind setting up another plate at the table."

"That won't be a problem," she answered. "I have heard a lot about you. I am finally glad to meet they guy that my husband has talked about for so long. You can come by for dinner anytime. I hope you like fried chicken."

Jake was hungry and replied, "Fried chicken is my favorite. Thank you for having me. You have a beautiful home and two beautiful children.

Henderson's wife smiled at Jake and said, "My wonderful husband always told me how nice you were, and I think I agree with him. You seem very nice and well mannered."

She walked toward the kitchen with her children and said, "Honey, dinner will be ready in a few minutes. Why don't you take Jake into the family room and catch up. I know you have a lot to talk about. The children and I will be in the kitchen and will give you some privacy."

Jake followed Henderson into the family room. Henderson went over to his liquor cabinet and offered Jake something to drink.

"No thanks," he answered, "I will take some water, though. I have been working out for the last two months and am trying to stay in shape and I'm staying away from the hard stuff." Both new there was a lot to talk about. Jake was about to say something, but they heard Henderson's wife call out to them that dinner was ready.

Dinner went by fairly quickly with not much fanfare. Henderson and Jake only talked about their fraternity days and how much fun they had while they were in college. Dinner was over and Jake and Henderson made their way back into the study.

"I will let you two have your privacy," Henderson's wife said. "It was so nice to meet you, Jake. Please feel free to come back anytime. Next time come and stay a few days. Good night." She left the room and took the kids upstairs to give Jake and Henderson some privacy.

"You must be a proud man, because you have a beautiful wife and two wonderful children. She is so nice and your kids are very well behaved."

Henderson nodded and smiled. "I am a very blessed man, but enough about me. I have a ton of questions to ask about you.

Where have you been the last ten years? Why did you lose touch with me? We were so close and you just took off and did not bother to even call. I tried to track you down, but I finally figured that you just wanted to be alone. What happened?" Henderson continued with more questions for Jake to answer.

Jake knew that Henderson needed some answers, but had no answers that he felt were good enough. "Honestly, Henderson," Jake answered, "there is really no excuse for disappearing. I was so upset with what happened, about us getting kicked out and all. I guess I should have been thankful that we still had our lives, but I felt that we were both owed something. You know me, I did not need any money, but I needed some sort of explanation. I needed someone to tell me why they did not want me anymore. You remember, we were treated like trash, thrown out on the curb. We did a lot for the agency and they treated us like scum."

Jake continued, "I tried for two weeks to see someone, anyone, but all the doors were shut in my face. I had enough and decided that to get away, not to come back home, though. I went out West, but I could never settle down, and got into some trouble with the law. I felt very sorry for myself. For some reason I just could not find time to call you. I know it was wrong, and I was selfish, but it took ten years and I am finally getting things under control. I have finally found my calling in life and I am happy. I had to come by and say that I was sorry for letting the years get by without at least making a phone call."

Henderson listened to what Jake was saying and started to laugh. "Listen, I know that you are sincere and I appreciated your apology. Look, I have never forgotten you. You were and still are my best friend. You do not owe me anything. I am just glad that you are still alive. You had me worried, but now it seems like old times all over again; just without all of the terrorist wanting to kill us."

Jake laughed, as well, and went over and gave Henderson a big bear hug. He was indeed sorry and was glad that they could leave the past in the past.

"Are you happy?" Jake asked Henderson, "I mean, it looks that you're very happy, but do you miss your past life."

Henderson knew where Jake was going and already had the answer. "The past is in the past. It was thrilling. There were places that we went to and things we did that I will never forget. I know what we did was right and it helped save lives, but I have too much to live for now. It is over for me and I am glad. To answer your question, I am very happy."

"I am glad to hear that," Jake said with a smile. "I need to tell you something, something that has changed my life."

Henderson perked up and told Jake that he wanted to know what he had to say. Jake told Henderson about how he was pulled over and arrested. He told him how he was put into an interrogation room and then woke up in some sort of training camp. He talked about Simeon and how he had gotten him into shape, not only physically, but mentally as well. He told him about H and how he played a part in both their lives. That caught Henderson by surprised. "What do you mean," he asked Jake.

"Henderson," Jake responded in a very serious tone, "H followed both of our careers. He was behind the scenes, but knew everything we did. He had our file."

"What file?" Henderson asked as he interrupted Jake.

"The file that was supposed to be deleted," Jake answered.

"How do you know it was ours?" Henderson questioned Jake.

"It was ours," Jake said as he walked over to look out the window in the study, making sure no one was watching them. "I looked the file over. It chronicled our whole career, from start to finish. I know you haven't forgotten about Iran, but have you ever wondered how we got caught?"

Henderson answered "Yeah, I know how we got caught. We were in the wrong place at the wrong time. I still can't believe we got out of there alive. What's your point?"

"My point is this, I trust H," Jake said as he was still staring out the window. "He has helped me, more than you know. He told me that we were getting to close to something and someone wanted us dead. Someone in the agency felt we knew too much. They tipped off the Iranian military, hoping that we would get eliminated."

Henderson stared at Jake and wondered why he kept looking out the window. "Is someone coming to get you?" Henderson asked, trying to be funny.

"Why do you ask that?" Jake responded.

"Because you keep looking out the window, as if someone is watching you. I remember how you were always paranoid about being watched. Nothing seems to have changed. You still are a little hysterical, thinking that someone is always watching us."

"You never know," Jake answered with a smile. "You can never be too sure. Anyway, getting back to my story, do you remember what we were there for?"

"I will never forget," Henderson answered, as he got up and started to walk over to the window to get a peek outside. He saw an empty street and turned around and said, "Did this H guy tell you who tipped off the Iranians?"

"He was close to figuring it out." Jake answered. "He spent five years trying to figure out how we were captured. Every detail that he found pointed to Higgins. He was about to confront him with the evidence that he had collected, but Higgins vanished. The agency swept it underneath the rug, especially since our file was deleted, and then said that Higgins just got mentally drained and took off. I have seen pictures of where he is and also what he has been up to. I know we both trusted him, but it turned out he was probably working for the other side."

Henderson had not thought of Higgins or the Iran capture in a very long time. He would have liked to have known more, but in his mind it was in the past and there was nothing he wanted to do about it.

"Jake," he said, "I know it should matter to me, but even if you did know more, what could I do. The past is the past. I really have no desire to go backwards. I have put that life behind me. I thank God that I am alive and really just want to continue doing what I am doing, and that is living a simple life."

"Henderson," Jake said as he finally walked away from the window and sat down on the couch. "I do not have a problem with how you want to live your life. My point was that we were set up. You remember that our job in Iran was to get in and get out without getting caught. We both wondered why we were there. The information that we got was different from any other mission that we had been on. Someone wanted us out of the agency and wanted us dead. Don't you wonder why or who?"

Jake was showing the same determination that Henderson remembered. That is why he liked Jake, because of how determined he was. He had followed Jake into the agency, simply because of his determination and loved the fact that he never had backed down to anyone. Once Jake put his mind to something, he always accomplished it. Henderson had forgotten about that, but listening to Jake talk about this conspiracy, made Henderson think more and more about what he could do.

"Jake, I want to help you," Henderson said, "but I am so far removed from that life, even if I wanted to get back in and help, I would not know where to start. If Higgins was responsible for us being captured, then hopefully he will be punished. I will support you from the safety of my home, but will not be able to do anything more. I am not like you, Jake. I let it go a long time ago and don't ever want to go back to it."

Jake was not there to bring Henderson back in. He knew that Henderson had wanted to leave long before they were caught, but just stayed in because Jake wanted him to. He definitely did not want Henderson to leave his wife and kids; that was not the point of his visit. He just wanted his friend to listen and agree with him.

"Henderson," Jake responded, "I know you can't do anything for me, but I appreciate you just listening. I would like to go after the responsible party, but there is no factual evidence pointing to Higgins. There are bigger fish to go after anyway."

Henderson had walked away from the window and sat down on his recliner. He leaned up after hearing that from Jake and asked, "What do you mean bigger fish to go after?"

Jake knew he had opened a can of worms and he knew that he had to tell Henderson what he had signed on to do. "This is classified, but I am back in the game," Jake said.

Henderson sat back in his chair and nodding to Jake to go on. Jake told Henderson about Code 7 and how H needed him to go into East Africa and rescue a missing agent.

"Doesn't he know that you have been out of action for a while?" Henderson asked him.

Jake answered by saying, "Do not forget that H had followed our career and knows what I am capable of. The problem is that there is not enough time to get me into complete physical shape, but if I don't go now, the agent could be killed."

"The agent may already be dead," Henderson said, "and you may get killed as well. You are not as young as you used to be. Aren't you just a little worried?"

"Henderson," Jake said, "one thing I know is that this is the life I want. This is the life I have always wanted. I have never forgotten anything that I ever did. I know that my instincts will take over. If I do not do this, than I will eventually die a broken man. They need me as much as I need them. You could be right and I may not come back, but at least I am doing something that I was meant to do."

"You were the best," Henderson said. "I know that you will do what you need to do and get back home safe."

Jake looked and nodded. He had forgotten how much he cared for his friend and he was very happy he had come by to see him, possibly for the final time, he thought. He knew it was getting late and it was time for him to get back to the camp and get some sleep.

"I have to go," Jake said as he walked to the front door. Henderson got up off the chair and walked Jake to the door.

"Jake, there is no way you will change your mind and not do this mission?"

Jake looked at Henderson and said, "I missed you my brother. Thanks for the hospitality and the talk. I should have done this long before now. I love ya' man."

Jake and Henderson hugged and Jake walked out to his car. "Take care and I will see you again. Be safe."

Henderson watched as Jake got in his car and sped away. Henderson was sad to see his friend walk away, but deep down he knew he would see him again. He shut the door and noticed that Jake had left a sheet of paper. He opened it up and read what was on it. He quickly tore it up and threw it away. He did not want his wife or children to see what was on it. He knew that his past life was over and he had no reason to talk about it ever again.

CHAPTER 9

An electric shock started up Jake's groin and went all throughout his body. He had never experience this type of pain before. He screamed in agony, but no one who cared heard him. He had been tortured for the last two weeks, but he would never break. He knew that he would probably die soon, but he would never give up any information that his captives wanted. The one thing that Jake did know, was the longer he kept quiet the longer he would live. This was put into his brain everyday during his training. Even though that he was in pain, Jake knew that he could withstand the torture as long as they dished it out.

Jake had been told that if he was caught during a mission, he would be on his own and that his life would not be spared by the agency. He was prepared; that is why he loved what he did so much. The excitement was thrilling and he had no desire to do anything else. He and had been so successful with their previous missions; the thought of being caught never entered his mind. The Iranian army caught him completely off guard.

"You will die soon, any last word," an Iranian officer laughed as Jake laid on the ground of a torture room. He was too weak to speak, but was able to hold up his middle finger, letting the office know how he felt of him.

"Take him in there and hang him with the other captive," the Iranian officer yelled to his private.

"Thank God," Jake said to the officer, "I think I would die if I had to look at your disgusting face for another minute."

The comment did not go over well with the officer. As Jake was lead out of the torture room and back into the dungeon area, he was hit across his back with some sort of stick. He felt that his back had been broken and yelled out in pain. "Keep your mouth shut or the next time I won't be as nice," the officer yelled out.

As the soldier tied his wrist together and hung him up, Jake was able to open his eyes and he saw his friend, Henderson. Henderson had been tortured, but he was able to wink at Jake before he passed out from the pain. Jake was very happy his friend was still alive and with the wink that Henderson had given him, he knew that his friend had kept quiet and not given up any information. Jake had suffered tremendous amount of pain and did not have enough strength to keep his eyes open. He shut his eyes and passed out.

* * *

"Get up;" H yelled to Jake. "It is time to get going."

H, as usual, had been awake all night. He rarely slept and because of the mission that they were about to go on, sleeping was not an option for him. He wanted Jake and Simeon to rest awhile, but he knew that the flight would be long and they could sleep some on the plane. H knew that they would not get much sleep during the mission and he had to prepare them for what he hoped would be a successful extraction of his agent. He felt that he could not sleep until his agent was back safe.

Jake continued to have flashbacks to his Iran capture. He had yet to tell anyone and knew that H did not want to discuss the capture until after the mission was over. Jake decided not to talk about it and hoped he would not have any more dreams about his capture and torture.

Even though H had been exiled from the CIA, he still had contacts that were very loyal to him. He was able to secure a plane. It was not a very large aircraft, but its engines were large enough to get them across the Atlantic and into Morocco.

Simeon walked up the small ladder into the aircraft. He knew that there was no turning back for him or anyone else.

He looked at Jake and said, "You know that this is your last chance."

Jake had no reason to back out now. As he climbed into the plane, he looked over at Simeon and touched him on the soldier and said with a smile, "I have been waiting for ten years for this chance, now let's get going."

H was the last one to climb into the plane. He looked back and said a quiet good-bye to his country, not knowing if he would ever come back. If the mission did not go as planned, he knew that this could be the last time the three of them would see America. It was a sacrifice, but all three of them were willing to go through with it.

H got in the cockpit. He had piloted many different planes and this plane was not any different any of the others. He started the engines and made sure that everything worked properly.

Before he took off, he turned around to Jake and Simeon and said, "I need you to familiarize yourself with this."

H handed both of them a folder containing the information on the last whereabouts of the agent they were going after. "Make sure you read this over and know it like the back of your hand."

Jake got the file in his hand and began to read over the file. It did not take him long to memorize exactly what he was asked to do. He looked over at Simeon and asked him if he knew his responsibilities. He wanted to make sure that they were both on the same page before they landed in Morocco. Simeon nodded and told Jake he would be ready. Jake had his doubts, but did not want to voice them to his new friend.

Even though it had been awhile, Jake had been in this situation on many different occasions. During his early years with the

CIA, he always knew exactly what he had to do. Simeon on the other hand had never been in the field. He always wanted to be a field agent, but H had felt that his expertise was better suited for training. Simeon got his wish, but he was unsure of what he was supposed to do. Jake sensed this and looked over at Simeon and said, "I know that you haven't been out there in action before. Once you get out in it, just let your instincts take over. Watch me when we are out there and follow my lead."

Jake had always been the one in charge of any mission he had ever gone on and this would be no exception. Even though it had been ten years since his last mission, he would take over the lead role and be in control of each situation that they would encounter. He would allow H to tell him what he ought to do, but once they landed and he was on enemy soil, he would be the one in charge. He liked it and would not have any other way.

"We will have a twenty-four hour layover once we land," H yelled over his back while flying the plane. "I will go over in complete detail what each one of our responsibilities will be. There won't be much time so sleep once we get to Morocco, so get some sleep on the plane. When we land, we will only have time to get supplies, and go over the details of the mission. If you need help sleeping, I have a couple of bottled waters, with a sedative in each one. Go ahead and finish the bottle and we will be there before you wake up. Sweet dreams, Gentlemen." Jake knew his adrenaline would be pumping, so a little relaxation was in order for him. He grabbed a bottle and looked at Simeon. They toasted to a successful mission and both of them finished off their bottle. Within the next five minutes, they were both fast asleep.

* * *

"Hey Mustang, wake up," Henderson yelled at his friend, who was hanging with his head down and eyes closed. "Man, you have been hanging there for awhile. Are you still alive?" Henderson and Jake had been hanging with their hands tied to shackles from a wall for almost two days. They were in what seemed like a dungeon with just a small crack of light coming in from the entrance way. Henderson began to worry about Jake. Both of them had been tortured for days, but it looked as if Jake had gotten the worst of it.

"Do you hear me, open your eyes man, come on I know that you are still alive." There still was no movement. This really worried Henderson.

Finally, Jake twitched a little. Henderson breathed a sigh of relief and the he saw Jake move his head and open his eyes.

"The pain is unbearable," he screamed as he held his head up and looked around at his surroundings. "Every bone in my body is aching, my head is pounding, and I think that my back is broken. I don't have any feeling in my feet."

"You need to try to move your feet around. I know you are hurting, but move your legs around, too." Henderson was in similar pain, but he had been conscious for over a day and had been able to move his legs around to get his blood circulating in his body.

Jake looked over at Henderson and said, "You look like that they got you good." Jake was referring to the black eyes and bloody forehead that Henderson had gotten.

"I am okay," Henderson replied trying not to let Jake see him in pain. "How about you? Are you going to be able to make it?" Jake winced in pain, but managed to blurt out, "yeah." Henderson knew his friend would be just fine.

* * *

Jake woke and looked out the window of the plane. He saw nothing but water below and knew that they must be halfway over the Atlantic Ocean. He figured that he had a few hours before they would land and saw that Simeon was still sleeping. Jake felt that this would be a good chance to get some information about his capture ten years ago. He got up from his seat and went to the front of the plane to talk to H.

"You're up," H said as he continued to fly the plane. "What brings you up here?"

"I have been having flashbacks about Iran, about being captured. I felt that I had put that horrible time behind me, but meeting you and hearing about my history, has brought all that back full circle into my life. I can remember almost everything. I remember every little detail and the more I think about it, the more I know how right you are. We were set up. I just need to know who did that to me."

H knew eventually he had to tell Jake what had happened ten years ago. He did not feel the time was right to disclose any more of what happened, but to have Jake focus on the job at hand. H looked straight ahead and kept flying the plane.

He said "I always felt some sort of responsibility toward you because of the way you were treated at the end. What's done is done. As you can see with me, the Agency credo is 'What have you done for me lately'. We both served the agency well, but something happened and changed that. I don't have the answers for you right now. Hopefully, we can figure these things out, but right now you need to be focused on the mission at hand."

H was not going to talk about the past anymore. He had made a point to Jake that he should forget about what had happened and move on. Jake knew H knew more, but he could tell that H was about to get irritated and felt that it was not the time to push the issue. He knew that there was more to the story, but knew he needed to focus and so he decided to just leave it alone. Jake knew that he would get to the bottom of it, but today was not the day. He decided to change the subject.

"What is your feel about Simeon?" Jake asked H, trying to feel him out about his trainer for the last five years. "Do you think he is ready for this?"

"Simeon has been with me for awhile now and he has done an excellent job of training. Even though he has not been in the field, I am confident that he knows what to expect. You need to be there for him, though. He will follow you. He sees the leadership in you that I do. One thing we both know is you never lose the instinct of being out in the field. I know once you land into the territory, your instincts will take over. You will have to put Simeon under your wing, but he will come into his own in just short time."

"What's his story," Jake asked hoping to shed some light on what type of person his new friend was.

"Simeon had a tough life growing up," H answered. "He never knew who his father was and his mother had been a drug addict. He had been shuffled through foster homes and did not have a place to call home. When he became an adult, he was arrested for an assault on an officer, then convicted, and had to serve two years in jail. Jail did not help him control his anger. He was going down the wrong path and got into the middle of a drug sting. He was arrested again, but it turned out that he was just a small player in the sting and the authorities decided that they needed him to help catch the bigger fish. He agreed and he was able to help bust one of the biggest drug stings of all time.

Simeon was later exonerated for his efforts and given a pat on the back. He liked what he had done and wanted to change his life. He later stumbled upon some more undercover work and the Agency started to pick up on what he was doing. I was handling world affairs at the time, but I stumbled across what he had been doing for the Agency. I met with Simeon and offered for him to join me and help form Code 7. That is pretty much it. Now, go back and get some more rest. You will need it."

Jake went back to his seat. He looked over and saw that Simeon was still asleep. Jake shut his eyes hoping to get a few more hours of sleep before they landed.

CHAPTER 10

After a very long flight, the plane carrying Jake, H, and Simeon finally landed in a small village right outside of Rabat, the capital of Morocco. H had been to Morocco on several different occasions and had met a few contacts. Unfortunately most had died or had left the country since his last visit. He had one contact that had not died or left and the contact was willing to lend a hand in their mission. H needed someone who would help him with fuel, supplies for the mission, and a shelter that would be home base. H wanted to get to East Africa as soon as possible, but he knew that Jake and Simeon needed at least one day of rest. The plane finally came to a stop and H looked out and saw his contact, Chafari waving them in. H knew that he could never trust anyone in the business, but had known his contact for over thirty-years and considered him a friend. H trusted him, but made sure Chafari did not know that.

"How was the flight," Chafari asked, as he helped the three of them off the plane. "It wasn't too long, was it?"

"Not bad, but it sure feels good to get that out of the way." H shook Chafari's hand and introduced him to Jake and Simeon.

"These are the two that I have told you about." H had been in contact with Chafari for some time now and let him know that Jake and Simeon were part of his small agency. Chafari was prepared for their arrival and made sure that H and his companions would be treated well.

"It is good to see you again, old friend," H said to Chafari as they shook hands. Chafari nodded and grinned and replied, "I am ready to get started."

Chafari was just out of college when he met H. H had been in the field on a mission in the Middle East and he needed someone who could get him some information on a situation that had developed in Lebanon. Chafari did not like all the violence in his country and wanted to help stop it. He was put in contact with H and both of them were able to bring justice to some very wanted terrorist. They continued working together for the next thirty years over all parts of the Middle East. Chafari was H's number one contact in the Middle East, but fearing that he may be discovered and killed, Chafari went to Morocco for refuge. He had made a home in Morocco and had been helping H with the planning of the mission.

"I have the safe house all set up for you guys." Chafari said as they walked to the Hummer. He handed each one of them a satellite phone and explained to H that he had the computers all set up the way he wanted them. They all got in the vehicle and left to the safe house.

They pulled up to the safe house. It was a small building, but it did not matter to them. They entered in the house and Chafari had it set up the way H had instructed him to do. There were two computers set up in the middle of the safe house. The main computer was set up with the most technical tracking device ever made. This computer would track the whereabouts of Jake and Simeon while they were in East Africa. H had paid a pretty penny for this computer and it had the best GPS system built into it. The computer would monitor Jake and Simeon at all times and it would also give H a map of the terrain of where they needed to go. As long as their communications were online at all times, H could tell Jake and Simeon exactly where they needed to go and who or what they would run into when they got there. The other computer was a simple back up, and it was equipped with the same GPS system built in as the main one. It had never been used and would not, unless the other computer went down.

The cell phones that Chafari had given the group were untraceable and the GPS chips that were usually installed in each phone had been disabled. H knew the importance of this, because he did not want his agents to be tracked by anyone. Chafari was an expert at developing small GPS devices and had come up with a tiny, clear chip that someone could put on their ankle and not even know it was there. Because it was so small and almost invisible it was very hard to be identified. Only H would be able to track the two agents as they went into the East Africa. If they got caught no one would know to remove this chip, because it could not be picked up by a scanner of any kind. H no longer had the use of a satellite like he did when he was in the Agency, so this would have to work for him. He wished he would have used this device on the agent that had been captured, but he did not and knew that a mistake had been made and that he would correct that mistake as best as he could.

"This will be a short stay for the two of you. So do not get to comfortable. We will fly out early tomorrow morning," H said, making sure that Jake and Simeon would be ready to go in the morning.

Jake sat down at the table and started to look at some different plans that had been drawn up by Chafari. "What is this?" Jake asked after looking at them for a few minutes. "That looks like a different escape route."

"Good observation. That is exactly what it is," Chafari answered. "I hope that things stay the course, but just in case we have two different plans. I was going to go over that in just a minute, but since you've seen it, let's go ahead and get prepared. Simeon, come over and let's get started on every possible scenario."

He laid out the plans and continued, "As you know this is what our original plan is and we will stay with this plan, but if something happens that changes the original then we need to be prepared to change quickly. I will then send you an emergency message that simply says 'Echo 11'. When you get the message, you will know that our original plan has changed and you will need to deviate from the plan and use the second route. This route is extremely dangerous, and I do not want to use it unless it is our final option."

Jake knew that the original plan was the only option and if the second plan had to be used, something had gone terribly wrong. He confided in Simeon, "Make sure we work together and that we are all on the same page and we will get out of there. Unfortunately, we really have no idea what it is like there since the oil was discovered, so all could be calm and we might slip in and slip out without ever being noticed."

Simeon knew that he could count on Jake to talk him out of any pre-jitters that he might have. "I will let you lead me to wherever you need me to go. I will always have your back."

Jake was very pleased to hear that from Simeon. He knew that, as long as he could trust Simeon that they would work well together. Even though Simeon was not Henderson, Jake thought to himself, he sure did come in a close second.

H was ready to get started. His computers were fully operational and he had everything in place. Chafari had informed him that his plane was refueled and ready for takeoff. All media outlets have been shut down in East Africa and all contact between them and the outside world had come to a halt. The last intel on this situation was that there was some communication between them and Iran. The U.S. had been trying to get information, but had been very unsuccessful at getting anything new on this situation. Other countries were unwilling to hand out any information about East Africa to the United States. These countries felt that the U.S. was now the evil empire and the CIA had been shut down. The Agency did not know about Chafari and that he worked with

Code 7. He had been able to get some information concerning East Africa. He explained to everyone that it seemed like that East Africa had turned the corner, but since this unbelievable discovery, all hell had broken out. There was chaos everywhere. He told them that they could use this chaos to their advantage. He showed them where he felt the captured agent was being held. He did not think that she has been moved, because he would have been contacted about it.

This did not bother Jake because he had been in hostile environments before. He had handled himself very well and been able to get in, get the job done, and get out without incident, except for the Iran debacle. He always felt that the more hostile the area was, the better prepared he would be. He looked on to hear H tell him more about the mission.

"Once you get to your landing point, you will contact me with you position." H said. "I will enter your code into this computer and with the small GPS device attached to your ankle, it will tell me where you are at all times. I will tell you which way to go, but unfortunately, I do not have a satellite feed and will not be able to tell you your surroundings. I will only be able to tell you where to go. You will need to move swiftly, but carefully. The area of East Africa that you will enter into has had a lot of activity, military activity, over the last two weeks. You are not there to engage in a fight, although you will be dressed for it. Here are you weapons. You will both be issued two handguns, one AK-47, six grenades, five plastic explosions, and a knife. Your extra ammunition will be in your bags. Jake, I want to make sure that you are still with me on this, because once you get back on the plane, there is no turning back. We have one chance to drop in and that will be it."

Jake understood what he had to do. He knew he was ready and would not back out. H was glad to see that Jake was ready to go.

He continued, "Chafari will be flying the plane. I will stay here watching your every move. The two of you will leave at two a.m. in the morning. The flight will be approximately three hours long. You will enter East African airspace at five a.m. and while be flying under the radar. Because you will be flying so low, you will not have a lot of time to pull your shoot after the jump. So make sure you are ready for this. You should land at these coordinates and then you will contact me. I will then let you know your next move. Do both of you understand."

Jake and Simeon both nodded in agreement. "Jake, I know that you have parachuted before, but to be on the safe side, I want both of you to jump together. This will insure that if anything happens, Simeon can help you out. I do not feel that this will be the case, but I want to take every precaution."

Jake agreed and knew that the big guy could take care of him if he needed it. "You have approximately three hours until you fly out of here. Inspect your bags again and make sure you have everything in there that you need. Also, put these chips on your ankles. This is vital. Chafari assured me that these devices will work, but let's try these out first."

Jake and Simeon both attached the tracking devices on their ankles and they instantly came up on the computer. "Great, this works. Remember, these devices are your livelihood. Make sure you do not remove them."

The final three hours blew by quickly and it was time for Jake and Simeon to board the plane. "Any last words that you have for us," Jake asked H.

"Good luck and God bless. I will see you at the extraction point in three days. Stay together and stay alive."

Chafari started the engine as they boarded and Jake looked back one last time at H. He took it all in and knew the next time he would be in a chaotic place with his life on the line. He took a deep breath and entered the plane. He was finally on his way back to the life he thought he would never have again.

CHAPTER 11

East Africa had become a very hostile environment over the last six months. Chafari knew this, but had received some information that there was an area where it still seemed peaceful. He made sure that H knew this and the plan was for the two of them to drop in this area, which was in the northern part of East Africa. The area was secure by all accounts. The plane flew low and the hatch opened. Jake and Simeon jumped out of the plane and landed in the northern part of East Africa.

It was a very dark and misty morning, but it did not hinder into Jake's plans. "Simeon, make sure you hide these shoots. We don't want anyone to know that we are here. Once you get those hid, come over and we need to do our first contact with H."

"One step ahead of you," Simeon said, "Go ahead and make the call."

Jake grabbed his cell phone and made the first call. "H, we have landed and are headed out." Jake said, "Is everything ready for us there."

"Yes, everything is put into place," H answered. "You need to get the contact before the sun comes up. Contact me when you reach the destination point and I will tell you what your next move will be, over and out."

Jake knew they had to move quickly. He knew that they needed to stay out of sight, but he also knew that they only had a little more than an hour before daylight. "This is when the training is going to kick in. Let's run." Simeon had already started.

They were on the way to Hal am, which was a fairly large town in East Africa. It was a very diverse city. H knew that Jake and Simeon could move around easily and not be considered out of the ordinary. They arrived right to the safe house and their contact was there to meet them. He gave them some clothes to change into and they were able to get a bite to eat. The safe house had been used by the missing agent a couple of months earlier. The contact informed them of where she had gone, but did not know where she was. He had information on how to get where she had gone and also had a vehicle for them to use. H had put his plan together very carefully and had every detail down to the minute. They left the town of Hal am and headed to the city of Turin.

Turin was located right outside New Helen, which was the capital city of East Africa. They left in an old pick-up truck heading to Turin. The contact drove them to the Nile River and they would go the rest of the way by an old house boat on the river. There had been a lot of reports of disappearances on the roads and it was safer to travel by river instead of the roads.

They got on the boat and took off down the river. It was an old clunker of a boat and did not go very fast, but at least they were safer than on the road. "Well so far so good," Jake said to Simeon as they road fairly slow on the old river house boat. The boat was old and run down, but it looked like the majority of boats that traveled down the Nile.

"How are you feeling? I know my adrenaline has been pumping ever since we landed." Jake was exited, but also knew to remain cool. He knew that Simeon would look to him and act the way Jake did. "My adrenaline is going through the roof right now."

Simeon replied, "Make sure you keep it under control. We still have a long way to go and you need to remain as calm as possible.

I know it is hard to control sometimes, but it is very important that you do."

They both were warned to be on the lookout for militia on the river. They also were told that the militia fired first and asked questions later. There was a hidden compartment in the boat, that they were shown and knew that if they needed to hide, that was the perfect place.

A few hours had passed and the boat continued to go down the river. They had passed by some small villages and nothing had looked out of the ordinary. They saw villagers on the riverbanks that had terrible expression of fear on their face. They knew that the villagers had been terrorized and that they feared for their lives.

They stopped in a small village about thirty miles north of Turin. They could see the fear in the villagers' eyes. The people in the village had recently been terrorized by one of Kier's militia. There was one woman who had survived that spoke some broken English and told Jake and Simeon what had taken place.

"Many men in uniforms came into our village," the women said in a fearful voice. "They killed most of our men and rape our women. This has not been the first time. We had peace for awhile, now we are scared for our lives."

Jake could tell that the woman was telling him the truth. The woman begged for Jake to help her. Jake knew something had to be done, but would have to worry about that later. He had a job to do and could not waver from the plan. They got water and some fruit and headed back down the river to Turin.

"What can you do for those people," Simeon asked Jake as they rode slowly down the river.

Jake replied, "I have seen this before on one of my earlier missions. I was in Yemen and saw all kind of murder and rape. We were there to rescue an informant who had been captured, a very similar situation that we are in now. We tried to bring hope to anyone we met, but we were there on a mission. We accomplished the mission and got out of Yemen. I turned over the information, but nothing was ever done. The killing and the rapes continued. I know that I am only one person, but I feel that something must be done. These are peaceful people. They cannot sleep at night for fear that they will not wake up in the morning. What kind of disorder is going on here?"

Simeon did not have an answer. East Africa was a country that had changed its landscape and they could tell that it had become a very fearful land.

"We need to find out what is going in this country." Jake continued his speech that there had to be something more that they could do. "The extraction window is so small that we just do not have the time that we need. We have to come back. I know that we could help these people."

Simeon agreed, but was hesitant when he answered, "I do think that these people need help. But what can I do?"

"Not much," Jake answered, "but if we accomplish this mission, I will not let these people continue to suffer. If I have to I will go to Washington and beat on any door that will listen."

The discussion continued as they kept puttering down the Nile. Simeon continued his rant on not being able to save the world when Jake interrupted him after hearing some sort of noise down the river. "Did you hear that?"

"Hear what?" Simeon asked as Jake shut down all but one engine of the house boat.

"That sounded like a gunshot." Jake had always been a keen listener. He could hear things that others couldn't. "Just stay alert. I think there might be some trouble ahead."

"Men," the captain of the enemy vessel yelled at his mates on the boat. "Quit shooting off your guns. There will be plenty of time for that. I want all of you to stay alert and remember that we have been ordered to board any boat on the river."

Kier's small navy, if one was to call it that, was a small military boat that was going up the Nile checking to see if anything was out of the ordinary. Jake and Simeon were headed down the river and into an ambush. "Look up there," one of the guys on the boat yelled. "I see a boat coming toward us."

"Remember," the captain said, "make sure we do not destroy the boat, just capture anyone who is on it and make sure that they are still alive."

The old house boat was coming down the river very slowly. "Turn off your engine," the captain yelled through a microphone. The boat continued its path. "Turn off your engines or you will be fired upon," he yelled again.

The boat still continued coming at them. They opened up fire on the vessel, unloading a few rounds of ammo on it. "That's enough. Remember, we don't want it destroyed, just a little damaged," the captain said. "Let's board it and see what we find."

They came up along side of the boat and one of the mates got boarded the house boat and turned off the final engine. "Anyone on it?" the captain asked.

"It looks that it has been deserted for some time. There doesn't look that is anything valuable on here. What do you want to do with it?"

"Let's burn it," the captain said. He lit a torch and handed it over for the soldier to burn the boat.

Jake looked at Simeon and motioned with his fingers. "On three," he said quietly.

One, two, three, the hatch on the boat floor lifted up. This caught the captain and the mates by surprised. Shots were fired and one man went down.

"Look out!" Jake yelled to Simeon.

"Shoot them!" the captain told his men. The men were not prepared for this attack and it showed. Simeon took another one out with an outstanding shot.

"Good shot!" Jake yelled as he moved over to the other side of the boat. Shots continued to be fired and there was major chaos all around, but Jake was able to take cover and take out another man in the militia. He knew there were four more. He had to take care of them or their cover would be blown.

"Simeon," Jake yelled. "Stay there I am coming over. Cover me!"

Jake moved swiftly over to Simeon as bullets went over his head. "That was real close," Simeon yelled as Jake sat beside him. "We need to take out the captain."

"I know," Jake answered as they were still being shot at. "They are over there hiding, trying to get to the radio. I have it covered. If they go for it I will be able to take them out. One more thing, there goes our quiet entrance."

Shots kept being fired by them and it seemed as if the shots would never stop. Jake noticed how erratic the shots were and figured that the men firing the shots were not well trained.

"I have a plan, cover me."

Jake knew that he did not have much time before others would hear the fighting. He decided to let his instincts take over. Jake got up quickly and moved to the other boat. A shot missed him by inches. He rolled over and got a great shot at the one who shot at him. He took him out and went to the back of the boat where he knew the other captain was. He crouched down and spotted the captain crouch over, hiding like a scared chicken.

"There are now two of us and just one of you. I don't want to kill you. Throw me your gun and lift up your hands."

The captain did not want to get captured, but did not want to die, either. "Don't' shoot, don't shoot, here's my gun," the captain said as he threw up his hands.

Simeon saw that Jake had captured the captain and had joined him on the other boat. "Good job," Jake said to Simeon.

The captain saw that Jake had taken his eyes off him and lowered his hands down and grabbed a gun that he had hidden behind him. "Watch out Jake," Simeon yelled as the captain shot toward him.

Simeon pushed Jake out of the way and was hit in the upper chest.

"No!" Jake yelled and shot back hitting the captain right between the eyes. He got down on his knees and grabbed Simeon's hand and said, "Simeon, talk to me. Keep your eyes open. I am going to get you some help."

Simeon knew that it was a matter of time before he was going to die. "Jake, there is no time. You must continue what you were doing. Please tell H that I saved you."

Simeon took one last breath and closed his eyes. Jake was in shock and could not believe his friend had died.

CHAPTER 12

New Helen, the capital of East Africa, had endured a rapid economic growth over the last ten years. The city had opened its doors to foreign investors throughout the world and had seen their economy double every few years. The city was the home of Mahmud Osman Kier the undisputed leader of East Africa. He was a revered and beloved leader not only with his own people, but others throughout the region. He had brought economic stability to East Africa and established the country as one of only two allies that the United States had in the region. The State Department believed he was a friend. Overnight it all changed.

The White House had asked all the major networks for airtime so that the President could talk to the American people. This would be a different speech than he had ever given. He had come into office three years before with the promise of peace and prosperity. The Iraq war had lasted a very long time and he knew that the American people did not want any more conflict. But after the biggest discovery of oil the world had ever seen and the United States not allowed any communication with East Africa, he knew the people would need some answers. He needed the air time so that he could set the record straight.

"Have you heard anything new on East Africa?" The President asked his chief of staff.

"No word as of yet, and their head of state has declined to talk," answered his chief of staff.

The President did not like the answer. He knew he had only a few more minutes until his speech. He was up for re-election and was under fire by the American people to solve the energy problem. His approval rating had always hovered around fifty percent, but recently it had gone to an all time high when the oil was found. The American people believed that the energy problem that they had been suffering through over the last decade would be solved. Unfortunately, he knew that just as fast as his ratings went up, they also could spiral down just as quickly if he could not get the crisis under control in East Africa. The President knew without the cooperation of late ally, the energy problem would still exist in his country and he would take the blame for it.

"I just do not understand what in the hell happened over there?" the President said in anger. "Our country had created this country ten years ago. We formed its new government. We sent billions of dollars to them and this is the thanks we get. That country was a great ally and now what are they to us? Their leader will not talk to us. They have the world is on their side, accusing us of all kinds of lies. I want to send our troops in there, but our people don't want another conflict. The U.N. has told us that they would take action against us if we go into there. You know all the problems that we have, but now I need some answers from you. What do I need to do to get this situation under control and keep the American people on my side? Give me some suggestions and calm my nerves."

The President was at his wits end concerning East Africa. He knew his hands were tied and re-election was just around the corner. The chief of staff knew that his job was on the line and he knew that the President's re-election depended on East Africa. Unfortunately, he did not have any answers the President wanted to hear.

He looked at the President and said, "We will still try to keep the lines of communication open, but as of right now nothing has changed. I would suggest that we sit back and let our some of our people find out what we need to do next. I just do not want to see you fall flat on your face because of this small insignificant country."

"I do agree that this country is insignificant, but right now they hold the keys to my re-election. So tell me, what info is the CIA giving us? I know that we are supposed to be standing pat, not letting anyone in our agencies go over there and investigate, but that is not my style. I need to know if we have anyone taking care of this problem for us?"

The President had resisted asking this question and did not want to know any detail about the any secret missions that might be taking place, but he knew that he was in dire straits and needed some answers.

"I was told that there was a mission, but I have not heard any more info on this matter," he answered.

The President became angry. He could not understand how his own chief of staff could not supply him with any more information than he was giving him. "Get on it. I do not want you to come back into my office until you have some sort of concrete information on the happenings of East Africa. We need to get them back as an ally. We need to set up a summit with them. If I have to, I will go there myself. Our political careers rest on their shoulders."

The President walked back to his desk and sat down ready to give his speech. Unfortunately he did not have any more information on this situation since East Africa separated itself from the United States. The President knew that his speech would either get him elected or send him on his way out. He enjoyed being President and did not want East Africa to be his down fall. He looked up at the teleprompter and began to speak to the American people.

"I address you tonight, differently than I have over the last three years," the President said in his deep, but enjoyable voice. "There has been a major discovery of oil in East Africa, our ally. We cooperated to the fullest extent and believed that this oil would help not only the United States, but the entire world with the energy problem. Unfortunately, East Africa, after tough negotiations with our State Department, has decided it does not need our help. East Africa has also requested that the United Nations step in and force sanctions on us if we send any advisors to their country. We are a peaceful country and do not want any conflict with anyone. We believe that East Africa can distribute the oil to any country it desires. We will not stand in their way to do so. We are working with their State Department at this present time to help any way we can, but I assure you that we will not force East Africa to do anything against their will. We will not tolerate any American interference or any other country for that matter. We will continue to talk with East Africa and the White House will keep the media informed. Thank you and God bless."

The President knew he did not have any answers concerning this matter and did not want a press conference. He was not prepared to answer any questions. He did, however, want answers and knew he could not stand by and not get his hands on the oil. He called his chief of staff again. "We need to keep quiet right now on East Africa. We need answers, but I do not want anything traced back to this office concerning East Africa. Find out all that you can about the mission and let me know, but again, be careful who you talk to. I do not want to be thought of as a liar. We cannot afford that."

"Yes sir," the chief of staff answered.

He was already one step ahead and had assigned a few men on the situation. He walked out of the oval office and made a call and asked if there was any more information concerning H and Code 7. "We cannot find him and his small agency," the voice answered on the other line. "It is like he fell off the planet."

The chief of staff reiterated that it was a matter of national security and that no would be allowed to rest until Code 7 was tracked down and eliminated.

"The people of East Africa will do as I have instructed," Kier's voice was heard over the loud intercoms that were all over the city of New Helen. "We have eliminated all of the infidels throughout our land. We are tired of being treated as second rate humans. The infidels came to exploit us and to take over our land. They wanted to change our way of life and our religion. We met it head on and have eliminated them."

These were speeches that were played every day in the capital city. They played at the same time with the same message. They were delivered for a simple purpose and that was to make sure the people would turn against the United States.

Two weeks after the oil discovery, Americans were asked to leave the country. It was a very chaotic time, but every American got out and had been accounted for. Everyone felt very lucky that their life had been spared. East Africa made sure that all Americans had gotten out safely and made sure that the U.S. had no validity to attack. The world came to East Africa's aid and offered support to the country. East Africa's government had become a very powerful player in the world overnight and wanted to keep it that way. They made sure to the world that they did not want any United States involvement and the U.N. had granted them that their wish.

The people of East Africa were promised peace and prosperity and for ten years under Kier, peace and prosperity is what they received. Unfortunately after the oil discovery, the past policies of peace and prosperity were destroyed, and the East African people now lived in fear and poverty. Murder and rape were rampant. Kier had turned the military over to his chief advisor, Qatar. Qatar loved his power and proved it by killing innocent people. He wanted the East African people to understand that he must be feared and ruled his military post with an iron fist.

Qatar had come into power when Kier took office. He was Kier right hand man and enjoyed his power. He took over the military and built it from the ground up. He needed a small group of men that he could trust and bring into his inner circle. He trained them and turned them into a regimented, terrorizing group that was his personal killing machine. He gave them authority to run his military.

Qatar had kept his men close to him for the last ten years, not giving them any responsibilities until recently. He unleashed his fury on the East African people and allowed his men and his military free range on the whole country. Qatar made sure that the people of East Africa knew that he was in charge of the military action and he knew that if the people feared him, then they had to respect his wishes. He would quickly make his point felt and made sure that the people lived in fear. The people needed to be rescued them from the tyranny of Kier and Qatar, but unfortunately there was nothing that could be done.

CHAPTER 13

Jake was in state of shock and was completely devastated. He had never lost anyone on a mission, especially a friend. He had developed a mutual respect for Simeon and would miss his friend. Jake stood in silence as he looked at the death around him. He was on the Nile River with two boats tied together. He had finally come up with an idea of disposing of the boats and of the bodies. But first he needed to find a place to bury his friend, Simeon. He then would burn the other bodies and the boats. He knew that he did not have much time and he would have to think fast and move fast. If he did not, he knew that other reinforcements would come looking for the dead officers and he did not want to be there when they did.

Jake had never been on the Nile River before and had no idea where to dump the excess baggage that he had. He got into the militia's boat and pulled his old house boat down the river. After a few minutes of traveling down the Nile, Jake spotted a perfect area to get rid of the boat and bodies. He drove the boats over to the side of the river and was able to tie up the two boats to an old rotted dock. He put all the dead bodies, except for Simeon's, into the boats, and dowsed them with gasoline. He lit them and watched both boats burn. They burned quickly and produced a lot of smoke. He knew he needed to get out of there because he felt that the smoke would attract some unwanted attention.

He hurried as he carried his friend's body up to the bank of the river and found a nice place under a tree. He felt horrible that Simeon had to be buried there, but Jake knew he had no other choice. He said a quick prayer, and placed a small head stone by the burial. Jake would miss Simeon, but had no time to reflect and he knew that Simeon would do the same and continue what they had started.

Jake knew his life was now in danger. He now had to travel by foot and had a long way to go, but only a short time to get there. He was not scheduled to contact H at this time, but he needed to tell him what had transpired. He grabbed his phone, and began to call, but it did not work. There was a bullet that was lodged in it and the phone was almost useless. He could not make calls, but felt that he could send a message to H to tell him what had happened. 'Simeon's dead, I am on foot. Phone is done. May not make the extraction time.' He sent the message, but the phone turned off and Jake had no idea if the message had been received on the other end. He got disgusted and threw the phone in the river.

Jake was still in shock. He was still agitated by his friend's death, but now he needed to focus on the situation at hand and get himself together if he was going to survive. He had never worked a mission alone and knew that he had to rely on himself and his instincts more than he had ever done before. He slapped himself in the face and began to talk to himself to snap out of being in shock. He knew he needed to get going, but before he was about to leave the scene, he heard a boat in the distance coming his way.

He needed to hide, but felt motionless. 'I have got to keep moving,' he thought to himself, but he just stood there. He had no communication, no transportation, and no plan. His original plans had changed and he felt helpless. The boat kept getting closer and Jake could see it. He knew that he had to hide or he would get captured. He splashed some water on his face and finally managed to snap out of it. He then moved down the river bank and hid in the brush.

Jake finally had his wits back, but it was too late for him to move. He had hidden in some brush and stayed low so that the oncoming boat could not see him. He could tell it was another militia boat and could see about ten different people on it. The two boats had completely burned and Jake was smart enough to make it look like an accident. He remained in his spot and stayed completely still and quiet. He listened intently on what was going on.

The boat came upon the wreckage. "What the hell is this," the leader of the vessel asked. "I do not know, but it looks as if these two boats collided into one another. The wreckage must have floated over to here."

"Qatar is not going to like this," the leader said. "It looks as if we lost some as well. Look at those bodies. They are burned to a crisp. Look over there; there looks to be a rope tied to the dock holding the boats. This may not have been an accident. Get out of the boat and check it out."

Jake knew he had forgotten to untie the two burned boats, but there was nothing that he could do about it now, but only hope that they would not look around for him. He only had a few more bullets left and knew that he could not take on all the men. He kept quiet as he hid in the brush, hoping he would not be spotted by the men.

"These boats did not just tie themselves," the leader said. "It looks as if we have an intruder. Get out and look around and see if there is anything catches your eye."

The soldiers got out of the boat, hoping to find something that would be out of the ordinary. "Hey look at this," one of the men said after spotting Simeon's grave site. "The dirt has recently moved. This seems fresh."

The leader ordered his men to continue looking. Jake was hidden very well, but he felt that there was only a matter of time before he was spotted. One soldier walked over looking in the brush and came within a few feet of where Jake was hiding, but the soldier left as he heard that Qatar had ordered them back to the capital. The search would have to wait and Jake escaped from being caught.

The men got back in the boat, and headed back toward the capital city. Jake got out of the brush and knew he needed to be on the move. He had a small map and it told him to follow the Nile River south. He would eventually make it to Turin, but now he was behind schedule. He had lost everything during the battle and would have to use his instincts the rest of the way.

Jake made sure he stayed on a small path that was out of view. During his walk, Jake thought back on his life. He had always treated his missions as a game. This made it easier for him to put things in perspective. Jake was not a complex man. He never planned for his future, always focusing on the present. He had always accomplished his main goal and that was to get out alive. He just hoped during the death defying mission, that he had made a difference in the world. He was trying to keep his mind off the death of his friend and continued to talk to himself, trying to keep himself pumped up. This helped him move on; he knew that would never forget about Simeon. But living in the present as he always did, he put Simeon's death in the back of his mind for now.

Jake had traveled through brush and thorns for almost a day, and he finally reached the outskirts to the city of Turin. Darkness had filled the sky and he was exhausted and very hungry. He stumbled upon a small run down shack. He walked inside and saw that it was abandoned. He would set up camp for the night and then get up in the morning to look for food. His day had been very long and now he just wanted to rest. He knew that had only two days left until the extraction and he wanted to be fresh in the morning. He tried to find a soft spot on the floor and lay down, but unfortunately the floor was made of dirt. He used his shirt as a pillow and shut his eyes. Jake did not know what to expect in the morning, but knew that he would be ready for whatever stood in his way.

The sunlight came through a small crack and hit Jakes eyes. He woke up, looking around to see his surroundings. Jake had slept through the night for the first time in a long time. He felt refreshed and ready to take on the world. The day before had taken a big toll on Jake, not only physically, but mentally. Jake got up off the dirt floor, rubbed his eyes and grabbed his map. He was ready to do what he came to do. It was his time all over again. He opened the door to the abandoned shack and headed to the city of Turin.

Turin was the largest city in East Africa with over a million people in the population. It had the most commerce in the country had the only airport, but unfortunately the airport was under the control of the East African military or Qatar. Qatar had stopped all international flights and the airport was in a complete stand still. Airspace was under control of the military and the military was ordered by Qatar to shoot down any plane that flew over this area. Qatar controlled almost everything in the country and he focused most of his energy in the city of Turin.

Jake entered into the city and was among the East Africa people. He noticed that the people were very peaceful, but he could also see the fear in their eyes. Jake had a hard time navigating his way through Turin. He wanted to fit in and not be out of the ordinary. He asked for directions, but no one he talked to could speak English. Even if he could get directions, he did not know where to go and meet his contact. He became frustrated and aggravated, but this was mainly from not eating. He saw a fruit stand and wandered over and grabbed an apple and sat down on a stone bench and began to eat.

"You look lost," a voice came from behind the bench that Jake was sitting on. Jake looked behind him and saw a young boy looking back at him. "Where are you from," the boy asked.

Jake did not want to tell the boy anything. "I am not lost," he answered." Just resting, go away." Jake did not want the boy around and hoped he would leave.

"I have been watching you for awhile, and you look as if you do not know where you are going," the boy said holding out his hand hoping to shake Jake's hand. "My name is Anteon, what is yours."

Jake held his hand out and shook his Anteon's, and said "Nice to meet you, now run along, I am busy."

Anteon replied, "You do not look like you are doing much, but eating an apple. I have been living on the streets for the last three years and know my way around the city. Ask me anything and I will tell you what you want to know."

Jake felt sorry for the boy, and wanted the boy leave, but Anteon hung around, not going anywhere. Jake got up off the bench and started to walk around in the busy streets, hoping that the boy would lose sight of him. Instead, Anteon was walking side by side with Jake and grabbed his hand and said, "Come on, mister, I will take you where you need to go."

Jake pushed the boy away, but Anteon came back insisting that he could help Jake. Jake wanted to continue to resist the boy's overtures, but knew the boy would continue to pester him. He finally gave in and said, "Okay, okay, you can help me."

"Great, where do you want to go first," Anteon ask him.

The streets were busy with people all around. Jake had no idea where he needed to go, he just knew he wanted to get off the busy streets. He saw an alley way and walked with Anteon over to it. He bent down and said to Anteon, "Well first, I want to know a little bit about you. You told me your name and where you live, but how do you know how to speak English?" Jake was simply amazed that the little boy knew how to speak English well.

"I learned from some Americans who use to live here," Anteon said. "They lived a few blocks from here and I would go over and talk to the American woman almost every day. She didn't have any kids, but really like me and she taught me how to speak her language. She also made me cookies and gave me milk to drink. I was hoping that she would adopt me, but one day I went over there and she and her husband were gone. I thought they would be back, but they still have not come back. It has been at least two months since they left. I guess they went back to America. They did not even tell me good-bye to me. Are you from America, because if you are then you might know them? She was very pretty and had blond hair, and he had a mustache. Do you think that you might know them?"

Jake grinned at him, but nodded his head no.

Jake could tell that the boy was hungry and he had an extra apple in his pocket. "Do you want this other apple," he asked Anteon.

"Yes sir, thank you, sir." Anteon was very well mannered and appreciated the apple. He still was eager to help Jake. First though, Anteon wanted to finish his apple. The little boy had not eaten breakfast and was very hungry. It did not take him long to eat whole apple and when he finished it he asked Jake, "I used to see a lot of people that looked like you. Now I don't. Where did they all go?"

Jake answered, "They were all asked to leave, so they left."

"Why are you here then," the boy asked.

Jake laughed. "Do not worry about that. Enough with the questions, I need you to take me somewhere."

"Where do you need to go," the boy asked Jake.

Jake handed the boy an address he had on his map. "It is real close by. Come this way and follow me." Anteon ran out of the alley and into the busy street.

"Hey, wait up," Jake yelled to the boy as he tried to keep up.

"Sorry, I am just so used to being able to get to places in a hurry." Jake hurried along and they made their way through the busy streets of Turin.

They got off the busy streets and started to walk to their destination, when all of a sudden Jake spotted a military jeep coming in their direction. He had come too far to be captured, so he grabbed Anteon and they hid in a back alley.

"What are you doing," the boy asked.

"Be quiet, there are people out there that don't want me here. I am not going to make it easy for them to find me. We will hide out in here until they leave. Okay."

Anteon understood. He was a smart kid, especially street smart. He had been living alone for awhile. His parents had been killed in a freak accident and Anteon was sent to an orphanage, because he had no other family. He hated the orphanage so he ran away. Anteon would rather live on the streets and take his chances, than grow up in an orphanage that he hated. He was a very outgoing little boy and he had made many friends on the streets. He knew where to go to get food and where to sleep safely. He was only eleven years old, but mentally he seemed much older than a child. He had experienced more things over the last three years than many people experience over a lifetime. Anteon just wanted a friend and he felt that Jake could be one.

"Those jeeps have been coming around more and more," the boy said. "I think there is going to be some kind of war. I hear things on the street that they have been killing innocent people for no reason. You are not the only one who needs to hide, because I always hide if I see them coming."

"Okay," Jake said. "They have gone. How much further is this place?"

"It is right this way," Anteon answered. "We will stay in these back alleys. I do not want us to be seen. Follow me this way and we will be there in a minute."

Jake followed the boy through a few more alleys and they finally came upon his destination. The door looked to have been beaten down and when they entered the building, they knew that someone had already been there. The place was trashed. Jake saw something out of the corner of his eye.

"Anteon," Jake said, "do not come in here. Stay outside and I will be right back. Do you understand me?"

"Yes sir," Anteon answered. He was a curious little boy, but he knew that Jake meant business and he did not want to angry his new friend.

Jake went to the corner of the building and saw a man lying on his back, bleeding all over his body. "What happened, are you still alive?" Jake asked.

The man opened his eyes and could barely breathe. He looked up at Jake and said, "They know that you are here. You are not safe."

Jake looked at the dying man and asked, "Who knows I am here? What do you mean? We need to get some help. Speak to me."

The dying man looked back and said, "There is not much time for me. You need to get to…"

"Get to where?" Jake asked, but it was too late. The man quit breathing. Jake could not believe that his contact was killed. Jake knew that someone knew he was here, but how in the world did this someone know where he was going or who he was meeting with. His whole mission rested on the contact, but now the contact was dead and Jake was a wanted man. He knew that he needed to disappear for awhile. He had come to hopefully rescue a captured agent, but now he just wanted to get out alive. He had no way to communicate with H and all he could do was hope that someone would be there to pick him up.

"Is everything alright in there," Anteon yelled at Jake.

"Yeah," he answered. "I am coming out. There is nothing to see in here." Jake came out of the building knowing he needed to separate himself from the boy. He did not want anything to happen to Anteon. "Thank you for all your help. You can run along, now."

"What do you mean run along?" he answered in a quick voice. "I can take you to any place in the city. Where else do you need go?"

"I don't need to go anywhere else. You brought me to the only place I was going to. Thank you, now run along."

Anteon was sad that his new friend did not want him around. "Okay," he answered "I guess I will leave. Don't get mad if you get sent to the same place that the other American got sent to. I tried to help you, but remember you did not need me."

Anteon began to run out of the alley. Jake scratched his head and wondered what he meant by other American. "Wait," Jake yelled back to Anteon. "What do you mean, other American? Do you know where the other American is?"

"You bet I do," the boy answered, "and I can take you to that place. We are a long ways off, but I know where that American is. Do you want me to take you?"

Jake was cautious and wanted to know how Anteon knew about the other American. "I want you to take me there, but how do you know this," Jake questioned the boy.

"If you live on the street, then you hear of a lot of things. Now come one let's go." Jake did not know what to think, but he had nothing else to go with and if the boy could help, he might as well let him.

CHAPTER 14

After walking for awhile, Anteon was tired and sat down in a back alley. They had been walking for five miles and it did not look as if they were going anywhere. Anteon looked over to Jake and said, "It is farther than I thought it would be."

Jake, noticing that Anteon was tired of walking said to him, "I will be back in a few minutes. Wait here."

A few minutes later Jake pulled up in a rusted old truck. "Where did you find that?" Anteon asked Jake.

"I am just borrowing it from an old man. I told him I would bring it back when I was done with it. Get in, let's go."

"We need to follow this road out of the city and into the jungle," Anteon replied, pointing to the north.

It took awhile, but they made it out of the city. "Pull over there; we have to walk the rest of the way. I do not want to let anyone know that we are coming."

They walked for awhile and came to the top of a large hill. It looked into what looked like a prison camp of some sort. Anteon said "Look over there. That is where they took the other American."

Jake squatted down so that he could be face to face with the young boy. He said in a very serious tone, "Are you sure that there is an American being held hostage in that prison camp?"

"I know that there is. I hear everything that goes on and I am positive that there is an American in that place."

Jake was a little uncertain about the whole situation, but had nothing else to go on. He felt that Anteon was a truthful kid and would not lead him down a dead end. He was not going to go into the camp and ask questions, but he wanted to get a closer look at what was going on.

"Anteon," Jake said, "you stay here. I am going to go take a closer look. Promise me you will stay here and out of sight. Do not wander off, because I do not want anything to happen to you."

Anteon promised he would hide and wait for Jake to return. "Make sure that you listen to me, Anteon, if I don't come back you run back into the city and forget about me. Okay."

Anteon nodded, and said that he would. He just hoped nothing would happen to his new friend. Jake went slowly down the hill hiding behind trees and overgrown weeds, trying not to be spotted by anyone in the prison camp. He got to the bottom of the hill and noticed that the camp was surrounded by a large electrical fence and had surveillance cameras ten feet apart on top of the fence. There were at least four guards at the main entrances. He did not see another entrance and was pretty confident that there was just one way in and one way out of the camp.

He knew he could not just go through the front gate and figured he needed to find another way into the camp. This was nothing new to Jake and knew exactly what to. He knew that he had to get into the camp to see if the American was indeed being held hostage. This was no easy task he thought, but he was there to do a job and leaving was not an option.

He watched the cameras for a few minutes and figured out precisely how many seconds he had to get by them without being spotted. Once that was accomplished, he then had to get through the electric fence. This was a little trickier, but he had done it before as well. He had been carrying a small shovel in his back pack and needed that to dig under the fence. He knew that he only had less than a minute to do that. He waited for just the right time and took off. He dug as fast as he could and finally had enough space that he could crawl under the fence. He did not want to get electrocuted so he laid his bag down and used it to brace up against the fence allowing his bag to take the electric shock. He crawled under his bag and was on the other side of the fence.

Jake had to get a feel for where he was. He did not want to go into a building without knowing which one the captive might be in. He did not have a lot of time to analyze the situation, so he had to make a quick decision on what he was going to do.

Jake got down low and got down on his stomach so that he would not be seen. He was able to see that the camp had six buildings in it. He saw that only one had bars on the windows, and figured that was where the prisoners were kept. He knew that is where the American would be if indeed Anteon was right. He had to maneuver quickly and had only had one chance so he ran as fast as he could to the other side of the camp. He was not as fleet of foot as he once was, but he did make it without being spotted.

Jake waited awhile and saw a few guards walk out of the prison building. It was a small building that looked as if it did not have many prisoners in it. The building was poorly built and had what looked like bamboo bars. It looked to have dirt floors and the structure was made out of cheap aluminum. He could see that the building had one main door and noticed that there was able to get a glimpse inside when one of the guards left. He saw two other guards in a room with guns. They looked like they were the only ones in there at the time. Jake knew that this was his chance to go into the room and eliminate them. He then could find out the whereabouts of the American.

He slowly walked up to the building and opened the door. He snuck in very quietly, staying low to the floor, hoping not to be notice. He crawled up close to the operation room and noticed that one of the guards was leaving the room. Jake stood up and hid on the other side of the door. When the guard walked out, Jake caught the guard by surprise, putting his arms around his neck and put him down the ground. He did not kill the guard, but only knocked him out. He grabbed the guard's gun and slowly made his way back to where the other guard was working.

Jake knew he could take the other guard fairly easy. He slowly walked up to the door and rushed into the room. The guard was completely surprised and before he could do anything to protect himself, Jake hit him over the head with the back of the other guard's gun and knocked him out. Jake moved the guard to the floor and looked at the map of the building that was laid down on a table. He looked at the map and noticed that there were only a few prison cells in the building. He memorized the directions and left to see if the American was in one of the cells.

Jake looked at his watched and knew that he was short on time. He headed down the dirt hallway that passed by a few empty bamboo barred cells. Jake finally came to the end of the hall and looked into the last cell. The cell had bamboo bars and a dirt floor, just like the others and there was hay in the corner of the room. He saw someone cuddled up in the straw that was in the corner of the room. He could tell that it had to be a prisoner and that the prisoner's arms and legs were tied up. It looked as if the prisoner was asleep.

Jake yelled into the cell, "Do you speak English?"

He did not get an answer. The prisoner looked dead and Jake did not know if the prisoner would answer him. He grabbed his knife and cut the rope that was tying the bamboo bars together. He then kicked down the bars and walked slowly over to the prisoner. The prisoner was laying face first on the ground. Jake turned over the prisoner and looked at her. The prisoner was a woman. She was filthy and looked malnourished. Jake had no idea who the prisoner was or if she was the agent he was looking for. H had never disclosed to Jake that the agent was a woman or what she looked like.

"Are you alive?" Jake asked the prisoner.

She opened her eyes and looked up at Jake. It was hard for her to focus on him and she was very weak and could hardly hold her head up. She had not eaten in a couple of days and seemed to be very dehydrated.

"I am here to bring you home." Jake told her with a smile.

She looked up and said in a very weak voice, "Great, now get me out of here."

"My name is Jake and I am an American. We have a long road ahead of us. Are you up for this? I mean, do you have enough strength to make it out of here?"

She felt very weak, but she was ready to do whatever it took to get out of the prison camp. "I will make it," she answered.

Jake picked her up and told her to hold on. He went back down the hallway and went out the door. The other guards that were at the front gate had no idea of the escape. Jake knew that he had to be careful or they would get spotted. He knew that if he could get back into the jungle, then they could hide for awhile.

"Hang on to me and I am going to run to the fence over there," Jake told the prisoner. "Do what I say and we can get out of here without being spotted. Do you understand what I am saying?"

She nodded yes. Jake could see that the guards had their backs turned away from him and he felt that that was their best chance to get away. He told her to climb on his back and he started to run as fast toward the fence of the prison camp. Unfortunately for them, a security camera that Jake did not account for spotted them and sounded the alarm.

Jake took a chance and it did not pay off the way he wanted it to. He did not have time to change his plan and when he got to the fence and yelled to the prisoner, "I am going to push you to the other side. Get ready."

Jake put his back pack up underneath the fence and shoved her under the fence. He looked back and saw the guards running towards them. He ducked down and went under the fence, but got stuck. Shots rang out at them and Jake finally pulled himself to

the other side. He grabbed his back pack and told her to run. She tried to stand, but she went she fell back to the ground.

Jake yelled to her, "Get on my back and hang on."

She climbed on Jake's back and he ran as fast as he could away from the fence and the camp. He could hear the guards behind him yelling at them and firing shots toward them, but they run out into the jungle and away from the gunfire. It was not the great escape that Jake had wanted, but they did get away and that is all that mattered to them.

Jake carried her up the hill to where Anteon was still hiding. He was out of breath and tired from carrying her on his back. Anteon came from his hiding place and asked, "Who is she?"

"She is the person that I came for, I hope." Jake still not sure if the woman prisoner was the agent he came to save. "Anteon, we need a safe place to hide until tomorrow. Where can we go?"

Anteon knew of a good place to hide in the city and he could also get them some food and water. "We need to get back to the city."

Jake knew that he could not carry her on his back all the way to the truck. He needed her to walk some, but she was dehydrated and did not have a lot of strength. They stopped to rest a while and he gave her his canteen and told her to take a drink of water. She was able to get some down and he told her to use as much energy as she could muster to try to run back to the old truck.

He felt that she was a tough person since she had endured a lot of pain. He did not know how long she had been in the prison cell, but however long she had, it looked to him as though she had persevered through it. They needed to keep moving and he asked her if she had enough energy to run. She nodded yes, though she did not have much energy. She ran with him, but secretly she kept her pain to herself. She still had her pride and did not want to look weak toward him. They continued to run as fast as they could back to the old truck that he and Anteon had hidden off the dirt road. Jake looked back and did not see anyone following after them, but did not want to take any chances of being caught. He slowed down to cover their tracks and it took a little longer, but it was the safest way for all of them.

They finally made it back to old truck and the three of them piled into it. Jake got in the driver's seat and drove them back into the city. He kept looking back expecting a military truck to pull up behind them, but nothing ever appeared. It did not make sense to Jake that no one came after them, but he did not mind and drove as fast as he could into the city.

"Where do I go?" Jake asked Anteon, as they arrived back into the city of Turin. Anteon pointed out the directions for Jake and after about thirty minutes of driving threw the busy streets of Turin, they finally arrived to their destination.

They pulled up to an old and run down hotel. It was made of clay bricks, and did not look modern like most building in East Africa, but it did have running water and electricity inside. Jake did not know what to expect, but Anteon seemed to know what he was doing. Jake did not like what he had to do, but he felt he had no choice, but to put his trust in the young boy.

Jake stepped out of the truck and helped Anteon and the woman prisoner out as well. The three of them walked up to front door with Anteon leading them. Anteon approached the door and knocked on it. A lady, who looked to be in her mid to late forties came to the door and peered out of the small peep hole to see who was knocking. She did not immediately open the door and motioned them to leave, but she saw Anteon so she decided to slowly open the door leaving a small crack so that only her voice could be heard.

"What do you want? I do not rent to strangers and anyway, I am out of rooms for the night."

Jake looked at Anteon and wondered why he had brought him to this old run down hotel. He was not about to grovel with someone who he had never met and obviously did not want them there. He just wanted a bed for them and possibly some food. He decided to leave and said to the lady, "I think this was a mistake, sorry to bother you."

Anteon tugged at Jake's leg and tried to explain that there was nowhere else to for them to go, but Jake did not want to hear anything about it. He was irritated that they had wasted their time so he turned around and took the prisoner by the arm and they started to walk away. The crack in the door widened and the lady stepped out of her comfort zone and said to them, "Wait, don't leave. My name is Diotrice, and I live here. I am sorry that I was rude, but I have to take precaution at all times. I see that Anteon has brought you to my hotel. He would only bring someone to me that would need my help. I can tell that you do need some help. What can I do for you?"

Jake turned around and said to her, "We need some food and shelter. I hate to intrude, but we have nowhere else to go. Anteon has helped me along the way. I want tell you where we have been, but I will say that he has led us to you, hoping that you could help us for the night. Is there anything that you could do for us."

"Sometimes Anteon talks too much," she responded, staring at the boy to let him know her displeasure with him bringing them to her hotel. "But since it is just for one night I might be able to find an extra room. Whatever your problems, I need you to leave them at the door. I do not need any trouble following you here."

"We just need one night and we will be out of your hair," Jake answered, assuring her that she would not have any trouble out of them or following them.

Diotrice nodded for them to that it was alright for them to come inside. She agreed that they could stay the night and had them follow her to an extra room that was vacant. "This is where you will be staying. You can come down and eat in a couple of hours. Dinner will be served at eight o'clock sharp."

Diotrice looked over the room and saw that everything was in order and left the three of them alone. Jake told Anteon to leave him and to go downstairs to be a lookout at anything that looked suspicious. He wanted him to come back to the room and report anything out of the ordinary. Anteon was eager to help Jake any way that he could, so he ran down the stairs and put a chair by a window, allowing him to see everything that was happening outside.

Jake purposely sent Anteon away so that he and the woman prisoner could be alone together. He wanted to find out anything he could about this mysterious person and make sure that she was the right person he was sent to rescue.

"How are you feeling," Jake asked her.

She was getting her strength back now that she was not tied up and lying in dirt. "I am better now," she answered, looking in a mirror to see what she looked like. "I was just very weak and dehydrated. Thanks for getting me out of there. I don't know how much longer I could take living in that horrible place."

She looked in the mirror and saw that she was still very dirty and looked as if she had not showered in months. "I stink, I need a shower. Do you mind if I can have some privacy."

"First I need some answers," he replied, not wanting her to take a shower until she answered him. She sat on the end of the bed and looked up at Jake and said in a very harsh tone,

"I am going to take a shower and then if I feel like it I will give you your answers." She stood up and walked to the bathroom door, where Jake was standing. "Please move."

Jake walked away, smiling and said, "Go ahead, I will be right here."

She walked into the bathroom and looked back at Jake and said, "I am an American," and she shut the door. Jake was glad to know where she was from, but still did not know who he had rescued. He did know that he had a fiery person, but still he need to know if she was the person who H had sent him to rescue.

The American woman had been locked up in the prison camp for more days than she could remember. She was given just small rations of food and water since she was imprisoned. She had lost some weight, and needed to get her energy level back up. She looked in the mirror again saw and saw how dirty she was and she could smell herself. She knew that the shower she was about to take would be one she would remember for a lifetime. She looked at her wrists and saw the marks left on them from the rope that had tied her wrists for so long. She looked down at her feet and saw the same markings. She was now at ease that she was out, but had no idea who this person was that had freed her. He did tell her his name, but that did not matter to her. She wanted to know more about him, but she would worry about him after her shower. She was just thankful to be out of the prison camp and wanted a moment of silence and relaxation. She would enjoy the time she had for a few minutes before finding out more about her rescuer.

She got out of the shower and started to brush her hair. While brushing her hair she finally had a moment that she felt totally relaxed again. It had been a month since she went into survival mode. She had almost forgotten why she had come to East Africa. It did not take her long to remember why she had come. She knew that she still had a job to do and had to figure out a way to finish what she had started. She had started her mission alone and she was captured, but now it seemed that Jake had come in and given her new life to help her accomplish her goal. She needed to find out a way for him to help her, but for now she wanted to eat and get her energy back, but she did decide to work on Jake immediately.

"Jake, you can come in, I am decent." Jake opened the door to the bathroom and was he was stunned how beautiful she was. He could not believe that the person who was crawled up in a ball on the prison camp floor was the beautiful woman in front of him.

"Are you speechless or something," she said as she looked at Jake gawking at her. "We do not have a lot of time and I need some information on you."

Jake had rescued her and he did not want to answer any of her questions. He felt he was entitled to some answers first and said to her "Listen, lady, I just rescued you out of some sort of prison camp and at least you owe me a thank you. After that, you need to listen to me and answer some of my questions. I am in charge here and my first question, what is your name?"

She did not like the tone in Jake's voice. She was on a mission and hit a snag. She was safe now, but did not feel that she owed this guy anything. She was glad that he had rescued her, but now she was ready to put that behind her and move on.

"Listen," she snapped back a Jake, "I do not know you and have a hard time trusting anyone. If it helps your ego, then thank you for getting me out of that prison camp, but looking back at it, it felt like a joint effort. I had to do a lot of running so we both weren't killed."

"Are you serious?" Jake retorted to her. "You were tied up and half dead."

"That was just part of the plan," she answered quickly back. She was not about to let Jake boss her around. She knew how to get a feel on people and she was just testing him. She needed to know what type of person he was and if he would put up with the crap she was giving him.

Jake did not know what to think of this woman he had rescued. He asked her again, not letting her skip out on the question and demanded her to tell him her name.

During her training, it had been instilled in her brain to never let anyone know her name, but this was a different circumstance. She did not know if H had or even would send anyone to rescue her, but her intuition took over in this case. She did not completely trust Jake, but she for some reason her instinct felt that it was safe to give him her name.

"My name is Sasha, o.k.," she answered him.

Jake now had a name and now he wanted to know what her role was and why she was here. For some reason, H had never given Jake the name of the agent, but he had to presume that she was part of Code Seven. He now wanted to know how she was captured and why she had remained alive. There was always a reason for everything and Jake knew that there was a reason for reason that she had not been killed. He went over and sat on the end of the bed and watched Sasha as she continued to brush her hair.

"I cannot remember the last time I brushed my hair," Sasha said as finished up, "but I can tell you that I will not take it for granted ever again."

Jake knew that she was stalling and did not want to get into a useless conversation. He got right to the point and asked, "How long have you been here."

"Listen," she answered quickly, making sure Jake knew that she could handle herself. "Jake, I do not know you. How do I know that you are just trying to get some information out of me? This is nice and everything, but how do I know I can trust you," Sasha said with a very serious look on her face.

Jake was losing his patience with her. He had risked his life to rescue her and now she was wondering if she could trust him. He felt like taking her back and giving her to the guards at the prison camp. "What do you mean, you can't trust me? I got you out of that camp, didn't I? I risked my life for you and now you say that you can't you trust me?"

Jake was irritated, but he did remain calm. He wanted to stay in complete control and would not allow her to see him loose his cool. Sasha could tell that Jake was not happy with how she was acting, so she decided to tell him a little about her story.

"I was in that camp for a long time," Sasha said as she walked over and got within a few inches from his face. "I never gave them one single answer to any of their questions. I was tortured, beaten, and starved, and still I remained silent. Now you come along and get me out of a prison, where it seems that we weren't even followed and you want me to spill my guts. I do not think so, Jake."

Jake knew that she did have a point, but was not about to let her know that. He was told by H that the agent might not be cooperative. He knew that Sasha was well trained and that he had to tell her the code word that only agents of Code 7 would know. He did not want to just spill the beans yet and wanted to know if she had her mental wits back to normal. He could tell that she had some spunk to her and decided that he would let her know why he was here.

"I know who your handler is and who you work for," Jake said to Sasha. "Does Code 7 ring a bell?"

Sasha did not say a word. She got out of his face and walk over to sit down on a chair in the corner of the room. Jake had to ask her a question before he continued telling her who he was and what he was doing in East Africa.

Jake continued by saying, "I am guessing that what I said rings a bell. Your handler is also my handler, as well. He told me that if I found the agent, then the agent would now the answer to a question. My question to you is simply this; what, if any, is the battle cry for the agency called Code 7?"

Sasha began to believe that Jake was on her side and figured that he was probably sent to rescue her and get her out of East Africa. H told her that if she was ever captured, he would send someone to rescue her, but never told her who that someone was going to be. He just gave her a code that the person would have to know to prove to her that he was legit. Jake had done just that. She knew the answer and knew that once she gave the answer that he would in turn say a code word that would let her know that he was indeed with Code 7 sent to rescue her. She stood up and said in a very stern voice, "War Eagle."

He looked back at her and winked, simply replying, "Seminole."

She sat back down in relief. She was overjoyed that H had not forgotten her and had sent someone to get her out of the terrible place. She was not out of the woods yet, but felt that she was half way there.

"Can you trust me now," Jake asked now grinning as Sasha nodded back at him. She did feel that she could trust him, but still she had some reservations as to why she did not know who he was. She knew that H's training took over a year to complete and wondered how Jake had gone through so quickly. She wanted to have a little fun with him and decided to say a few things to get to see if she could rattle him a little.

"H must be desperate or something."

"What do you mean," he asked.

"Isn't it obvious," she answered. "You did not go through the necessary training. It shows and I am kind of wondering what you are trained in. He must have just found you off of the street. You are clearly out of shape. You could not even carry me all the way to the truck. He must have let you go through the elderly version of the training to get you through so quickly."

Jake got a little upset by what she said, but was not about to lose his cool. He knew that she was trying to get him riled up, but he would not let it. He walked over to Sasha and got a few inches from her face. He looked right into her eyes and said told with a soft voice, "I am going to let you think about that for awhile. Right now we need to get ready for our extraction."

Anteon came up to the room and knocked on the door and said, "It is time to eat."

Jake looked at Sasha and said, "I guess we are saved by dinner."

"Yes, but I will get some answers out of you, either the easy way or the hard way," Sasha said back to him with a grin on her face.

"I might like it the hard way," Jake said with a laugh.

She shook her head and grinned. Jake walked out of the room and was happy that he could get a grin out of her. She wasn't as bad as she thinks she is, he thought as they walked downstairs to get a bite to eat.

Sasha had not eaten in a couple of days and was very grateful to get some solid food into her system. "I can't wait to eat. I have been getting by with a little water and some crumbs," she said to Diotrice, who was sitting at the head of the table.

"Diotrice," Jake said, "I want to thank you for your hospitality. We will be gone by tomorrow morning, and to have a place to eat and sleep is truly an honor."

Diotrice looked up at Jake and nodded. She remained silent and looked at Anteon to answer for her. She did not want to know who they were or why they were there. She only cared about Anteon and his well being. If he ever got into trouble, she was always there for him. She wanted him to stay with her, but he was a stubborn little boy and wanted to take care of himself. Anteon would disappear for awhile, but always came back to the old hotel and Diotrice would always give him food and shelter. This was the first time he had brought anyone with him, and she was hesitant, but Anteon assured her that they would be gone in the morning and as long as they were true to their word, then she did not mind giving them a little food and a roof over their head.

"Diotrice might not say much," Anteon said, "but she knows that you appreciate this."

Jake looked over at Diotrice and again thanked her. She nodded back at Jake. "There are some clean clothes for you to wear. I will pack both of you a bag of fruit for tomorrow. Be safe."

Diotrice got up from the table and went into the other room. She wanted to leave them alone and did not want to know anything about them. It did not bother Jake or Sasha for that matter and they continued to eat.

Anteon, with his mouth full of bread that he had just eaten, said to Jake and Sasha, "If you need me to take you to where you want to go tomorrow, I will."

Jake knew that there was a short time frame for them to get to the extraction area and if they missed it, they could get stuck in East Africa for awhile. "I am going to take you up on the offer," Jake said to Anteon. "You have been a great help to me. Be ready early in the morning. We will leave before the sun comes up."

"Yes sir," Anteon answered with a big grin on his mouth.

Sasha had been eating at a rapid pace. She wanted to make sure she got her energy level back to where it needed to be. "Are we all done here?" Jake asked as he saw Sasha try to get one more piece of bread in her mouth.

"One more bite," she answered. Finally, she finished and Jake told them that they needed to get back upstairs to the room. He knew that they had a long day ahead of them and knew that they needed their rest.

"Anteon," Jake said "remember, six o'clock sharp. Do not make me get you up."

"I won't be late," he answered and then turned to go back to his look out spot.

Jake and Sasha went back to their room. "What side of the bed do you want?" Jake asked Sasha.

Sasha could not believe the arrogance of Jake. She was grateful of what he had done, but the nerve of him wanting to sleep in the same bed with her. "You must be joking," she said with an obnoxious laugh. "I will give you a couple of pillows and you can sleep on the little couch in our room."

Jake did not like the thought of sleeping on the couch, but gave into her. He did not want to get into an argument and he also felt sorry for her, knowing that she had been sleeping on dirt for the last couple of months.

"We never finished our conversation from before," Jake said as grabbed the pillows and walked over to the couch.

"I thought we did," she answered.

"You know we didn't," he answered back. "I tell you what, I will start if you will finish. Do we have a deal?" Jake said as he sat down on the edge of the couch.

"I guess, but I have to like what I hear from you," she said.

"Since it is still early, I will give you the long version," Jake said to Sasha as she sat on the bed.

"I have all night," she answered with a grin.

Jake started telling her about his college days and about his friend, Henderson. He told her about being recruited right out of college and about the ten years he had put into the agency. He told her of his capture in Iran, and about his release from the agency. Jake felt comfortable with her. She looked as if she was hanging on to every word that he said. He did not know if he completely trusted her, but she did seem like a trustworthy person to him. He continued and told her about his troubles over the last ten years and how he yearned to get back into the business. He told her about H and Simeon tracking him down and training him for his purpose to come and save her.

"I am very appreciative of you saving me out of that prison camp," Sasha said. "I loved Simeon. He was a tough trainer, but he taught me more than I thought I could ever learn. How is he?"

Jake had hoped that it would not come up, but knew that he had opened a can of worms when he mentioned Simeon's name.

"We were raided on a houseboat on the Nile. Unfortunately, Simeon did not make it." Jake said with a small tear forming in his right eye. Sasha had a hard time believing that her trainer was gone. She saw Jake tearing up. "He was so strong, I thought nothing could ever stop him," she said watching Jake wipe away the tear.

"He was strong, but he told me to continue on. He wanted me to save you." Jake had gotten control of his emotions. He did not like for anyone to see him tear up, but on the other hand, he wanted to make sure Sasha knew that he cared for Simeon. Sasha could tell that he was upset and she too was hurt by Simeon's death, but knew that death was part of the business that she had gotten into and had to put it in the back of her mind for right now.

"I think that Simeon would be proud of you. I know that he would be proud of both of us, but you are right. He would want you to keep going. He would want me to keep going. Your job was to get me out of here and if Simeon was here that would be his job as well."

Jake knew that she was right. He did what she said and put it behind him. He could tell that Sasha wanted to get out of East Africa and as fast as she could. He also felt that she was not telling him everything, either, not only about her capture, but something else entirely. It was late and he wanted to let her rest, but felt that it was her time to talk without interruption. He found a comfortable place and told her to tell him everything that she could.

After finding out about the death of her trainer, Sasha did not want to tell Jake of her mission in East Africa. She had come to East Africa to accomplish a goal, but she had not finished what she had started. Her choice was to take the extraction that Jake was giving her and leave or finish what she started. She looked in her heart and knew that Simeon would want her to finish. He had instilled into her to always finish and finish strong. It was in her blood and she could see in Jake's eyes the same desires that she had. She knew that he could help her if she asked him to. She did not know if it was the right decision, but she decided to tell Jake her story, and so she started from the beginning.

CHAPTER 15

The agency needed to get into East Africa and get any information it could on the leader of the country, Mahmud Osman Kier. The agency was on strict orders from the administration that anyone who went in to East Africa, went in alone. They needed answers, but did not want to know how they got them. The President was not completely out of the loop. He made sure that his name was not involved with any overt operation concerning East Africa, but that something was going to get done concerning the small nation. He had too much riding on the outcome and knew that East Africa's oil could help drop gas prices in half almost overnight, thus helping to bring an end to the energy crisis. The President knew that his approval ratings would go through the roof, if only he could get could get control of the oil.

His re-election campaign was about to start and knew that it would be a battle for him to be re-elected, if he could not get a grip on the energy crisis. He also knew that it would be a cake walk if he was responsible for ending the crisis as well. Not only was his re-election in jeopardy, but also his legacy was as well. He did not want to go down in history as a President with lost opportunity. He wanted to be adored and loved not only by the American people, but also the world as well. The President knew that this would only be accomplished if he could find peace with East Africa. He informed his advisors to go in to East Africa, but to make sure nothing came back to his administration. He would not be responsible if something went wrong. He knew the repercussions of his actions, and did not want the United Nations, or the American people's wrath toward him and his administration.

The agency did not want this to stain its credibility worldwide so it came to H and let him know what was at stake. H had never backed down to anything and knew that Code 7 could handle any challenge. This is what his agency was all about and he went to talk to Sasha about it. He trained her for these types of missions and when he looked into Sasha's eyes and he knew that she was ready for this kind of mission. He knew how Sasha had worked and knew that she could accomplish the anything that she put her mind to. The agency did make it clear that if the mission was compromised, then Code 7 would be shut down. H assured the agency that nothing would be compromised and that Code 7 would accomplish its goal. He prepared Sasha and he mission was on.

Sasha had never gone on this kind of mission before. She had done some other missions in the Middle East, but this one was different. She had to go it alone. She had been accompanied by other agents from the agency, but this time the agency wanted only one agent to go in to East Africa. They felt that one agent could handle the situation and H agreed.

He told her that at any time she would have to change course and do something that she had never done before. That single reason was why H believed in her so much. He saw how she could change direction and blend in with anything that was put in front of her. There were some logistics to go over, but the agency wanted Code 7 to leave immediately. They had two days to get things in order and Sasha had to be in East Africa in less than forty-eight hours. Every minute that passed was more time for the other candidates to bash the President. The President wanted some good news to give to the American people.

They left and arrived in Morocco. Everything was set into place and Chafari was there to meet H and Sasha as they got off the plane. Simeon had stayed in the States like he always did because H needed him for in America to be his eyes and ears in the states. H did not trust the agency and made sure that Simeon would keep up with anything that he saw or heard. Chafari had everything set up for Sasha, her cell phone, weapons, and her global positioning system, otherwise known as GPS. She would leave by plane and parachute into East Africa. Once she arrived she would communicate with H's contacts that he still had. She flew out in the morning and landed safely in a small city in the northern part of the country.

Sasha's mission was for her to go to the capital city of East Africa. She got her supplies at the safe house and stayed for a few days to learn the lay of the land from a contact that H had set her up with. She then traveled in secret for two days until she made it to New Helen, the capital city. While she traveled to the capital city, she met people who told her stories of the mass murder and rape that had been going on for the last few months. She found out that the military was the culprit and they were getting their orders directly from the capital. She also became aware that Kier, the President of East Africa, was only communicating by video and that he had gone into isolation. He had been for the people for the last ten years, but now no one ever saw him in person, only through the video that was plastered all over the capital city.

The agency and Code 7 had gotten her a safe house that was located right outside the capital. She had one week to get information and to set up contacts concerning any information that could help her. She knew she had to work quickly because the clock was ticking for her to get out of the country.

"I hope your guy is good," the head of the agency said to H by phone on a secure line that went to headquarters of the operation in Morocco, where H had stayed behind to monitor Sasha's whereabouts at all times.

"She is the best," H responded. "You have nothing to worry about. She has made it to the safe house outside the capital. She seems to have gotten a lot of useful information."

"What kind of information?" the agency commander demanded.

"Listen," H said. "I will gather this information and get it back to Washington as soon as possible. I need to follow standard protocol."

"You need to hurry up," he interrupted to let H know that he meant business. "This is no time to go slow. I am under a huge deadline and you are slowing me down."

The head of the agency was not a happy. He was not a patient man and H knew that he would not be happy until Code 7 got the information that he needed. This put more pressure on him, but he remained calm and made sure that Sasha continued to stay on course with the plan.

Sasha got back to the safe house after checking out a report concerning a local village. The village was very small, but the activity and information she had gathered was enormous. She hurried to tell H what she had gotten.

"H," she asked. "Do you copy?"

"I am here," he answered hoping for some positive news.

"I have been at a small village," she said. "I was told that it was a great place to observe things. I cannot believe what is going on over here."

H could hear fear in her voice. He hoped that she was safe. "Are you alright?" he asked Sasha. She did not answer right away. It seemed that there was a little break up in her line. "Sasha, Sasha, answer me," he said, but got no answer. H got anxious. He kept calling her name, but did not get an answer.

Sasha dropped the phone as she felt the metal barrel of a gun that was pressed against the back of her head. She put her hands up and slowly turned around to see three men in uniforms. She had backtracked and made sure she was never in any danger. She never saw anyone behind her, but it seemed that they had always known that she was there. Now in her safe house, for reasons that she could not explain there stood three men with guns pointing right at her head.

"Who are you and what are you doing here?" One of the men asked her. She looked at him as to tell him she did not understand what he said. "We know you speak English, woman. Quit acting like you do not understand me."

The men began to come towards Sasha. She knew if she reached for the gun she would be shot. She turned around and ran out of the back door. Unfortunately, there was another man in uniform waiting for her. He hit her on the head with the back of his gun. She was instantly knocked out and fell to the ground. "I got her," he yelled to the others as they came out the back door.

"What do we need to do with her," one of the men asked. "We were told to take her to the prison camp down in east part of the jungle. She will serve a good purpose and maybe they can get some answers out of her."

They picked Sasha up off the floor of the house and carried her outside and threw her in the back of the jeep. "Go ahead and burn down the house and everything in it."

Two of the men got some gasoline and poured it in and around the house. They lit a torched and threw it in the house and began to burn. It did not take long until the safe house had burned to the ground.

* * *

Sasha woke up with her hands tied above her head, hanging from bamboo poles in the middle of a prison cell. She had a headache, but knew she could not concentrate on the pain. She could not believe that she had been captured and felt that her mission had been compromised by someone. She had taken every necessary step to make sure that she was never followed. She knew that no one knew that she was in East Africa, outside of Code 7, but now she was hanging by her hands in a bamboo cell. There was no way for Sasha to contact H and she did not know if she would be rescued, but she knew she had to maintain her survival skills for her survival.

A guard entered into her small cell and pulled out a knife. Sasha's first thought was that he was going to slash her throat, but instead he used the knife to cut her down. Sasha fell to the ground and because she had been hanging for so long, she had lost feeling in her arms.

"Get up!" the guard demanded. She rolled over and tried to stand, he kicked her back to the ground. "Get up I said!" he yelled again.

She looked at the guard and started to get up, but rolled over on her back and kicked the guard as hard as she could between his legs. He tumbled to the ground in excruciating pain. By this time she had regained feeling and some strength in her arms so she was able to grab his gun and she headed out the cell. Her instincts took over and she headed toward the door. She got to the door and opened it, but unfortunately for her, there were ten guards in front of her with their guns raised toward her head. Sasha knew there was nowhere for her to go so she dropped her gun and raised her tied hands.

"I thought you would see it my way," a voice said to her.

She looked up, but could not see who was speaking. A man in a general's uniform, decorated with at least ten different metals, appeared and directed his men to drop their guns.

"Who are you?" Sasha asked as one of the guards walked over to her and picked up the gun that she dropped.

"I do not think that you are in position to ask me questions," the general responded. "I will be the one who will be asking you the questions. I think it is in your best interest to answer them." The general was very direct with Sasha. He would not tolerate anything but the truth. He was feared by his men and was known by his men to kill anyone who did not obey him.

He told one of his men to grab Sasha and to take her down to the interrogation room. The general had some questions that she needed to answer. The interrogation room, otherwise known as the dungeon, was not a place that one would want to go. The prisoners knew that if anyone ever went into the dungeon, that person never came out alive. Sasha had not been there long enough to know anything about the dungeon, but knew that where ever she was going, was not going to be a fun place.

She had been prepared for torture from the training she had gotten from Simeon, but she had no idea what was in place for her. The guards took her to a small building that was located in the middle of the prison camp. They opened the door and they walked down stairs into a small room, not much bigger than the cell she had been in. There was a wooden chair in the middle of the dark and damp room. She sat down in the chair, having her hands tied behind her. Her legs were also tied to the chair. She could barely move, but she had to prepare for pain she was about to get.

There was a small light that came on and glared right into her eyes. The light was so bright that she could not see anything in front of her. "I am not going to blind fold you because I want to see the fear in your eyes," the general said as he lit a cigar, blowing smoke into her face. Sasha said nothing and kept looking straight ahead. "I will ask you easy questions, at first," he continued. "If I like the answers, we can all leave happy and I will let you go, if I don't then I will introduce you to a friend of mine. Are you an American?" Sasha said nothing. "Did you hear me," he demanded, "Who are you and what is your mission?"

Sasha was not going to answer any of the general's questions the way he wanted. She grinned sarcastically and gave him an answer she knew he would not like. "I am here as a tourist. I have never been to East Africa before and I am just here taking in all your wonderful sights."

The general thought that he could be cordial to her, but he had heard enough of her lies that he could handle. He would not tolerate anything coming from her mouth, but the truth.

"I have tortured plenty of people," the general said as he continued to smoke his cigar. "I get the most pleasure out of torturing women. Especially, women who do not like to cooperate with me."

He walked over and grabbed to his electric shock treatment. He ordered one of his men to hook up her up to the machine. He then threw a bucket of water on her.

"As you can see, I did not like that answer," the general said to Sasha. "I want to introduce you to my friend," pointing to the electric shock machine. "This machine does not talk back. He does what I want, when I want it. Because I am a nice guy, I am going to ask you the same simple question. This time I would like the right answer. Why are you here and what is your mission?"

Sasha was not going to tell the general anything. She knew that she would always put country first and would not give in to him, no matter what he did to her. She looked back into the light and said, "If you did not hear me the first time than you are deaf. I am here as a tourist, you low life son-of-a-bitch."

Sasha's words upset the general. He had distaste for unruly women, and what she said did not eliminate his hatred for them. He would not allow any woman to try to belittle him in front of his men. He was going to make her pay for what she said. The general got a few inches from her face and blew more smoke from his cigar at her. She did not flinch and continued to look straight ahead. "You are a very stubborn person," he said to her as he continued to puff on his cigar. "You will pay for being very stubborn."

The general pointed at one of his men to turn on the electric shock machine.

"Wait!" Sasha yelled. "I have something to say, but it is for you and you alone."

The general leaned downed and put his face right in front of Sasha's face. He got so close to her face that she could feel the air coming out of his nostrils as he breathed. He was not happy with her for continuing her charade, so he blew more smoke into her face. She wanted to cough, but looked into his eyes with pure hatred.

"What do you want for only my ears to hear," he asked again as he inhaled more from his cigar.

She kept herself very close to the general and did not want for him to move. She opened her mouth looking as if she was going to say something, but instead she spat right into his face. "I just wanted to make sure you knew how I felt about you."

The general, humiliated in front of his men, slapped her across her face. He grabbed a handkerchief out of his coat pocket and wiped the spit off his face. He walked away from and motioned to the guards to go ahead with the shock treatment. The machine was turned on and the general paused. He looked at one of the guards and grabbed the button that controlled the machine from his hand. He wanted to be the one that made sure she suffered for what she did.

An hour had gone by and Sasha could barely hold her head up. She had endured enough pain, that she felt dead. She was seeing double vision and had no feelings in her arms or legs. The general did not stay around after the initial shock. He felt that he had better things to do and turned the torture over to his guards. He did inform the guards not to kill her, because he needed her for information.

The guards had tortured Sasha long enough for one day. They grabbed her off the chair and carried her back to her cell. She was thrown to the ground and tied back up. She had no desire to move. She knew that physically she had no strength, but mentally she needed to stay as strong as she could.

She was very hard headed and she had already made up her mind that she would rather die than give up any information. The one thing that she had learned in training was that if she ever got caught, the odds of survival were slim to none. She knew that she would be killed even if she told them what they wanted to know. She wanted to hold out as long as possible and live another day.

She was able to endure the torture for the next two months and did not give them any information.

During her two month stay in the prison cell, Sasha was able to make a friend in the cell next to her. He passed food and water to her to help from time to time so that she could keep her strength up. The prisoner had been in the camp longer than Sasha and any torture that he got was not as bad as what Sasha experienced. He wished he could do more for her, but he was able to keep her spirit up and reminded her every day that she was alive.

Finally Jake came and rescued Sasha. She would never forget the experience and would never forget the prisoner that had helped her. He had been moved and she could not help free him that day, but she hope that she could help him one day the way he helped her.

CHAPTER 16

Jake had listened to Sasha story and realized that she was sent to East Africa for a purpose that she had yet to accomplish. During his first tour of duty in the agency, he never left a mission unfinished. He did not care what it took; he always finished what he had started. He did not want her to leave her business unfinished either. Jake knew that he was sent to this country to rescue her, but now there was something else on the table for them to finish. He knew that their time frame for the extraction was less than a day away and that he did not have a lot of time to think about what he wanted to do. She had mentioned that she only needed a few more hours to accomplish what she had started. He knew that they would have enough time to accomplish her mission and still make it to the extraction zone.

Jake went back and forth on the issue, but he had always lived for the excitement in life and never wanted to leave anything on the table. He made up his mind quickly what he wanted to do. He walked over to Sasha pulled up a chair so that he could be face to face with her. He looked into her eyes and with a very serious tone in his voice, he said, "Sasha, your mission is not over."

She was startled by what he had said and did not understand what he was getting at. He saw this and quickly said to her, "Hear me out. I believe that I was sent her for another purpose than just to rescue you. You know the lay of the land. You know where we need to do to make your mission a success. You were sent hear for something, and I can see the fire in your eyes that you want to finish it. I want to help you finish what you started. I know that if we work together, we can accomplish what you have yet to finish."

Sasha had been through a lot over the last month. The electric shock had taken a toll on her body and she did not feel that she was at full strength yet. However, she knew that if she left out of East Africa, she would never return to finish what she had started. Jake gave her the opportunity that she wanted. She felt obligated to H and Code 7 to get the information that they had sent her to get. She knew that if she did not take this opportunity that Jake presented her, she would never get a second chance. She wanted to get back at the general and knew that she would see him again. She knew exactly where to start.

"Jake," Sasha said. "I know that I can do it, but I need to know that you are one hundred percent sure you want to go through with this."

Jake was never more sure of anything in his whole life. He had lived for these moments and was not about to let it pass him by. "I have been waiting for this my whole life," he answered.

"What about the extraction?" Sasha questioned Jake.

"We will deal with that tomorrow." He answered, "We need to get to sleep. We have a big day ahead of us tomorrow."

Jake began to think about what his next move would be. The extraction was still scheduled for the next day. He felt that finishing the job that Sasha had started would help Code 7 get out of the trouble that it was in with the United States government. He decided that they would go to the extraction, explain their case and pick up need supplies. He went to sleep feeling very confident that everything would work out for the best.

Jake woke up the next morning and immediately began to go over the plan with Sasha. The extraction time was later in the evening and Jake asked her if there was anything that they could do in the meantime.

"Yes there is," Sasha responded. "We need to go to the safe house."

Jake was puzzled. He said to Sasha, "I thought you said that the house had burned down."

"I believe it was, but there is something we need to get. I stored in a safe place and I know that it did not burn with the house. We need to see if Anteon can direct us there from here."

Jake went downstairs and woke Anteon up. He asked him if he could take them to the safe house. Anteon was excited to help anyway he could and knew exactly how to get to where they needed to go.

Sasha told Jake that they needed to go as soon as possible, so they packed their things and headed out. On the way out the door, Jake and Sasha thanked Diotrice for her hospitality. Diotrice packed a bag for both of them that included bottled water and some fruit. They were very appreciative and the three of them left the old hotel and got into the pick-up truck. They left the city and went in the direction of the safe house. Anteon knew all the back roads and they all agreed that it was best to stay off the main roads for fear of being spotted by the East African military. It took longer than expected, but it paid off as they made it to their destination without any incident.

Jake drove up a small dirt road and made his way to where the safe house used to be. He stopped the truck and Sasha got out. Jake followed and told Anteon to stay in the car. The house was gone, having been burned completely to the ground. There was just a couple of old burned up pieces of wood left. Jake shook his head, felling that they had wasted their time coming back. He looked at Sasha and said, "Do you think there is anything that could have survived this burn. It seems to me that not only did it burn down, but someone came back and burned it some more."

Sasha looked at Jake, chastised him for having little faith, and walked into the middle of the burn rubble. She walked over to where the front door use to be and began to pace toward the middle of the burned down safe house. "Come here over here, Jake," Sasha hollered. "I need some help digging, but before you come, see if you can find anything to help us dig."

Jake looked around, but saw nothing, but then he remembered that there was a shovel in the back of the truck. He grabbed it and yelled back to Sasha with his smart aleck response, "Will this help?"

She looked up and saw Jake holding a shovel. "Yes, it will, I am so happy that you found something. You're my hero, now get over here. We need to dig right here."

Sasha was pointing straight down. Jake walked over with the shovel and moved some debris away. He started to dig, but then stopped and looked at Sasha and asked her, "What are we digging for."

She answered, "I was always taught never trust anyone and to always know that even if you take every precaution you can, you are always being watched. I did take precautions, but I was caught. Before I was captured, I decided to have a small undetectable safe installed in the special compartment in the ground of the safe house. Any information that I received, went into it."

Jake nodded, knowing that she was not only beautiful, but intelligent as well. "Are you sure the safe is right here," he asked pointing at the ground with his shovel.

"Yes," she answered. "I made sure to measure before the house burned down. I did not bury it too far down in the ground. It should be right here."

Jake continued to dig and after awhile he hit something very hard. "I think I have hit something," he said.

"Good, now move away the dirt. Hopefully the combination is still good." Jake got down on his knees and moved away the dirt with his hands. He had uncovered the safe. It was surrounded by concrete so he could not pull it out, but the lock was still attached. Sasha turned the lock with the combination and opened the door.

"Great," she exclaimed as she put her hands into the safe. "All the information is fine." She grabbed into the safe and pulled out a small black metal box. "I think this box will help us in our mission." Sasha had her foot pointed right where Jake's shovel was.

Jake started to dig and he dug as fast as he could. He was eager to see what she had in the safe. His shovel hit something hard and Jake got down and moved the dirt and ash away from the metal box. It was not heavy and he picked it up and handed it to Sasha and asked, "What is in the box?"

Sasha knew that eyes and ears were everywhere and wanted to get out of sight. "I will tell you later," she said. "Right now we need to get out of here. I just do not feel safe."

Jake agreed with her and they hurried back to the truck.

"Alright, Anteon," Jake said after hurrying back to the truck. "We need to get us to the extraction area. Do you know how to get there," Jake asked while pointing to an area on the map he that he had not lost.

Anteon knew exactly where to go and they go back into the truck and headed out. It was later in the day and Anteon knew that the military would have most of the roads blocked off for check points. He knew that Jake and Sasha would not be safe so he continued to have them stay off the main roads.

They had been going down an old dirt road for awhile, when Jake looked out of his side view mirror and notice another truck following them. "It seems that we have run into some trouble," he said as the truck got close to the rear bumper.

"It's probably nothing," Sasha answered. "See if they want to pass."

Jake slowed down and put his hand outside; hoping that they truck would pass them. Instead the truck bumped Jake's back bumper. "That wasn't good," Jake said as he started to speed up.

"This doesn't look good," Sasha exclaimed. "What do you think that they want?"

"I do not want to find out," Jake answered as he put to hands on the wheel, determined to out run them.

The trucked pulled up beside them. Jake looked over and could see five guys in the other truck with guns. They motioned with their guns for Jake to pull over. Jake swerved over trying to run them off the road. He then sped up trying to get away from them. Unfortunately, Jake's action made the men open fire at them.

"Hang on," Jake said.

He continued to swerve over and try to run the other truck off the road. It almost worked, but the other truck pulled back and tried the other side of the road. Jake, who had exceptional driving skills, knew he could not out run them in his old clunker that he was driving. However, he knew that he could out drive them.

The Nile River was on their right hand side of their truck and jungle was to the left of them. Jake slowed down hoping that the other truck would pull up against him again. The truck continued firing shots, but this did not deter him.

"Make sure ya'll stay down," Jake yelled at Sasha and Anteon. "We are in for a little bumpier ride than expected."

The other truck did not pull up against him like he wanted them to do, so Jake kept the same pace and kept swerving around on the dirt road so he could avoid the gun fire that seemed to be coming from all different directions. He saw a sharp left turn coming and felt that this was his only chance that he would have to get away from the other truck. He knew that it was just a matter of time before one of the bullets that were being fired at him would eventually hit his truck.

"Listen," Jake said to Sasha and Anteon. "We are not going to be able to out run these guys. I thought I could run them off the road, but it doesn't look like that is going to happen either. I just hope that you know how to swim."

"What do you mean?" Sasha asked.

Jake looked over at her and said, "There is no time to explain, just hang on."

Jake could hear the bullets go over the roof and finally one hit the glass, shattering it. "Okay guys, this is it. Hang on!"

Jake put his foot on the accelerator and the old pick-up truck hit a bump in the road and took off into the air. The truck and everyone inside landed in the Nile River. The truck that was chasing them came to a screeching halt. They did not quit shooting at Jake and the others, but they had floated too far down the river.

"Is everyone alright?" Jake asked as the truck continued to flow down the river.

"I guess," Sasha answered. "Was this the best you could come up with? You could not at least try to run them off the road."

"Listen, I am just glad we are still alive and in one piece. But I guess I will take that as a thank you. Anteon, how are you doing?"

"I am fine," he answered.

Jake responded, "Good, we need to get off this truck and we need to get out of the river."

They flowed down the river, allowing the rapids to get them closer to their extraction point. They all jumped off the old pick-up truck and began to swim through the rapids. They all had made it to shore and the extraction point was only a few hours away. Hopefully, the extraction was still on scheduled, Jake thought. If not, they were in a lot of trouble.

CHAPTER 17

Jake, who had not swam in a long time, could feel the effects of the river and was completely out of breath. He looked over at Sasha and saw that she was sitting up, not looking nearly as tired as he felt. He tried to play it cool so that she could not tell that he was exhausted. He quickly put the focus toward her and asked, "Did you make sure you got that box before you jumped out of the truck?"

"Yes, I got it. It was not easy swimming with it, but that is something that I did not want to leave behind," Sasha answered.

She put the box down and laid on the riverbank. Jake and Anteon decided to join her and all three laid on the river bank. They were all out of breath and decided that it was a good idea to rest for a few minutes before they hiked up to the extraction area. The hike was not going to take very long, but they had to go to higher ground and it was going to take a toll on all three of them. Jake knew that they were short on time, but felt that everyone should and take a breather.

"Anteon," Jake said as he reached for his map in his back pocket. "You do know where this is, don't you." He was pointing at a spot on the map. "It looks like a lot of jungle out there. I hope you don't get us lost."

Anteon was young, but he had learned how to navigate and knew the area very well. He assured Jake that they were not that far and he had nothing to worry about. Anteon was able to handle himself and did not let any of the adventure over excite him. He had been very cool and collective during the car chase and acted like it had not been that big of a deal, even though it was. He looked up to Jake and wanted Jakes approval. He wanted to prove to Jake that he was a huge asset to him.

"You are a good boy, Anteon," Jake said as he took a sip of water out of his canteen. "I just want know that none of this could have ever had happened, the rescue and all, had not been for you. You got us a place to sleep and supplied us with some food and water. You have truly been a God send. I am very appreciative of everything you have done for us."

Jake never gave out many compliments and this came from the heart. The boy had started to grow on Jake he knew how much the boy meant to him and the mission. Anteon loved hearing how proud Jake was of him. He had never grown up with a father figure and needed any encouragement or acknowledgement he could get from a man. He wanted to please Jake as much as possible.

Anteon turned to Jake and said, "You're welcomed. I just hope you don't forget me when you leave."

Jake got up and walked over to Anteon and gave him a big pat on the back. He would not forget Anteon and assured him that he would do everything in his power to take care of him.

Sasha had caught her breath and got up and told the group she was ready to continue. Jake saw her get up and said, "Let's go. It shouldn't be much further. We have about two hours before the extraction. When we get there we can rest a little more."

They walked up the mountain, through very thick parts of the jungle and arrived at the extraction point. It was a small clearing in the brush. Jake felt it was safer to stay in the brush and not go out into the clearing until the helicopter appeared. He did not have a great feeling about the situation. The car chase had kept him uneasy and felt that they were being watched.

"Guys," Jake in almost a whisper. "We need to stay out of sight. I do not have a very good vibe out here. Things do not seem right."

Sasha nodded at Jake and agreement. "I have the same feeling. It just does not feel right out here. I agree with Jake, let's stay out of sight and stay quiet."

They laid low and stayed out of sight in the brush for the next two hours. Jake would occasionally put his head up and look around, but he did not see anything out of the ordinary. He still did not feel that it was safe for them to move from where they were. He whispered to them after taking one last look, "Only a few more minutes, hopefully this will all go smooth. I still have a bad feeling about this situation. Anteon, you might have to come with us. I don't want to leave you here. We will bring you back later, when we come back to finish what we started, but the safest plan for you is to get on the helicopter and get out of here for a while."

Anteon got excited. He looked over at Jake and whispered, "That's fine with me. I have never been on a helicopter."

Jake grinned and said to Anteon, "Kid, it won't be a joy ride, but it may feel like one. Just follow me and I will tell you what to do when the time comes."

Jake looked at his watch and saw that it was only a few minutes until the helicopter would be there. He had a flare in his back pack and he threw it into the clearing. Red smoke filled the clearing and a few seconds later they heard the helicopter coming towards them. The helicopter reached the clearing and Jake stood up and told Sasha and Anteon to follow him, but for them to remain as low as they could to the ground. They followed Jake and ran into the clearing. Nothing out of the ordinary happened and Jake started to feel that maybe he was overreacting and hopefully nothing bad would happen to them.

The helicopter was now hovering right over their heads. The clearing was not big enough for it to land so Jake motioned for them to drop down the sling. He wanted Anteon to go first. Jake yelled over the helicopter noise to his little friend to not be afraid.

He let him know that he was right behind him and that everything would be just fine. Anteon was a little skittish about being hoisted up in the air, but he trusted Jake and knew that he would not let anything happen to him. The sling dropped down and he strapped Anteon in safely. Jake looked into Anteon's eyes and said, "You will be fine. Trust me. I will be up there before you know it."

Jake motioned to H's men who were flying the helicopter to take Anteon up. Anteon grabbed on to the straps for dear life. Jake could see the fear in his little friend's eyes, but knew he would be up before long. He watched as Anteon was raised in the air and finally made it into the helicopter. Anteon came to the edge and waved and gave Jake the 'o.k.' sign with his hand to let him know that he was fine. The strap was lowering to the ground for Sasha to come up next. Jake looked back up toward the helicopter and saw a big smile on Anteon's face.

"I told you everything was going to be fine," Jake screamed hoping Anteon could hear him over the noise from the helicopter. The strap hit the ground. Jake looked at Sasha yelled, "It's your turn. Come here and let me strap you on."

All of a sudden, Jake saw something in the corner of his eye.

"Sasha, get down!" Jake screamed as he pushed her to the ground.

Jake pointed to the pilot of the helicopter to leave, but it was too late. Jake saw a missile launcher come out of the woods and fire upon the helicopter. The missile did not miss and the helicopter blew up sending parts all over the jungle. Jake grabbed Sasha and ran for cover. Jake saw the helicopter explode, sending it straight down to the ground.

"No!" Jake yelled as he saw it hit the ground. He got up and ran over to it, but the flames were to hot and he knew everyone was dead, even his little friend Anteon.

Jake could not believe that he lost Anteon. He lost it and started to yell and scream. Sasha came over and grabbed him, slapping Jake across the face for him to get a grip on the situation.

"We have to get out of here," she yelled, hoping he would follow her. Shots were fired at both of them as they began to run into the jungle.

Jake was not completely with it and yelled out "Why? He was just a little boy."

Sasha looked back and told Jake to keep running. They ran as fast as they could, hearing behind them the enemy getting closer and closer.

"It is no use," Jake yelled back at Sasha. "Where are we going to run to?"

"Just keep running, we will think of something when we get away from these guys chasing us. Look there is a clearing up there. Maybe that will lead us somewhere."

The two of them kept running and finally made it to the clearing. The clearing turned into a road, but unfortunately for them, the road was occupied by the East African military. The soldiers were waiting for Jake and Sasha. Jake and Sash had nowhere else to run, because there were guns pointed towards them from all different directions.

They put up their hands, both hoping that they would not be shot. They heard a voice come out from a distance, "You can stop running, there is nowhere for you to go. We have many guns aimed right at your heads. There is no escape. You can come with us, or we can carry your dead bodies to a grave; your choice."

Jake knew the voice was right and he and Sasha were trapped. They could not outrun the army and had no weapons to fight them. He looked at Sasha and grabbed her hand. "Okay, we surrender," he said. Sasha knew that Jake had done the right thing and knew that there was no escape.

"Good," the voice said. "Now drop to the ground and lay still."

Jake and Sasha were forced to drop down to their knees, having their face facing the ground. A soldier came over and tied each of their hands together. He also made sure that they were tied together. "Get up off the ground," the voice said to Jake and Sasha.

They stood up and Jake looked out and yelled, "Whose voice is telling us what to do. I sure would like to see a face to the voice."

The same man, who had tortured Sasha only days earlier, came in front of his men and said, "I am the general and head of the army. My name is Qatar. I am a very powerful and do not like these disturbances that you have caused in my country."

He walked over to Sasha and grabbed her by the hair and pulled her head back. She let out a yell in pain and Qatar pulled back even further. "I thought that I had ended this little disturbance a couple of days ago," he said looking at Jake, "but you came in and ruined my plan."

Qatar was referring to his earlier encounter with her. He then turned over to Jake and said, "I told your government to stay out of my country, but obviously they did not listen. You have come in and done some damage to my country."

He turned and looked at Sasha, grabbing her back the hair again and yelling, "You will pay for what you have done. Now give me that black box you are holding. It must be important for you to break out of my camp to go after."

Sasha was not going to be intimidated by him again and spit in his face for the second time. That aggravated Qatar immensely. He was tired of being humiliated by her in front of his men and he reached back and back slapped her across the face.

"That will be the last time you spit in my face," he yelled. "I will guarantee that you will die an unpleasant death and I will be there to watch it."

He grabbed the metal box out of Sasha's hands and said, "Like taking candy from a baby. This is my box now." He pushed her over so that she fell on her side in the dirt.

He walked over and put the metal box in his jeep. Qatar then went over to Jake and looked him up and down. "Is this the best the States have to offer? You are a joke and you have no idea what you have gotten yourself into. I guess you don't mind the same fate as her."

Jake was angry. He had no desire to talk to the general. He stood there and looked at the general, but did not say anything to him.

"The cat must have your tongue or you must be stupid," Qatar said, laughing at him.

Jake was in no mood to have anyone get smart with him, but he knew that the best thing for him to do is to continue to remain quiet.

Qatar walked back over to Jake and he saw the anger in his eyes. "What is wrong with you? Why are you mad with me? You are the one in my country that is not invited. I am just trying get rid of the garbage."

Jake stared down Qatar and finally said, "You are responsible for my little friend's death."

"I killed no one," Qatar snapped back and got within a few inches of Jake's face. "If anyone died it is because that person is a traitor to my country. All traitors will be killed."

"He was just a kid," Jake answered back. "He did not hurt anyone or betray anyone. He only helped me."

Qatar started to laugh. "You are funny, my friend. That kid was a traitor in my eyes. He should not help an unwanted spy. Remember, my friend, if you had not come here, he would still be alive. Not only are you responsible for his death, I will find anyone else that helped you along the way and have them share the same fate and then both of you will soon die as well. Take them away; I am tired of looking at them."

Jake had one more thing to say before Qatar walked away. "Qatar!" Jake yelled. Qatar slowly turned around and looked at Jake. "This is not over for us. I will make sure that Anteon did not die in vain. There is blood on your hands for his death, and I will make you pay for what you did."

Qatar walked back over to Jake and again laughed at him. He pulled back his fist and hit Jake in the face. Jake head jerked back and pain took over his body. "Unfortunately for you, there is no one else that can rescue you and her. You will die and I will be there to see it."

Qatar walked back over to his jeep and got in. He sped off down the dirt road. Jake looked at Sasha and shook his head. "Sasha, I am so…"

Before he was able, to finish what he was saying to her, a soldier hit him in the back of his head with a gun and knocked him out.

"No!" Sasha yelled out.

The soldier walked over to her and looked as if he was going to hit her as well, but instead she was blindfolded and was put in the back of a truck along with the Jake, who was knocked out.

* * *

"Wake up!" yelled Sasha as Jake hung from his hands. "Please, Jake wake up."

He was still motionless and had yet to move for the last hour. "I know you are still alive," she continued. "Please wake up."

Jake finally started to move. He opened his eyes and he looked around the room. His vision was blurry and he had a terrible headache. He had no feeling in his arms or legs. It all felt like a dream to Jake and thought that he would wake up at anytime. But then Jake looked around the small cell and saw some light coming through a crack in the wall.

He heard Sasha say, "Jake, I see you moving over there. Can you hear me?"

Sasha was hoping Jake was okay. She saw the gun hit him in the back of his head and thought it might have been a fatal blow. She knew that he was in a lot of pain and was thankful that he started to move around.

"I can hear you," Jake responded, "but I am hearing ringing in my ears. I can barely see and I feel that my vision has been blurred. I am aching all over and don't have any feeling in my arms or legs. Other than that, I think I am fine."

Sasha was relieved to hear that Jake had not lost his since of humor. "How long have I been out?" Jake asked her.

"It seems like a couple of hours," she said. "I am glad to hear you say something. I think you suffered a concussion."

"Thank you doctor Sasha for you diagnosis. I think I am cured now."

"You do not have to get smart with me," she answered. "I was a little worried about you, but now I could care less about you."

"I'm sorry," Jake said. "I did not mean to hurt your feelings. Thanks for caring. By the way, how are you feeling?"

Sasha's body ached as well. She was also hanging from her hands tied above her and had been hanging just as long as Jake had. She felt that she had lost feeling in her arms and legs as well. "I have felt worse, but I am used to this by now. It seems to me that we are back where I started. This is not the same cell, but it seems to be the same prison. Oh, one more thing, thanks for the rescue." She started to grin.

"Don't mention it," Jake returned a smile, "Anytime you need to be rescued, don't hesitate to call me. I will get you out and back in within twenty-four hours." They both started to laugh, but the pain set in and both decided that it would be better to quit laughing.

"No more jokes," Jake said, "I don't think I can take it. It hurts too much."

They both hung there trying not to laugh, but could not control themselves. "I cannot believe this," Jake said as he continued to laugh.

"What do you mean?" Sasha asked as she finally quit laughing.

"I rescued a beautiful woman, only to get captured again and I never had a chance to make a move on you." Sun light had come in and lit up the cell. Jake had been talking to her in the dark, but now could see Sasha and looked over to her and smiled as his hands hung over his head. "It is amazing how hot you look with your hands just hanging above your head."

"Listen Jake, this is not the time or place for all your pleasantries. Even so, what makes you so sure that I would have allowed you to hit on me?" Sasha said.

Jake looked over at Sasha and said, "I have seen you looking at me. You know that I am irresistible."

Sasha started to laugh again, but this time she got flushed a little. "You are so full of yourself." She started to mumble words together, "What, I mean, I would never go for a guy like you. You are not my type. I, well, I just wouldn't go for a guy like you."

Jake just shook his head. He knew that she liked him and knew that she did not want to admit it. "I will make you a deal," Jake said to Sasha, "when I get you out of here, you will owe me a date. I will take you to this little restaurant in my hometown of Montgomery, Alabama, called the Supper Club. It has the best food in the whole state."

Sasha grinned and said, "If you can get me out of here again, I will go where ever you want. I still expect you to buy though." Jake nodded and said, "I wouldn't have it any other way."

Even though both were tied and hanging from the roof, it did not deter them and they continued to talk to one another. Their arms and legs were in pain, but this was the first time that they got to get to know each other. Neither one knew how much longer they would be alive, so they put aside their pains to chat.

"You really liked Anteon, didn't you?" Sasha asked Jake.

"He was just a boy, just trying to help me," Jake replied. "He did not have to help me, but he did. He had a lot of potential and lived on the streets. I told him nothing would happen to him in that helicopter and to trust me. That was the last thing I said to him. I know he is in a better place now, but he was too young to go. I think the same thing for Simeon as well. He trusted me and I let him die, too. I have never had this happen to anyone."

"Listen, Jake" Sasha said. "It wasn't your fought. You did all you could do. Simeon saved you. He took a bullet for you. He obviously cared about you. And Anteon looked up to you. He trusted you too. There are not many people in life that will get the trust you got from to great people in that short of time of knowing them. Be sad that they are gone, but do not be angry at yourself. Remember that their lives should not go in vain. We need to get out of here so we can get whoever is responsible for what happened to them." Sasha was never the one who gave comforting advice, but she felt differently toward Jake and wanted to try and cheer him up.

"Thank you for your kind words," Jake said. "They were good guys. I will never forget them."

Jake and Sasha bowed their head and shut their eyes. They remained quiet, letting their silence be a tribute to Simeon and Anteon. After a few minutes had passed, Jake raised his head and opened his eyes. He asked Sasha, "I've wanted to know, what was in that metal box that got us back in this mess."

Sasha had kept quiet on the matter because she did not want to tell Jake anything about it, but now they were hanging in a prison cell marked for death and she thought to herself that it did not matter if he knew or not.

"Jake," she said, "Do not be made at me, but I never actually looked in the box."

Jake was stunned. He hung there a little while longer not making a sound. He wanted to make sure that he responded in a way that she knew he was not happy, but did not want to come on as yelling at her.

He said to her in a very harsh voice, "What do you mean you did not look in the box? I do not understand. I am biting my tongue right now. This is not fun and games to me. I am upset." Jake was angry. He could not believe that they put their lives on the line for nothing. "Sasha, I was beginning to like you, but know I kind of wonder what you were thinking."

"Listen, Jake" Sasha answered, "Hear me out. I was given the information, told to put it in the metal box, and told not to tell anyone about it."

"Who told you that?" Jake asked.

"Be patient, I am getting to that." She answered.

Jake was getting more impatient by the minute. His arms were hurting more than ever and he could not believe that she was not more up front with him. Jake was very upset with her, but held his tongue. He twirled around so that his back would be toward her. "Jake," she said, hoping he would give her a chance. "Turn around. Please hear what I have to say and make your judgments afterwards you hear me out."

"Okay," Jake answered as he swung his body back so that he could see her eye to eye. "Go ahead and say what you have to say. It's not like I am going anywhere."

Sasha was getting irritated with Jake and felt that he was belittling her. "If that is how you are going to act than I will keep my mouth shut."

"I thought you would never do that, thank God."

Jake continued to make some smart aleck remarks, but Sasha interrupted him. "Just shut up, Jake, I thought you were sort of a nice guy, but you are just jerk."

"We'll excuse me. I am not the one that got us caught and hung up here in a dark prison cell, with our death sentence a couple of days away. I was just sent here to rescue you and get you home. I should have left you where I found you. I know I would be better off, if I would have done that." Jake really did not mean to say that, but was angry and the words just flew right out of his mouth.

"Jake that was a mean thing to say. Quit talking to me, please," Sasha said and then looked away. Jake knew that he had hurt Sasha's feelings.

"Listen, Sasha," Jake said, "I did not mean, I mean that just slipped out. I did not mean to say that."

"Well you did, now just stop talking to me."

Jake did what she wanted and stopped talking to her. He felt that it was for the best because his whole body was hurting and talking did not do it any favors. He hoped that someone would rescue them, but knew that it was unlikely. He just hoped to lie on the ground, but that did not look like it was going to happen either.

CHAPTER 18

Jake and Sasha both fell asleep during the night. Jake kept falling in and out sleep during the night as he hung with his hands above his head. When morning came, he opened his eyes and saw that Sasha was still asleep. He had not spoken to her all night, letting her catch up on her sleep and also hoping that she would forget about how mean he had been to her.

His arms were killing him and he knew that Sasha's had to be hurting her as well. Jake could not take it any longer and began to yell uncontrollably, hoping a guard would hear him. But no one came, and this just made him yell louder. Still no one came so Jake started to swing with his legs back and forth. He felt the tension in the rope starting to loosen as he went back and forth in the air. He was able to push off a wall with his legs and it helped him swing higher with more force. He began to jerk with his arms down hoping the rope would pull off the ceiling of the cell. After jerking for almost half an hour, the knot loosened, allowing him to free his hands.

Jake braced himself as he fell to the floor. He knew he should have done that earlier, but he was thankful that his feet were finally on the ground. He laid down a minute to get the feeling back into his legs and arms. His back was killing him, but he knew that Sasha was in the same pain so he got up off the ground and went over to Sasha and woke her up.

Jake shook her ever so slightly to gingerly wake her up. She opened her eyes and saw Jake grinning.

"Good morning," he said and she quickly forgot that she was mad at him. She just hoped he could get her down. "This might hurt a little," Jake said as he tugged at the rope that was holding her in the air. Jake pulled on the rope, putting all his weight on it and the rope came loose from the ceiling. Sasha fell on top of Jake, but was just thankful to finally have her feet on the ground as well. She crawled over to the corner of the cell and sat up. Jake followed her and sat down beside her.

"I said some mean things to you last night and I know I hurt your feelings," he said, hoping she would accept his apology. He held her hand and said in a very gentle voice, "I am sorry and I mean it."

Sasha stared back at Jake and could see that he was sincere. "Just don't say that to me again," Sasha said and then she started to grin.

Jake kept staring at her and he said, "You are a very beautiful woman. Hopefully you will take me up on that date when we get out of here."

Sasha responded by saying "I would love to, but one small problem. We are stuck in a prison cell in the middle of East Africa. It looks as if we have no way of escaping and we could be killed at any time. I hate to be the doom and gloom, but it doesn't look good for us."

Jake knew that he had to come up with something in a hurry. His arms were still sore, but he knew that he could not use that as an excuse. He was never one to give up and until his heart was not beating anymore he would find a way for them to live another day.

He told her to follow his lead. "What are you going to do?" she asked.

"I am going to get up out of here," he answered. "I really want to eat at the Supper Club again, and I really want you to come with me."

He yelled again hoping to get a guards attention. He told Sasha to lie on the ground and pretend that she had died. Jake yelled again, but this time heard someone coming. He knew that he had gotten someone's attention and he told Sasha to go ahead with the plan. She got down on the floor in the middle of the cell acting as if she had died.

A guard came to the cell, yelling for Jake to be quiet. He did not get a response, so he looked into the cell and saw Sasha lying on the ground, but did not see Jake anywhere in the cell. The guard yelled down to another for him to come help him.

"What is it?" one of the guards as he ran down to the cell.

"Look in there," the other guard answered. "I see one of the prisoners lying on the ground, but I cannot see the other one. I don't understand where he might have gone. We have been here all night long and I did not see him escape, did you?" The other guard looked in the cell and could not see Jake anywhere. "Open the door and check it out. I will go get some more help."

The guard opened the door and entered the cell as the other guard ran down the hall to get some help. The guard came in and bent over to check Sasha's pulse. He could tell that there was nothing was wrong with her, but before he could yell for help, Jake dropped from the ceiling landing on the guard. He had been holding himself up in the corner where the guards could not see him. Jake got up and hit the guard across the face with a quick right handed hook. The guard fell to the ground and Jake quickly grabbed his gun as Sasha moved to the other side of the cell.

The other guard heard the commotion and ran into the cell. Sasha caught him by surprise as she kicked him in the back of his head. He fell to the ground in shock and pain. Jake made sure the guard stayed down by hitting him in the back of his head. The force from Jake knocked the guard out. Jake motioned to Sasha to use the rope that they were tied up with to tie up the guards. He grabbed the other guard's gun and gave it to Sasha.

"That was pretty fun," said Sasha, as she tied up the guards' wrist to one another. "We make a good team."

Jake nodded and said, "We do indeed, but that was the easy part, now we got to get out of here."

After tying up both of the guards, Jake and Sasha, being very cautious walked very slowly out of the prison cell. They got outside the prison and realized that they were back in the Qatar's prison camp. Jake's first thought was to escape as he did the first time, but he had nothing to brace under the electric fence to absorb the shock. He knew that the only way to escape the camp was to go through the front entrance. Unfortunately, that would be a little tougher than going out the other way.

"We need to stay out of sight for a little while," he said to Sasha. "Let's hide over here," as he pointed towards some brush in the corner of the camp.

"We will talk about how we will get out of here and we will try to escape without anyone realizing we have left this awful place."

Sasha nodded in agreement. She knew that she could be as quiet as a mouse and this was one of those times. They crept over to the brush and hid out of sight.

"Sasha," Jake whispered, "I am going to create a diversion."

"What kind of diversion?" she whispered back to him.

"You will know when it happens," Jake answered in a quiet voice. "And when it happens, I want you to run as fast as you can to the entrance of this camp. Do not look back. Get outside the gate and keep out of sight. I want you to get back into town and go back to Diotrice's place. I will meet there."

Sasha stared into Jake's eyes. She could tell that he was a trustworthy person. She had never trusted many people, but she had faith in Jake and knew that he would get them out of this mess.

"Alright, here we go. Are you ready?" Jake asked Sasha as he was about to leave and establish a distraction.

"Yes," she answered and then Sasha gave him a little peck on the lips. "

What is that for," he asked as Sasha smiled at him.

"That is for luck."

He stared back at her and said, "I will take that any day of the week. Now remember to stay here until you hear the diversion."

"What is the diversion going to be," she asked.

"Don't worry about what I am going to do. You will know it when you hear it," he answered. "All I want you to do is run like the wind and the next time that I will see you will be at a meeting place."

Jake kissed Sasha on the top of the head and left before saying another word.

Sasha sat quietly in the brush wandering what Jake was about to do. Her heart was racing as she became very nervous. She knew that she had to control her emotions so she started to think about Jake. She had not had a romantic encounter with anyone in a very long time, but she felt that there was a spark between the two of them. She could sense that he was a good man and hoped that she would see him in the near future. She could only hope that they would both make it back to town safely.

Sasha had let her mind wander a little, but she came to very quickly as all of a sudden there was a very loud explosion in the western part of the prison camp. Sasha figured that the explosion must be the diversion that Jake caused. She looked toward the entrance of the camp and saw that the guards were running toward the explosion and away from the front gate.

Jake had spotted an old gas truck that was near a building in the western part of the camp. He was able to light a small flame and it turned into the diversion that he hoped. He could only hope that it was enough for them to escape.

The fire was out of control and it took most of the men in the camp to try and contain it. Sasha knew that this was her chance to get out of the camp without being noticed. She ran as fast as she could out the gate. She looked over her shoulder as she ran and saw that all the guards were still manning the fire. No one saw her leave the camp. She had escaped for the second time from the prison camp. Sasha decided to hide in the jungle for awhile so that she could catch her breath, hiding in some brush. She did not mean to, but Sasha fell asleep for a few minutes. She got up refreshed, ready to make it back to town and back to the old of hotel that Diotrice owned. She was going alone and had to hope that Jake made it back safely.

Sasha found her way to a road that looked as if it would lead back into town of Turin. She was walking beside the road, staying out of sight of any of Qatar's men that would be looking for her. She heard a truck coming down the road and she hid behind a tree so that no one could see her. The truck hit a curb and something fell off the back of it. It stopped and someone got out of the truck and grabbed the item and put it back onto the truck. Sasha felt that this was her chance to catch a ride without the driver and passengers knowing about it. When the truck started, Sasha ran and hopped into the back of the truck. She was able to squeeze herself behind some barrels, staying out of sight. Though the trip back to town was not as comfortable as she wanted it to be, she made it back to town without being noticed by anyone.

The truck came to a stop in the middle of town and Sasha jumped off the back of it. She looked around and saw the streets busy with people. She noticed that there were soldiers, more than she had seen before, walking around and asking people questions. She needed to stay out of sight, so instead of going right to Diotrice's hotel, she went through back alleys also hiding out in open doors. It took longer than expected, but she finally made it back to the hotel. She could only hope that Jake had made it back safely as well. She had not seen him since they left the prison camp, but in her mind she felt that he had made it back and was safe.

Sasha had walked well over an hour and was exhausted. She had been through a lot and every time she had a minute to rest, she was on the go again. She stayed outside the hotel to make sure that no one had followed or seen her. She had waited for awhile and she felt that it was safe for her to walk up and knock on the door. The door opened immediately and Diotrice appeared. She told Sasha to come in as if she was expecting her back. Sasha did not feel that everything seemed normal, but did as she was told. She saw Jake and he seemed quiet, not really excited to see her. She knew that something was wrong, but put it aside and ran to Jake to make sure he was fine.

"You made it," Jake said smiling, and then he fell straight to the floor.

Sasha bent down, grabbing for Jake, but he would not move. "What happened?" she said turning to Diotrice, hoping for an explanation. Unfortunately for her, she never got the chance to get an answer. Qatar came around the corner waiting for her.

"You think that you can get away from me? The two of you have been a pain in my side for the last time," Qatar said with a snarl.

He went over to Jake lying in pain and reared back his boot and kicked him in the ribs. Jake, who was already in excruciating pain, had barely enough strength to yell.

"Go ahead and say your good-byes," Qatar said to the two Americans, "You will be hung tomorrow morning in the town square. I will show all my people what we do to spies."

Qatar grabbed Sasha by the arm and got within a few inches of her face. He said to her in a very low, but intimidating voice, "I will never forget that you spit in my face, not once, but twice. You will know your place and you will finally suffer the consequences."

Sasha wanted to puke from the smell of Qatar's cigar breath, but stood there and did not say a word. He looked at her for a few more seconds and then walked away, ordering his men to tie her and Jake up together.

* * *

It was pitch black dark and Jake could feel the dampness in the air around him. He tried to move his arms, but he realized that they were tied up behind him. He was seated and tied to a chair. He could not move. He knew that he was a pretty bad predicament, but tried to move anyway, seeing if he could get his hands untied.

"Jake are you awake? You have been out for awhile. How are you feeling?" Sasha asked as she could feel him moving around. She was tied up to a chair as well and had her back to Jake.

"I am ok, but have a small headache," he answered as he continued to work and try to get his hands free. "This is beginning to be a very long day. I am beginning to thank that this day may never end. By the way, where are we?"

Sasha had been out for a few hours as well and had no idea where they were. She told him that she had no idea. All she knew was that it was very dark, wherever they were. Sasha wanted to pass the time and ask Jake what had happened to him when he left the prison camp. "How did Qatar capture you," she asked. "Did he follow you or was he there waiting on you."

"I do not know," he answered. "I saw you get out of the camp and my plan was for me to get out and follow you to town. I had gotten the guards attention with the explosion and they were too worried about putting out the fire than looking for me. I got out of camp and made my way back to town and found the hotel. I waited to make sure that I had not been followed and also I was hoping I would see you. But you never came, so I figured that you must have gotten to Diotrice's before me and that you must have been inside. I went and knocked on the door. Diotrice came and let me in. Before I could explain to her what had happened Qatar came with his men and captured me. I felt like they knew exactly where I was at all times."

Sasha interrupted and said, "Why did you feel that way."

Jake continued, "He hinted it to me. He said that what he knew about me led him back to the hotel. He asked me more questions, and of course I did not answer anything. I barely remember anything after that, but I can't imagine that he was nice to me after that."

"Do you not remember me coming into the hotel," Sasha asked.

"Vaguely," Jake answered. "I just thank God that you are alright, Sasha."

He tried to stand up, but his head hit the top of the ceiling of whatever they were in. "Don't bother trying to move," Sasha said. "It feels as if we are in some kind of big wooden box."

Out of nowhere, they started to move. It felt as if they were moving on the back of a truck.

"Are you wet," Jake asked Sasha.

"Yes, I am. They must have sprayed us down with water."

The two of them had no idea what was going on. The big metal crate that the two of them were in was on the back of a truck headed to a middle of town. Qatar wanted to show the people of East Africa his power by executing the two Americans in the middle of Turin. He knew that this would frighten the East African people even more if they saw two Americans executed. He was a powerful man, but he was not the leader of East Africa. He wanted to be the leader and knew the only way to the head of the table was for him to be a ruthless military general. He needed loyalty from his men and fear from the East African people. He did not care who stood in his way and he was willing to kill anyone who tried to stop him.

"We are still moving," Jake said as the truck made its way into the middle of town. "I guess there is not much more that I can do. I am sorry, Sasha. This is not the way that I wanted things to end. I hope it is not the end, but we need a miracle."

Sasha knew that things were not good and that it was just a matter of time before the truck stopped and they would be killed. "Jake," Sasha said as the back of their heads touched. "You have no reason to be sorry. We tried our best, but there was something in our way that did not want us to succeed."

Jake knew that being negative would not help them get out of the situation that they found themselves in. He knew for them to have a chance to survive, he would have to change his attitude.

"I will not let us go down like this, Sasha," Jake said. "I will come up with something to get us out of this."

Sasha had not given up completely as well, but she knew that Jake needed to come up with something quickly or they would not be alive much longer. The truck came to a stop and they could hear the commotion of the crowd that had formed in the courtyard that had been designated as the execution area. The top of the crate opened and the light from the sun came into it. Jake and Sasha were lifted out of the crate and cut loose from their chairs. Jake looked out into the crowd and could see that everyone in the city had come to his and Sasha's hanging. He saw the wooden platform with two nooses hanging down and knew that those were for them. He did not like the fact that they would hang to the enjoyment of all that was there to witness this. Jake looked up on the platform and saw Qatar smiling and waving to the crowd. He was behind a podium and it looked like he would give a speech. Qatar turned his head from the crowd and looked over at his guards and gave an order with his hands to have the two Americans put on the platform.

The guards pushed Jake and Sasha up the platform. Their hands were immediately tied behind them and they were positioned under each noose and stood there as Qatar turned around and looked at both of them. He walked away from his podium and got within a few inches of Jake's face.

"You look pretty helpless," he said laughing as Jake squinted eyes, trying to keep the sun out of his eyes. "Do you still think that you are going to kill me, because right now you do not seem to be going anywhere but down."

He started to laugh and he walked over to Sasha and got into her face as well. "It is such a shame that I have to kill such a beautiful woman like you, but I will still sleep well tonight."

Sasha stared right into Qatar's eyes and did not say a word. She hated the general and did not want to give him the pleasure of her voice. Jake on the other hand, said one more thing to him. "I made a promise to you Qatar that I intend to keep."

"And what may that be," Qatar asked. "I will kill you. Mark my words, I will kill you."

Qatar started to laugh and raised his hands and gestured to Jake to take him right now. "Come on, come get me," he said as he continued to laugh.

He went back over to Jake and pulled his fist back and hit him right in the stomach. Jake bent over in pain, trying to catch his breath. "You are the one that will die today, not me. The world will know my power and they will know what we do with spies. I am becoming a very powerful person and you should have never messed with me. This will be your final hour." Qatar walked away and back to his podium.

Jake leaned back up, still out of breath, and looked over at Sasha. "Is this you plan?" She asked. "It sure isn't getting us out of here."

Jake said while continuing to catch his breath, "I am still working on it."

"Well," Sasha answered. "You need to work a little faster."

Qatar went back up to the podium. He was going over his thoughts wanting to make sure he gave his best speech he had ever given. He made sure the East African television cameras where there, because he wanted his speech and the execution to be televised only in his country. Qatar was very particular on how he wanted himself portrayed. He wanted the East African people to fear him, but he did not want the world view to make him look like a crazed lunatic.

"People of East Africa," Qatar spoke into the microphone. "I stand here before you today because we have been under attack by the United States of America. We have asked this country to leave us alone, but they have refused and have sent spies to our country to try and take our oil. We spoiled their plan and have captured two of them and now we will show everyone what we do with spies."

The crowd started to applaud and yell. Qatar was a good speaker and knew how to get the crowd on his side. "This will be the first of many executions that will be done to anyone who does not abide by our law."

The crowd continued to applaud and yell. Qatar was quiet. He loved to hear the applause of the crowd. He knew that his plan was working and in only a matter of time that the two Americans would be out of his hair and he would be well on his way as becoming the new ruler of East Africa.

CHAPTER 19

The sun was blaring down and the heat was exhausting for both Jake and Sasha as they stood there in front of the people who had come to see them hang. Qatar continued to talk and it seemed as if he was talking for hours. Jake had heard enough of him. He knew that if he was going to do something to get out of this situation he and Sasha were in, he needed to do it quickly. He saw that there were two guards on the platform with him and Sasha, and he began to watch their every move. He looked around and saw more soldiers down below the platform. He looked over a Sasha and saw her sweating from the heat that was coming from the sun.

He smiled at her and said, "Are we still on for the Supper Club?"

Sasha looked back a Jake and answered, "Only if you get me out of this situation." He smiled back at her and winked.

Jake knew that he had a huge dilemma in front of him. He had no idea what he was going to do, but he wanted to keep Sasha's spirits up. Qatar said his last word and finished his speech to the huge crowd. The people continued to cheer and roar. Jake looked and saw huge monitors telling the people to cheer for Qatar. He knew that Qatar could not get the people to cheer for him. He knew that Qatar was a weak man. Jake now had to figure out a way to get out of the soon to be hanging that he was scheduled for.

Unfortunately, Jake's time had run out as he looked over and saw as the guards slipped the noose around Sasha's neck. The guards then did the same to Jake. Qatar turned around and looked at the nooses around the two American's. He was pleased at what he was about to do and felt that would give them one last request.

"Do you have anything else to say," he questioned the two. Sasha responded by saying that he was a pig. Qatar smiled at her and told her that he could not wait to watch her neck break as she grasped for air.

Jake had enough of Qatar and yelled, "Mark my words, you will die and I will be responsible for it."

Qatar had heard enough. He turned his back to them and turned toward the crowd and said through the microphone, "This is what happens to spies."

Qatar turned to the guards and gave the signal to them to pull the switch that would open the door and have Jake and Sasha hang to death. All of a sudden, in the north corner of the courtyard, a huge explosion erupted. There was another explosion in the western part of town. Jake looked over and saw a one of the guards that was guarding him, went down with a gunshot wound between the eyes.

"Sasha," Jake yelled. "Get down!"

There were multiple explosions going on all over town. Sasha was able to elbow the guard beside her in the groin, sending him falling off the platform. She crawled over to Jake.

"Was this your plan," she asked.

"Not really," he answered. "But I will take it."

They looked over as bullets flew by the head and more explosions went off in town and noticed Qatar ducking for cover and rolling off the stage. Chaos had broken out in the crowd and they were running in all direction. There were more explosions erupting all over the city and bullets were still flying out of the sky.

Jake knew that this was his chance to get Sasha and himself out of there. There was so much chaos going on around them that the guards were preoccupied with saving themselves than worrying about Jake and Sasha.

"Can you untie this rope?" Jake asked Sasha.

"Yeah, I think so. I am going to have to use my teeth so stay still." She answered as she crawled over to the knot. She managed with her to get his arms free and then he untied her.

"Come on," Jake said. "We are getting out of here. Stay low and let's mix in with the crowd. Hopefully, we can find some sort of an escape route."

Jake and Sasha jumped off the platform and got into the pandemonium that was going on in the crowd. Jake looked around to see if he could see Qatar, and saw that he had gotten into a vehicle and sped off. He knew that he was right and that Qatar was coward. He knew that he would have to meet him another day, but now he needed to get out of town and lay low with Sasha for awhile. They continued to run through the crowd, with the explosions still going off all over town. Jake had no idea where these explosions were coming and it seemed as if they were coming from bombs over head, but Jake looked up and did not see any planes flying over them.

Jake wondered who had set up this diversion, and was amazed at the excellent job of keeping the soldiers off balance. The explosions came from the northern part of town, and then a few seconds later there would be another one in the southern part, or western part or eastern part. The explosions were very loud and it seemed that East Africa was under attack. The explosions did not stop and Jake felt that they needed to hide out for awhile until all the commotion died down. He did not want to run into an explosion so he told Sasha to look for a place where they could duck down into.

"Let's hide in here," Jake said to Sasha as they came to an old run down building. "We need to stay out of sight for a little while and this will give us some time to figure out where we go from here."

Sasha agreed and they entered the old building. They ducked down under a window and could see soldiers running all over the place in hysteria. Jake felt that he and Sasha would be safe. They had not been followed and were very well hidden.

Right when Jake felt that they were safe, the door opened to the abandoned home. Jake looked over and saw someone enter into the building and he motioned to Sasha to stay down and out of sight. Jake crept slowly and was able to sneak behind the person who had entered into the building.

He jumped on him and grabbed him by the neck. "Are you ready to face your maker, because that is where I am sending you," Jake said as he was about to break the strangers neck.

The stranger yelled out, "Wait; hold on, Jake it's me. It's Henderson."

Jake could not believe his ears. His friend had come back. He pulled back the turban that was covering his friend's face and sure enough it was Henderson. Jake was exited that his friend had come back. He was so excited that he was at a loss for words. That was very unlike Jake. He tried not to choke up, so he just looked at Henderson with a stunned look on his face. He then grabbed Henderson and gave him a big bear hug.

"You got nothing to say," Henderson said in amazement to Jake, who had yet to speak.

"I am simply amazed that you are here," Jake finally said to his friend. "Now let's get out of here."

"Let's remain in here for a little while longer," Henderson responded as he motioned to Jake to squat to the floor.

"Wait a minute," Jake said, "I need to know what is going on. How did you know we were here and what is up with all the explosions. This is not making any sense. What is going on?"

Jake was puzzled and became a little aggravated. He was happy to see his friend, but wanted answers from Henderson. Henderson was going to give Jake the answers he wanted, but he knew that now was not the time. He wanted everyone to lay still, stay out of sight and remain very quiet as well. He knew, along with Jake, that Qatar would order his men to track them down and Henderson did not come over to East Africa to be captured before he could get everyone to safety.

He looked at Jake and said, "I want you to trust me."

"You know I do," Jake answered. "I trust you with my life."

Henderson whispered, "I will tell you what you want to know in due time, but right now, let's just stay here and out of sight."

Sasha had stayed still and quiet, and figured out that they must know each other. She motioned to Jake to let him know that she wanted to know what was going on. Jake crawled over to her and explained to her about Henderson and their past and that he was here to help rescue them. Sasha nodded and the three lay and waited for the next hour, without talking or making a noise.

Henderson stood up and leaned against a wall, then took a big breath. It had been a long time since he was in action, and he wanted to take it all in. Jake looked over at Henderson and saw that his friend was enjoying the moment. He could see the determination that he used to see in his friend's eyes. He knew that Henderson was excited to be back in the game. But still, Jake wanted to know how his friend found him and what the plan was from here on out. Jake knew the plan was not for them to sit around keeping quiet the rest of the day. Jake felt that he had waited long enough and he needed some answers.

"Henderson," Jake said as his friend was still leaning against the wall in the deserted building that they were in. "You have got to give me something, man. How in the world did you find me? I guess I am saying, what in the world are you doing here?"

Henderson looked over at Jake and grinned. "I've missed this. You were right, Jake, what a rush." Jake nodded and grinned back at Henderson, but that was not the answer he was looking for.

Henderson began to stall at Jake's question and asked, "Who is the pretty girl you are with?"

Sasha said in a sharp voice, making sure that Jake did not speak for her. "My name is Sasha. It seems that we are all in this together now. Jake was sent here to rescue me, but I guess I might need to thank you, since I still haven't been rescued." Sasha was getting impatient and Henderson could tell.

"Kind of feisty, I see," Henderson said. "I like that."

"She is feisty," Jake said, "I will give her that, but she is just as good as we were and hopefully still are. She has some great intel on the whole East African mess we are in. Anyway, you got her story Henderson, now you need to quit stalling and tell us what is going on."

Henderson knew he had stalled enough. He knew how impatient Jake was and knew if he did not tell him anything, that Jake would pester him until he did.

"Okay, Jake," Henderson said, "Here it is. It all started the day you left my house and came over here. I will admit that I was intrigued by the story that you told me about everything that happened to us ten years ago. I was not completely convinced that it was accurate and needed to know if there was any validity too it. I never told you, but I still had a contact over in the agency. I had never asked him about our situation, but decided to when you left. He did some research concerning our case and found out that you were indeed right. Our records and identity had been deleted in the system, but he was able to open up a file that went over some details of our Iran situation. He could not give me a concrete answers, because most of the content was deleted, but by his account the file showed that we were set up in Iran. The contact told me that it had to be someone very close to our situation, because whoever set you up, knew that all of our missions were kept top secret."

Jake had always thought that they had been set up. H had told him that they probably were, and now Henderson was giving him the same answer. He knew that someone in the agency wanted them out, but never could imagine it be anyone other than Higgins.

"Go on," Jake said, "I am still listening."

Henderson continued and said, "I became concerned for you. Since there was someone who was close to us and our secrecy in the agency, I thought that you were walking into trouble. I immediately thought of two people that might want to get back at you. One was Higgins, as of right now no one seems to know where he is and the other, of course was this guy H, who you said knew all about our history."

Jake looked at Henderson and shook his head in disagreement. "H is a good guy. He would not try to set me up again. He is the one who was looking for Higgins to prove that Higgins was the rouge agent."

Sasha interrupted and agreed with Jake. "H is a father figure to me. I cannot believe that he would try to hurt Jake or me for that matter."

Jake continued to nod his head in agreement with Sasha, "It has to be Higgins. H has been good to me and given me my second chance. I would not be here without him."

Henderson nodded and said to them, "I like the fact that you are taking up for your friend, H, but I am not accusing him. I am just pointing out the fact that it could be him. Anyway, the story is not over."

Jake interrupted and said, "Yeah, you need to tell us how you got here and how you got involved with rescuing us from Qatar's clutches."

Henderson continued, "If you would not keep interrupting me I could finish a lot faster. Continuing my story, I had just gotten off the phone from my contact when my doorbell rang. It was someone who I had never met before. He told me he knew who I was and that he was sent by a special agency called Code 7."

Jake could not help himself, and had to interrupt again. "Who was the guy? What did he look like?"

"Just let me finish," Henderson said as he shook his head. Jake gave him the thumbs up and promised he would not interrupt again. Henderson continued, "The guy would not give me his name, but he showed me a satellite video feed of what happened at your extraction. I saw the helicopter go down and saw that you had been captured. I could tell that he was telling me the truth and said that you needed help and that I was the only one that could come. He briefed me of the East African situation and how the U.S. was told not to interfere. He also said that Code 7 was being hunted down by the Agency and because of this, for me to be careful. I don't know for sure, but I think that he was a double agent who worked for both the CIA and Code 7."

Jake started to think back when he started with Code 7, and remember that H told him that whatever happened between the two agencies, that he had someone that he could trust in the CIA. H never told Jake who he was, but to Jake this had to be the person that H referred to. Sasha looked at Jake and nodded her head. She had been told the same thing by H and wanted him to know that this was legit.

Henderson looked at both of them and knew that they wanted him to continue. "This person told me that if I wanted to help you, then I would have to leave immediately."

"Obviously, you left Henderson," Jake interrupted. "I would like to know what you told your wife and kids."

Henderson grinned at Jake and said, "I have never lied to them, but I did not think it would go over well if I told her that I was a secret agent going overseas on a dangerous rescue mission. So I told her that there was a big science fair convention in Las Vegas and the person that was suppose to go had come down with a terrible illness. I was called at the last minute and I had to go to take his place, and unfortunately I had to leave immediately. She told me to stay out of trouble and to have a fun time. Who knows, I may just be able to do that."

Jake started to laugh. He knew Henderson could tell some wild stories and knew that whatever he told his wife must have been a lot more detailed than what he had gotten. He knew that he got the shorter version, but if he asked for more information, he felt that they would be there all day.

He was still laughing when he answered, "I will make sure that I remember that one, so if I ever need an excuse to go anywhere, I will tell them that I am going to a science fair convention. I think you may be turning into a dork."

"I did what I had to do," Henderson said with a big grin on his face.

"Okay, that was funny, but seriously finish the story, about how you got here," Jake demanded and was running out of patience.

"Your right," Henderson answered, knowing that Jake was getting impatient. "I left right away and flew to Morocco and met up with your friend, H. He is a nice person, but for some reason I sense that something's not right about him. I will have to take your word about trusting him. Even though I had my reservations about him, I sat down and he caught me up to speed on what was going on. Thank goodness you had not taken off your GPS device on your leg. This helped us track you where you were."

Jake looked down at his leg and saw the little device that he had completely forgotten about and realized that it was a life saver. "Thank God for this life saving device," Jake said as he looked over at Sasha.

She smiled at Jake and was also thankful that the small device had helped Henderson locate them. She had remained pretty quiet up to this point and felt it very intriguing, watching how Jake and Henderson interacted with each other. She had never had any close friends, but could tell that these two were close. She felt that she could learn a lot about Jake, by watching him with Henderson. She started to feel very comfortable about who Jake was and wanted to let him into her life a little more. She knew that she definitely wanted to go on that date, but still would play hard to get.

Henderson looked down at Jake's leg and said "I know that you grown fairly close to that device, but I need to do this."

He grabbed the small GPS device off of Jake's leg and smashed it into the floor with the back barrel of his gun. Jake looked at

Henderson and had a bewildered look on his face and said, "What the hell was that for!"

Henderson looked at Jake and said, "I will explain later, but right now we need to get out of here. I want to introduce you to the people who help me set up this little swarray. Let's be careful, because we are not out of the woods just yet."

The three of them left the disserted building and followed Henderson down a back alley. They continued down different alleys until they came to an old clay house that looked disserted. Jake looked at Henderson and said, "Are you sure about this?"

"Just wait," Henderson said, "Everything is alright. There is someone I want you to meet."

Jake and Sasha stood together and waited. Henderson knocked on the door. An eye slit opened and shut quickly and then the door opened. It was Diotrice. "Wait a minute," Jake said looking over at Henderson, "What is going on here."

"Calm down and take it easy, Jake," Diotrice said, "I am on your side."

Jake did not know what was going on and who to believe. This was the woman that had turned him over to Qatar. "You must be wondering what is going on and why I handed you over to Qatar," she said to Jake and Sasha.

She continued, "You have to let me explain. It is quite simple. First of all, there was little that I could do. He got here just before you and he threatened me. I probably could have done more than I did for you two, by I did not want to lose my cover. He believes that I am a loyal follower and I wanted to keep it that way."

Jake was following her and it seemed as if she was part of the Agency. He wanted to interrupt her, but she said, "I will answer any questions you have, but first hear me out. After the two of you were taken away from my house, I immediately started working on a plan to free you. I have been working with H for some time and I immediately contacted him to let him know what had happened. I also sent out some of my foot soldiers to find out what was going to happen to the two of you. That is how we were able to set up all the explosions to go off right before your execution was to take place. Henderson arrived before the show began and we were able to execute it to a T. I told him to approach you and bring you back here, because I do not think that you would have believed me. Hopefully, there are no hard feelings for me."

Jake and Sasha could not believe what was going on. Both wondered why H had not told them about Diotrice. "Why didn't we know about you?" Jake asked.

Diotrice looked at Jake and knew he needed and answer, but it was not the right time just yet. She answered Jake by saying, "I will tell you the whole story, but not now. I need to talk to you about something else right now. We are all in this together and you will learn about other details at a later time."

Sasha looked over at Diotrice and asked, "What are you talking about by saying that we are all in this together. I just want to get out of this country. We have escaped death more than I can count and I would like to take the first flight out of here."

Jake nodded in agreement. He had enough of East Africa. He had lost two friends and had almost lost his life. He did not know what Diotrice was talking about and did not want to find out.

"What is up with this Qatar character," Jake asked Diotrice.

She explained to them that he had come into power with Kiir over ten years ago. He was Kiir right hand man and the only way to communicate with Kiir was to go through Qatar. Qatar had surrounded himself with twelve men, who were his own personal military. Over the last two years, he had let his men terrorize the country. He had power, but was power hungry, Diotrice explained. Qatar was a dangerous man and had killed anyone who dared to get into his way. Diotrice told them that there had been attempts on his life, but that they were unsuccessful, simply because he has surrounded himself with his men. It is impossible to get him alone.

Jake was getting tired of hearing about Qatar, the man who was responsible for two of his friends' deaths. All he could think about was revenge and Henderson saw that his friend has something on his mind and knew that he had to intervene.

"Jake and Sasha," Henderson said trying to ease the situation. "This started out as a rescue mission, but now it has become much more than that. I know what is going on, and I will try and explain it to you. Sasha, you started something that you do not even know how big it really is. Now, you can stay here and listen to what we have to say and help change the world or I can signal in the extraction team to come get us. Jake you always told me that this is when heroes are made. Right now I need both of you to be heroes."

Jake always liked to listen to Henderson's speeches. It had been a long time since he had heard one. They did motivate him and he knew that he had the leadership skills that Henderson enjoyed. He knew that Henderson needed him and that they had always done their missions together. Jake knew that he could not let Henderson go it alone and would stay to do whatever needed to be done.

Jake looked over at Sasha and could tell that she was tired, but he wanted her to be a part of whatever they needed, especially if that meant getting a crack at Qatar. Jake walked over to her and said with his hand on her shoulder, "They need us. I feel that I owe it to Simeon and Anteon to stay and finish whatever there is to finish. Do you want to stay and help me?"

"Just like that," Sasha said, "you made your decision?"

"Henderson has been a brother to me and if he needs me, I am there for him. He would be there for me as well. I do not want you to do something that you do not want to do, but I would love it if you would come along for the ride with me."

Sasha looked into Jake's eyes and saw the persuasiveness in them. "As long as you continue to get my back, I will stay on this mission."

Jake loved her answer and looked over at Henderson a said, "Well, we are both in. Now I need to know, what do you have for us?"

Henderson said, "Come with us and see. I know that you are going to love this."

CHAPTER 20

The ride back to New Helen, the capital city of East Africa, was a very long one for Qatar and his men. He was not happy at what had happened and lashed out at his men for the botched hanging attempt on the two Americans. The driver did not answer for he knew that if he did, he could take the Americans' place. Qatar knew that his leader would not be happy about the situation and he wanted to blame on anyone but himself.

Unfortunately, it did not matter who he blamed, because he would be the one that had to take responsibility for what had happened. He felt that the hanging was going to be his shining moment, but instead it turned into a chaotic scene that showed him as an incompetent leader. He knew that he had to turn things around into his favor, not only to prove to his leader that he was competent, but also to the whole country of East Africa. He wanted to become the leader East Africa and needed to be known as a strong and fearful man. He knew that this would build toward his ultimate goal and that was to become the leader of the Middle East and Northern Africa, which he knew would become the center of power in the world.

Qatar's black hummer and his convoy of vehicles pulled up to the palace. The palace was not only where Qatar did his day to day operation, but his leader did as well. Qatar controlled the first floor of the palace while the leader of East Africa controlled the second floor.

Qatar got out of the hummer and walked into the palace. His first thought was for him to assemble his men and come up with a plan that they could tell the leader.

Qatar went into his office and slammed the door, leaving his men to wonder what was going on in his head. He did not have the patience for anything to go more wrong than what had already happened. He opened his office door and yelled for his top aide to come into his office. The aide entered in to see that Qatar very upset and angry.

Qatar looked at him and said, "Can you believe what happened today? This was supposed to be my time to show to my country what type of leader I am. It turned out to be a circus. Explosions going off all over the place, and I barely got out of their alive. I was the target. I know I was. My life could have been over. Whoever was responsible for that treacherous act was gunning for me. Did you see what happened to me?"

Qatar thought a lot of himself. He wanted to believe that it was not a rescue attempt for the Americans, but an assassination on his life. Once the first explosion occurred, Qatar left the scene in a hurry and had no idea what had happened. He wanted everyone to believe that his life was in danger and to forget about the Americans that had escaped. He also needed to make sure his leader believed his story as well. The aide nodded and agreed with Qatar. He wanted Qatar to know that he supported him, because he feared for his life. He did not want what had happened to others who had not shown support Qatar, happen to him. He had only heard stories, but what he heard kept him up at night.

"Answer me, you insignificant bug!" Qatar said as his patience with his aide quickly subsided.

The aide was scared for his life. He did not know what to say, but finally a few words did trickle out of his mouth. "It was very hard to tell what was going on. The reporters said it was technical difficulties. I assumed that your life must have been in danger and I was very relieved that you came back alive."

The aide was very quick on his feet. He had survived a long time by being Qatar's punching bag and today was no different. Qatar looked at his aide and said, "What did you tell our leader? Did you tell him the same thing?"

The aide had made up an excuse for Qatar and his actions. He had done it plenty of times before. He told Qatar simply, "You left me here for good reason. You have treated me well and I thank you for that. I could not lie to our leader and I informed him that our job was compromised because your life was in danger. He was not happy, but I was able to convince him that you had a plan that was in the works to capture the spies."

Qatar looked at the aide and said, "Why did you tell him that? Why would you think that I had a plan?"

The aide did know he had to come up with something quick. He answered by saying, "You are a great a powerful leader, yourself. You are always prepared for the inevitable. I have great faith that you have a plan in place if something like this happened. It did and I know with your great intelligence, that your plan will work and the spies will be captured and killed."

Qatar looked at the aide and remembered why he had kept him around so long. He needed someone to remind him how great he was. Qatar's aide did this for him. Qatar was known to send people away to his prison camp just for looking at him the wrong way. The aide did not want to die anytime soon and made sure that Qatar needed him all the time. Qatar told the aide to leave. He needed to be alone for a little while so that he could get his words right when he spoke to the leader. He did, however, make sure that his men were on the same page with him and let it be known that none of them should step out of line.

The leader of East Africa had become a recluse since the oil had been discovered in the northeast part of the county. He was no longer reachable face to face and the only way to communicate was by a private telephone that was installed only in Qatar's office. No one really knew where the leader was located. He had moved into the western part of the palace on the second floor and had two guards at the door at all time. Only food was entered in and garbage was let out. Qatar and his aide were the only two allowed to talk to him by phone. Qatar had not seen him for a while, but could feel his wrath if something did not go the way the leader wanted. The leader might be a recluse, but he still his power was still endless in East Africa.

Qatar's private phone rang and he knew that it was not going to be a pleasant conversation.

"Qatar," the leader said as he answered the phone. "I have been waiting for you call, but I had to call you. You know that I do not like to call anyone, especially you. I know what happen today and I want an explanation."

Qatar knew that he had to come up with something quick. His leader was not a patient man and would make sure that his vengeance would come down on Qatar if something was not done to rectify what had happened.

"My leader," Qatar answered and paused for a minute before continuing, "As you know, my life was in danger. I have reason to believe that I was the target and the Americans escaped because my men were too busy protecting me. As you know, we have all been well trained on what to do if something like this happened. I want to assure you that this problem will be taken care of immediately and I will give you these spies' heads on a silver platter before the end of the week."

Qatar heard no answer on the other end of the line. The silence was deafening for and seemed to last for hours, but it only lasted for a few seconds. The leader finally answered and said, "If not theirs, yours. It doesn't matter to me."

The leader hung up his end of the phone. Qatar knew that the leader meant business and that he had only a few days to capture the two Americans or he would lose his life.

He called to his aide to come back into his office. "Get my men together," Qatar said, "we are going on a nationwide manhunt."

The aide nodded and left the room. He returned a few minutes later and informed Qatar that his men would be at the front of the palace within the hour. Qatar was pleased that his men were sticking with him. He knew that his men were loyal to him and that they would find a way to accomplish his goal of capturing the Americans and anyone else that was involved. He knew exactly where to start. He told his men that they would go to Diotrice's hotel and question her first. He would be in charge and take care of her, personally.

The hour past and all his men had come to the palace. With his men gathered around him in a circle, Qatar stood on the palace's steps and gave a speech.

"Early this afternoon," he spoke in his deep voice, "we were under attack. The explosions were generated by spies who want to enter our country and take over our government. We have repeatedly told them to stay out, but they want to take over our oil supply. They come to destroy our cities and rape our women. We cannot allow this. We tried to show the world today what we do with these people, but instead they used terroristic tactics to escape. This will be their final stand and we will capture these Americans and give our leader their heads on a silver platter. Now let's go and remember, not to disappoint me. Your life depends on it."

Qatar wanted to make sure that the two Americans would be captured and he could use this as a stepping stone to prove his leadership and seize control of the country. He knew that the people of East Africa still supported their leader, but Qatar knew that things could change very quickly. He had helped the leader take control of the country ten years earlier, but now it was his time to take charge of the country. He blamed the United States for handing over the leadership to his counterpart and never understood why he had not been given a shot to lead. He hated America for leaving him out in the cold and wanted to take it out on the two Americans who had escaped.

He knew he had to wait a little longer to take over the leadership of the country. He was going to make sure that everyone knew what he was going to do and knew that if he could get the problem taken care of, he could finally get the support of the East African people and eventually it would lead to him taking the leadership away from the present leader. He wanted the power and knew with the new found oil that he would not only be a powerful man in East Africa, but also throughout the world.

Qatar ordered his me to get into their vehicles and follow him back to Diotrice's hotel. He had already captured the Americans before their escape and he felt that she wasn't completely honest with him concerning them. She knew too much about the Americans and he felt that she had deceived him. He would not stand for any kind of deception and would return there to get to the bottom of the situation. He did not have the patience to make the trip a long one and ordered his driver to get there quickly. Qatar told the driver that he would lose his feet if they did not get to the hotel within the hour.

After only a forty minute drive, Qatar and his men arrived at the hotel. The hotel looked deserted from the outside, but Qatar believed that there might be some evidence inside the hotel that might give him a hint on where Diotrice had gone to. He ordered one of his men to enter into the hotel and to check to see if he could find any type of evidence of where she might have gone to.

The man entered into the front door of the hotel and went inside. He looked around and noticed that a lot of things were missing. He scoured through the hotel, but did not find anything that could tell them where anyone had gone. He was about to leave the hotel, but there was one room that he had not checked. He walked over to the room and tried to open the door, but it was locked. He decided to kick in the door, but that was a bad idea. Once the door was kicked in, it set off explosives. He noticed what he had done, but it was too late for him to get out of the hotel.

The explosion was a very large blast that blew up the entire hotel. Qatar was blown almost twenty feet in the air into the side of his hummer. He was knocked out for a few minutes. When he came to, he saw that the hotel was completely destroyed. The explosion so big and magnificent, that it brought other spectators to the scene. Qatar was delusional, basically in a daze, stood up and saw the people that had come to see the explosion. He did not want to look bad again in front of anyone so he told his men to get the people out of the area. He yelled at one of his men to come over to him.

He walked slowly over to Qatar and said, "Yes sir. What can I do?"

Qatar had lost his cool and wanted to take out his frustration on someone. He felt that the Americans were playing games on him and making him look like a fool in front of his men. He wanted to make someone pay for his humiliation and wanted blood for this outrage. If he could not get to the Americans he would go after the first person that he saw.

He ordered one of his men to come to him and shouted to him, "Get me that person." Qatar was pointing to one of the spectators who was looking on and seem to be laughing at the situation. He grabbed his man by the shirt collar and yelled, "Get him and bring him to me! No one laughs at the great Qatar and gets away with it!"

Qatar's man went over and grabbed the spectator and brought him to Qatar. "This is what happens to people who mock me and do not do what I ask them to do," Qatar said as he grabbed his pistol and pointed it at the stranger's head. The man begged for his life, but Qatar would have none of that. His mind was made up and he pulled the trigger. The man, who was an innocent bystander, fell to his death.

Everyone in the crowd that had gathered looked at the horror that had just taken place. They all ran in hysteria to get away from the scene. Qatar meant business and he did not care who he had to kill to get the people's attention.

"Now," Qatar said "I need answers to what happened here. Do I make myself clear?" His men knew he was serious. "I will wait here for a few more minutes until one of you tell me what is going on. If I do not get the answers that I want, then your fate will be the same as this dead man who lies at my dirty feet." He was hovering over the man that he had just shot and killed. "Now get him out of my sight and give me something to go on. I need to find these Americans."

Within a few minutes, one of his men came to him with another local and let the local tell Qatar what he knew. The local told him how Diotrice had set him up and that Diotrice was probably the one who had helped the Americans. Then man was very scared at what might happen to him. He did not want to give Qatar bad news because he knew this would make Qatar even more upset. He was right. Qatar got his gun and shot the local across the eyes. "This is what we do with traitors," Qatar yelled.

Qatar had no idea if the local was a traitor or not, but he did not like hearing that one of his foot soldiers had betrayed him. He believed that Diotrice was now hiding the Americans and that the bomb that blew up her hotel was meant for him. He knew that time was against him and he not only needed to capture the Americans, but Diotrice as well. Qatar, again, gathered his men together and told them that their clock was ticking. He made sure that they knew to take care of anyone who got into their way and for them to ask questions later. Qatar's time was ticking as well and if he did not have anything concerning the Americans shortly, his fate could be sealed as well.

Qatar did not care about anyone, but himself, and would eliminate anyone that slowed him down or got in his way. The Americans were two people who were an obstacle for Qatar and now Diotrice was on the list as well. He would not make any more mistakes concerning his handling of them and would kill them without wasting time when he had the chance. He knew that it was only a matter of time before he would capture them and he would be able to extract his revenge on them at that time.

CHAPTER 21

Jake and Sasha followed Henderson and Diotrice down into the basement of their new headquarters. Jake's mission had completely changed in just a few hours. He was sent to rescue Sasha, but now his old buddy Henderson had come to East Africa to save him. Jake still had a lot more questions, but felt that it was best to go with the flow and find out everything later.

They all made into the basement and Jake could see that there were weapons of all sorts. He had not had any weapons in awhile and the site of this put a smile on his face. He also notice three computers that look to have some sort of satellite images on them. There were also a set of plans that were on a table and Diotrice motioned for everyone sit down at the table.

Jake looked at Sasha and could tell that she wanted the same thing that he wanted and that was answers.

"Henderson and Diotrice," Jake asked with determination in his voice, "please inform us what is going on. I feel like a pawn in a chest match and I don't like it. I would like some answers and I would like them now."

Henderson started to laugh at his friend. He knew that Jake wanted to be in control and at the present time he was not. Henderson was always on the other side of the coin, letting Jake lead him through all their earlier missions, but this time he knew more than Jake. He knew that it was killing Jake inside and he wanted to relish in the moment a little longer, but this was not the time for him to play games.

Henderson nodded to Diotrice which was his way of allowing her to go ahead and tell Jake and Sasha everything. She nodded back. Diotrice had a lot of things to say and hoped that they would be patient enough to hear her out.

She sat up straight and looked at Jake and Sasha and without her accent she said, "I speak perfect English. The accent was just a disguise for me to blend into the East African culture. I was born in America and came over to this country ten years ago. I work for the CIA and have been part of the agency for over twenty years. When I started, my handler was Higgins."

Jake rose up in his seat. He could not believe that she knew Higgins. He was about to say something, but Diotrice cut him off and continued with her story.

"I know that you have a lot of questions and I will get to that, but first hear me out. I trained under him for ten years, doing special operation work in the Middle East. He had never mentioned the two of you by name, but hinted that he had two agents in the field. He never let us cross paths for some reason, but ten years ago he sent a message that I needed to come back home. He told me that two of his top agents were killed in Iran and felt that I was not safe in the region anymore. Higgins decided to send me to this country shortly after getting me out of the Middle East to set up a base for contacts here in this country. I felt it was my duty and gave up my life as an American and took on the role as Diotrice, an East African inn keeper who took care of the indigent and wayward children. I have been living this life since I arrived a decade ago. I feel that I am a patriot and I am here for my country, the United States to do good in the world."

Diotrice took a sip of water and continued, "Higgins told me that I was his number one agent in the region and I communicated with him extensively for the next five years, giving him any information about what was going on in this new country and also any news concerning the surrounding countries. He constantly led me to believe that I was very important to him. One day I went to contact him and I got no answer. This went on for week and I figured that he would contact me at some point. Unfortunately, he never contacted me again and my file was basically deleted."

She paused a second and took another drink of water. Jake, Sasha, and Henderson were now very interested in what she was saying and sat very quietly listening to every word. She continued, "I had lived here for five years and had given everything that I had to this country. I could not go back to the United States, because in their eyes, I do not exist. I decided to continue doing the work that I was doing and reach out to the indigent and orphan children of this country. I had lived a peaceful, uninterrupted life for the last five years until I was contacted by H three months ago. He explained to me who he was and how he had worked for Higgins. He told me that he needed someone on the inside and knew how to navigate through this country. I listened and accepted, but I had some rules. I would help set up the mission for Sasha and I would keep tabs on her while she was here, but she could not know of my existence. H accepted and you were sent over here to do your job. I knew that you were being followed and sent word to you through one of my men who works for me, but it was too late and you had already been captured. I am sorry that you had to stay in that prison camp as long as you did. I wanted to get you out myself, but we both agreed that we could not sacrifice my cover."

Sasha interrupted, and said, "I understand what you're saying, but why did you not let me know of your existence? Did you not think I would trust you?"

Diotrice answered her by saying, "As you know in this business, trust is hard to come by. We both agreed that there was a job for you and one for me. He wanted you to get information and wanted me to shadow you. That is what I did. I followed your every move.

After the safe house burned down, I went and got the information that you had uncovered from the black box."

"But we went back to the house and retrieved it." Sasha said. "Unfortunately, Qatar took it from me. If what you are saying is truthful, what was in the box that he stole from me?"

"Basically, a bunch of gibberish," Diotrice answered. "I had to put something in the box, just in case Qatar or his men spotted it. The information that was in the black box is going to help us with our new mission."

Jake had sat in his chair listening to ever word that Diotrice had to say. He was amazed by the story that she was telling. He wondered why she had not told him any of this before. "Why are you telling us this now?" Jake asked, "You could have told us this earlier when we stayed with you."

Diotrice nodded her head and agreed with Jake, but said, "I know I could have, but I had a suspicion that you were being followed. Unfortunately, I was right. As you both know, you were followed and that has given me reason to believe that there is a mole in our operation. Your every move was followed from the day that you came into the country. Your GPS device could only be tracked by our system and it seemed that someone either hacked into the system, which seems very unlikely, since no one knew that you were here, or we had someone informing Qatar of you whereabouts. I believe the latter and that is why I wanted your device removed. You did get it off your leg and destroy it, didn't you?"

Jake nodded head, yes. He now knew why Henderson removed it and smashed it. Sasha had never had one, so she figured that she wasn't tracked; only Jake was tracked.

"Who in our agency would want to track us?" Sasha asked.

Diotrice looked at both of them and answered, "Unfortunately, I have reason to believe it is H. The reason I believe this, is that he is the only one who had access to anything concerning this mission."

"That does not sound like the man who sent me over here," Sasha said with a puzzled look on her face.

Henderson looked over at Jake and said, "That is what I was trying to tell you. How well do you know this guy? It seems to me that there is more to H than both of you know."

Sasha started to shake her head again. She had known H personally longer than anyone sitting at the table and it was hard for her to believe that H was a traitor. She looked at Diotrice and asked, "You said that you trusted H."

Diotrice nodded her head, "No, my dear, I never said that I trusted him. I simply said that he trusted me. I have been in this business long enough never to trust anyone, but myself. Everything that has happened since both of you have been here has lead us to believe that H is behind it, and he is the one who knew where you were and could track you. How in the world did Qatar know that both of you would end up back at my hotel, had he not been contacted by someone who knew where you guys had been before. I just can't understand why he did not let Qatar know about my role before now. I know that Qatar has probably been informed by now, but had he known early, we would all be dead."

Neither Jake nor Sasha wanted to believe that H had set them up, but the evidence in front of them pointed toward him. The events of the last few days had Jake and Sasha questioning the difference between the truth and untruths. Jake knew that Henderson would tell him the truth. He needed a minute alone with Sasha and and asked his friend and Diotrice for some privacy.

They got up from the table and walked away so that Henderson and Diotrice could not hear them. Jake whispered to Sasha, saying, "I know what is going through you mind right now. You have questions and they are the same questions that are going through my mine as well. I need you to trust me with your life and believe me when I say this, Henderson and I have gone through hell and back. He would never tell me anything that was not the truth. I hope that H is innocent, but right now we cannot trust him or anyone else for that matter. I still have a problem trusting Diotrice, but Henderson is here to help us and I have to believe my friend. I have trusted him with my life in the past and he has never disappointed me. I know that I am right on this one."

Sasha answered Jake by whispering so that Henderson and Diotrice could not hear her. She said, "I hope that you are right. It is hard to believe anyone right now, but for some reason, I do trust your judgment and if you trust Henderson, than I do as well. All I want to do is get out of this country with my life still intact, so let's go back over to the table and listen to the rest of what they have to say."

They both came back to the table and sat down. Henderson looked over at Jake and asked, "Is everything alright? Are you guys on the same page as us now?" Jake looked back and nodded a yes.

"Go ahead Diotrice," Jake said, "Finish what you were saying."

Diotrice continued, "Before Higgins' disappearance, he and I would communicate usually once a week. I would be debriefed on all the information I was gathering. I always wondered why he picked East Africa for me, but I never questioned him about it until right before he left. He got angry with me and did not like the fact that I question him. He said that I was challenging his authority and that I had not right to ever question what he wanted me to do. I had never seen that side of him and then I never heard from him again after the incident. That happened five years ago. He was my handler for five years and just vanished from my life. As I said earlier, I decided to make it my life's work here in East Africa to help the indigent and orphan children. I had not done any work for the agency for the last five years and thought that I had been forgotten, until H contacted me.

He told me that my file was not deleted, which I thought and that he had reviewed if and that he knew the good job that I had done. He informed me that he had been Higgins right hand man. He did not say anything more to me concerning that and I did not ask. H was very direct to me and all he wanted me to do was to give him updates on what was going on here in East Africa, since the United States had been isolated. I told him that my time in the agency was over and I had other passions that were taking up my time. He then informed me that he was sending an agent here to do the things I used to do and if I could shadow her. I was hesitant at first, but he was insistent. I finally gave in and informed him that I would shadow her and would keep him abreast of anything out of the ordinary. I told him of Sasha's capture. I did not hear from him for over a month, but he then contacted me and told me he would be sending in another agent on a rescue mission and to make sure that I look after him as well."

Jake knew that other agent was him. Sasha looked at him and said, "Jake, you did not run into Anteon by coincidence. He was sent to look out for you. I had him show you how to get to the prison camp, but I told him not to bring you back to my hotel. At first I was upset with him and thought my cover would be blown, but I knew that the two of you had nowhere to go, so I let you in. I hoped that you would make the extraction on time, but I know that there was no extraction and that Qatar was responsible. I know what happened to Anteon and I was devastated by his death. Before you left, Anteon told me how much he looked up to you and wanted to help you. I know that you did not know him long, but I could tell that you cared for that little boy and know that his death devastated you as well.

I felt that my job was done, but after what happened to Anteon, I could not sit on my hands any longer. I started to put things in motion because I wanted Qatar's head on a platter. One thing we all know by now is that he is a very evil man. Once he captured both of you, I knew that it was my duty to put a rescue plan together. H contacted me and told me he was sending one more agent to help me. Henderson came within the next twenty-four hours and we put the plan in place."

Henderson interrupted Diotrice and said, "I showed up and there was no time to lose. These two," Henderson pointing at two young men who were working diligently on the computers, "helped me navigate through the city and put the explosives in the right place. We put the explosives in places where we knew there would be minimal damage and hopefully no deaths for the innocent bystanders. After the explosions went off, I watched you and Sasha escape and run over to the abandoned building where I found you.

We had other people in place that were also on our side. I had them shoot at Qatar and his men to keep them at bay. The plan worked perfectly and we got both of you out of there with minimal damage and no casualties. I am pleased with the outcome."

Jake looked at the two guys working on the computers and asked Henderson who they were. Henderson told him that he would get to their story in a minute, but wanted to let Diotrice finish first.

Jake and Sasha were glad that the plan worked perfectly and that no innocent people were harmed, but they wanted to know why they were not extracted right after the rescue. Diotrice told them that there was more to the story.

"I have reason to believe," she said, "That Qatar is running the country. At one time he was a simple cleric in Sudan, but then he got involved in creating this country and helped Kier become leader. He knew that he could never have the support of the people, because their loyalty is towards Kier. But as long as the people think that Kier is still the leader, Qatar could do what he pleased. Then the discovery of oil changed the political atmosphere of this country. Qatar has made his presence known more strongly and Kier has disappeared; only making appearances by television. Kier has done more for this country than any other leader could have done and he used the United States to build a strong country. I know it is my opinion, but he knows what the United States has done for this country and what they would do in the future. For him to just throw out all U.S. support is just ludicrous to me. Someone, and that person has to be Qatar, must be pulling his string. Sasha was close, but I need more concrete information. The information is at the capital city, but I need someone to get it for me."

Jake knew what she was alluding to with that statement but asked anyway to make sure he was correct. "Are you saying we need to go to the capital city and get proof that Kier is no longer in charge and that Qatar is ruling this country without anyone's knowledge."

"Jake," Diotrice answered, quickly saying. "I knew that you were smart. That is exactly what I want. The three of you have all been well trained. I know that you can all work together and we can help bring order back to East Africa. This country was on the verge of greatness and I believe it still can achieve that, but not with Qatar trying to rule it. He will ruin this country, if someone does not stop him. I am an American by blood, but if feel that this has become my country now and I want to save her."

Jake, Sasha, and Henderson did not say a word. They all looked at each other in amazement feeling that Diotrice was insane to think that they could save the country. Jake and Sasha wanted to get out of East Africa, and Henderson was just a six grade science teacher. They wanted to get home as quickly as possible.

"Before you make up your mind, there is more to the riddle," Diotrice said and was not finished with what she was saying. "Even though I have been away from agency work for awhile, I did not mean that I had quit working. I have always kept my ears open to rumblings that were going on around me. Listen to me. This is very important what I am about to say. The oil discovery was not discovered three months ago. It was discovered almost two years ago. You might find this hard to believe, but believe it because it is true."

Jake interrupted and asked her, "How do you know this."

"Let's just say that I have my sources," she answered. "Again, I have kept my contacts and I hear everything that is going on. Going back to the oil discovery, whoever was in charge of this, and I am guessing Qatar, wanted to make sure everything was in place before announcing it to the world. It took two years for this to happen and that is the same amount of time that Kier became a recluse. Do you think that this is a coincidence, I think not. Again, I know Qatar's actions and I know that he wants to be not only the leader of East Africa, but in his sick mind he feels that he can be the leader of this region. Again, I have sources that have informed me of this. I also have reason to believe that Qatar duped the United States into investing a lot of money into this country. He then kicked the U.S. out before it could reap the benefits of its investments. Our job is to prove that Kier is not in charge and that Qatar has brought this destruction and anarchy to this land. I cannot do this alone. I need the three of you to help me and the question I have for you is, are you with me?"

Henderson looked at Jake and Sasha and said, "I have a family at home, but feel it is my calling now to help out Diotrice and East Africa. But remember I have only twelve days left until my science fair camp is over."

They all started to laugh, but each one knew how serious this was and what she was asking. Jake lived for these moments, but he was older and tired. He needed to motivate himself a little more than he used to in the past. He did however want to team up with his old friend Henderson and continue to make history and that was motivation enough. He then knew adding Sasha to the equation would help them accomplish what they were set out to do.

Sasha had come a long way in the last couple of years. She knew that her purpose was far greater than she could ever imagine. She had always had something inside of her that pushed her to take a chance. That is why she joined the agency in the first place and why she teamed up with Code 7. She knew that her mission was not over and knew that this would be her time to help restore order to East Africa and get rid of Qatar. She looked over at Jake and said, "I have a great feeling that the three of us will make a great team."

Jake knew that this decision could change not only his life but his best friends' as well. He knew that failure would not be an option and all their lives depended on him. He loved a challenge and knew that this time he would not fail. He wanted to leave Iran incident behind him and he knew that only a successful mission would accomplish that. He looked at everyone sitting at the table and said, "This could be a life threatening mission. Henderson, can you handle that?"

Henderson nodded yes he could.

"How about you Sasha, do you still want to do this?"

She nodded yes as well.

"Diotrice," Jake said with a smile, "It looks as if we have a team put together to save this country. When do we start?"

CHAPTER 22

Diotrice wanted to introduce the new team of three to her two partners. She brought them over to one of her partners who was working on the computer and said, "This is Jerdan. He is a computer genius. He will be able to monitor all of your activity with a new GPS system. He will explain to you who it works through the satellite system."

"How do you have a satellite system?" Jake said addressing Jerdan.

"We don't," Jerdan answered in a quick, quirky voice. "But the beauty of this satellite system is that I was able to intercept the code to get on the U.S. satellite for this region. We are able to use their feed without their knowledge. "

"That is pretty risky, don't you think." Henderson said.

"You would think so, but not now," Jerdan answered. "Because of the sanctions the U.N. put on the U.S. to stay out of East Africa, there is not much risk at all."

Henderson nodded and agreed that it was a pretty good idea. He figured that Jordan obviously knew a lot about computers and did not bother trying to pick his brain.

"Over here we have Haritos. Obviously his name is too hard for any of us to say so I shortened it to Hare."

Hare looked up at the team and nodded. He was quiet person, but meticulous on what he needed the team to do. He made sure that each piece of weaponry was inspected and ready to go into battle. He made sure that he got things done.

"Hare is our weapons expert and specialist. He will get you all your weapons and ammo. Both of these guys will be your life line. I will let them tell you how you will communicate with each other. It is fascinating."

Diotrice was ready to put her plan into action. She had stockpiled funds that she had received from the CIA over the years that enable her to purchase some weapons that would help them with their mission. The computers were old holdovers from her earlier days, but with Jerdan on board, they did exactly what she needed them to do.

"I want all of you guys," Diotrice said "to get familiar with one another. Take a few minutes and talk and get to know each other. You will need each other's help so that we all will stay alive."

Jake was excited to get his hands back on a gun again, but he still did not know what all the weapons were for. He wanted Diotrcie to sit down and go over exactly what their mission was going to be. Diotrice assured him that in due time he and the others would know exactly what they were going to do, but first they needed to familiarize themselves with one another. Jake felt that her answer was sufficient and walked over to Hare. He wanted to check out all the weapons that Hare had.

Hare was glad that Jake had asked. He was holding a device in his hand at the time. "This right here is a semi-automatic rocket launcher. Before you ask, I did say semi-automatic. You can load up to four rockets and shoot them within five seconds of each other." Hare then showed Jake how to use the weapon.

"You load the four rockets in the bottom here, and press this button to load one into the launching area. It loads quickly and then you press this button to launch the rocket. Also there is a scope here."

Hare pulled open the scope, and continued by saying, "It is also shoots a red laser toward your target. You should never miss you target because you have pin point accuracy."

Jake really liked what he saw and wanted to hold it. Hare wanted Jake to have it and gave the rocket launcher to him. The weapon was not heavy and he could strap it to his back and move around very quickly.

"I will take it," Jake said as he took the rocket launcher and put it to the side, "Now, let's see what else you have."

There were all kinds of different weapons Hare had to show the three the Americans. He had semi-automatic guns, small hand guns, sawed off shotguns, grenades, basically anything you could think of that could arm a small army. He wanted to explain to each how to use the weapons, but Sasha looked at him and said,

"There is no point at wasting your breath with telling us how to use these weapons. We are all very well versed on what they do and how to use them."

"I think we have enough weapons and ammo to feed an army," Henderson joked, then looked at Jerdan and asked, "What do you do."

Jerdan explained to them why he was the computer genius. He had worked with Diotrice for the last three years. He was from Iraq and learned his computer trade in his home country, but left for his safety. He told them how terrorist had taken over the region where he lived and had murdered his family. He was able to escape and he fled to Sudan, who at the time was taking in refugees. He did not like living in the country and decided to go north to East Africa. He had no place to live and always struggle to find food. He lived on the streets for a few months until Diotrice saw him and took him into her hotel. He showed her his talent with computers and she brought him into her operation. He had worked for her ever since.

"As I told you earlier, I am able to get the satellite feed for our whole country. I can zoom in to wherever you are and communicate with you through this device." It was a very tiny earpiece that was undetectable once it was put into one's ear. He handed it to Henderson and told him to put it into his ear and walk into the other room.

Henderson stuck it in his ear and walked away. Jerdan then said, "Testing, one, two, three. Can you hear me?"

Henderson answered back, "Yes, can you hear me?" Jerdan answered "Yes, I can. Come back I have more to show you."

Henderson walked back in and Jerdan showed him more of his devices. He held up a small device and said, "This is a small camera. It is not that big, but very powerful. This little camera can zoom in on an object almost five hundred times stronger than any other camera. Push the red button to take a picture and push the green button to see what you took, and push the blue but to send it to me."

Henderson was very impressed, but was a little puzzled by what Jerdan just said. "I do not have to hook it up to a computer to send a picture? All I have to do is push the blue button?"

"Yes," Jerdan answered. "The digital picture will come to my computer without being attached to a computer. Do not ask me how I came up with that, it would take me all day to explain."

Jake and Sasha had been listening and they were impressed by the small operation that Diotrice had put together. Jake looked at Henderson and said, "They have come up with a lot more sophisticated toys since our last mission together. Some of these things would have come in pretty handy, especially this rocket launcher."

Henderson nodded, yes to Jake and walked over and looked at some more weapons. Sasha then said to Jake, "Is that the only one because I wouldn't mind firing a couple of shots Qatar with it."

Jake laughed and said, "Let me take the first shot and you can have it after that."

Diotrice had come back down from upstairs and looked to see everyone getting along and laughing. She interrupted by saying to everyone, "I am glad that we all seem to like each other. Now it is time to get down to business. Come on over to the table so that we can go over what everyone's responsibilities will be."

Everyone came over to the table and sat down. Diotrice started by saying, "I want to key everyone in that this is a life threatening mission. As you know, not everything is fun and games, and one mistake could cost you your life."

Jake always being impatient, had to interrupt and ask a question. "What exactly are we going to be doing? I am very intrigued, but I am sick and tired of being left in the dark. I have yet to been given a real explanation of what you want us to do."

Diotrice could see the frustration in Jake's eyes. She did not have time to tell Jake what he wanted to hear. "Jake," Diotrice said. "I do not have all the answers that you need right now, but I believe that if you can accomplish this mission you will probably find an answer to all of your questions."

Diotrice continued to focus on the mission and wanted to make sure everyone was on the same page. "As you know, Kier and the government do not want any U.S. involvement in East Africa. I, on the other hand, believe that is not the truth. We are led to believe that Kier is still the leader of this country, but there is no real reason for me to believe that. Since the oil find, Kier hasn't left the palace. Actually, things started to change before the oil discovery and his sightings have been nonexistent. We have had satellite surveillance on the palace and show no activity of Kier. I have reason to believe that Qatar has either killed him or has imprisoned him inside the palace. There had only been a few video addresses by Kier and no one is certain that it is actually him.

The reason that I have brought you here is that I need the three of you to go to the capital city and get information for us. I will be able to send this to our intelligence in the United States. Anything that you find will enable our government to go in front to the United Nations and argue that East Africa indeed needs our help. Remember, I have lived here for a long time, and I have seen that over the ten years that this country was under Kier's control, it has flourished it an industrial and wealthy country. Our streets were safe, our children had a future, women had rights, but now it has all changed. I want to help this country get back to the way it was going under Kier's leadership. As we all know, if Qatar is running this country, he is leading this country down his own path of evil and nothing good can come of that."

Diotrice continued by saying, "Jake, I am making you the leader of this mission. Sasha and Henderson will look to you to take charge. Do you think that you can handle this?"

Jake knew that he was more than capable of leading this mission. He looked at Sasha and Henderson and asked if they were ok with the decision. Both nodded yes. Sasha knew that Jake had more experience than she, and she wanted him to take the lead role. Henderson had always let Jake be the one in command over all their missions and he worked better when Jake was in control.

Diotrice continued pointing at a map, "Here is where we are going to start. The capital city is a good hour drive from here, and unfortunately Qatar and his men will be looking for you all over the place. You will have to ride in the back of cargo truck. I have confidence that they will not stop the truck and it will pass through to the capital city so do not worry about being caught. When you get into the capital city, you will meet with one of my contacts. There you will have a place to stay for the night and also you will be able to contact us about what you can see about the happenings of the palace."

"Can you not just get that with the satellite feed?" Jake asked.

"That is a good question," Diotrice answered. "But they are smart and they know when the satellite feed is on them. We need some up close and personal sightings of what is going on in the palace. We need you to get into the palace and take pictures. Jerdan has a blueprint of the palace and can talk you through where you need to go."

"When do we leave," Sasha asked as she stood up ready to get going.

"We need all of you to get your weapons and be ready to leave within the hour," Diotrice answered, motioning them to go ahead a get up from the table. "We do not have a lot of time. I have gotten some information that something big is going to happen and I do not know what it will be. I have some clothes for you to wear so that you can stay disguised. Go ahead and get ready to go. We will load up some other things that you will need on the truck."

Jake, Sasha, and Henderson gather up the weapons that they would need and made sure their earpieces worked. The time was not on their side and the ride would not be a comfortable one, either. They would have to ride in the back of a cargo truck and it would be very hot, bumpy ride. Jake and Henderson had ridden in worse, so they were prepared. This mission would not be for the faint of heart. All three had been on many different types of mission, but none of them had been on a mission where so much was a stake. They knew that the United States' hope of working with East Africa rest on their shoulders.

None of them wanted to make a mistake. None of them knew what they were walking into, either. They had to rely on Diotrice and her team to get them through the mission and they did not know how reliable that they were going to be. There were many questions, but the three of them had to believe in the new team that they had formed and had to hope that everyone would be on the same page. The mission was about to start and the three of them were ready to go.

Jerdan and Hare had gotten the cargo truck packed and came back into the room and told Diotrice that the truck was ready to go. She called them over and told them that there was a lot at stake. She did not want to over bear them with the pressure, but knew that they may be the last chance to help East Africa.

"Remember," Diotrice said, "Only trust your instincts. There is no room for misjudgments and no room for error. I do not know how deep this may go, but I am sending you to find out. Please be careful and come back safe."

Jake, Sasha, and Henderson all shook Jerdan's and Hare's hand and wished them good luck. They got into the back of the cargo truck, but before the door was shut, Jake looked back to Diotrice and said, "This will work. This truck will get us to our destination and we will accomplish our goal."

Diotrice replied, "I am sure that you will be safe until you get to the capital city and the truck will not stop until you get to my contact. But if you stop before hand, be prepared to fight your way out of there. I have complete faith that you will get in and get out safe."

The three gave her the thumbs up that they were ready. They knew that they if anything did go wrong and they had to fight their way out of the back of the truck; they would probably not make it out alive. Jake looked at his friends and told them to say a small prayer before they left. It is always good to have God on your side than on the other side, he thought.

The truck started and Diotrice started to lower the hatch to the back. "One more thing," she said to them, "I want you to know that I believe in you."

The hatch shut down and it was completely dark in the back of the truck. "I am sure glad she believes in us," Henderson said. Jake could not see him, but said to Henderson, "Well it looks as if we are together again. I pray that things will be different than the last time we were in the back of a truck."

"That is the only reason I came back," Henderson said. "I want to go out on top. I did not like leaving the agency the way we did. I always felt that we had unfinished business. I know it looked like that I had put it behind me, but I never did. I had to come back and prove this to myself. Thanks Jake for giving me the opportunity."

Jake knew that there was a lot of pressure on him, but he would not have it any other way. He not only had to protect Henderson, but Sasha as well. The three sat silently taking in the long ride to the New Helen. It was hot inside, but it did not bother anyone. The ride was going smooth and nothing had happened so far and Sasha finally said that she was getting thirsty.

Jake had made sure that his canteen was full before he left. He handed her his canteen and said, "Have some of my water. You will need your strength."

Jake reached for Sasha and touched her elbow to pull her close to him, whispering into her ear. "I want you to stay close to me. I do not want to lose you."

Sasha could hear the care in his voice. She appreciated it, but knew that they could not do their mission properly if she was tagging along side Jake.

"You are not going to lose me, but you have got to let me do my job. I have a mission to accomplish and we all have objectives to do. I will be fine," She answered.

"You have to promise me one thing," Jake whispered back.

"You name it," she answered. "That first date that you promised me, I want to take you to the Supper Club."

"When this mission is over and we make it back to the United States, I will go on a date with you to the Supper Club. I promise you that."

Jake was satisfied. He could not hold her down and knew that she could hold her own. He could only hope that Sasha would remain safe and knew that only time would tell.

The truck finally came to a complete stop. They did not know if they had made it to their destination or what was going on. It seemed that they had been traveling for over an hour, but because there was no way to communicate with the drive they had to hope that they had it to their destination. The hatch opened and they all grabbed their guns ready to fire on any enemy that they might face.

A voice yelled into the truck, "Welcome to the New Helen. Please, drop your guns. I mean you no harm. Get out of there and come with me. We have a lot of worked to do."

It seemed that they had made it without incident, but still, they had a long road in front of them. Jake, Sasha, and Henderson jumped out of the back of the truck and looked at each other. Each one could see the determination in their eyes. Jake knew that with the team he had, no one could stop them. They were going to find out what had happened in the palace and help bring an end to Qatar and his men. There was no turning back now. A new journey had started for all of them.

CHAPTER 23

"There are no signs of the Americans, sir," said one of Qatar's men when asked the status of Jake, Sasha and Henderson. Qatar was upset with the answer and could not understand why no one had seen or heard the intruders. He and his men had scoured the city for two days, but no there were no signs of the whereabouts of the Americans. Even worse for Qatar, his secret contact that he was getting information from on what the Americans were doing, had not contacted him in over three days. He felt that it could not get any worse, but unfortunately for Qatar it did. "You are requested back in the capital city," one of his men said to him. "I have word that the leader would like to see you."

Qatar was getting tired of being ordered back and forth, especially now since he did not have anything to report to him. He knew that this would not go over well with the leader of the country and he knew he needed to come up with some sort of plan and it would help it he came up with as soon as possible.

"Call all my men," Qatar order, "And tell them to meet back here as soon as possible. We need to get back to the capital city and quickly. I have a feeling the Americans have left the city and I will inform our leader that we have lead them into a trap. We smoked them out and they will be on our turf now."

His men did exactly what he said and left the city as fast as they could. They knew that Qatar was not a patient man and knew that they could lose their lives if they did not return as quickly as he wanted them too.

Qatar had many reasons to return, but the main reason was to get back on his private line and talk to his contact. He knew his contact for awhile now, and knew that he had not called him for a reason. Qatar felt better about keeping the lines of communication open in the capital city. He could use his private line to contact him and hopefully get some much needed information. It was never good to go to the leader empty handed and needed something that he could go on.

It did not take long and they all arrived back to the capital city and came back to the palace. Qatar knew that he did not have the answers that the leader wanted, but knew he had to give him something. He came into his office to get on his private line and called the leader. The leader knew who it would be before he picked up.

"Qatar," the leader answered in a very questionable tone, "Do you have any news for me?"

Qatar did not want to tell him anything at the time, but he knew that the leader probably knew the answer to the question. "It seems as if the Americans have left the city," he answered. "We scoured the city, knocked on all doors, and could not find them anywhere. We did not get any answers from anyone. I know that the Americans did not vanish into thin air, but they have disappeared for the moment."

The leader had enough of Qatar's mistakes. He sent him to do a job and it was obvious to him, that the job was not accomplished. He hated failure and did not have the patience for anymore mistakes.

"Qatar," the leader said in a very condescending voice. "I am tired of your excuses and mistakes. I sent you to do a job and it seems as if you a failed. What am I to do with you?"

Qatar quickly answered in a frightful voice knowing that his life might be a stake. "I have been your loyal servant for the last ten years. I just need a little more time. I promise, I will deliver the Americans. Just give me more time."

There was a pause on the other end of the phone. Qatar had no idea what the leader was thinking. Finally the leader snapped back to Qatar, "You have twenty-four hours, if I do not have the results that I want, you will be punished. Do you understand what I am talking about?"

"Yes, I do. Thank you," Qatar answered back. "I will make sure that you will be happy with the results. I can guarantee it."

Qatar hung up the phone to the leader. He knew that would be the last time he would talk to him, if he did not find the Americans. He needed to call his secret contact and find out what was going on and to see if he had any idea of what had happened to the Americans. He made sure that he was on a secure line and made the call.

"Qatar," the contact on the other line answered. "I thought I had given you all the information that you needed."

"Obviously, you have not heard what has happened," Qatar asked his contact.

"It is like a fortress over there in East Africa. No one can get any information out of there. Tell me what has happened since the last time we have talked," the voice asked back.

"The Americans escaped and they have disappeared. No one seems to know where they are. That is why I called you. I need to know where they have gone. I need the information and I need it now."

Qatar was not in the mood for small talk and giving explanations. He did not have much time and needed answers quickly. The contact answered back, "I do not have a have any information on them at this time, but I can tell you that you are looking for three instead of two. They have added a new one."

This was not what Qatar wanted to hear, but he knew that it helped to know that a third American had been added to the mix. Qatar asked, "When can you give me some information concerning their location? I do not have much time and need to know in a few hours."

The contact answered, "Give me two hours and contact me again. I will have the answer that you need."

Qatar hung up the phone. All he could do was hope that his contact would come through for him. He had not failed him so far and felt that he did not have much to worry about, but knew that time was not on his side. He called his men and told them to be ready in two hours. He informed them that he was coming up with a plan and would let them know what it was that that time. Qatar knew that he had a chance to capture the Americans, save his life, and get rid of the leader all at once. He just needed to come up with a plan and was relying on his contact to get it started for him.

* * *

"Let me get all of you some water and something to eat," the man said who had lifted the hatch for them to get out of the truck.

"I know that you were probably very hot riding in the back of that truck. By the way, my name is Benjamin and I am the person that Diotrice told you about."

Diotrice's contact in New Helen was a middle age man, in his mid to late forties. He seemed to be very nice and hospitable or so it seemed the Americans. He told them that he had worked as a contact for Diotrice for the last three years and had done so, because he did not like the way the country was headed. He had seen a change at the palace, not in a good way and voiced his opinion in some secret circles. He was introduced to Diotrice. She brought him into her small secret rebellion and was her contact in the capital city.

Benjamin continued to tell them how he had to keep a low profile over the last three months because of all the chaos that was going on. He still gave help to Diotrice's cause and was very important to her and her organization.

Jake did not know what to think of Benjamin, but he knew he did not have time for any more small talk. He wanted to get started on the job at hand and get in and out of the palace without incident.

"We are ready to get started," Jake said as they entered into Benjamin's small hideout.

Benjamin did not have much to offer them, but there were three cots for them to lie down and plenty of water and food. Jake got the blueprint of the palace and put it on a table in the corner of the room. Benjamin brought in some fruit and water for them. Jake asked him what had been happening over at the palace over the last couple of days.

Benjamin sat down. He told them all to sit down as well and explained to them that there had been a lot of commotion over at the palace the last few days. He had seen Qatar leave with his men two days before and come back earlier in that day. He figured that he was out looking for the Americans and had no not found them. He had never seen all Qatar's men gather at the palace as they had done and figured something bad was happening. He explained to them that Qatar came and went from the palace as he pleased. He told them that this had been going on for the last three years. Qatar looked as if he had more authority than he had ever had. He told them that it did not look like Qatar took orders from anyone and beat to his own drum. He knew that if Kier was still in charge, Qatar would not be allowed to do the things that he had been doing.

He then told them of how the locals were hearing rumors that Qatar and his men were going to go door to door and kill innocent people if they did not have information of the missing Americans. He could not believe that after ten years of peace, all that went through his people's minds was death. Benjamin reiterated that life meant something to Kier and that he brought hope to the country. He had met him before and he knew that Kier was a good man.

Benjamin knew that money was the root to all evil, but found it hard to believe that the oil would change him over night.

This raised the interest in the three Americans. They could tell that Benjamin had been around. He had seen how East Africa was formed and that it had become big allies to the United States. He tried to explain that Kier would not turn on the United States unless there was another force behind him, such as Qatar pulling his strings. Benjamin could only hope that Jake, Sasha, and Henderson wanted to help him and his cause.

So he continued and said, "Qatar was a priest ten years ago. He did help Kier take over the country, and I know that Kier felt loyalty toward him, but I do not believe that he would allow him to ravage through this country like he has done the past six months.

I believe and have told Diotrice that Kier is either dead or is being held captive in his palace. People are too scared for their lives to ask question and just go on day to day like hoping that they do not die by Qatar's hands. I did ask questions and got a warning that I would be killed if I continued. That is why I have gone into hiding. I still keep tabs on the palace, but still I have not seen Kier. We need to get you into the palace and looking at the blueprint of it, there is only one entrance and that is through a heavily guarded front door to the palace. I believe that you all would be sitting ducks if you went through that way. However, I know of a secret passage way into the palace that is not on this blue print."

Hearing about the secret entrance was music to Jake's ears. He was not interested in going through the front door. "Tell us more about the other passage way," Jake said.

Benjamin continued, "I did work in the palace a few years back. That is how I got to know Kier. I could tell that he was a strong leader, but that he also had compassion for his people. Unfortunately, I heard some things that I should not have heard and had to hide in the palace for fear of getting caught. While hiding, I stumbled onto a passage way and a tunnel that lead me to the center of the city. That was three years ago and I never told anyone about what I heard or about the passageway. I never tried to go back, but I believe it is still there."

"Benjamin," Sasha asked. "What did you hear and why were you scared for your life? You just told us that Kier was compassionate and cared for his people."

"I do believe that he is compassionate, but I was at the wrong place at the wrong time. I was doing my job for Diotrice and gathering information, but came across a secret room and some very interesting files. Since it was supposed to be a secret room, obviously, I was not supposed to be in there. I was able to take some pictures of the file, but I heard some voices and I hid in a small room so that I would not be discovered. I forgot to close the file drawer and the two men saw that the drawer was still opened. They discussed what was in the file and said that if this got out than it could destroy them and their plan. I waited for a long time in that room and finally was able to escape and never went back. I do not know if they figured out who I was, but I did not want to take a chance. Diotrice understood and allowed me to do work outside the palace. After that incident, the palace has been locked down ever since."

After listening to Benjamin and his story Henderson needed to know more. "What did they say? What was in the file?" He asked.

They all wanted to know, but it seemed as if Benjamin did not want to say. They could see the fear in his eyes. "I have witnessed firsthand what Qatar and his men are capable of. I treasure my life and will take what I saw and heard to the grave as an old man. All I can tell you is that if what they said comes true, East Africa will be a more dangerous place than it is now."

"Why can't you tell us?" Jake asked.

"I will tell you this," Benjamin answered. "You go into the palace and see what you can find, come back with some information and we can compare notes. I believe in Diotrice's cause, but I do not trust many people and I need to find a way to trust the three of you. You get some information concerning what I speak of and I will help you a little on the way. Is that fair?"

Jake wanted the information now, but did not want to rattle this guy's boat. He and his counter parts would go into the palace and see what they could find out. He had the plan, now he just needed to carry it out.

* * *

Two hours had passed and Qatar was getting anxious. He had not heard from his contact and needed something concerning the Americans. He was upset that his contact had not called him and could wait no longer. He picked up his private line and called his contact.

"I need some news on the Americans. Where are they?"

Qatar's made sure that his contact could hear the anger in his voice. "I have found out through many reliable sources," his contact answered, hoping that it would be good news for Qatar. He continued, "That the Americans have entered the capital city. I have in fact heard that they are currently there in your city now and are planning to come after you."

Qatar was indeed happy to hear the news. He knew that he had a better chance at locating them and felt that he would set a trap for them.

"That is very interesting," Qatar answered with a smirk in his voice. "Tell me, do you know where they are at this time."

The contact answered "No, I do not know. My sources indicated that they snuck into the city, but did not know how or where they might be at the present time. My sources are positive that the Americans are there to come after you and I know for a fact that they are going to come to the palace within the next twenty-four hours."

"Are you sure that they are coming to the palace?" Qatar asked the contact.

"Yes, I am positive. I have been informed by many credible sources that they are coming to the palace. For what reason, I do not know, but I presumed that they are coming after you. I do not need to tell you to be prepared, but I do need to warn you that these three a very well trained soldiers of some sort. You need to get your men together and be ready for them. They are armed and know how to use what they have. That is all that I have right now, over and out."

The contact hung up his line. Qatar knew if he needed any more information, he could rely on his contact to come through for him again. He had never steered him wrong over the last ten years of dealing with him.

Qatar would be ready for anything that the Americans would come after him with. Qatar grabbed his radio and radioed out for his men to report to the palace immediately. It did not take long for them to report back to the palace. Qatar gathered them together at the steps of the palace. He stood on the top step do that he could look down on his men, like he always did. He then began to explain his plan.

"As I predicted," he started with a grin on his face making sure that his men knew how right he was. "The Americans are here in our city."

"Tell us where to go and we will take care of them," One of his loyal servants said.

All the men started to follow suit and started to yell that they all wanted a piece of the Americans. Qatar held up his hand to quiet his men and said back to the, "I want to preach patience to you. I have good information that we do not need to go anywhere. We will stay here and they will come to us."

Qatar looked at his men and said with a very loud voice, "No one is coming into my city and trying to eliminate me. I have worked too hard to get where I am today. We will wait here and set a trap for them. They will not be expecting us and we will pounce on them. It will be my finest hour and their capture and eventual death will help us get back into favor with our leader. Be patient men and look to me for I will give the word when to capture them."

Qatar was proud of himself. He knew it would only be a matter of time before he would capture them and turn this catastrophe into a triumph that would eventually lead him to his ultimate goal, and that was becoming the leader of East Africa.

* * *

"Do you have your weapons of choice?" That was the question Jake asked Henderson.

He had always asked him in the past, because during one mission Henderson had forgotten his gun and had to borrow one of Jake's.

Henderson looked at Jake and with a smart aleck remark said, "Yeah I do. Thank you for keep reminding me. Just because I forgot them on one mission, you will never let me forget it." Henderson looked at Sasha and she started to laugh.

"Oh really, you forgot your gun," she said with a big grin.

"Remember, Sasha, never forget anything. Jake will never let you live it down." Henderson was trying to joke around, but Jake did not want to hear any of it. He was all business and knew that there could be no mistakes. He did not want to forget anything and if meant a little ribbing on his case, he was fine with that.

"Okay guys," Jake said. "All kidding aside, I want to go over what we need to do first." Jake got the map he had drawn next to the blue print. "We will enter here," Jake was pointing at the secret entrance that he had drawn. "It looks as if you will come out in this area, which seems to be on the east wing of the palace. Isn't that right Benjamin?"

Benjamin was looking on and said, "You are correct. One thing I want to point out is there is surveillance all over the palace and what I can remember is that there is a camera pointing right at that small area. I do remember that the camera goes back and forth so you will be able to calculate the exact seconds you will have to move out of there so that you will not be spotted."

"Thank you for that little tidbit," Henderson said. Jake nodded to say thanks as well.

"Finishing what I was saying, we will come out here." Jake was continuing to point at the area at the end of the secret entrance. "The question is, where do we go from there? Benjamin, you are familiar with the palace, where do we need to go to get the needed information?"

Benjamin looked over the blueprint. He pointed to it and said, "Right here. This is where you can find what you are looking for."

"Where is that?" Sasha asked.

"It is the room that they were building right before I left. I will tell you that I over heard someone say that this would be a room to keep very important things. The important things are what I do not know. It could be anyone's guess, but that is where you will find your much needed information that you are looking for."

Jake figured that Benjamin was probably right. He felt that Benjamin was a bit sketchy, untrustworthy, and he did not appreciate the fact that he would not tell him what he knew, but Jake figured he would get it out of Benjamin at a later date. Jake was here to do a job, get out of there alive, and pass the information along to people who could help out the situation.

"Let's get ready. Night fall will be here in a few hours and we need to be prepared to go into the palace at that time."

Sasha and Henderson agreed and started getting prepared for anything that could happen to them. "Read out loud the check list to me," Sasha said to Henderson. After going through each item, they all agreed that it seemed that everything was in order.

They could only wait for the time to pass. Even though it was only a two hour wait, it felt as if they waited for two days. Finally the time had passed and it was time for them to go to the secret entrance.

They got into Benjamin's truck and headed to the middle town, where the secret entrance was located. They pulled up to where a manhole was located. Benjamin explained to them that they had to go down the manhole and it would lead them to another entrance where that would lead them to the palace. The three Americans got out of the truck and Benjamin looked at them as they left. He gave them the thumbs up and told them good luck. Jake looked back and said,

"We do not need luck, but thanks. We will see you when we get back."

They all went down the manhole and found where the secret entrance was located. It was covered with some old rotten wood. Henderson pulled back the wood to the entrance and said, "This is it, no turning back now."

Jake took Sasha by the hand and said, "Are you ready for this."

She answered, "I told you that I am a big girl. I can take care of myself." "I know, but I just…"

Henderson interrupted and said, "I hate to interrupt the two love birds, but we need to get this party started."

Jake said, "Thanks, man for the comment."

Sasha said, "I thought it was kind of sweet."

Henderson responded, "O.k. enough is enough. Let's get moving."

Jake nodded to both of them and said, "Let's go. We will remain as quiet as we can from here on out."

The three entered into the secret passageway not knowing what they would encounter. Hopefully, Jake thought to himself, they would all come back alive.

CHAPTER 24

Jake took the first step down a latter that led to a dark tunnel. He hoped that it would lead him and his team to the palace and hopefully solve the mystery of Kier. When he got down to the bottom, he could tell that the tunnel was pitch-black dark and had no visibility in front of him. Jake turned on his flashlight that he had strapped on the top of his head. He was able to look around and could that tell the trip to the palace would take a little longer than he originally thought. The tunnel that the three of them were about to walk in was some sort of sewer system. The smell made Sasha gag and Henderson could hardly breathe. Jake knew that there was nothing that he could about the smell and wanted them to get moving. He looked at both of them and used his hands to tell them to calm down and made sure that they were on the same page. He did not want to run into some sort of ambush and not be prepared for it.

He motioned them to follow him and they all started down the tunnel. The smell was nauseating, but they endured it and walked for almost a mile. After the long, unbearable walk, the three of them came to the end of the sewage infested tunnel. Jake used his flashlight to see a small crawl space that was fenced in. There was water running through it and pouring into the tunnel that they had walked through. Jake knew that there had to be a starting point for the water and figured that the crawl space seemed to be the entrance that would was the lead them into the palace. He turned around and motioned to Sasha and Henderson that they would enter into the crawl space and for them to be careful.

Jake would go first followed by Sasha and then Henderson would bring up the rear. The crawl space was a very tight fit them and there was no room to turn around. Jake crawled slowly, but deliberately through the space. He had left some of his weapons behind and though he was not happy about it, he knew that he would not have fit in the crawl space with them attached to him.

The three of them had crawled for awhile and Jake saw a light that was coming up in front of him. He turned off his flashlight off and continued to crawl toward the light. Jake crawled very slowly and cautiously to where the light originated from. He noticed that there was a vent that was covering the end crawlspace. He motioned to Sasha and Henderson to stop. The two of them laid in the crawl space, covered in sewage water, waiting on Jake to get them out of the situation that they were in. Jake noticed that the vent had two small tubes coming into the crawl space that pumped the sewage water into the crawl space that they were lying in. He looked and saw that the vent could be removed and the pipes could be moved. He could tell that there was a small storage room on the other side of the vent and did not see any cameras positioned in the room. Jake knew that once the vent cover was removed and the pipes moved, that the three of them could get into the storage move and be able to devise a plan on how to move around in the palace.

Jake saw that the vent cover was screwed on and grabbed his trusted screwdriver that had carried around for just these types of occasions. Unfortunately, it was screwed on from the inside of the storage room, but this was not a problem for Jake. He did not have an ordinary screwdriver. It turned on a side angle and made jobs that looked impossible, very easy. He then very carefully and quietly unscrewed the vent. He moved the pipes out of the way and held the vent by his fingers so that it would not fall to the floor. Jake laid the cover down and slid out into the storage room. Sasha and Henderson soon followed. The three of them sat quietly, smelling like sewage, in the storage room. Jake knew that they were now in the palace and the first part of their mission was complete.

Qatar sat in the palace, smoking his cigar. He was setting a trap for the three Americans and he could sit back and wait for their capture. His contact had not let him down and he had informed his men to be ready. He wanted the Americans to be captured alive and informed his men not to shoot to kill. He had placed his men at all the corners of the palace and there was nowhere for the Americans to escape, if they did indeed come into the palace. He knew that his leader would be pleased with the capture and knew that this would help him with any chance of him becoming the leader of East Africa. Now all he had to do was sit back and wait for it all to unfold. He smoked on his cigar again and continued to smile.

* * *

Jake knew that there had to be a security camera that was located outside the door of the storage room. He knew that opening the door would blow their coverage, so he used a small mirror and slid it under the door. He could see the camera and noticed that it went back and forth from the right and to the left, stopping only for a few seconds until it started again. Jake knew that there was not much time for them to get out of the storage room and out of view of the camera. He calculated that they only had twenty seconds to get out of the room and out of view of the camera.

Jake motioned to them that they did not have much time and would have to work together for them to all get out of the room without being seen. Jake counted down and at the approximate time he opened the door. He ran quickly to the corner as Sasha and Henderson followed his lead. It seemed that they had gotten themselves out of the storage room without being seen.

The palace was empty. They had not made it to their destination, but so far they had not run into anything or anyone. Jake was satisfied so far, but still wanted to make sure they stayed quiet. He was ready to get back on the move and motioned to Sasha and Henderson to follow him. He continued to use hand signals to communicate, wanting to stay as quiet as possible. Jake walked out in front, while Sasha was in the middle, between him and Henderson. Jake had studied the blueprint and knew exactly where to go. He wanted them to continue to follow him and walk slowly and cautiously making sure they stayed out of sight of the cameras. They stayed glued against the wall as they walked with their guns held ready to fire at anyone who got in there way. That was the last thing on their minds, but they were ready to protect themselves if they needed to.

The palace was beautiful inside. Even though it was dark, they all could tell that money was not an object when the palace was built. The floor that they were walking on was made of marble. The walls were decorated with all kind of expensive art and there were many statues throughout all the halls. Though they noticed all the wonderful and expensive things the palace had to offer, they were not there to sight see. They were there to get the information that they came for and get out of the palace without being seen.

They had not encountered anyone up to this point. They remained close to the inside wall and were getting closer to their destination. They came to an intersection in the hall and Jake held up his hand and motioned them to stop. He felt that things were not right. He turned to Henderson and motioned him to go to the other side of the wall and for Sasha to follow him.

Jake looked on the other side of the wall and it looked as if the coast was clear. He motioned for Sasha to go across very quickly, but for Henderson to stay put. Sasha quickly scampered across and seemed to make it to where Jake wanted her to go, but suddenly something was triggered and there was a loud alarm that sounded. There was a heavy metal chain door that dropped down and trapped Sasha on one side hall and Jake and Henderson on the other side.

She ran to the door that had dropped in front of her and grabbed Jake by the hand, hoping he could help her. He knew that there was nothing he could. He motioned to Henderson and they tried to pull on the door, but nothing happened. The door was grounded and it did not matter how much they pulled on it, the door was not going to budge.

They continued to pull on the door, and it seemed that they were making some progress by lifting it a little big, but unfortunately, they heard voices coming.

Sasha looked at Jake through the door and said to him, "I will take care of myself. You need to get out of here."

Jake told her that he wanted to stay with her, but she insisted that it would do no good for the three of them to be captured. She insisted that for Jake and Henderson to leave.

Jake continued to shake his head and said, "The three of us came in together and the three of us will leave together."

Sasha looked at him, "I have been captured before, and I was rescued. You cannot save me again, if you are captured with me. Now go, get out of here. Hurry up!"

Jake could see the men coming on Sasha's side of the hall. He knew that there was nothing he could do for her. He looked into her eyes and said, "Trust me; I will come back for you."

"I know you will, now go!" She yelled as she pushed on Jake to get out of the palace and to save himself. Jake turned around and motioned to Henderson to run. Sasha watched them as they turned the corner. Before she turned around, she felt the barrel of a gun to her back. She knew that there was nowhere for her to run so she dropped her gun and held her hands above her head.

Jake and Henderson continued to run to the way that they had come into the palace. Jake took one last look over his shoulder as he ran and saw some men take Sasha down to the floor. He could only hope that she would not be killed and was determined to rescue her again.

Jake and Henderson made it back to storage room and to the crawl space. They could hear footsteps running behind them. "Get in," Jake yelled to Henderson. Henderson went head first into the crawl space and Jake crawled in right behind him. They crawled as fast as they could and finally got back to the sewer.

"Let's go, hurry!" Jake yelled to Henderson as they ran away from the crawl space and into the tunnel. Jake and Henderson knew they needed to get out of there in a hurry, because they could here men coming behind them. To both the delight of Jake and Henderson, the tunnel was dark and whoever was following them could not see anything in front of them. Jake and Henderson hid in the darkness staying completely quiet. Jake could only hear three different voices and knew that the closer they men came to them, the easier he and Henderson had a chance to eliminate them.

Jake and Henderson stayed in the darkness and crouched down and laid low. They waited for whoever was following them and wanted take them out. They heard one of the men's voices say, "I think they went this way. Radio in and have them meet us at the other side. It is too dark to go down there. We will just trap them in and flush them out. Let's go back the way we came and go back into the palace." The men ran back the way they came.

Making sure that the men had left, Henderson whispered to Jake, "We need to get out of here and do it quick."

"I know, I know, let me think a little." Jake replied.

Henderson whispered back to him, "We don't have time right now. We need to get out of here."

Jake knew Henderson was right. He just was not ready to give up on Sasha, but knew that he had to let her go and fight that battle another day. He said to Henderson, "You are right. Let's get out of here before this becomes our grave."

Neither one wanted to be sitting ducks, but if they did not get out of the sewer in a hurry, that is exactly what they would be. They ran back to the ladder that led to the surface and Jake got up very quickly. He removed the top of the man whole and looked out. The streets looked quiet and there was no sight of trouble.

"Come on up Henderson, I do not think that we have much time before they come for us."

Henderson came up as fast as he could. They looked around and saw headlights coming toward them. Jake looked at Henderson and said, "You know what to do. Let's split up and meet back at Benjamin's hideout, when this blows over a little bit."

They both ran in different directions, with Jake running to the west of the city and Henderson running to the east of the city. Unfortunately, Benjamin's hideout was located in the northern part of the city, but they both felt that they wanted to throw off their attackers and could easily meet up there later.

Jake ran as fast as he could. He could feel that the training that he had gone through with H and Simeon was paying off. He was running for his life and was not wearing out. Before he got too far away, he looked back over his should and saw that Henderson getting away as well. He knew that Henderson could get away and hide for days if he had too. Jake was more worried about himself getting away than Henderson hiding out. He knew that his impatience could get him caught and knew that he had to get that under control. He remembered that Henderson could remain calm and that he needed to calm himself down as well.

Jake ran down an alley and he could feel the vehicles coming up from behind him. He did not want to look behind him because he knew that would slow him down. He was still running as fast as he could and could hear shots being fired and could feel the debris of the ground splash up against his leg from the bullets that missed him. He knew he could not stop or he would be killed.

Even though Jake was running, he was able to see a door that was opened, that led into a building. It was still early in the morning and realized he ran into an apartment building. There were people sleeping all over the place, many were on the floor. Jake laid on the ground trying to be as quiet as he could so that he would not wake anyone that was asleep. He could hear the vehicles that were chasing him come to a stop and then he heard doors open and slam shut.

"I saw him run in here. Look the door is still cracked open. I know he is still in there." The two men that were chasing after Jake walked in front of the building. Jake knew that they would be coming in soon so he grabbed someone who had been sleeping on the floor and woke them up. The person woke up and wanted to scream, but Jake was able to put his hand over the stranger's mouth to keep him quiet.

"I am not going to hurt you, but I need to get out of here. Is there a back door so that I can get out of here unnoticed."

Jake could only hope that the stranger understood him. After the man calmed down and realized that Jake was not going to hurt him, he pointed toward the back entrance. Jake ran through the entrance to the door and opened it. The door led to another alley and he ran down it hoping it lead toward the hideout. Unfortunately for Jake the ally lead to a dead in, but at the end of the alley was a huge dump with garbage that seemed almost two stories high. The smell of the garbage was putrid and Jake wanted to vomit, but instead he had an idea. He would use the stench of the garbage to his advantage and decided that this was his chance to lay low for awhile. He could only hope that whoever was after him would overlook the garbage pile and look for him elsewhere.

Jake decided to jump into the garbage. The stench was even greater in the middle of the pile. Jake figured that the garbage had probably been accumulating for at least a couple of months. He had been in some dumps before, but this by far was the worst smelling he had ever been around. He buried himself down deep in the garbage heap and he made sure he had a small opening so that he could breathe and see out of. He felt that he could not be seen and had to lay and wait and hope that no one wanted to check to see if he was stupid enough to hide in the garbage pile.

Jake had been lying in the garbage for what he felt was hours, but only a few minutes. He noticed some vehicles drive by the opening of the alley. One of the vehicles stopped and turned around and came down the alley that Jake was hiding in. The vehicle stopped and two men got out.

"Man does it stink down here," one of the men said to the other.

"Did you see which way he went?" The other guard asked.

"I was told he went this way, but it looks like the alley dead ends down there and that looks like a big pile of garbage and it stinks."

"It does stink. That smell is atrocious. Go down there and see if you see anything."

"Hell no man, if he went down there to hide, than he will die from the stench. I say we leave it alone, but let's tell Qatar we scoured through it, and secured the area, but there was no sign of the Americans. Let get out of here and go down the other way. There is no way he would be stupid enough to hide in there."

They got back into their vehicle and backed out of the alley. Jake looked and could see that they headed in a different direction. That was a very close call, Jake thought, but he knew that he was not out of the woods of garbage just yet. Even though he was getting sick from the smell, he knew he had to tough it out for a couple of more hours. He waited for daylight and needed people up and moving around so that he could move more easily around town without being spotted. He did not want to be the only person out on the street because he felt that he would be a sitting duck. Jake knew he could sit in the garbage for days if he had to, but time would not allow him to do that. Sasha needed his help. Jake wanted to get out of there so that he could go back and rescue her yet again.

* * *

Qatar's men had been driving around the city for hours and had no sign of the two Americans that had gotten away. They did not want to go back to the palace and face Qatar empty handed, but unfortunately for them, he radioed out for them to come back to the palace.

Qatar was waiting on the steps of the palace for them when the five Hummers filled with his men, pulled up.

"What is the report?" Qatar asked one of his men.

"The report is not good, sir," one of his men answered knowing that Qatar's wrath would probably come down on him. "The American's got away and we could not find them."

Qatar, who usually would be upset with that information, started to laugh. "We do not have to waste our time looking for them in the city, they will come to us."

"How do you know this?" One of his men asked him.

"Because we have something that they will come back for," Qatar answered with a grin on his face.

He looked over at the palace door and one of his men brought Sasha out from the door way. She was tied up and gagged. Qatar grinned and started to laugh again. His men knew that she was a very big commodity for them and understood why Qatar was laughing. He yelled to one of his men, "Throw her in the palace's prison with our other prisoner. She will be very useful to me."

Qatar knew that he was going to use Sasha as bait and set a trap for the other two Americans. He knew that it was just a matter of time before they would come back for her. He would be more than ready this time around and would make each of them pay with their life. He knew this would make his leader very happy and it would help him reach his master plan even more quickly. He knew that his time as the new leader of East Africa was within his reach. He started to laugh even more.

* * *

Jake had waited for over two hours in the garbage pile. He saw that the sun was coming up and could hear people out on the street. He dug his way out of it and tried to clean himself off. He was able to get the trash off of him, but the smell was a different story. He would have to deal with it so he decided to run out of the alley.

The streets were busy people and he felt that he could fit right in, but he needed a change of clothes. As he walked by the locals, they looked and stared at him. He knew he stunk, but there was nothing he could do about it. He walked through the busy streets and came across another alley. He noticed a clothes line hanging. He felt bad that he was about to take something that was not his, but he knew if he did not change his clothes, he would be recognized and could lose his life. He went over to the clothes line and made sure no one was watching him. He grabbed a robe off of it. He put it on and immediately seemed to fit right in with the locals. He knew that he needed to get back to Benjamin's as soon as possible and hoped that Henderson had beaten him there.

Jake walked through the city, trying to take in the sights and sounds. He could tell that the people of East Africa wanted a peaceful way of life. With his face hidden, he was able to see Qatar's men riding down the streets and making threats to some locals. He could tell that this must be the way of life that the East African people were having to endure. He started to think about Sasha and what she was going through. This made him want to get back to Benjamin's hideout as soon as possible.

It did not take Jake that long to get back to the hideout, and when he got there he looked around the outside of the place and did not see anyone. He did not know if he should go inside or stay outside. He got to a window and looked inside of the hideout. He looked in the windows and could tell no one was inside. He went around the back very slowly, ducking down so that he could stay out of sight. He saw someone in the distance and could tell that whoever it was, that that person was trying to hide.

Jake walked up very slowly and meticulously behind this person, trying to surprise him. Jake pulled out his gun and put it to the back of the intruder's head. "One bad step and I will blow your brains out," Jake said.

The stranger held up his hands and said, "Wait, wait, wait, Jake it's me, Henderson. I saw you from a distance and thought I would let you sneak up on me. I guess that makes us even." He was referring to when he snuck up on Jake during his rescue in the city of Turin.

"Yeah right," Jake said. "You know I still can sneak up on the best of them. Good to see you, anyway how did you get away?"

"I will tell you in a minute," Henderson exclaimed as they shook hands, "I can barely concentrate right now because of the horrible stench you have. You roll over the dead with that smell, where in the world did you pick that smell up from?"

"Never mind my smell," Jake answered. "Yes, I do stink, but we are both here and alive. As you know, not all is good in our world. Sasha's been captured and we still have a mole that we need to flush out. Speaking of the mole, Have you seen that SOB, Benjamin?"

Henderson could tell that Jake was upset with what had happened to Sasha. He knew that Jake wanted to take it out on Benjamin and he did not blame him, they just had to find him first.

"I have been here for at least thirty minutes," Henderson told Jake, "But I have not seen that slimy individual. I say we wait for him awhile and while we do, I think that you need to go rinse yourself off and try to get rid of that smell before I pass out."

"Good idea," Jake answered. "Let's go inside and see if he turns up."

Jake and Henderson went into the hideout and as they thought, Benjamin was nowhere to be found. It did not look deserted as they thought earlier, but it did look as if he had not been there all night. Jake found a towel and damped it. He tried to wash the smell off, but the smell would not wash away. He figured that he needed a good cleaning to get the horrible smell off of him, but this had to do.

He would have to worry about that later. He had more important things to take care of before he could take a shower.

He walked back into the room that Henderson was in and was about to say something to him, but Henderson held his hand up and motioned to Jake that someone was coming. Jake grabbed his gun and hid behind the door as Henderson hid on the other side. The door opened and Jake pounced on the person that entered in the hideout.

"Don't kill me, please!" The stranger yelled out, fearing for his life. Jake was lying on his back and turned the man over to see who screamed out for his life. It was Benjamin. Jake got off of him, wanting to hurt him, but held back. Benjamin got down on his knees and begged that Jake and Henderson would not hurt him.

"We aren't going to hurt you," Henderson yelled. "You look pathetic. Get up off your knees. Be a man." Benjamin stood up, while Jake and Henderson deliberated what to do to him. They had interrogated a lot of people during their time and they had always played good cop and bad cop. Jake could tell that this was exactly what Henderson wanted do and he decided that they were going play the game again.

"You might not hurt him, Henderson, but I am going to kill him," Jake started, as he looked right in Benjamin's eyes.

Henderson took that as his cue and said, "He might not know anything. Leave him alone."

"He has played us as a fool, now he is going to pay." Jake put his gun to Benjamin's head and said, "You got to the count of three or only two of us is leaving this place alive. You don't have a gun, but we do. One, Two,..."

Benjamin looked at Henderson and begged him to step in, but Henderson let him know once Jake gets started that there was nothing he could do. Jake was very close to saying three when Benjamin started to cry and begged to Jake, "Okay, okay, wait a minute. I am on your side. What do you want me to tell you?"

Benjamin knew that Jake meant business, and was just buying himself a little extra time.

"Listen you SOB," Jake yelled, "I am tired of the games. Since I signed on for this mission, I have been arrested, drugged, run to death, lost two good friends, gotten no sleep, ate very little and slept in garbage. Now my new girlfriend has been captured for the third time and I have a short amount of time to save her. I am have lost any patience that I might have had. I am tired of the games that you have been playing. We need some answers and we need them now."

Henderson interrupted, "I want to go back a little bit," referring to what Jake had said to Benjamin. "You think Sasha is your girlfriend?"

"Well I haven't asked her, but it is just a matter of time. She knows that I am the real deal." Jake winked at Henderson and cracked a little smile, but he continued to hold his gun at Benjamin's head.

"In your dreams," Henderson cracked as he tried to be serious, but let out a little laugh.

"Wait and see," said Jake, "But first I need this SOB Benjamin to give us some answer, and if he does then maybe we can find out." Benjamin just looked up thinking that both of these guys were crazy. The only thing that he could hope for was to get out of this situation still alive.

Jake's patience had run out. He looked at Henderson and said, "I am tired of this guy. He has gotten on my last nerve. I am about to pull the trigger."

"Wait minute," Benjamin screeched out, holding back the tears again. "Ok, ok, I will tell you what I know." He was so scared that he urinated in his pants.

"We go a wet one," Henderson cracked, trying to hold back from laughing.

Jake looked over and saw what Benjamin had done to himself, and he shook his head. "Man, you have got to get control of yourself. Here, take this and dry yourself." Jake threw Benjamin his towel that he had used to dry himself off. "Now, tell us what you know, I do not have all day." Jake pulled his gun back and put out a chair for Benjamin sit down in.

"It is a long story, so bare with me," Benjamin started. Jake and Henderson sat down to listen to what Benjamin had to say. He started again, "I have known about both of you for a long time. I knew about you ten years ago, when you were wanted men in the Middle East. I also knew that the two of you were captured in Iran."

Jake and Henderson looked at each other and got stunned looks on their faces. Henderson asked him, "How do you know about that?"

"Well," Benjamin said. "I know that the both of you were getting close to something someone did not want you to know about. I know that you both were set up to be captured."

"How do you know this?" Jake asked.

"Because," Benjamin said with a very distinct voice. "I have worked for the agency for a very long time. I know a lot of things." Jake and Henderson could not believe what they were hearing. It shocked both of them that someone in East Africa knew their story. Jake wanted to hear more and said to Benjamin, "Go on, finish what you were saying."

"I needed help here in East Africa, and I was instrumental in bringing you back in to this way of life. There is more to this than just a rescue mission. You were brought here for something far greater than that."

Jake and Henderson wanted to know. They felt that they were on the brink of finding out something that had eluded them for the last ten years. "What were we brought here for?" They both asked at the same time.

"I want to tell you everything," Benjamin continued. "But I do not feel safe right now. I never saw anyone, but I felt that I was followed. We need to get out of here and go to a safer location."

"Listen, Benjamin," Jake interrupted. "I do not have time for this, go ahead and finish. We are fine right here."

"Seriously, Jake," Benjamin said. "I am not feeding you a line. I know that I was followed and we need to get out of here. I don't feel safe." All of sudden, Benjamin's head fell face first on the table. Blood went everywhere because he had been shot in the head from a sniper outside. Jake and Henderson got down under the table. They crawled on the stomachs, staying down and hiding behind a wall. They could only wait for the sniper to go away.

"Are you kidding me," Jake yelled to Henderson. "Right when we are about to find out what the hell we are doing here, this SOB gets shot."

"Well at least we know that he was telling the truth," Henderson said. "Now let's get out of here before we get shot." They crawled out the back door and headed toward a safer location. They could only hope that they would get some sort of help from someone to get Sasha out of the palace. They found an old truck and borrowed it to get out of town. They both knew that there was only one person that they could trust and that person was Diotrice. Hopefully, they could find her.

CHAPTER 25

Sasha had been captured for the third time since she had been in East Africa. This time though, she had been captured in the Kier's palace and was put in a small cell in the palace's basement. It seemed to be a cleaner cell than the cell at the prison camp, but still it was a cell and very uncomfortable. She was tied to a chair and was gagged in the mouth with a rag. She looked around in her cell and could tell that the walls were made of brick that were painted white. There was a small window, more like a small opening, in the door of the cell. She figured that it must be where the food, if she received any, would be pushed in. The opening also gave her a little bit of light that trickled in as well. She tried to peer out the small opening, but it was difficult for her to see anything. She did hear at least one guard that was located outside her door. She figured that there were more guards outside her cell, but she knew of only one.

When Sasha was brought down to her cell, she was able to see that there was another cell located beside hers. She also noticed a television camera lined up in front of the cell that was beside hers. It caught her eye, because it was so out of the ordinary. She did not understand what it was being used for, but she sensed that something was going on in the cell next to her.

Sasha's only hope to get out of this situation that she found herself in was for Jake to come back for her. He had rescued her before and she had faith that he would rescue her again. She was tired and her emotions were out of control. She wanted to get some sleep so she closed her eyes and started to think about all the things that she had experienced since she first arrived in East Africa. She never expected that all these events that she had experienced would happen to her, but knew without her training she would not be alive. She felt in her hear that H was a good man and he was not the mole. Since she had not talked to him since her arrival, she did not know what to believe.

Even though she questioned her mentor and had issues with trust, Sasha knew that she could trust Jake and Henderson. She would continue to use what she had learned and remain silent if she was interrogated again. She knew that there would be risk and felt in her heart that she was willing to die for her silence. She was a strong woman, mentally, before the mission, but had grown even stronger with everything that she had experienced. She desperately wanted to be in her own bed back at her house in the United States, but she remained undeterred. She tried to put out of her mind anything that might happen to her and decided to dream of white sandy beaches and lying in the sand, soaking in the sun.

Sasha had finally found her special place and was quite content, but then her cell door slammed open, interrupting her train of thought. Five men walked in with another man who was blind folded. They sat him in the corner of the cell, while Qatar walked into the cell. He had his big grin on his face and was puffing on a cigar.

"We meet again, my sweet, sweet love," he said as he blew cigar smoke out of his nose. He walked over and pulled chair up to her and sat down so he would be face to face to her. He came within an inch of Sasha's face and blew smoke into her eyes. She wanted to cough, but held back, not wanting to let Qatar get a leg up on her. He reached and grabbed her gag out of her mouth.

She finally had a chance to say something and took full advantage, saying, "I am not your love, nor will I ever be sweet to you."

Qatar started to laugh and looked at his men. They all began to laugh as well. "Silence!" Qatar yelled to them all. "Someone has to pay for your little break in into the palace. I will only ask you this one time, and you better be honest with me. What were the three of you trying to accomplish?"

Sasha would never give an answer to Qatar. She stared right into his eyes, staying completely silent. He became irritated with her and slapped her across the face. She almost tipped over from power of his slap, but she endured the pain and stared right back at him.

"Does the cat have your tongue?" Qatar questioned her, almost at the point of yelling to her. She continued to remain silent. He became angry and said to her, "I have had it with you. You will pay for your silence."

Qatar pointed to one of his men and him to bring the man who was blindfolded over to him. They picked him off the floor and brought him over to Qatar. He had his hands tied behind his back and was bent over on his knees. Qatar untied the man's blindfold and removed it, leaving the man bent over on his knees. Sasha saw the man's eyes and could tell that he was scared for his life.

He looked down at the strange man and pulled his head back so that he could see Sasha. "I want you to see the woman who is responsible for your life. You need to beg her right now for your life. She has the power to let you live or die."

The man looked at Sasha and started to cry for his life. She had never seen the man before, but all of a sudden, she felt a huge responsibility for him. She did not know what Qatar was about to do, but she did not want to reveal her mission, no matter the cost.

Qatar got his gun in his hand and put the head of the barrel against the man's head. "I am going to give you to the count of three and then I am going to blow this man's head off. Do you understand me?" Sasha knew that Qatar was not playing around, but she did not want to tell him anything.

Qatar started to count. "One, two,.." "Wait, hold on," Sasha yelled out hoping to stop Qatar from shooting the man. "All right, don't shoot him. I will tell you what you want to know." Qatar knew that Sasha, like most Americans, had some sort of conscience. He knew he could play on her conscience to get her to talk. He had tried using shock therapy, but since she had not said anything before, he figured that he would play toward her emotions. It had worked exactly like he thought.

"Alright, I will wait," Qatar said. "I will ask you again, but if you do not answer me truthfully, this man will die and his blood will be in your hands. Now tell me, why are you here?"

Sasha had been in this sort of predicament before, but this time it was different. She had never had someone else's life depend on what she had to say. She did not want to be responsible for his death, but on the other hand, she could not reveal anything about the mission. She continued to go over the pros and cons silently in her mind. She knew that she could not live with herself, if she was responsible with someone's death. Ultimately she decided that she would let the man live so she gave Qatar what he wanted.

She told Qatar why she had come to East Africa and what her mission was. She only gave him short answers and did not go into anything to specific. She told him that her main mission was to see who actually was running the country and that by all accounts it looked as if he was now the leader of East Africa. She was told him that she should have left the country and taken her information to United States authorities, but was captured and imprisoned. She did not want to tell him anymore than she had too and felt that Qatar had heard enough. She wanted him to let the man go and not do anything to him.

Qatar looked into Sasha's eyes and said, "Now, that was not that hard. That is all I wanted to hear from you."

"Since you are now satisfied from what I said, let the man go." Sasha pleaded.

Qatar had never had any intentions of letting the man go. He pulled out his gun again and put it to the man's head. He pulled the trigger and the man fell to his death. Blood splattered all over Sasha.

"I told you what you wanted to know and you killed him anyway," Sasha said in astonishment. "You are an animal. You got the information you wanted and told me that I would not be responsible for his death if I did what you said."

Qatar started to laugh at her. "Thank you for your cooperation. I did not however say I was going to let the man live. The man was a traitor, and I have wanted to kill him for some time. He was going to die no matter what you said. But, if it makes you feel any better, you are not responsible for his death."

"You are a wicked man, and you are going to rot in hell for what you have been doing." Sasha hated Qatar. She wanted to be the one responsible for getting him to hell, but she would have to wait.

He started to laugh at her again. All his men laughed along with him. "Would you guys shut up! Now pick up this guy and get him out of here. I have one more thing to say to her. Now leave!"

The men knew that Qatar meant business and picked up the dead guy and hurriedly took him out of Sasha's cell. Qatar got up into Sasha's face and said to her, "I know what is going on in that pretty little head of yours. You think that your friends are going to come and save you. Then you will try to come after me. We will be more prepared for them this time. I am using you as bait and I will just fish them out to bring them here. They may think that they are saving your life, but in the end all three of you will be captured and put to death. How does that make you feel?"

Sasha would never talk to Qatar again. Looking at him made her sick. She turned her head so that she would not see his disgusting face.

"I guess you have lost the ability to speak. Just know that you will be the reason your friends will be caught and killed. You will be responsible for that. Oh, by the way, thanks again for the information. It will come in handy." Qatar walked out of Sasha's cell. She could not believe that she had given Qatar any information. She did not give him everything, but did not like that she had given him any at all. She needed a way to warn Jake and Henderson about Qatar's plan, but unfortunately, she was tied to a chair in a concrete brick cell.

She continued to try and thank of a way to warn Jake and Henderson, but her thought process was interrupted by the commotion going on outside her cell. It was hard for her to hear, but she could see out of the small opening on her cell door that there was a lot going on. She began to jump in her chair allowing her to get as close to the cell door a she possibly could. She looked out of the small opening and notice that Qatar and some of his men had another prisoner that was blindfold and tied to a chair. She could see that one of the men was behind the television camera and also that they had sat the man with the blindfold on behind a table.

She could not make out what was being said, but she could tell that the blindfolded man was asked to say or read something into the camera. His blindfold was taken off and he was dressed in some sort of military fatigue. Sasha saw the light come on the television camera and saw the man start speaking into it. He looked like he was reading something, but she could not tell what he was reading. She noticed that whatever he was reading, it took awhile for him to finish.

What looked like an interview to her was finally over and the man was lead back to his cell. She looked at the man and recognized him. He was the same prisoner who happened to be at the prison camp when she was there. He was the prisoner who helped her. She knew that it had to be him. He seemed to be a very nice man and she wondered why he was here at the palace, doing a televised interview.

Sasha had wondered what had happened to him and was happy that he was still alive, after thinking that Qatar had killed him. She knew that Qatar only kept people alive to further his agenda and knew that when his use for them was over, he would eliminate them. She did have faith that Jake would come to rescue her, and when that happened she would make sure that she would also free the prisoner in the cell beside her.

Sasha was able to scoot her chair back into the center of the cell, away from the door. She put her mind to work and tried to figure out what Qatar was up to, but unfortunately she knew that she could do nothing about it. The only thing that she could cling to was hoping that Jake and Henderson were on their way.

Qatar was finished with the interview and had left the cell area and gone back to his office. He knew that his leader would want to know an update on everything that had transpired over the last couple of days. He also needed to talk to his secret contact to find out what the other Americans were plans were. He picked up his private line and called his leader.

"I have been anticipating your call, Qatar." The leader said when he answered the phone. "I understand that you have captured one of the Americans. I would like to be the first one in congratulating you on your hard work." Qatar was happy to hear that his leader was pleased. He knew it was always a good thing for the leader to be happy. "But before your head gets too big," the leader continued, "I am not happy that there are still two Americans out there that have not been captured. That is not good thing. We don't need them running around our country, especially our capital causing havoc. I need to know how you are planning to capture them and stop all this chaos."

Qatar knew that his leader would ask him that question and he was ready to give an answer. "We are ready for them and plan to play a little cat and mouse game. I have the mouse and the trap is set. Now we just have to sit back and wait for the two of them to come to us. I do not want to waste our energy running around the city trying to locate them. That is like trying to find a needle in a haystack. We both know how these Americans act. They can never leave anyone behind. I know they will come and try to rescue her and I assure you, we will be ready."

The leader was pleased to hear that his pupil had come up with a splendid idea. "Make sure that you will be ready and then I want you to bring them to me. Everything is going the way we want it to go. I do not need these Americans to mess anything up. You know how important these next three days will be. Make sure that your plan works. If it doesn't, you will have to answer to me. I do not think that you want that."

Qatar reassured his leader that everything was in place and that it would go as planned. They hung up the phone and Qatar became very upset. He was sick and tired of being talked down to from his leader. He wanted to eliminate the leader, but it was not time yet. He needed everything to continue as planned. First, he needed to locate the Americans and capture them and he would deal with the leader at a later date.

Qatar picked up his secure line and called his contact. "Do you have any news on the two American's," he asked his contact.

The contacted replied, "Not at this time. The last I heard was that they had left the city, but I do not know if that is a fact as of yet. Give me some more time and contact me again. I will have you the information that you want."

Qatar did not like that he had to wait, but knew that his contact had never let him down and his information was always correct. "Remember," Qatar said, "if everything goes according to plan, you will have a part in my new government."

"I have no doubt that I will," the contact answered. "I will have you some information as soon as possible."

"Don't let me down," Qatar answered. "This is vital to all of us."

"I know," the contact said. "I will make sure that you will have everything that you possibly can to capture these guys."

Qatar hung up the phone and knew that it was just a matter of time before his plan went into action. He sat back in his chair and felt that everything was coming together. He knew that it was just a matter of time, but he needed to be patient, but unfortunately for Qatar, patience was not one of his strong suits.

As the night came, Sasha closed her eyes. She had not had much sleep or quiet time for that matter, and though she was tied to a chair and locked in a concrete cell, she enjoyed the quietness. She knew that waiting would be hard, but somehow, some way, Jake and Henderson would come to her rescue. She needed to be patient and hopefully her time would not run out.

CHAPTER 26

Jake and Henderson had traveled to the outskirts of New Helen. They had escaped from the gunfire, but Jake thought it was odd that there was only one person shooting at them. He thought that Qatar would send a lot more than one person after them, but was happy he and Henderson got away without incident.

"You did say that Diotrice was going to meet us here, didn't you?" Jake asked Henderson.

"Yes," Henderson replied, "Be patient she should be here any minute."

Jake had a hard time trusting her, but knew that there was no other place to turn. The clock was ticking and every minute that passed, gave Jake less hope that Sasha would stay alive. He wanted to do anything he could to get Sasha out of the palace, even if it meant dealing with someone he did not trust.

The two of them were told to meet in a small village outside of the capital city. The village seemed to have been deserted for some time. It looked as if Qatar and his men had come to the village and burned most of it, but there was one straw hut that was still standing. They decided to wait outside the small hut waiting on Diotrice.

There was some dust blowing up in the distance. Henderson saw it and said, "She's coming. Before jumping her case, Jake, let's see what she has to say."

Jake was clearly upset. He knew they had been set up at the palace and that caused Sasha to be captured. He wanted to let Diotrice know how he felt about the situation, but knew that nothing would be accomplished if he got upset, so he was glad that he had Henderson there to calm him down. If he did not have him there, he did not know what he might be capable of. Diotrice had parked and got out of her vehicle. She walked up to them outside the straw hut and told them that it was not safe to talk outside and for them to go inside the hut. She could tell that Jake and Henderson were upset.

Diotrice, in a very sincere voice, said to both of them, "I am very sorry that Sasha was captured, but I want to let both of you know that I have been working on a way to get her out of there."

Jake was very anxious to hear what she had to say and said, "What is your proposal?"

"First of all," she answered, "I have stated this before and I know now that there is a mole in our ranks. This mole seems to know our every move. For that reason, we need to take special measures when we do anything from here on out. From now on, only the three of us will know what the two of you will be doing. Do not discuss anything with anyone else."

They both nodded their head in agreement. Henderson then asked Diotrice, "Do you have the any idea of who it might be?"

"I do not," she answered. "We have completely shut down all talks with anyone outside of our inner circle. I felt that the mole got his or her information from us talking through unsecured lines. I just want to let you know that we have to be careful how we plan our next move. I am tired of the mole knowing what our next move will be before we do."

Jake knew that every minute that they did not get back to the palace, it was on less minute that Sasha had to live. Time was running out and he needed for Diotrice to tell them what their next step was going to be. "I know we can flush out the mole and that is a big problem that we are facing, but right now Sasha is in the palace and God only knows what is going on in there. We need to get in there and do something. I am ready to go now."

"I know we need to hurry, but it's not like we can just go rushing into the front door asking them to give her back," Henderson said. "We need some sort of plan."

"Ever since I got to this country, I have always had some sort of plan, a purpose, whatever you want to call it," Jake said. "But nothing has gone the way I wanted it to go. I never thought in a million years I would be outside New Helen in a straw hut trying to rescue someone I have already rescued on two other occasions. It just hasn't made sense for me."

"Jake," Henderson said, "you know that plans always change. It's been like that since we got in this business over twenty years ago."

"I know," Jake said. "That's why I am proposing what you just said. We both know that Qatar and his men are waiting for us to go in there and rescue Sasha. They think we are going to try to slip in and try to do something under the radar. I say we do something that they least expect. We just go right through the front door during the middle of the day. I don't think that they would ever expect that. I am tired of sneaking around; we need to go back to our old school ways. Just hit where it hurts and least expect it. That will be slapping Qatar right in the face."

Diotrice liked what Jake was saying. "I think you are on to something," she said. "I like it. I think the two of you should do that, go right through the front door. Qatar would never expect that. With that in mind, do you still have the rocket launcher?"

"Yes I do," Henderson answered. "I have it right here."

He had the launcher in the back of his bag and got it out and showed it to both of them. Jake thought that he had left it at Benjamin's hideout, but Henderson picked it up right before they ran out of there.

"Good, cause you're going to need it," She replied.

"What are you proposing?" Jake asked.

"I am proposing exactly what you said. I want to kick Qatar right in the mouth. I want the two of you to go through the front door with your guns aimed and ready to shoot up the place if you have to. They know that you are coming, so like you said, why make it a surprise."

Henderson thought the idea was a little farfetched, but on the other hand Jake was smiling and nodding. Henderson said, "I do not want to go down in a blaze of glory. I want to save Sasha, but I do not want to die trying to get her out of there. I think that this is a crazy idea."

Jake looked over to Henderson, "I know it is a crazy idea, but I am tired of going by the rules. Why let them sit back there and wait for us to show up and then pick us apart. You know that Qatar has to be using Sasha as bait and he knows that we are coming back to get her. We have the expertise to take out a lot of his men, but we need some sort of diversion. I promise you Henderson that you will not have to worry about losing your life and you know that I have never let you down. Have I?"

Henderson looked at Jake and said "Well…."

"Don't answer that," Jake said, "But you know what I mean." He looked a Diotrice and said, "Can you create some sort of a diversion for us. I do not care what you do, but we need to get their attention away from the palace so we can get in there and move around a little easier."

"I am already one step ahead of you," She answered. "I know a few people that can help me with that. They are good people and they will help us make this work. I do need the two of you to remember not to speak of any of this when we leave this hut. The mole is out there and I do not want to give Qatar any hint of what we might do."

Diotrice started to walk out of the hut, but Jake grabbed her arm and said, "I need to know one thing, can I trust you?"

"Do you have a choice?" She replied.

"I guess not." Jake said. "I just do not want this to blow up in my face again. This is my only chance to make it work and I am depending on you. I need to know that you will come through for me."

Diotrice walked over and looked the two of them in their eyes and said, "Remember it is my ass on the line, too. Maybe I should be asking if I can trust you the two of you."

She then turned and headed out of the straw hut. She got to the doorway and turned around and said, "Give me three hours. Go back to New Helen and wait for me. I won't contact you, but you will know when it is time to go back into the palace. Remember, guys, three hours."

She turned around and left the hut. Jake and Henderson looked at each other and knew what they had to do. They immediately got their things together and headed out of the hut. They had been given three hours and wanted to make sure they had some time to spare.

Jake knew that he had no choice but to trust Diotrice. He could only hope that she would come through for him. He knew that he was right about something, and it was that the clock was ticking and this would be his only shot.

"Your right we need to get going. I would like to say that I do not know what to think about Diotrice, but up to this point, she has been pretty reliable." Jake said, "Though I would like to know what she might be planning."

"Well," Henderson replied. "You know that we have nowhere else to turn. I have a good feeling that she will come through for us. Remember, Jake, without her, you would have been killed by Qatar. She was the catalyst that got you out of that situation. I just came in at the end."

Jake had not thought of that, and it did put his mind to some sort of ease. He still knew that it would be hard to really trust Diotrice until the plan unfolded, but still he knew that Henderson was right. He had to trust her and believe that she would come through for him.

They gathered what was left of their weapons and headed out of the straw hut. They strapped on the ammo all over their chest and had their guns strapped on as well. Both looked like a couple of cowboys who were going into a shootout in the old west. "We need to get some native clothes so that we will blend in. I think we stand out just a little bit." Henderson said referring how they look like.

"You're right, that would be a good idea." Jake responded. "This place is deserted; hopefully we can find something around here."

They scoured the small village and found some native clothing. Henderson was putting on a robe, when he notices someone running past the hut and trying to hide out of sight. He looked at Jake and motioned that someone was watching them. Jake acknowledged him and motioned for Henderson to go one way and he would go the other. They would then meet each other in the middle and flush out the person that was hiding.

Jake went around one side of the hut. He could see the figure trying duck down to hide. He saw Henderson slowly moving in on the figure. Jake and Henderson motioned at each other and knew that they had the surrounded the hiding figure. Jake had gotten behind the person and put a gun to his back. "Don't move," Jake said to the stranger. "Stand up and put your heads over your head."

"Don't hurt me," the guy said as he rose to his feet. "I am a villager. Please do not take me away like they did the others."

"We are not here to take you away," Henderson assured the frighten individual. "What are you doing here?"

The man looked shaken and very nervous. He did not know what Jake and Henderson's intentions were, but he was very frightened and went ahead and answered them. "This was my village. They came and took all my people, my family, the leader of the village, and put them in some trucks and took them away. Then they then burned down the village."

Henderson asked the man, "How did you get away?"

"I did not have to escape. I was down at the river getting some water when I heard these men in trucks pull up, so I hid from them. I have been hiding here for a long time now, with not much food or water. I had hoped that someone would come back, but you are the only people that I have seen for some time. We all trusted in Kier, our leader of this country. He came in and promised us all that life would be different from what we had before they formed this country. He actually came to our village and told us that instead of living in huts that we would get houses. That day has never come. Not only did we still live in these huts, he then sent his men to burn them down and take our families. He is only interested in his own power. Since the oil was found, he has not been for the people like he said, but only for himself. I am only one man, and I now have no family, but I am begging you to help me find them."

Jake and Henderson did not understand what motive Kiir would have to burn down the village and haul all the people out of it. This was very similar to earlier villages that Jake had seen with Simeon off the Nile River. He told Henderson about what he had seen and felt that they needed to help this poor man. Jake and Henderson wanted to help the stranger, but it would create a problem for them. Their time was limited and Jake's main objective was to get Sasha out of the palace.

"Give us a minute," Jake said to the man. The two of them walked away from him so they could talk in private.

"What do you want to do with this guy?" Henderson asked Jake.

"I do not know," Jake answered. "He seems sincere about what he says, but how can we trust him. He might work for Qatar for all we know."

Henderson agreed, and said, "Let's pick his brain a little bit more and see what we can get from him."

Jake liked what Henderson had to say. They walked back over to the man, who still looked scared to them, and Jake said, "Tell us more about your village and your family."

The man did not know where Jake was going with his question. Jake and Henderson could tell that the man became flustered with the question. Jake asked the same question to the man and wondered if he understood him. He became upset and did not know what Jake and Henderson wanted from him.

Henderson said to the man, "Why don't you want to answer what we asked you. It is a simple question."

The man became very irritated and started to walk away from the two Americans. Jake held up his gun and told the man to stop. The man started to run, but Henderson was way ahead of what he wanted to do and tackled the man before he got started. He got on top of him, and Jake tied the man's hands behind his back. They stood him up on his feet and Jake held his gun to him.

"Who are you and what do you want?" Jake asked the man.

"Listen," the man said as he quit putting on his act for them. "I have been following you guys for a while. I live in the capital city. I am trying to gather information about the two of you and take it to my small rebellion."

"What are you talking about?" Henderson asked.

"My name is Trahan Kiel," the man said. "I am the leader of a small rebellion that we have established in the capital city. I needed to know what your roles were here."

"Did you shoot Benjamin?" Jake asked.

"I did not. I have my people looking into that. I knew that I needed to follow you when that happened. We all know that Qatar wants you dead, but from what information we have gathered, we know that the shot did not come from any of his men."

"How do you know this?" Jake asked, hoping that Trahan could fill in the pieces of what was going on.

"I have a small organization of rebels that have been together for almost two years. I had my men get in touch with all their

contact and through them I have been informed that there are other facets that want you dead outside of Qatar."

"How can the two of us believe anything you say?" Jake questioned him. "It is very hard for us to believe anything that anyone tells us, especially someone we found hiding in the brush."

"That is true," Trahan said. "I know that it is hard to believe what I have to say. If I were the two of you, I would not believe me. I have always live by the slogan, 'Do not believe anything you hear, and half of what you see.' I want you to at least let you believe in half of it. I want to take you back to the capital city and show you my little operation."

The two of them did not want to believe this person, but they both believed that if the Trahan was telling them the truth, his organization could help with Diotrice and her distraction.

"I tell you what," Jake said to Trahan. "If you are telling me the truth, I know that Diotrice could use your help. We need a distraction, and you may be the ticket that will help us."

Trahan told Jake to go ahead and get in touch with her. Jake made the call back to Diotrice and told her of what he and Henderson had uncovered. She was very interested and she headed back to the disserted village. It seemed that there was a plan coming together. The time was ticking and they only had two and a half hours left.

Diotrice arrived back at the village and Jake and Henderson filled her in of what Trahan had told them. She needed a small army of rebels and Trahan might be the ticket that she needed. She did not know if she should trust him, but wanted to see what the man had to offer. They decided that Diotrice would go with Trahan and Jake and Henderson would stay with the plan. They did not have much time left in the deadline and needed to get the show on the road.

Jake and Henderson left Diotrice and Trahan at the small village for the two of them to devise a plan and headed toward the capital. "Can you believe all the twist and turns we run into,"

Henderson said to Jake as they continued their journey toward town. "It is amazing to me what is going on here in East Africa. It is hard to trust anyone, but if what they say is true, we will be able to save Sasha. I really believe that."

"You are right about that," Jake said. "I am just glad that you came along for the ride. You are the only person that I can trust. I would not be here had you not come to East Africa. I just want you to know that you are the only true friend I have ever had. Thanks."

Henderson knew what Jake was saying. He had missed Jake and was glad that they had gotten back together even though this could end up being a life or death situation. He knew that Jake always had his back as he had Jake's. He looked at Jake and said, "The reason I got into this in the first place is because it seemed like it would be a lot of fun. It is, but it wouldn't be any fun without doing it with you. I guess what I am trying to say is that, well, you're welcome. Now let's go save your girlfriends life. Are you with me?"

Jake looked over at Henderson and said, "You know it brother." The diversion was less than two hours away. They were close to the capital city and both were focusing on the mission at hand. It was only a matter of time.

* * *

The broadcast started and Kier, as usual, came on to the millions watching in his native land. The earlier broadcast had only been seen in the East Africa, but Kier decided that he wanted the broadcast to be carried on any station that wanted it. The President of the United States was told earlier in the day that it would be on. He knew that East Africa was the key to his re-election and he was very eager to hear what was going to be said.

"Any news what he might say?" The President asked his chief of staff.

"We have been monitoring this situation all day and have heard nothing," the chief of staff answered.

The President was not happy with his answer and let his chief of staff know his displeasure. The President almost lost his temper. He was upset that everything was crashing down around him. He was even more upset that the leader of a small African nation was holding all the cards, especially chance to his re-election.

The media kept the American people well informed of what the oil discovery could do for the economy and energy crisis. The broadcast was big news in the United States and was on the Front Page all the major newspapers. There were graphs and charts explaining the impact of how the gas prices would go down. The newspapers explained how the only way for the energy crisis to go away, was for the current administration to find a way back into East Africa's good graces. All the news papers criticized the administration of not doing enough to help with the crisis and East Africa, and the American people took note. Because of all of the bad reports, the President's approval was at an all time low.

The President was well aware of the press, but he was more anxious of his approval numbers. He knew that if his administration could get East Africa back as an ally and help bring the gas prices down, his approval numbers would sky rocket and he would easily be re-elected. If during this telecast, the United States was told to remain out of East Africa, then the chances of his re-election was slim to none. The President knew that his political life could be over in a matter of minutes.

The President was frantic and he could barely control himself. His chief of staff came in and gave him a scotch and told him to relax. The drink was welcomed and they sat down in the oval office and turned on the television. The broadcast was picked up by every major television network. They turned to the television to one of the news broadcast and the anchor came on and said, "This is the most anticipated broadcast that has ever been carried by this television station. If anyone did not know, East Africa, a country formed by the United States over ten years ago, has had a discovery that could change the world's economy as we know it. Gas prices are at an all time high and it seems that there is no end in sight. But East Africa had a discovery over two months ago that could end not only this country's energy crisis, but the world's as well. The largest oil discovery that the world has ever seen was discovered in this tiny country located in the eastern part of the continent.

Many experts have determined that this discovery could help lower the gas prices the prices of the late 1980's and 1990's. This could mean that the prices at the pump could make a gallon of gas be under a dollar. Yes, you heard me right. This oil discovery could help drop prices back to below a dollar a gallon. That brings back memories of gas prices in the 1980's and 90's.

The President's re-election could be decided by the end of the night. East Africa was once a very strong ally with the United States, but unfortunately the United States was asked by the East African government to leave the country and that our country was no longer welcomed there. The United Nations has backed East Africa and sanctions would be levied against our country if we disobeyed the order. That is why the broadcast of the leader of East Africa is so important. We hope that he will share some light on what our future holds with their country."

The President did not enjoy what he was hearing. He let his chief of staff know of his displeasure by saying, "This guy is a real jerk. He has made our administration look like buffoons. You know that we had nothing to do with us leaving that country. All we did was help East Africa, but would he tell the American people that. No, he didn't. I need some air time to explain to the American people what really happened. At least I would tell them the truth."

The chief of staff shook his head. He knew that there was nothing he could say to make the President calm his nerves. He did not want the President to take up air time to defend himself. He knew that nothing good would come of that. He only could hope that the broadcast of Kier would be good news. He told the

President that before becoming to irrational, that they needed to hear what Kier had to say. They would devise a plan after the broadcast. They sat there as the broadcast came on.

Kier was sitting at a table in his military fatigues. He had nothing behind him but a white wall and an East African flag. He seemed to have tired eyes, but when he spoke, he did with a lot of energy. He started the broadcast off by saying, "This is a taped message. I am constantly under death threats that I have had to go into hiding. I do not go outdoors anymore and run my country from the safety of my palace. Many of the threats that I receive come from the United States. I have asked for their cooperation and they have not honored my wishes. We, the people of East Africa, believe that the United States is the real enemy of the world.

The government of the United States raped our land of resources for last ten years and I was not about to allow them to continue with our oil. They have secretly used our country to better their military bases in our region. We cannot allow them to get away with this any longer. East Africa was formed to be a survival nation and will be able to survive on her own now. We have many strides as a country over the last ten years and do not need the United States and its influence over us any longer. We allowed the American people living in our country to leave peacefully. All we wanted in return was the respect that they not come back into our country. Unfortunately that has not been the case.

The current administration has not held up to their end of the bargain. My feelings for the United States were indifferent until two American spies were located causing havoc in our country two weeks ago. These American spies are still at large. They will be captured and we will broadcast their hanging to the world. Because of what has transpired over the last two weeks," Kier paused for a minute and then the camera focused on his face, "Let me put it this way, the United States will never get any of our oil. I guarantee you that."

The broadcast was over. The President scooted up into an upright position in his seat, with his arms crossed. He was very upset and made sure that his chief of staff new that he was. "Turn that crap off. That is not what we needed to hear. This has got impeachment written all over it."

The chief of staff wanted to say something, but the President was not finished. "Who was in charge of sending the so called spies over there in the first place? How in the hell did they get caught and what is going on over that. Do you realize that both of our butts are on the line for this?" The chief of staff knew there was no answer that would appease the President.

"I cannot believe that you allowed spies to go over there. Not only will I not be re-elected, but I may be impeached. You know that the House and Senate will want an investigation into this." The chief of staff of staff continued to listen to what the President was saying. "You have got to make this right and put the blame toward some other branch of the government. Fix it! Now get out of my sight!"

The chief of staff left and returned hours later with news the President had been waiting for. "What do you have for me?" The President asked him.

The chief of staff answered, "The CIA has been on this situation for some time. They have assured me that Kier is not telling the truth. There is no record of any agent being in East Africa at this time. The CIA will continue to monitor this situation and notify the White House on any progress concerning this matter."

The President nodded to his chief of staff, but knew that his fate was set with the American people. He did not want to hear any recent poll number and could not understand how a small country had so much control over his re-election. "What does this guy have against me and the United States of America? We have done nothing but help that country and this is the thanks we get."

The chief of staff wanted to say something but the President was not finished with what he was saying. He looked at his chief of staff and said, "What do we need to do to rectify this situation?"

"Sir," the chief of staff answered, "We need to go on the offensive. A guilty man hides and says nothing, but an innocent man takes his battle to the street. We need to hold a press conference and ask every television station to give us air time. You need to go on television and tell the American people everything that the United States has done for East Africa. You need to be determined and show the American people that they used the United States to better their country and forcefully kicked us out for no reason. Also show anger in your voice concerning how Kier deceived not only you, but the whole country. We can get the American people back on your side, but you have to pronounce our innocence toward this situation and we have to do it quickly."

The President knew that his chief of staff was right. That is why he made him chief of staff in the first place, the President thought, because he always came up with ideas to make him look better than he really was.

"That is an excellent idea," the President said. "Go ahead and make the call to the networks. I want to start on my speech to the American people right away. The sooner the better and we may still have a shot at keeping us in office."

The chief of staff left the Oval Office and went to make the call. All was not lost for the President, but he needed a miracle for him to stay in office.

CHAPTER 27

Jake and Henderson drove back quickly to New Helen and left the truck that they had borrowed back were they had found it. It was midday and the city was crowded with people. They were well disguised, since they had changed their clothes, and mixed well with the local people. They had a little more than an hour until Diotrice's distraction took place and they wanted to get to a hiding place and settle in. They also needed to discuss their final details of exactly what they wanted to do. They knew that they had to be on the same page, because one tiny mistake could cost them their lives. They knew that the palace would be heavily guarded, but this was not that big of deal to them, because they had been on similar missions before.

During the ride into the city, Jake and Henderson had talked about previous missions and how they overcame insurmountable odds before. They both had looked death in the eye and somehow escaped with their lives. This situation was just another story that they would remember, but as of now, they had no idea how the last chapter would be written.

Jake and Henderson had made it to the area of where the palace was located. They had settled into a nice secure place and were able to see armed guards that were guarding the palace door.

Henderson got his binoculars so that he could get a better look at everything that was going over at the palace.

"It looks as if Qatar has bumped up security a little bit," he said as he counted ten more guards than they had seen before.

"At least he respects us a little bit more this time around," Jake said with a smile.

Jake was pumping himself up to go into the palace. He knew that the three hour window that Diotrice gave them was almost over. The time was ticking and Jake and Henderson were very anxious.

"We need to try and stay calm and be focused on our objective," Jake said as Henderson was trying to get comfortable. "I know I am getting anxious, but we have been in this position before and everything went the way we wanted it to. I will stay focused and Henderson, I need you to go to your happy place. Think of something else right now. I will let you know when it is show time."

Henderson agreed with Jake, but wanted him to be quiet. He was very anxious and needed to calm down and knew the more Jake talk to him the less chance he had to relax. He shut his eyes and began to think of his family and knew that it would be only a matter of time before he saw them again. Thinking of his family got him into a different state of mind. Jake liked the fact that Henderson was relaxing and looked as if he was in a complete state of serenity. Henderson had always done this in earlier missions, especially before they went into a situation so life threatening. Jake thought back and enjoyed the moment. He knew that his old school ways were coming back, and now in a few minutes their past would become their present all over again.

* * *

Diotrice knew that this day would come. She had been preparing for this attack for almost two years. Now she had more to work with. She had never met Trahan, but had heard things about him.

She did not know what to believe, but now had the chance to find out what Trahan was all about.

Trahan was born and grew up in Sudan. He left the country and was educated in Oxford, England. After school, he came back to Sudan and joined the military. He moved up the ranks and learned how to be a leader. During the revolutionary war ten years earlier, he was shot and injured. His superiors left him to die, but he was a survivor his whole life and made his way to an old village and the people of the village nurtured him and helped him recover. He remained in the village for many years, getting married and living off the land.

During the years that he lived in the small village, East Africa was formed and Kier was put in charge of the country. He had known Kier, since he was in the Sudanese army, and never felt that he had the leadership qualities to lead the new country into the future. He put that aside and just concentrated on his marriage and being a goat herder. Later, his wife became pregnant, but she died at childbirth along with the child. This left Trahan a bitter man. He left the village and became a wanderer, never settling down.

After two years of wandering between three countries, he came back to the capital city of East Africa. He could see the change that the country had gone through, becoming an industrial country from the agricultural country that it was when it was formed. He was able to find work in construction and help build the new palace that would house Kier. Since he had disappeared from society for so long, no one knew who he was or that he had been in the Sudanese army.

While building the palace he heard all kind of things concerning the government and the changes that were in store for East Africa. He continued with the project, but when he finished, he knew that his life mission had changed. He quickly set up small secret meetings and told people that came to them of what was to come in the future. He was able to put together a small militia and because of his military training, he was able to train them and get them ready for any change that might take place. He accumulated a small stockpile of weapons and had hidden the weapons in a covert hiding place in New Helen. He knew that a revolution might eventually come and he felt that he had the forces to combat that, but he did not have a plan.

Trahan brought something that Diotrice had lacked, and that was a militia and more weapons. She had been working for the last two years with Jerdan and Hare on a plan that would bring the end to Qatar and his men. She had seen what Trahan had predicted and that was a complete change in the East African government. Diotrice knew that this was their chance to step in and help stop the violence that had been taking over their country. The only problem was that they did not have many people willing to fight wither them. She had what Trahan wanted, a plan, and Trahan brought the forces to deliver the plan. They knew that they would make a good team.

Trahan and Diotrice headed back to the capital city. It did not take that long for them to get back and during their ride they continued to talk about what they wanted to do. Trahan drove into the city and went to an abandoned warehouse that housed his operation. He brought Diotrice to the warehouse and she got a chance to see his small militia. It was a group of about fifty men that he had gathered together for just such occasion. She looked over the small group of militants and was pleasantly surprised of what they looked like. They all seemed to be in good shape.

Diotrice noticed that all the men were well built men. Trahan had told her earlier that they he had all his men in tip top shape and she knew that he did not disappoint her. She saw men ready to go battle if they had to, but still she did not know if they how they would react in such a short period of time. Trahan promised her that her men were ready and that they had been sitting on their hands for some time now.

"We only have a few hours before our plan comes together and Jake and Henderson go into the palace," Diotrice said to Trahan. "Are you sure your men are ready."

Trahan looked at his men. The men were sitting with their weapons on their shoulder. He walked around the warehouse, looking at each one of their eyes. He knew that they were well trained and that they were ready for a fight. He walked back over to Diotrice and looked into her eyes and said to her, "This is their time. They are ready. Just give them the word and you will not be disappointed."

Henderson was in complete meditation. He was relaxed and had no worries. Jake also was in control of his emotions. Even though patience was not one of Jake's strongest virtues, he remained calm and waited until Diotrice's so called distraction. He had only been waiting for a few minutes, but it felt like hours. The sun was hot and it was bearing down on both of them.

Jake put his binoculars up and could tell that nothing had changed with the guards at the palace. He wanted to get in the palace and save Sasha, but he knew that he had to wait. He looked over at Henderson and could tell that he was exactly where he wanted to be. He never woke Henderson out of his trance until they were ready to go. He was not about to change those plans.

Jake looked out into town and would let the noise and the commotion of the city, help him pass the time. He watched as the merchants on the street corners haggled with their customers over prices of their merchandise. He also could see Qatar's men walk by these same merchants and just take things away from them. He saw as the merchants try to fight back, but were beaten down and almost shot. He knew that they could not do anything about it. It was sad, Jake thought. There was no law and order. Jake could only hope that Sasha was still alive.

* * *

Diotrice had given Jake and Henderson her word that she would create a diversion and get Qatar's men's attention away from the palace. She knew that a small army launching an attack on the palace would be a great distraction. She felt that her plan had to come together perfectly if Jake and Henderson had any chance of rescuing Sasha and all of them getting out of the palace alive.

She, along with Trahan had gotten the men together. She brought in Jerdan and Hare to go over them the logistics of the mission. Though the militia was not very large, Diotrice knew that she could get her job done. She also felt that once she proved the truth, others more would join her for her revolution. She thought of herself as someone who had a higher calling and thought that she could bring peace and prosperity to East Africa.

Diotrice and Trahan knew that time was becoming more and more of a factor and that their three hour window that she had promised to Jake was almost over. They only had a few more minutes, but she was very confident that they could get everything in order and everyone in place on time. She looked over to Jerdan and asked how everyone's demeanor was. Jerdan gave her the thumbs up. She then looked at Trahan and told him that this was it. This was the beginning of a new East Africa. The only thing left was for her to pray that the rescue would happen the way she envisioned.

CHAPTER 28

KABOOM!! There was a huge explosion in the northeast part of the city. Jake looked up and saw the fire and smoke that had form.

"What was that?" Henderson asked as he awoke from his relaxation nap.

"That was our diversion," Jake said.

"Well I guess that means we are up," Henderson replied knowing they needed to get moving so that they could get to the palace quickly.

"Let's go," Jake said as another explosion happen near the first one.

"Hopefully," Henderson said as he was ducking his head, "These explosions are not going to get in our way to the palace. Make sure you watch yourself."

Jake was in too much of a hurry to hear what Henderson was saying. He just raised his hand and made sure that Henderson followed him. The two ran toward the palace. They could see that most of the guards had left their post and had run toward the explosion. This excited Jake and he felt that Diotrice had come through for him and her plan was working exactly the way they wanted it to.

"It looks like we won't have to deal with as many guards, now." Henderson said to Jake as more guards ran toward the bedlam that Diotrice had created.

"That can only be good news for us." Jake replied. "This will make our job a lot easier."

There were only two guards in front of the palace doors. The guards were disheveled and Jake and Henderson could tell that the guards did not know what to expect. Because of this, they felt that getting by the first two guards would not be difficult, but once they got into the palace it would be a different story.

"Henderson," Jake said as they continued to run toward the palace, "Follow my lead. I will take out the first guard and then you can take out the second one."

All of a sudden, there was another loud explosion, but this time it was in the southwest corner of the city. That part of the city was very populated and it caused people to start running all over the city streets. There was a lot of confusion all over the city streets. It was very similar to what had happened a few days earlier, when Henderson helped free Jake and Sasha from the clutches of Qatar.

"She has got them running all over the place," Jake yelled to Henderson. "Now it is our time to go in there and make some explosions of our own."

Jake and Henderson got close to the palace. They crouched down behind the side of the steps so that no one could see them coming. Jake used his hands to tell Henderson what to do. This was their time, Jake thought. He looked at Henderson and nodded his head. Henderson gave him the thumbs up. Jake counted down from three and they ran up the palace steps.

One of the guards came at Jake to attack him, but Jake beat him to the punch. He threw a right punch and landed it across the guards face, causing the guard to fall to the ground. Jake went down to the ground with him and then rolled over and got on top of the guard. Because of the sneak attack, Jake was able to knock the guard out.

Henderson saw his opportunity to take the other guard out. As Jake was putting the finishing touches on the first guard, the second guard pulled his gun out and was about to shoot Jake in the back. But Henderson was ready and he had already pulled his gun. He was able to shoot first sending the guard down to the ground. Henderson knew the guard was dead and knew his first job was accomplished.

"Thanks, man," Jake said as he nodded to Henderson. "You are always there to get my back."

"That is what friends are for," Henderson said with a wink and a smile. "Besides, you said that you wanted to go back to our old school ways and I was just answering the call."

They both picked up the guards guns and hurried to open the palace door. They thought that they would probably have some resistance once they went into the palace, but once they got the door open, by their surprise, there was no one there.

"I don't like this, it is just too quiet," Henderson whispered to Jake.

"You're right," Jake said. "It is too quiet. Let's make sure we watch each other's back and don't separate. Remember, we need to find out where they are hiding Sasha and get there, but let's not rush into a trap."

"Look over there." Henderson said as he was pointing to what looked like a surveillance room. They both looked cautiously around and did not see anyone, so they entered the room. Jake went over to a computer monitor. He sat down and started to plug in information, hoping the computer would tell him Sasha's location. Henderson stood by the door, holding his weapon aimed toward anyone that came his way.

"Have you been able to find out where Sasha is?" Henderson asked Jake as he kept his eyes focused on anything that might come their way.

"It looks as if they are holding her in the new wing," Jake answered. "It is on the other side of the palace. I cannot tell how many guards are over there, but it does show that there are a few. I am glad that you brought the rocket launcher. That will come in handy."

There were still explosions going on outside the palace. Jake and Henderson knew with all that was going on outside the palace, it would keep most of Qatar's men occupied.

* * *

Diotrice looked over a Jerdan and Hare. She was amazed how they were able to plant the explosions all over the city. She was very proud of them and gave both huge props at helping Jake and Henderson accomplish their goals. She could tell that they were busy communicating with everyone who was responsible for the havoc that they were causing throughout the capital city.

She radioed to them and asked, "How are our guys holding up."

"So far, there have not been any casualties," Hare radioed back to her. "I will tell you one thing, though this chaos has awakened the city. If you do not know already, Qatar's men are running all over the place. They have no idea where we are coming from. This is definitely a surprise hit."

Diotrice was pleased. She knew that she and Trahan had definitely put together the ultimate surprise attack. She was still worried about the two Americans who had gone into the palace and radioed back to them, "Any word from Jake?"

"Nothing yet," Hare replied. "I will let you know as soon as I hear anything."

Diotrice could only hope that Jake and Henderson had gotten into the palace and were on their way to save Sasha. She did not know how long they could keep their small attack going and hoped that they could get out of the palace in time.

* * *

Jake and Henderson began to walk slowly down the palace hallway toward the new wing where Sasha was being held. They were able to hide in the doorways, taking all the precaution that they could, but both continued to be amazed that they had not run into any enemy forces in the palace. Jake was ahead of Henderson and suddenly stopped and held up his hand for Henderson to do the same. Henderson knew the signal well. He knew that Jake with his amazing hearing must have heard something. Henderson repositioned himself in one of the doorways, making sure that he would be ready for anything that might come his way.

They could see that two guards were walking down the hall, going toward the main entrance. They had radioed to the other guards at he entrance, but had not gotten an answer, for obvious reasons. Jake was hiding in one doorway, while Henderson was in another. When the guards walked by, Jake jumped on the first guard and took him down. Henderson wasted no time and immediately hit the other guard on the back of the head, before the guard could react, taking him down to the ground as well.

"Are you trying to show me up or something?" Jake said jokingly to Henderson as they grabbed the bodies and hid them in an empty room.

"You know I learned from the master. I can't let you have all the fun." Henderson answered with a smile. They began to walk slowly again toward the west wing of the palace and made their way to a stairway.

"We need to go downstairs," Jake said. "That is where the map on the computer showed where Sasha is located."

Henderson motioned to Jake that he would go down first and Jake needed to cover his back. Jake nodded and pointed for Henderson to go. They crept down slowly and got to the bottom of the stairs. Henderson held up his hand, motioning Jake to stop. They positioned themselves in the stairway so that no enemy guard could see them, but unfortunately the way they positioned themselves left them minimal vision to the hallway.

Henderson used a mirror that he had in his bag and attached it to the end of his gun so that he could see if anything was happening down at the other end of the hallway. He held up his hands to Jake and counted out that there were six guards. Jake grabbed out a grenade and looked at Henderson with it in his hand showing that he was going to toss it down to the end of the hallway. Henderson nodded, but noted that everyone would know they were here.

Jake smiled and whispered to him, "That's why I love what we are doing, because it is more fun when there is a challenge." He pulled the pin and rolled the grenade down the floor.

The guards were all talking to one another, not paying attention to anything that might be coming their way. One of the guards heard something rolling down the hallway, but when he looked, he could not make out what it was. When the object came to a stop, the guard realized that it was a grenade.

The guard yelled at the top of his voice, "Get down! Grenade! Grenade!"

The guards all scattered, but it was too late. The grenade exploded, and killing a couple of the guards, leaving the rest in shock looking for their weapons. Jake and Henderson took full advantage of what had just happened. The two of them came running through the smoke, finishing off what the grenade did not.

"That was loud explosion. We can only hope it blended in with all the other explosions going on outside the palace," Jake said as he removed the weapons from the dead soldier's hands.

"That is wishful thinking, and I doubt it, so be ready for anything that comes our way," Henderson replied.

After the smoke settled down, the two Americans noticed a solid steel door. Jake knew that Sasha had to be on the other side.

"Henderson," Jake said with excitement. "This has to be where they have been holding Sasha. The door is the only one that is made out of metal."

"Do you think that we can penetrate it?" Henderson said as he continued to wave the smoke out of his eyes.

"It will be tricky, but I am pretty sure that I can do it," Jake replied.

"You know that we don't have much time so you need to get on it." Henderson assured Jake that he would cover him as he worked to unlock the door.

"It looks that I am going to have to blow up the lock. That is the only way in." Jake grabbed his explosives that Hare had given him and puttied them on to the door. He yelled for Henderson to take cover as he ran away from the door, waiting for the explosives to detonate. Jake hid behind the corner as the door blew up and shattered all over the place. Smoke filled the hallway and Jake yelled to Henderson to make sure that he was alright. Henderson replied that he was alright.

"Go in and see if you can find Sasha," Henderson said as he coughed from all the smoke that had filled the hall from the exploding door. "I will stay out here and get cover your back."

Jake held up thumb and nodded to Henderson and entered through the doorway. All he could do was hope that he guessed right and Sasha was in the room unharmed.

* * *

Qatar called to one of his men on his radio, who was outside the palace. "What the hell is going on out there? It sounds like we are under attack."

The guard told Qatar that they had yet to pin point what was going on, but it was very chaotic and people were running and screaming all over the city streets. Qatar believed that his country was under attack and had gone down to his bunker for protection. He continued to believe that his life was always in danger and did not want to take a chance of being killed.

He began to think that he might have been tricked. When he heard all the explosions, he immediately fled down to his bunker. He had it built a few years back, for just this occasion or what he thought was an attack. He began to think that if might be a diversion for Jake and Henderson to come into to the palace. He thought that he was prepared, but never dreamed that they would come for their rescue attempt during the middle of the day. His contact said that they always attacked at night. He tried to radio to the other guards that were at the front door of the palace and there was no answer. He now knew something was going on. He needed to get out of the bunker and back into the palace as quickly as possible. Before he left his bunker he made a call to his leader.

"Sir," Qatar said as the leader answered the phone. "It looks as if the Americans have come in our palace to rescue the girl. We will be able to get this little situation under control, but right now it is chaotic around here."

The leader was upset and the quietness on the other end of the line was deafening. All Qatar could hear was the leader breathing heavily. Finally the leader answered and said to Qatar, "I will be ready for them, if they decide to come up here, but I would rather you dispose of them. Do you think you can handle that?"

"You do not have to worry," Qatar assured him. "My men and I will have this under control very shortly."

Qatar hung up and could only hope that he could get this chaos under control. He did not want the leader's wrath to come down on him if he could not.

* * *

Diotrice check the status on the so called attack and was told that they had run out of explosives. She had figured that she had, because she had not heard one go off in a while. She knew that she had done what was expected of her and had gotten Qatar and his men's attention.

"How are we doing?" She asked Jerdan. "So far we have the guards running all over the city completely unaware of where we are positioned. They do not know what hit them."

"Fantastic!" Diotrice replied. "Now we have got to hold them off a little while longer. Make sure that we tell the men to hide behind anything that they can find. Qatar's men are well trained, but so are we. It is terribly important that we hold them off as long as possible, for our fate is no longer in our hands."

Diotrice knew that her fate was in the hands of Jake and Henderson. Whatever happened in the palace would eventually make its way onto what was now her battlefield. She had all the faith in the world that Jake and Henderson would rescue Sasha, but could only hope that they would rescue her as well.

CHAPTER 29

Once the smoke cleared there was an opening where the door once that lead to the prison cells. The explosion was such a huge blast and it threw Sasha onto the floor. She could not see what was happening and felt that she was under some sort of attack. She go off the floor and looked out and saw Jake running into the prison room. He yelled her name, hoping that he had picked the right area. Sasha was a little lightheaded and started to cough, but got herself together and was able to answer that she was in a cell.

Jake turned to the cell that he heard her in. He could only hope that she was unharmed and asked her, "Are you alright? Are you hurt?"

"I am o.k." She answered, still feeling the effects of the explosion. "I was a little startled by the blast, though. It tipped me over and now I am lying on my side." Sasha was still tied to a chair and was very irritated with the situation she had been in.

Jake yelled back to her, "I am going to get you out of there. I just need to find the keys."

"I think the keys are over in the corner of the room." Sasha said. "

Which corner?" Jake responded.

"I can't see, because I am lying on my side. Just look all over and I know that you will find them." Jake could hear that she was irritated and he tried to hurry his search. He saw some keys on the floor and figured they must have fallen down during the explosion.

"I found them." Jake yelled into her cell, hoping that would put her to ease. "Hopefully, one of these keys will get you out of there."

As Jake was going back to get Sasha out of her cell he saw the other cell beside her. He looked in and saw another prisoner who was tied up and gagged. Qatar must really have something against this guy, Jake thought as he continued to try different keys in Sasha's cell.

"Have you found it yet?" Sasha asked as she was still lying on her side.

"I am trying," Jake said. "I want to get you out of there. We do not have a lot of time. I have Henderson watching the hallway. He will gun down anyone who tries to come after us. I am sorry that I cannot find the right key. This is irritating."

"Calm down just a little," Sasha said as she tried to make sure Jake was not getting to anxious. "Try the biggest key. I think that is the one that they always unlock my door with."

Jake fumbled around on the key chain and finally found the biggest key on the chain. He put it in and it fit in the lock. "Got it!" Jake exclaimed as he unlocked the door and the he opened the door. He ran into the cell and sat Sasha back up. Jake used his knife to cut the rope that was wrapped around her legs and arms and stood her up.

"Thank God you are here," Sasha said as she rubbed her wrist to soothe the pain that her wrist had gone through. She looked up into his eyes and gave him a small peck on his lips. "I was very worried about you Jake."

"You were worried about me?" Jake replied in astonishment. "I have not slept because I was very worried about you. I did not know what was going on in here. I knew that your life was in danger and all I could think about was to get here as fast as possible. I just thank God that you are alright."

"I am fine," Sasha said with a smile. "Now since you know how I am, I have to know, how did you get in here?"

Jake smiled back at her and said, "I will tell you later, but you will like the story. We don't have a lot of time, so let's get out of here."

They began to run out the doorway, when Sasha stopped, turned around, and walked over to the other cell. Jake saw her turn around and asked, "What are you doing?"

Sasha replied to Jake as she looked into the other cell, "I know that this guy is in a lot of pain. He has been shuffled in an out of his cell many different times. I could not tell what they were doing to him, but I did see him having to talk in front of that camera over there a few times." Sasha was pointing to a television camera that was in the corner of the room.

Jake saw the camera and said to her, "I saw him tied up to a chair and that he was blindfolded and gagged. I just presumed that he must have made Qatar very angry. I am sorry that he is in that situation, but we just do not have the time to carry anyone else along."

Sasha ignored what Jake had said and got the keys out of her cell door and was thumbing through them trying to find the one that fit in the other cell door. Jake continued to tell her that there was just not much time and they had to go.

Sasha quit thumbing through the keys and turned to Jake and said, "Do you remember the guy I told you about who had helped me when I was in that other prison camp."

"Yes, I do." Jake responded, still having one foot toward the exit.

"Well," she said, "As you remember, I woke up one day and he was gone. I never thought I would see him again. I was wrong. That is him in there. He is the same guy. I would never forget his face and I know that is him."

"Are you sure?" Jake asked. "I mean, how can you tell? He is blindfolded and gagged."

"I was able to scoot close to the door and look out one day." She said. "I saw his face and I swear that is him in there. The funny thing is, they had him talking into that camera. He must be someone that Qatar cannot stand. That alone is reason to free him."

Jake knew that there time was limited and that Qatar's men could be on their way at anytime. He yelled out the door to Henderson to see if he was alright. Henderson yelled back that he had them covered, but he wanted them to hurry up. Jake said they were on their way, but had gotten a little side track. He said that they would be out in less than a minute. Jake took the keys from Sasha, "I will open the door and you run in and get him."

He found the right key and opened the door and told Sasha to go in and help the guy out. She entered the cell and bent down and whispered in the prisoner's ears that she was there to help him and for him not to worry, that they were going to rescue him. She took the blindfold off the man's face and instantly knew that he was the man from the prison camp.

"Let's get out of here," she said as she removed the gag in his mouth and cut the rope off his hands and feet.

The man was weak and somewhat confused. He looked like he was drugged up on something. He had trouble gathering his speech and could not utter the words of appreciation for her. Jake looked into the cell and could tell that the man did not have enough strength to hold up his head. He knew that the man could not get out of the cell by himself so Jake ran into the cell to help and told Sasha to head towards the exit.

She looked at Jake and grabbed his arm and said, "Thanks for understanding."

Jake smiled back and grabbed the man and put him over his soldier. Jake followed Sasha out of the cell and to the exit of the cell area. Henderson was still at his post and saw them coming. He saw that Jake was carrying someone else.

Before he could say anything, Jake yelled to him, "Change of plans. We need to find an empty room and put this guy down. He seems to be very weak and he seems to be is dehydrated. Sasha knows him from her days at the prison camp. No questions, just find us somewhere to go."

Henderson knew that Jake was not messing around. He knew that all their lives were at stake and he had to get them out of there and into an empty room. He gave Sasha a gun and told her to stay behind him, but to be sharp and take out anyone that moved. They needed a room that was secluded that they would not be found. Henderson just hoped he could find it, before it was too late.

* * *

Qatar got back above ground and could see the havoc that was happening inside and outside the palace. He radioed to his men that were outside to get back to the palace and as fast as they could. He told them that they were not under attack and that it had been a diversion to get them away from the palace. Qatar knew that the two Americans had probably located the cell area and had freed Sasha. He knew that he could not let them escape and he needed to get rid of them or his leader would try and eliminate him instead.

The bunker that Qatar had locked himself into was below the palace. It took him awhile to get out of the bunker and back above ground. He went straight to the palace's main entrance and saw that the two guards that had been at the entrance were slain. He became enraged with anger and knew that the Americans would be on their way out of the palace. He wanted to do anything he could to keep them in the palace until his men came back from the inner parts of the capital city. He sat at the entrance watching to see if he could get a glimpse of the Americans coming, they never appeared. He looked back out of the entrance and saw his men coming. He only counted five of his original twelve.

"Is this all of my special forces that are left," he asked with astonishment.

"Yes sir," one of his men answered. "The other seven were left inside to help guard the palace."

"A lot of good that did," Qatar answered in a very angry voice. "The two American spies have entered into the palace. They have killed two of my men, and possibly more. We need to find these terrorist and take them out. Most important thing though, is to keep them in the palace. If they escape it will be the end of all of us. Do I make myself clear?"

The men knew exactly what Qatar was talking about. They either killed the Americans or they would die themselves.

"Check the monitors and find out where the Americans are." Qatar said, pointing to one of his men.

The man went into the monitor room and looked at the ten different monitors that were attached to different cameras throughout the palace. He went through each monitor, hoping for a glimpse of the Americans, and finally he spotted them in the new wing. He rushed out to tell Qatar the where the Americans were located. Qatar informed his men that this was going to be an all out war to take these two Americans on. He wanted his men to make sure that they had plenty of ammunition, because they were going to need it..

"Sir," the man who had spotted the Americans on the monitors, said to Qatar. \

"What is it?" Qatar answered, wanting the man to hurry up with whatever he had to say.

"It seems as if the Americans have doubled in size. I counted four, instead of two. They must have freed the other prisoner as well."

Qatar grimaced in pain. His ulcer that he thought had gone away, flared up again. It only seemed to flare up when he got bad news. He could not allow the Americans to escape, but now the thought of the other prisoner escaping as well left him on edge.

"Men," Qatar said in a very determined voice as he looked to them. "I want you to shoot to kill. No one leaves this palace alive. Do you understand me, shoot to kill!"

Jake had rescued Sasha from another cell, but he knew that was the easy part of the plan. The hard part was finding a way to get outside the palace. The other prisoner put a small kink in his plan, but Sasha had other ideas and wanted to save him. Jake thought about it a little bit and did not have a problem with that. He wanted to make sure that she was happy and also that they were helping someone. Jake had not forgotten why he had gotten into the business in the first place. That was simply to help out his fellow man and give them a better way of life. He knew that he would be able to sleep better at night, knowing he had helped his fellow man.

Henderson had located a small, empty room. They all entered and he locked the door behind them. They all knew that they did not have much time to make up their minds what they needed to do. Jake told the group to give him a minute to think and told Henderson give the prisoner some water out of his canteen. He continued to think, but said nothing. Time was ticking and the enemy could be on them at anytime. Finally, Henderson could not take the silence and spoke out.

"I think we need to go the same way we came in, but we need to be more careful." Henderson knew that was risky, but really had no alternative.

Jake did not agree and said, "Do you think that is wise, I mean it seems that Qatar has probably located us and will be waiting for us."

Henderson responded by saying, "I don't think there is any other way. I remember the blueprint and it said there was only one way in an out of the palace. They shut off our way through the secret entrance, so that is out of the question. I have a feeling that we just need to be ready for anything that comes our way."

The prisoner, after drinking from Henderson's canteen, interrupted them and said, "I don't mean to change your plan, but I do know of another way that we can get out of here."

This was the first time that he spoke and it amazed the three of them that he knew anything about the palace. He was still dazed and weak, but he felt strong enough to voice his opinion.

Sasha could tell that he was out of it, so she said to the prisoner, "You need to rest and preserve your energy. We will get you out of here. Don't worry; we will take care of you."

The prisoner took another swallow from Henderson's canteen. He was a little out of breath from drinking, but he was able to continue what he was saying. "I know I look in terrible shape, but trust me, I know how to get out of here."

"How do you know how to get out of here?" Sasha asked him.

"Just like you said earlier," the prisoner responded with a slight smile, "it is a long story, and I will tell you later, but right now we need to get out of here before Qatar's men come get us."

Jake did not know how this prisoner knew anything about the palace, but if he had an alternative then going back out the front door, he was all ears. He knew that any other way would be a lot better than running into Qatar and his men and possibly getting shot.

"Okay," Jake said, "Let's hear what you have to say."

The prisoner told them that they needed to go back up the steps to the second level of the palace. The palace had three different levels and many different rooms and it could get confusing if you did not know where you were going, but the prisoner knew how to navigate his way through the palace fairly easy. There was a crossway on the main level and if they could get by there without incident, they could get out of the palace unharmed. The problem he told them was getting by the crossway.

It did not seem to difficult to Jake and the others, so they felt that they would take the prisoner's idea and go out the way he suggested. Jake asked if the prisoner was up to the challenge and he nodded his head that he was fine. The four of them headed out the way he suggested and made their way through the palace.

They came to the crossway that he had told them about and Jake held up his hand for them to stop. He told all of them to get down and to be quiet. He had a sense that something was not right. He turned to Henderson and asked for his mirror. Henderson handed it to him and he attached it to the end of his gun, like Henderson had done earlier. He positioned his gun so that he could see around the crossway from the mirror if anyone was waiting for them. He could see Qatar and his men were set up waiting for them. Jake motioned to his counterparts that there was trouble, but unfortunately Sasha could not help but sneeze. Their cover was blown. The same trap door that had trapped Sasha earlier in, dropped down behind them. They could not go back the way they came and had to continue forward.

"We are going to be sitting ducks," he said to the prisoner as he was showing his frustration with the situation.

Qatar wasted no time and had his men opened fire them. Jake and Henderson shot back, but neither side had much luck hitting their targets.

Jake looked back at the prisoner and after taking a few shots toward Qatar, asked him, "I thought you knew where you were going? You have led us right into an ambush."

"I do," the prisoner answered, "I told you that this area would be a problem. We can still get out. Just have to wait a little longer than I expected."

Henderson looked over at Jake and said, "We are sitting ducks. This guy doesn't know what he is talking about. Let's get ready for a fight. I got your back."

Sasha was not ready for that and looked at the prisoner and said, "There has got to be a better way. We don't have time to wait. What else do you know about this place?"

"Make sure that we stay behind here," Jake said as he put his hand on Sasha, making sure that she stayed behind him. "At least we are safe for a little while, but who knows for how long."

The prisoner remembered that they did have another option, but a small one at that. He knew that as long as they stayed where they were, they could be picked off by Qatar one by one.

Jake was tired of waiting on the prisoner to come up with any more foolish ideas and decided to take matters into his own hands. He grabbed for a grenade, but forgot he had used the only one he had. He wanted to use the rocket launcher that Henderson was carrying, but knew that there was not a lot of room and it could kill them all. They were indeed stuck and Jake had no answers for what to do next.

The prisoner looked across the hall and saw a small opening in the wall. He looked over at Jake and said to him, pointing at the opening, "Look over there."

Jake looked and saw the opening and asked, "What is it?"

"I believe it is some kind of chute that will lead us down to the basement level," the prisoner answered. "It might be tight, but we will all fit. We need to run over there and jump down it. I know that Qatar and his men will not follow us in there, because if they do, they will be the sitting ducks."

Jake knew that this was probably the only thing that they could do. He still was skeptical and asked the prisoner, "How do you propose we do this. They are shooting like mad at us. We have no shot of getting across without being hit by a bullet."

The prisoner knew that it would not be easy and he did not want to risk anyone's life, but on the other hand, he also knew that the longer they sat there, Qatar and his men would eventually inch closer and try to eliminate them.

"Jake," the prisoner said, "Do you see that statue over there?"

"Yeah, I see it," Jake answered.

"I am going to run over there and move it close to the chute. I will position it by the chute so that the three of you can run across and dive in. It is hard for Qatar and his men to hit a moving target. Just trust me, do not think about it and go head first. Another thing, the opening does not look big enough for you to jump in with your guns, so you will have to discard."

Jake did not want to be unarmed, but knew that he was right. He did not want to be completely unarmed so he would carry at least his hand gun. He turned to Henderson and Sasha and told them what they were going to do. They nodded to Jake and told him that they were on board with it. Jake told Sasha that she would go first, Henderson would then follow and he would go after them. He hoped the prisoner could make it as well, but his first priorities was for their safety.

"Okay," the prisoner said, "We have got to do this in a hurry. Are you with me?"

The three Americans nodded and gave thumbs up. "Alright, here I go!" The prisoner yelled as he ran as fast as he could toward the statue.

The three shot toward Qatar and his men, giving a nice cover for the prisoner. He had made it without being shot and move the statue I a great position. He motioned over to Jake and told him to come. Qatar and his men continued to shoot at them, but Jake was undeterred. He knew that it was time for them to make their exit.

"Sasha," Jake said, "I got you covered. Once he opens the chute door, you run like the wind and dive in. Do you go it?" She nodded and Jake looked at her and said, "We will be right behind you, now go."

The prisoner had opened the chute door and Sasha ran as fast as she could. She could hear the bullets pass by her, but she made it across and jumped head first into the chute.

"It looks like she made it," Jake said to Henderson. "Now it is your turn. Stay low and don't get hit. Good luck my friend and be careful."

Henderson ran across and made it to the chute. He jumped in head first as well. Jake was happy that they both made it and knew that it was his turn to run across. He dropped his gun and started to run. He had almost made it, but all of a sudden he felt a great pain in his right arm. He did not have time to look at it and he jumped in the chute. The prisoner saw Jake jump in and knew that he had to go in or he would be killed. He took his chance and jumped in following close behind Jake.

Qatar witnessed all four of them jumping into the chute. He could not believe his trained men could not hit at least one of them. He was angry and lashed out at his men. "How could you guys let them get away? Now who wants to go down after them?"

Qatar knew that none of the men would do it. He was so mad that he almost threw one in there just for the heck of it, but knew he could not sacrifice anyone else. He was down from twelve men to five men and needed all of them.

After securing the hallway, one of his men came carrying the Americans weapons. He said to Qatar, "It looks as if they had to leave their weapons behind. Look what I found."

Qatar was happy to see that and knew that he had the upper hand. Even so, they needed to get back downstairs to cut the Americans and prisoner off before they escaped.

"Let's get back downstairs," Qatar said. "At least we know where they are and that they are unarmed. There is only one way up and we will be waiting for them. Remember, no one leaves here alive." Qatar knew he had them trapped and grinned at the thought of killing them all. He knew that this would please his leader as well.

CHAPTER 30

Diotrice and her small militia continued the fight in the streets of the capital city. They were holding off Qatar's small army and were gaining confidence. Diotrice hoped that there would not be many casualties and she asked Hare if he knew the count. He informed her that the count was reasonably low and that the militia had Qatar's men off balance and confused. The only problem was that they were running low on ammunition. Diotrice knew that her attack would end quickly if they ran out of ammunition. She hoped that they could hold on as long as they could.

She looked over at Jerdan and asked if Jake had contacted him. Jerdan shook his head no. Diotrice did not want her men to die in because they ran out of ammunition. She wanted to end this conflict as soon as possible. Jake should have contacted them by now and she felt that he was in some sort of trouble. The plan was for him and Henderson to rescue Sasha and get out of the palace within twenty minutes, but that window was long over now. It had been almost thirty minutes since the conflict started.

She felt that she could help them out. She had to get to the palace and knew that she could navigate easily through the city to get there. She told Jerdan and Hare her plan, but they resisted and told her that it was too dangerous for her to leave.

Diotrice looked at both Jerdan and Hare and said, "I owe it to Jake to help him if he is in trouble."

"What about us?" Jerdan asked, "What if you do not come back?"

Diotrice knew that Jerdan and Hare could take care of themselves and along with Trahan could finish the battle. She motioned to Trahan to come over and so that he could hear what she was about to say.

"Listen, without ammunition, we will all die. I believe that when I find them, they can help end this conflict. I promise you, I will be back, I have to come back. When I get back I will make sure that this conflict will end. But if I do not come back, you know how to take care of yourselves. Get out of the city, and take care of our men. I have to go, but I assure you I will be back. While I am gone, Trahan, you are in charge."

Diotrice left and went toward the palace. She hid behind walls and buildings, continuing to duck bullets that were coming by her head. The three that she left wanted to believe that she would be back, but knew that anything could happen to her. Hopefully, they thought, she would deliver on her promise and bring an end to this conflict.

* * *

The prisoner landed head first into a big pile of dirty laundry. He looked up to see that Jake was bleeding from his arm.

"Are you alright?" He asked as Jake grimaced in pain.

"I will be o.k." Jake responded. "I think it is just a flesh wound. The bullet did not enter my arm, but just scraped by."

Sasha was concerned and grabbed a sheet out of the laundry pile and tore it into a bandage size. She tied it to Jake's arm to help stop the bleeding. Henderson could see the compassion that she showed Jake, but still had to crack a joke.

"You don't have to mommy him," he said to Sasha.

She did not like the comment and snapped back at him by saying, "Someone has to take care of him. We need someone to lead us out of here."

Henderson nodded and said, "You are right. I am trying to loosen up the seriousness that we are in. Go ahead and finish helping him out."

"Thank you," Sasha said, hoping that she got her point across.

The sheet that covered Jakes arm seemed to do the trick and the bleeding had subsided. Jake knew that they needed to get out of the laundry and turned to the prisoner and said, "We are in here and we need to find the fastest way out of here. You seem to know a little about this place. Which way do we need to go?"

The prisoner responded, "Unfortunately, there is only one way out of here and it is up those steps. Qatar and his men could take a while to get here so we need to get moving."

Jake interrupted and said, "We will be no match for him. Remember, we had to ditch our weapons. We need something to combat him with."

Henderson showed Jake the one item he held onto and did not unload when they jumped through the chute. He held up the rocket launcher. Henderson handed it to Jake, and Jake held it in his hand. He really wanted to use it, but he knew that the small confines they were in, firing the weapon of that magnitude, could kill them all. He handed it back to Henderson and told him to keep it. He would get it back from Henderson later. They now needed to get up the steps as fast as they could and get out of the palace.

As they stood up and headed toward the steps the prisoner yelled out, "Hold on a minute! I might know of another way. Come with me."

Jake wanted to take control of the situation. He was tired of following this stranger, and told him that they needed to get out of the palace in a hurry. He was tired of the games and felt they were getting nowhere. The prisoner pleaded with Jake and told him that he would not be disappointed to what he was about to show him. Jake looked at Sasha and Henderson and they nodded that they would be willing to give the stranger one more chance. They decided to follow him up a few stairs. He stopped and pulled back a part of the wall. All of a sudden a keypad appeared. The prisoner entered in a code of some sort and a doorway opened.

"Let's go in here," the prisoner said to them as he entered into a dark room. "I cannot believe I almost forgot about this place."

The three Americans followed the prisoner into the dark room. There was no light, so Jake lit a lighter that he had been carrying around for awhile. He stopped the prisoner and turned him around. He had to know who this guy really was and how he knew so much. "You have got to tell us what is going on and who you are." Jake demanded.

The prisoner looked at Jake and said to him, "If you want to live, go with me into this room and I promise that we will be safe for awhile. I will tell you what you want to know and I do not think that you will be disappointed."

Jake followed Sasha and Henderson into the secret room and the prisoner shut the door behind them. He found a few chairs in the room and had them sit down. He was ready to tell the three Americans what they wanted to know.

* * *

Qatar knew exactly where the chute went to and he also knew that there was only one way that they could escape. They would have to come up the stairs that led to where he and his men had positioned themselves. He told his men to go outside the doorway to the stairway and wait for the door to open.

"Fire on them as soon as the door opens," Qatar ordered. "They have no weapons. I want them all dead."

Qatar knew that his time frame of getting rid of the Americans and the prisoner was shrinking. He knew the longer that they were alive the shorter he had to live. He had to get rid of them in a hurry. He had been in these situations before and had always gotten the job done, but this was different. The Americans seemed to always be one step ahead of him and it was driving him crazy. He felt that they were getting help, but he had not been told by his contact who was helping them. He could not worry about that at this time, because he felt that he had them exactly where he wanted them.

Once he eliminated them, he knew that this would bring order back to the palace. He then would turn his attention to the chaos that was going on outside. He looked outside into the capital streets and noticed the mayhem that was continuing. He felt that the Americans had brought some sort of civil war to his capital. Qatar became outrage and knew that he could not let the Americans get away with the chaos that they started. He would take care of them himself if his men could not finish the job.

Qatar continued to look out the window at the conflict. He was still outraged and could not believe that the Americans and prisoner had not come up to the main floor. "Have any of you seen anything?" He asked one of his men.

"Nothing yet, we are still waiting for some sort of movement, but there has not been any."

Qatar looked his second in command and asked, "You have been at the monitor, have you seen them exit the palace."

"No, I haven't," he answered.

Qatar was getting anxious. He knew that there was no way that they could have gotten out of that room without them knowing about it. He just presumed that they were hiding on the stairs, hoping that he would just forget about them. Qatar was not about to forget about them. They were the ticket to his ascension into leadership of East Africa and he was not about to let them slip through his fingers.

Qatar became tired of waiting for them and ordered two of his men to go down into the stairway and find out what was going on. The two men crept slowly down the stairway. Qatar did not hear anything and wondered what had happened. A few minutes passed and the men emerged from the stairway empty handed. They did not have the news that Qatar wanted to hear.

"There is no sign of them. We know that they came down the chute, because we found this," they were holding up the torn a bloody sheet from Jake's wound. "But we do not show them leaving. It seems that they just disappeared."

Qatar was furious. First of all, he knew that people just did not disappear. Second, he had trained these men and he could not believe that they were this stupid. "Obviously, they are still in the palace. We just need to find them. If you cannot do this simple task, then you will get their fate. Do I make myself clear?" The men knew exactly what Qatar was talking about. They were supposed to be the most trained military minds in Sudan, handpicked by Qatar and now they were down to five guys. They were getting tricked by three Americans and a prisoner. They were not about to fail Qatar. They knew that they could not let anyone escape or they would not see tomorrow.

*   *   *

After following everyone into the room, Jake turned on a light and sat down with all the others. The room was not very big, but it was made entirely of steel and brick. Jake knew that the room must be some sort of a safe room and that they would be protected for at least a little while. Jake was impressed with the room and started to look around. He was startled and almost fell out of his chair when he saw all that he had been missing. He saw all kinds of different guns and ammunition for these guns located throughout the room.

"Now this is what I am talking about," Jake exclaimed with excitement.

Jake and Henderson got up from their chairs and grabbed two hand guns and clips and strapped them on to each other.

Henderson kept the rocket launcher on his back, just for the simple fact that he had kept it for so long. Sasha was also impressed with what she saw and she went and picked out a gun for herself as well.

Jake came back to the table and sat down. He was simply amazed by what had gone on and where he was. After all he had been through he now found himself in a room full with weapons. He could not believe his luck. Just when Jake thought he and his team were in trouble and could lose their lives, they now were in a safe room with more weapons than he knew what to do with. Was this just coincidence, Jake thought to himself as he looked at the prisoner? He knew this person was not an ordinary prisoner, but someone who must no more than he was letting on.

Jake continued to look at the prisoner and finally asked, "So what is your story?"

The prisoner looked at Jake and answered, "It's a long one, but as long as we are in here, we are safe. I should know because I had this room installed and no one knows about it."

"What do you mean that you had this room installed?" Henderson interrupted.

"I did say that my story would be very long," the prisoner replied. "Everyone might as well sit down at the table and listen to what I have to say."

Jake, Sasha, and Henderson were very intrigued to hear what this prisoner had to say. They sat down with Jake as the prisoner took the head of the table. Sasha grabbed his hand and told him that they were ready for anything that he had to say.

"First of all," he began, "I want to thank the three of you for getting me out of that cell. I have been in prison cell for the last two years. This is the first conversation that I have had with anyone outside a barred room for that long as well. I thought that I was losing my mind, but somehow I kept it together and I knew one day that I would be freed."

Jake nodded and said, "We are not out of the woods just yet, but it we are getting close."

"You are right," he answered. "But I am a lot further than I have been in quite awhile and I think the three of you can get us all out of this mess."

Sasha grabbed his hand and asked him, "Why have you been imprisoned for so long?"

"That is an easy question to answer," the prisoner with a smile. He then removed Sasha's hand and sat back in his chair. The three Americans listened intently. The prisoner continued by saying, "Two years ago, I was sleeping in my bed and I was awoken in my sleep by a loud sound at my door. I can remember so vividly that it feels like yesterday. It was probably the worst day of my life. Anyway, I awoke and saw five armed men come into my room. I immediately sprung to my feet, but it was too late to do anything. One of the men hit me in the back of the head and I fell down to my knees. Another kicked me and I fell to my back.

Before I knew it, I was tied up and they put a blind fold over my eyes. Even though I could not see, I felt that they led me outside. I was put into the back of a vehicle and after about an hour or so drive I ended up at some sort of prison camp. It was strange, because the camp was fairly big, but I was the only prisoner. It was not hard to figure out that the camp that had been secluded and that was supposed to be kept secret. They kept me in my cell and fed me one meal a day. I was also put through terrible torture and drugged. This is the most sober I have felt since I was captured and imprisoned. I have not been drugged for the last two days and I can thank you guys for that."

"Why do you want thank us for that?" Jake wondered.

"I believe that they forgot to drug me, because they were too busy worrying about you." Jake looked back at the prisoner and asked. "Who is they?"

The prisoner said, "I will finish the story and tell you who they is. I had been in the camp for almost two years until Sasha was put into the cell next to me."

He then looked at Sasha and said, "I knew you were there and tried to help you, but I was incoherent most of the time."

Sasha grabbed his hand again and said, "You helped me more than you know."

The prisoner smiled again continued, "The guards caught me trying to communicate to you. They came in real late at night when you were asleep and blindfolded me once again. I was then brought back to the cell that you found me in. I have been there for the last month or so."

The prisoner was very calm as he spoke. As he had said, he had not talked to anyone in almost two years and he felt that they were trustworthy and that he could tell them anything.

Jake interrupted him and asked, "I want to go back to the beginning. Why did they kidnap you? What did they want?"

The prisoner looked up to them and with a very serious face said, "They wanted my power."

Henderson was sitting on the edge of his chair listening to every word the prisoner was saying, but now he needed to know what he was talking about. "What power could you possibly possess?" He questioned.

The prisoner leaned up in his chair and said in a very serious tone, "The power that I am talking about is being able to change the world."

Jake could not believe what this guy was saying. He laughed a little under his breath and felt that the drugs had yet to wear off him yet. He decided to play along and see if he was really off his rocker. Jake asked the man, "How can one man change the world?"

The prisoner looked at all three of them and said, "By finding a discovery that could single handily abolish the energy crisis the whole world has been experiencing over the last ten years. This discovery would also bring peace and prosperity to a country that has been poverty stricken for much of its existence. I was poised to help this country accomplish that, but I was taken away against my will and locked up in a prison cell."

The Americans knew exactly what he was talking about, but only Jake asked, "So what you are saying is that you are…"

The prisoner interrupted and said, "I am Mahmud Osman Kier, the leader of East Africa. I have not been able to say that for the last two years, but it fell off my tongue as easily as it did two years ago when I was not imprisoned."

The three Americans were shocked. They knew of the leader and Jake and Sasha had even seen pictures, but now they were sitting across the table from him. They three Americans looked at each other and were nodding finally seeing that the prisoner did resemble the pictures that they had seen. This was the leader of East Africa, but he looked weak and frail. He was not the powerful man he once was. They still wanted to know why he had he been imprisoned for the last two years.

Henderson looked at Kier and explained to him how he had come onto the scene. He gave Kier the shortened down version and quickly finished his story. But he still wanted to know more of the Kier's story. He then asked Kier, "Is Qatar behind all of this?"

Kier hated hearing that name and nodded his head in disgust. He answered Henderson by saying, "That name makes me sick. I knew him for over ten years. He was my right hand man, but I will admit that my first mistake with him was trusting in that man from day one. I brought him into my government because he was so helpful to me early on in my career, but little did I know he was planning to betray me when he had the chance."

"I just don't understand how you could let that happen," Jake said abruptly.

Henderson put his two cents into the conversation. "I agree with Jake. How could a smart guy like you let someone like that come in and take over your leadership?"

"I truly believe," Kier responded "that it was his plan from the day that we met. Looking back on it he was never very helpful. Back then, Qatar was just a cleric and he came to me with a promise to help take East Africa to greatness. I was young and naïve and allowed him to do anything he wanted."

Kier continued, "Qatar and I took my message of hope and prosperity to the streets and almost overnight people were on board with me. Because there was no election we were able to take over this newly formed country. Since Qatar had shown me so much loyalty, I promised him whatever he wanted. He chose to create a small military force that he alone would control. He told me I could not ask any questions as long as he did not break any of the countries laws. Unfortunately, I agreed. That was my downfall. Since then, it has been downhill. I admit it now that I was wrong. He has done nothing, but over turn all my policies. I just hope that my country can recover."

Jake could see the hurt in Kier's eyes. Jake always seemed to have a good since for people and he could tell that Kier was sincere and he seemed like a good man. "Go on," Jake said as he wanted to hear more of what Kier was saying.

"I did allow Qatar to form a small militia. He controlled it and did what he wanted. I never questioned him, because he did not break any laws, until two years ago."

"What did he do?" Henderson asked. Kier looked toward Henderson and said, "He took over the oil find and killed people. The people that were killed were my friends, they were close to me. I finally found out about it, but by that time it was too late and I was imprisoned by his men."

"You said that you were imprisoned for almost two years," Sasha said. "If that is true, and the oil wasn't discovered about six months ago, then how did you know anything about it?"

Kier grinned, "Because, we discovered it over two years ago."

Jake, Sasha, and Henderson were could not believe it. They were led to believe that the discovery was found only a few months back, but instead they found out that East Africa and Kier had known about this for some time.

"Did you want to keep this a secret?" Henderson asked."

Kier looked at the three of them and with a very serious look on his face said, "I was planning on sharing the discovery with the world, but Qatar had different plans in store for it and me. I was planning on a news telecast, to tell the world of this discovery, and then telling the world about Qatar and his antics. Unfortunately Qatar had gotten wind of my idea and obviously did not want me to share that information. I felt safe, but he had someone in the inside. He was able to slip his men past my guards and into my room. As I told you earlier, the next day I was in a prison camp. I had not seen his evilness until then. He went to the oil find, killed my people and had me imprisoned. He had a very good plan and carried it out to a t."

Jake had to know one thing so he asked, "How did you find the oil in the first place?"

"I had an American confidant," Kier answered. "He was one of the smartest men that I had ever known. He brought in the best engineers that the world had to offer and they did testing for almost three years. They found a lot of activity in the northeast part of the country. They set up drills and before long they found the oil."

"What happened to the American and the engineers," Sasha asked to Kier. "Why did they not tell you what they had found?"

Kier looked at Sasha and said, "Unfortunately, those were the friends that Qatar killed. He did not want them to tell their story."

"Qatar must be stopped. We have to take care of him and send him to his Maker," Jake said as he looked at all of them. "We need to get you back to your leadership and get rid of this guy."

Kier looked at all three and let them know that there was more to the story. "During my tenure, I brought the United States into the country. I opened up our doors and allowed the United States to come in and become our ally when no other countries in our region would. The United States helped us more than anyone really knows. They not only brought in business, but they helped build hospitals across the country, helped with our infrastructure, and gave us billions of dollars. I welcomed them with open arms and had my countrymen welcome the Americans as well. I believed that even though the oil was found in our country that the United States had a right to it. Qatar, on the other hand, did not have the same views that I did."

* * *

Qatar and his men continued to look over the entire palace and still could not locate Kier and the Americans. As usual, Qatar became angry and called to one of his men that was checking on the one of the monitors.

"Any sign of them?" he asked.

"I have checked every monitor and there is no sign of them anywhere," the man answered.

Qatar called another guard and asked, "Are you sure that you sealed off that secret entrance that leads to the outside?"

The man was nervous, but had to answer the question. He said, "Yes sir, there is no way anyone could get out that way. The entrance is completely bricked in now and we have a guy watching it just in case. I believe that they still have to be in the palace somewhere."

Qatar became angrier. He started to yell at his men. He paced up and down the floor with a gun in his hand. He called to one of his men in his militia to see how the battle was going on outside of the palace.

"Have you not eliminated the rebels yet?" Qatar asked.

"We are bogged down right now," his man answered as explosions continued in the background. "They hit us with those explosives and it put a little dent into our situation. I am feeling better about this now, but I will let you know when we get the upper hand."

Qatar became outraged. He was losing the battle inside and outside. He needed to find the four escapees and he needed to find them as soon as possible. If he did not find them then he knew that he would pay the consequences. He knew that he could not let the prisoners escape.

"You keep your eyes on those monitors," he demanded, "and if you see any movement you let me know. Any movement, do you understand?"

The man knew that Qatar meant business and answered him with a loud, "Yes, sir!" Qatar left the room and went back into the hallway of the palace. He needed to keep his composure and at this moment, that was very difficult for him to do.

* * *

The hidden room had been a life saver for Kier and the Americans. They were all able to get out of a situation where their lives were in danger and were able to get their focus back to the job at hand, and that was escaping. There was just one hitch, and that was that they were still here to do a job and that job was eliminating Qatar.

Jake asked Kier, "I wonder why Qatar has kept you alive for so long? I hate to be so blunt, but the way he kills people that get in his way, why not kill you and move on?"

Sasha could not believe Jake would ask that and looked at Kier and tried to apologize with her eyes.

Kier understood what Jake was saying and he responded by saying, "That is a good question. I wondered that myself, but one night while I was at the prison camp, Qatar came to my cell. I could tell he had been drinking. I asked him the question that you just asked me 'Why not just eliminate me.' He said that he wanted to, but that he couldn't. He said that I was too valuable and that eliminating me would mess up the major plan. He did not go into any more detail and he left without answering my question."

The three Americans listened very intently. Since Sasha had been in the prison camp, she could relate to what Kier had gone through. She continued to show compassion and asked him to continue with his story.

"As you know I live on a dirt floor," Kier continued. "But that was not the worst part. I was tortured every day. I was also drugged to the point that I was mostly comatose for weeks on end. I had no idea who I was or what I was doing."

Sasha now understood why Kier became a puppet to Qatar. "What was the reason for all of this? Why did Qatar do all these things to you?" She asked.

Kier looked her in the eye and answered, "Because, he needed me to do his dirty work."

Jake said back to him, "You did do all this against your will, didn't you?"

"Not exactly," Kier answered.

"What do you mean," Henderson asked, feeling left out of the conversation.

Kier continued, "I did not want to die. Between my moments when I was not drugged up, and they were few and far between, Qatar told me that as long as I cooperated, I would remain alive. This is something that I am not proud of, but I have been afraid of dying my whole life. It had become a game to me. I had to prove to myself that I could overcome my fear of death, but I could not and put myself in front of my country. I was not willing to die for my country."

Jake did not like Kier's answer and asked him, "How bad was your torture?"

Kier, the great leader of East Africa, looked down at his feet and said, "I was tortured and belittled. I thought to myself, here I am, the leader of East Africa and I was treated no better than a dog by a man that I trusted for over ten years. Unfortunately, instead of fighting back, I gave in to his wishes. I have regretted that and after my last telecast, I told him that was my last one. My fear of death had passed and after seeing the three of you in action, I have a new approach to the way I will do things in the future."

"What will that be?" Sasha asked.

"It is hard for me to explain, but I feel that you will see me differently from now on."

Jake had a hard time respecting Kier. He was thankful to him for getting them out of harm's way, but Jake could never give in to anyone, no matter what the cost. He did not want to throw stones at Kier because he knew that all people were different and that some people did not have his strong will. He felt in his heart that Kier would need their help in regaining control of his country. It was not going to be easy, but he knew that the three of them could help him.

Getting back to the story, Sasha asked, "Why did Qatar have you do the telecast? Did he ever give you an answer for that?"

Kier shook his head, "Qatar never gave me an answer, but I can tell you that he had a plan. The plan was a simple one, but a grotesque one at that. First he would eliminate our people. He wanted to make sure that I still looked as if I was in charge so that I would take the rap for all the rape, murder, and any other terrible thing that he and his men did to our people. East Africa was becoming a prosperous country and I was very popular, not only with our people, but with the United States as well. He knew that he could not take over power without the support of the people and he also knew that the United States would not stand for him taking over. The second part of the plan was to get the United States out of our country. That is why he had me hold the press conference to get them out of our country and go to the United Nations for help. I did not want to do that, but he gave me no choice."

Kier continued, "Qatar wanted to make it look as if I was power hungry. He knew that East Africa could become a powerful country with the oil discovery. He also felt that if he made it look as if I was responsible for all the horrible things that my people were experiencing, they would want to revolt against me. He would be there to save the day and become the leader of the revolution. Since he already had me captured, he would lead me out into the people and they would be the judge and jury. I would be found guilty and possibly hung. He then would take control and become supreme leader of East Africa. That would be his final act of the plan. The only problem is that he did not foresee the three of you coming in and messing everything up."

Henderson gave his point of view, "That seemed like a good idea for him, but as you just said, we have put a little dent in his plan."

"Exactly," Kier said, "That is why we have got to get out of here and get to the people. That is the only way to stop him and his evil antics."

Jake could read people fairly easily and knew that Kier was not telling them everything about the palace. He looked over and said to Kier, "You know a lot more about this palace than you have told us."

Kier wondered what he was talking about and looked back at Jake and said, "Why do you say that?"

Jake answered, "I feel that you brought us into this secret room and let us refuel and get our energy back. I know that you have a different way for us to get out of here."

"Jake," Kier said back to him, "You seem to read me like a book. You are right. There is another way out of here. I do not think that this way will get us out of the palace, but it will get us to another section of the palace. Hopefully, we can surprise our enemy and take them out, one at a time."

Kier got up from the table and told the three of them to gear up. He wanted to make sure that they had all their weapons loaded and ready for action. He then walked over and pushed a button that was hidden behind a frame on the wall. Another door on the other side of the room opened. Jake looked at all the others and said, "That's our queue; let's go get 'em."

CHAPTER 31

It had been an hour since Kier and the three Americans were last scene. Qatar was losing his patience and wanted a report from anyone with good news for him. His men were too frightened of him and did not want to come forth with the bad news that nothing had changed.

Qatar knew that time was running out on him and needed someone to give him and update. He yelled to anyone who would answer, "What is the status on the missing prisoner and the Americans."

No one dared to answer him and fearing the worst. This angered him so he grabbed one of his men by the collar and yelled at him, "I am sick and tired of all your incompetence. I do not care what you have to do to find them. Tear these walls down if you have to but I will tell you that if the prisoners are not found within the next five minutes, someone is going die and it is not going to be me! Now get going and find me those prisoners." His men did not move as quickly as Qatar wanted them to and he yelled again to them, "Get moving, you sons-a-bitches!"

* * *

The four escapees were walking through a dark and tight entrance way when Jake mumble under his breath to Kier, "Where are we going."

Kier told him not to worry, just to trust him and they would come out of their hiding place soon. He let them know to be prepared to face Qatar and his men and reminded the three of them that no one was a friend, in the palace. They should be prepared to shoot and not hesitate to take a person out if they had to. Jake knew after what had transpired earlier, that the three of them would ready for anything that presented itself to them.

*   *   *

There was still no visual on the screen of the four escapees. The man responsible for the watching the monitors, approached Qatar and let him know that he had good news for him. Qatar smiled and told his men that this is what he had been waiting for and let the man know that he had his full attention.

The man said, "I have studied the monitors and the tape and have not seen anyone outside of us. Because there is only one way in or out of the palace, I believe that there is no way that they have left this building. They are still somewhere in the palace. Because I have not seen them in any room or hallway, I have reason to believe that they are in an area that cameras are not located in. We need to get our hands on the blueprint of the palace and figure out what room that might be."

Even though Qatar did not get a location of the escapees, he still felt that this was the first bit of good news that he had heard about this situation. He nodded to the man and told him to get a blueprint of the palace and to figure out what room did not have cameras located in them. He then radioed to everyone that was in the palace to expect the prisoners to be hiding in some sort of secret room. The men wanted to start shooting at the walls, but Qatar held back on that idea. Deep down he wanted to shoot up all the walls, but did not want to damage the palace, especially if he was planning on living there. He let them know to keep their eyes open and to be ready for anything that might come their way.

* * *

The three Americans and Kier were coming to the end of the long dark entrance way. He wanted to make sure that they had the guns loaded and that they would be ready for anything. Kier was the first on to the doorway that led back out into the palace. The door had a small peep hole on it so that he was able to look out and see if there was anyone outside the door..

Qatar's men were scattered individually throughout the palace. One of Qatar's men was walking down the hall checking rooms and looking for them. He had turned the corner and had his back turned from the doorway of the secret tunnel. Kier motioned to Jake on what to do and he quietly opened the door. The moment it opened, Jake jumped out of the entrance, landing on the guard and covering the guard's mouth. Henderson followed Jake and hit the man on the back of the head, knocking him out and sending him to down to the ground. They tied him up and hid him in a room.

Unfortunately, they could not stay out of sight of the cameras. There were too many of them all over the palace and that they had been spotted. Jake informed three others to be prepared for what was about to happen.

* * *

"We have located them, sir. They are in the northeast section of the palace." Qatar was informed from the man watching the palace monitors. "Unfortunately, I have bad news. We are another man down."

Qatar was relieved that they had located the escapees, but could not believe that he had lost another man. He knew that he and his men had to get together and act quickly. They were going

321

up very experience tacticians and if they did not get together, they would be eliminated one by one.

"We need to get ready for them and fast," Qatar said to his head man. "Get on the radio and inform all of my men that are in the palace where the prisoners are. Let's face the head on."

Qatar's head man radioed the three remaining men in the palace and informed them that they had located the prisoners. They were to meet back at the west wing of the palace and regroup. They would get the instructions from Qatar on what to do when they all back together.

* * *

Jake was determined to get the four of them out of the palace and started to make his way to the door. He did not want anything to happen to Kier so he made him stay close behind the three of them as they all moved slowly and diligently down a hallway. He knew that Qatar and his men could be around any corner and could strike them at any time. He wanted Kier to be protected, because it was vital for the leader of East Africa to survive at all cost and get his power back. Jake knew that He could put his policies back into place and eliminate all the things that Qatar had done in the country.

They continued down the hallway and came to a corner of the palace. Jake raised his hand and motioned all of them to get up against the wall. He eyed Henderson and motioned to him that he felt that Qatar and his men were on the other side of the wall. Henderson nodded and motioned for Sasha to make sure she took care of Kier. She looked back at Henderson and gave him the thumbs up. Jake back at Henderson and motioned with his fingers that they would strike on the count of three. Jake held up one finger, then two, then three. Jake turned the corner and found nothing in front of him.

Henderson smiled at Jake and said, "I guess you're losing your intuition, but hey, at least it got my adrenaline pumping."

Jake scowled at Henderson, hoping that he would become more serious in the job at hand. Henderson understood that scowl and knew what Jake was telling him, even though he did not speak the words. Jake might had been wrong about the corner of the hallway, but he still felt that Qatar and his men were close. He pointed to Sasha and Kier and told them stay close and up against the wall. He wanted to continue to make sure that both stayed out of harm's way. Even though Sasha could take care of herself, she obeyed and kept her hand on Kier. She wanted to make sure that he was protected at all times.

*   *   *

Qatar assembled his remaining men and went over his plan to capture the escapees. Qatar made sure the trap doors were raised because he wanted easy access throughout the palace for not only himself, but for Kier and the Americans. He knew where they were located and knew that the only way out of the palace was to come toward him and his men. Qatar would not be caught off guard this time around and would not make any mistakes. He knew that this would probably be their last chance to capture them because if he did not and they escaped, he knew that his leader would eliminate him. Qatar had other plans and dying was not one of them.

The monitor showed Qatar where prisoners were located and where they were going. He knew he had to take advantage and go after them at this time. He would not let them get by and informed his me to shoot to kill.

He wanted to make sure that his men knew the seriousness of the situation at hand. He said to them, "The American's will kill you. They have a prisoner who is insane and had informed them to not stop until all of us are dead. You have no choice but to strike them down. I will not have it any other way."

The men took their places behind walls and in doorways. Qatar told them that this would be their greatest triumph and that they will continue to hold on to the palace. His men's loyalties were unquestioned. They were willing to die for him, but the question still remained, how loyal was Qatar to his men?

* * *

The battle outside the palace had been going back and forth for the last three hours. People who lived in the marketplace, where the battle was raging, had evacuated for their own safety. Jerdan, Hare and Trahan saw that their militia was not only running out of ammunition, but their spirits were becoming low as well. They had never been in a fight like this, especially for their life and it was taking a toll on everyone that was involved.

"How are our guys holding up?" Jerdan asked Hare.

"Not good. We never expected this long of a battle. We have lost a few men and the heat from the sun is really weakening them," Hare said.

Trahan agreed and said, "This might be the case, but our men are resilient and are still able to hold off Qatar's men. I don't know for how long, but I feel that we can continue until the morning. I will continue to inspire them. Hopefully they will continue the great feat that they have been able to do so far."

The heat from the daylight sun was still upon them, but it was late in the afternoon and night fall was just around the corner. Trahan knew that when night came, it could give him and his men a break. He had not heard from Diotrice, since she had left for the palace and only could hope that what he and his men were doing would eventually help her in her quest to save Jake.

* * *

The four escapees had made it to the other end of the palace without any combat. They had only run into one of Qatar's men at the beginning, but eliminated him from the equation. They knew that getting out of the palace was a different scenario. The four of them got to another hallway and could not see the end of it. Jake had been in these situations in his past and his intuition told him that Qatar was on the other side waiting on them. Jake motioned to Henderson and explained to him what he wanted to do. Kier knew what he wanted to do, but told him of another way.

"We know that Qatar and his men are waiting for us on the other side of this wall. Let me try talking to him and reasoning with him. He did work for me for ten years. He may listen to what I have to say."

Jake was a little reluctant, but felt Kier knew something that he did not about Qatar and decided to give it a try. Deep down, Jake knew that reasoning with Qatar would be a lost cause, but he knew Kier would not back down and decided to give him a chance to have it his way. Jake told Kier to wait a second and then he yelled out, "Qatar! I know that you are on the other side of the wall. I would like to talk a little bit."

Qatar heard what Jake had said and looked at his men and motioned to them that they needed to keep quiet. His men acknowledged him and remained quiet. Qatar did not want to talk, but let his actions take care of anything that needed to be said. Jake continued to yell to Qatar, but Qatar refused to answer. Kier continued to encourage Jake to continue calling Qatar. He knew that Qatar would eventually answer back. Jake felt that it would not work, but continued to yell, hoping Qatar would say something back to him. Finally, after about ten minutes of screaming his name, Qatar finally yelled back to him.

"What in the hell do you want to talk about!"

Jake finally got Qatar to say something and knew that would buy them some time. He wanted to open up a line of communication between them. Jake felt that the more that Qatar talked the better chance they had to thinking of a way of escaping.

"Let's talk about your day. How has it been going?" Jake said in his smart aleck tone of voice.

Henderson and Sasha just shook their heads. They knew that the comment would not make Qatar easier to work with. Jake waited and did not get a response. Henderson whispered to Jake to get to the point and to quit playing around. Jake knew that he was right. He was not used to talking out of a situation like this. He always settled the matter with his gun, but for Kier's sake needed to try a different way to open up the lines of communication.

But before Jake could correct himself, Qatar yelled back, "I do not have time for your jokes. I say we just all settle this with a little gun fight."

That is what Jake would have wanted ten years ago, but things had changed. He was not the only one involved now. He had already lost two friends during this mission and did not want to lose anymore. He looked over at his friend, Henderson, and all he could think about was his friend's wife and children. Jake could not chance his friend's safety, especially if there was another way to solve this small crisis.

Jake then looked at Sasha and knew that he had a chance for a relationship, something that he had yet to experience in his lifetime. He knew that he did not want to lose her in a gun fight. Finally he saw Kier, the leader of East Africa, a country that could single-handily eliminate an energy crisis that the United States had been suffering for the last decade. He knew that if Kier was no longer around than the country of East Africa would lose all hope and the energy crisis would get out of control.

Jake did not want to get into a war of words with Qatar. He knew that he could never appeal to Qatar, but felt he could appeal to his men. First he wanted to attack Qatar. He knew that Qatar would become angry at anything that attacked his psyche. He would first go after Qatar, then move to sway his men.

"Qatar, what kind of name is that, Qatar. Did your mother give you that name? That just sounds like a name you would give to someone who just dropped a load in their pants, don't you think. "

Qatar became incensed. He was tired of Jake and would not allow him to humiliate him any longer. Jake was a pain in side and wanted him dead. He yelled back to Jake, "You have gotten on my last nerve and now you will die by my hands."

Jake rolled his eyes and started to laugh at loud. He knew that he was getting under Qatar's skin and wanted to keep baiting him. He yelled back to him, "Qatar, your leadership is second to none. You have done wonders with this country since you have taken over. I know that you want to eliminate all of us, but we all know that is not going to happen. But somehow if you did succeed, what would you do next? What do you have on your agenda for the future of your men and this country?"

Henderson gave his friend a surprised looked on his face, and had no idea where Jake was going with what he was saying, but he had seen him in action to many times to ask any question. Sasha wanted to Jake to stop, but Henderson stopped her and whispering to her that Jake must have a plan. He wanted it to play out and she was reluctant, but agreed to let Jake continue.

Qatar did not know what Jake was trying to do, but decided to play along and said to him, "First, I would just kill you, your two friends, and the prisoner. I would not allow you anytime to live after I captured you. Just take a bullet and put it between your eyes."

Jake had been instructed by Kier that Qatar liked to talk, especially about himself. He felt that he had an in and would play this to his advantage.

"You mentioned the prisoner that we have with us," Jake said. "How do you know him and why don't you call him by his name?"

Qatar was getting irritated with Jake and did not like the question. He yelled back at Jake, "What do you know about the prisoner?"

Jake could hear in Qatar's voice that he was becoming upset. He knew that he must have hit a nerve and responded, "I know that that the prisoner has something that you crave at night. He has something that you have to kill to get. What he has, you will never have, and that is being the leader of this great nation. He has been forced by your hand for the last two years to do what you want him to do. That will end today. He will get his leadership back and you will be the one who will suffer."

Qatar did not like what Jake had said. His men could see the anger in his eyes. "That is not how I see it," Qatar said. "Right now I am exactly where I want to be. I am not the one running, trying to escape. It seems to me that you have to get by me to get out of here."

Jake wanted to keep Qatar talking. Kier continued to urge Jake on as he kept nodding his head, encouraging him. Jake continued to egg Qatar on, "Have you told you men the truth about yourself. Better yet, have you let them know what will happen to them? What will happen to their fate? We have all seen the plans that you have in place. We all know that you want to become dictator and eliminate your men if you had to?"

Jake had no idea what Qatar would do to his men, but he wanted them to at least think about it. He knew that they could hear what was being said and hoped that what they heard, would open their ears a little.

Qatar's men looked at him to see his reaction. Qatar did not like the accusation and yelled back at Jake, but was not as authoritative as he had been. He said, "You do not know what you're talking about."

Jake could hear the indecisiveness in Qatar's voice. He knew that his men had to be looking at Qatar, following every word and seeing if they would be any part of Qatar's dictatorship.

"Qatar," Jake yelled. "I know exactly what I am talking about. I might have been out of the game for a little while, but I have run into guys like you. Actually, you are small potatoes next to who

I have run it to before. These guys have much bigger balls than you could ever dream of having and they all want the same thing; Power. They will eliminate anyone who gets in their way. They will do what has to be done, no matter what it takes, even if that means turning on your friends."

He waited on Qatar's remark, but heard nothing. Jake had worn thin on Qatar and he had enough of what Jake was saying. He yelled to his men, "I am tired of this guy. Let's take him."

His men did not follow his orders. They heard everything that Jake had said and seem to be wavering a little on what they were going to do. They had been by Qatar's side for a long time and seem to struggle at what they wanted to do. They did not want to move and wanted to hear what Jake had to say. Qatar had never had his men disobey him and he became outraged, but tried to stay under control. He knew that if he did not maintain his composure, he would lose their loyalty. He had to think of something fast and was about to say something, when Jake interrupted his plan.

"Cat got your tongue, Qatar?" Jake yelled back after not getting a response. "Are you worried that whatever you say, your men might not believe? If your men haven't realized that you can't be trusted, I can assure you that they will not have a problem realizing it now."

Jake changed the tone in his voice and then addressed Qatar's men, "I do not know how long you have worked with Qatar, but I will tell you that he will turn on you in a heartbeat. He worked and pledged his loyalty for ten years to Mahmoud Osman Kier, the true leader of East Africa, only later to betray him. You wonder to yourselves what I am talking about. I will give you the answer. Your so called leader, the one that you have followed and gave your loyalty for so long, betrayed the true leader of East Africa. He kidnapped him, kept him locked up like a caged animal, and forced on him, drugs to control his mind.

You need to look deep into your soul. Qatar has murdered and raped your countrymen to get to where he is. The fact that you're still alive is simple. He needs you right now, to do his dirty work. When he finally gets what he wants, he will do to you what he has done to everyone else that has ever gotten in his way, and that is eliminating them. That is what he tried to do with the real leader of East Africa, Mahmoud Osman Kier. Unfortunately, we spoiled his plan and rescued Kier before he had a change to kill him."

Qatar's men heard every word that Jake spoke and it did make them think. Even though they had been loyal to Qatar for so long, there was never a night where they felt safe and could sleep, wondering if they would wake up the next day alive. What Jake had to say, did resonate in their minds.

One of the men yelled out, "How do we really know what you say is true. How do we know that who you speak of, is really Mahmoud Osman Kier?"

The men all wanted to know the answer to the question. Qatar had never been truthful of what had happened to the leader of East Africa. Qatar had told his men that Qatar had lost trust in the world and had secluded himself in the top floor of the palace. He told them that the prisoner was a look alike of Kier, and that the real Kier had him do the video press releases. He had them convinced that Kier became a recluse and did not want anything to do with anyone.

He also told them more lies of Kier. He told them that Kier eventually wanted him to be his successor, but the people of East Africa would never accept it. He told them that Kier ordered the rapes and murders, and that they had to do what Kier told them to do. He told his men that Kier had gone crazy and that they were going to overtake him within days. His men had believed Qatar for the last two years, but now it seemed to them that it might be a lie.

Jake yelled back to one of the men and said, "Obviously, your leader has not been truthful to you. As I said earlier, he has kept your true leader, Mahmoud Osman Kier, locked in prison cells for two years. He has tortured him, belittled him, and forced him to put on telecast, making him to be a ruthless dictator against his will. Listen to me, the man that we rescued out of the prison cell downstairs, is the true and only leader of East Africa."

Kier knew that he had to approach the men on the other side of the wall. He knew that this would be the only way that they would believe what Jake was saying. He hoped that if he approached them, that they would drop their weapons and could help bring Qatar to justice.

Kier looked at Jake and nodded as to say that Jake had done a good job speaking to the men. He knew that he had to speak up and tell them who he was. He yelled to the men, "I am Mahmoud Osman Kier, the true leader of East Africa. I have acted cowardly over the last two years towards my country. I have only cared for the safety of myself, putting my life in front of yours and all the people of this wonderful country. I will not allow myself to do that anymore. You may find it hard to believe, but it took three Americans to risk their lives for me to see my mistake."

Kier did not get a response from the men and because of that reaction, he felt that this would be the ideal time to convince them who he was. He slowly walked around the wall toward the men. Jake reached out to stop him from making a mistake, but Kier shook his head to Jake and told him that this was the right thing for him to do and to let him go on. He assured Jake that this is what he needed to do and he hoped it would make the situation right again.

Kier did not know what his fate was going to be when he got to the other side of the wall. He did not know if he would be killed on the spot or accepted as the leader of East Africa. He was willing to accept what met him on the other side of the wall. He turned the corner, leaving the three Americans to wonder what his fate would be as well.

Qatar could tell that his men were not listening to what he telling them anymore. He knew that he had lost his men and figured that they were going to turn on him. He looked up and saw that his men were watching Kier walking towards them. He knew that this would be his best chance to leave while he still could and slipped out a doorway nearby that went upstairs to the upper level of the palace. This was an area that no one had ventured, for fear of the leader's wrath.

Kier walked toward the men, continuing to talk them and assuring them who he was. Once he got to them, they all knew that he was Kier and he was their true leader and the leader of East Africa.

They immediately dropped their guns and got down on their knees and said, "Sir, please forgive us. We had no idea. We felt that we were doing only the things that you wanted us to do."

The men stood up and embraced Kier. He told each one of them that he did not fault them for what they did. Kier took complete responsibility in what they had done. He wanted to make sure that each one of the men could trust him again.

Kier yelled to Jake, Sasha, and Henderson, telling them that it was safe to come around and join him. The three of them walked slowly around the wall, holding their guns up aimed and ready to shoot, not taking any chances. After they realized that Kier was safe and the men had dropped their guns, they lowered their weapon. Jake could see that all the men were smiling and enjoying the moment. He almost forgot about Qatar, but quickly remembered and noticed that he was missing.

"What happened to Qatar?" he asked the group of celebrating soldiers.

Kier looked at the men and wanted to know answerer as well. No one knew what had happened. There was so much commotion that was going on around them, that they did not realize he had left.

Jake looked at Qatar's men and said, "Qatar left you here, not caring for your fate and it seems now he is just trying to save his own neck. This just shows you what type of person he really is. He is nothing but a coward and I will make him pay."

Jake saw a door that had been left open. He asked Kier what the door led to. Kier explained to him that it led to the upper level of the palace and that it led into a big banquet room. There was also an exit that led to the roof. Jake knew that Qatar had gone through the door and was planning on escaping on the roof. He knew he did not have much time and needed to go after him. Kier tried to convince Jake that he wanted to go after him, but Jake had none of it. He needed Kier to go to the streets and end the conflict that was going outside. Jake knew that he could take care of Qatar and did not want to put Kier into anymore danger.

Jake told Henderson to go with Kier and help bring an end to what was going on in the streets. He also told the men to go and for reinforcement and to protect Kier. He wanted Sasha to stay behind in the palace, but she knew that Jake did not want her to do anything. She did not want to do that and demanded that she go with Jake. She persisted to the point that Jake finally agreed as long as he was in front of her at all times. She reluctantly agreed and picked up her gun and was ready to go.

Jake wished Henderson luck, but before he left he grabbed the rocket launcher that Henderson had been carrying around. He felt he might need it more than Henderson. Henderson did not like to part with it, but let Jake take, though he wanted Jake to know that he had grown attached to it. Jake assured Henderson not to worry and that he would have it back very soon. They gave each other high fives and headed out in different directions, Henderson took off outside to the capital's streets, while Jake and Sasha headed to the upper level of the palace. Neither of them knew what to expect.

CHAPTER 32

Jake and Sasha went through the doorway that led to the steps to the second level of the palace. Qatar had gone up to the top of the stairs and saw them coming after him. He fired a couple of rounds at them, but Jake and Sasha were ready for his attack and easily ducked out of the way.

Jake continued to get under Qatar's skin and yelled at him, "Is that the best you got. Why won't you come down here and face me like a man? It seems to me that you would rather run and hide like a scared little puppy dog."

Qatar was tired of the games Jake was playing and yelled back, "You can come up here and get me. I will be waiting." He then ran up the remaining stairs and out a doorway. He then disappeared on the second floor of the palace. Jake wanted to run and catch him but he decided to be more cautious and he and Sasha went up the stairs at a very slow pace.

Jake and Sasha had not been alone for a long time. There had been a romance that was brewing between the two earlier on when they had met, but neither had pushed the issue. Now that they were together, even though it was under extreme measures, Jake decided to talk to her a little more about their relationship. He said, "I know that this is not every girl's fantasy for a first date, but we can at least pretend it is."

While walking slowly behind him up the stairs, Sasha responded, "Why are you calling this a date? I mean, how do you know that I would accept any type of proposition from you."

"First of all," Jake responded with a smile, "I have rescued you on several occasions. That right there deserves at least one date. "

They continued to go up the steps watching and making sure that Qatar did not come out shooting at them again. "Second of all," Jake continued, "I know that you have the hots for me. I am good looking, have great self confidence, and I am very intelligent. The question you should ask yourself, is really would I even ask you out in the first place?"

Sasha could not help it and had to let out a laugh. "You seem to be pretty sure of yourself? The only thing that I see in you is a little immaturity."

Jake turned around and smiled at her. He started to laugh a little as well. "All girls like a little immaturity in some men. I might be a little immature, but I can tell that you like it in me."

Sasha had started to like Jake, and even though they were on a mission, she still liked to kid around with him. She hoped that she could get to know him better when all this was over. "I tell you what, Jake," Sasha said, while still grinning, "When we get Qatar, ask me out again and I will give you an answer."

Jake smiled back and said, "That gives me all the more reason to get the bad guy. Now I have to get serious, let's go get him."

Jake turned back and continued upstairs. Sasha followed slowly and cautiously behind him. They made it to the second level without incident; however, the door was shut and when they went to open it, it was locked. Jake told Sasha to stand back as he was going to kick the door in. He started to kick the lock and it did not budge. He put down his gun and backed up. He ran at the door and leaped towards it with his should smashing into it. He hit the door with such force; it knocked him down to the floor. The door did not swing open, but it did jar it and loosen it so that it could be opened. Instead of waiting for Jake to get off the floor, Sasha opened the door and went in to the second level first.

Jake had hit the door extremely hard and almost knocked himself out. He got up off the floor, picked up his gun and realized that Sasha had gone ahead of him. He knew that she hated Qatar and wanted to be the one that took him down, but he did not like the fact that she was in the room alone. It had been less than a minute when she went through the door, but Jake knew that was all the time that Qatar needed to overwhelm her. He opened the door and rushed in.

When Jake went through the door, he saw Sasha, but he also saw Qatar. He was holding her with his arm around her throat and a gun pointed at her head. He felt that might happen if one of them rushed in the room alone. He reached for his gun, but before was able to point it at Qatar; he felt a sharp pain on the back of his head. He started to black out and then his knees started to go out below him. He fell to the ground and passed out. Qatar threw Sasha to the ground and walked over to an unconscious Jake lying on the ground. He stood over Jake and began to laugh. He looked over at Sash and saw her lying on the ground as well and said to her, "I am still on top and always will be. Now get up and come with me."

* * *

Henderson and Kier had made it to the streets of the capital city. The tide had turned into their favor, and now they had Qatar's men under their command. As both of them suspected, it was chaotic, with gunfire sounding out all though out the city.

"We need to see if we can get these guys to stop shooting at each other," Henderson shouted to Kier hoping he could hear him over all the gunfire. "How do you think we can do this?"

Kier, who had been locked up over the last two years and had been completely stripped of any of his leadership, did not waste time taking charge again. He looked at one of the men and commanded him to get him in touch with the leader of conflict. The man could tell that Kier meant business and wasted no time in do exactly what Kier wanted. The man called the head of the conflict, got him on the radio and told him what was going on. The man then handed the radio to Kier. Kier told him who he was and that the fight was unnecessary. The leader of the conflict was hesitant to believe him. He did not want stop the conflict. Kier became upset and turned off the radio.

"That guy doesn't believe it is me," Kier yelled to the man who had handed him the radio. "Take me to him."

The man knew where the leader of the conflict was and had Kier and Henderson follow him. It was a quick walk and they came into the small bunker that the leader was in. They walked down into the bunker and everyone in the bunker looked up and saw Kier coming down into it. They all quit doing what they were doing and stood up. The leader had his back to him and did not see Kier come in. He started to yell at his subordinates, wondering why they had all stopped working. He turned around and saw Kier staring at him. He shut his mouth in awe as he thought he was dreaming.

Kier looked at everyone in the bunker and addressed them. "It is me, Mahmoud Osman Kier. I am alive and well." He then looked at the leader and said, "Is it you who I spoke to on the radio."

"Yes, sir," the man answered in a shriveled voice.

Kier was not upset, because he knew that it was hard to believe that he was indeed alive. He looked at the leader and told him that there was no harm done, but they needed to end the conflict immediately. Kier ordered him to end the gunfight. The leader made the call and reported that his men obeyed and they were now ducking bullets from the other side.

Kier turned to Henderson and said, "I did my part, now you need to do your part."

Henderson agreed and went over to the radio and made a call to Diotrice. Trahan answered the radio to Henderson dismay. Henderson got a little worried that something had happened to her and asked Trahan, "Where is Diotrice. Why did she not answer the call?"

Trahan could tell that Henderson was worried and immediately explained to him that she had not been injured, but she had left to go to the palace to give help to him and Jake. He was concerned that Henderson had not seen her. Henderson would worry about Diotrice later, but he needed to make sure that his militia would stop the fighting as well. He explained to Trahan the situation and told Trahan to call off the fighting. Trahan was relieved that Kier had been rescued and assured Henderson that they would call off all gun fire.

Henderson yelled over to Kier to inform him that he had gotten in touch with the leader on the other side of the conflict and that they had ordered a cease fire and that the shooting would be stopped. Both Henderson and Kier were relieved. It seemed that everything was getting back to normal. Henderson felt he had done his duty and knew that his friend would need him. He explained to Kier that he needed to get back to the palace as soon as possible. Kier agreed and told Henderson that he had the situation under control. They shook hands and Henderson headed out of the bunker.

* * *

Jake had been out for awhile, but finally started to open his eyes. He could see in front of him and he tried to stand up, but could not. He looked down and saw that his hands and legs were tied to a chair. The back of his head was throbbing. He realized that he must have been hit in the back of the head with something that knocked him out. He then began to wonder how long he was knocked out and did then he started to remember seeing

Sasha being held at gun point by Qatar. He became worried that something bad had happened to her. His vision had not completely come back to him and he could not see very far in front of him. He decided to yell out her name, hoping to hear her voice. He did not hear her voice, but heard someone else's voice.

"Calm down," the voice said. "She is fine."

Jake could tell that the voice came from behind him and that it was not that of Qatar's. Jake tried to turn his head around, but still could not see who it was. He felt he had heard the voice before, but could not remember from where.

"Quit struggling," the voice continued. "You are not going to be able to go anywhere. You may as well get comfortable. It seems that we have a lot to talk about."

Jake looked out of the corner of his eye and saw a figure come out from behind a doorway. Jake could not tell who it was, but it did not take long for him to figure it out.

The figure who was continuing to come towards Jake said, "Hello Mustang. Yes, it is me, Higgins. It has been a long time hasn't it Jake."

Jake could not believe that Higgins, the man who had kicked him out of the agency ten years ago, was standing in front of him. He had always wanted to face him, to tell him what he thought of him, but he never thought it would be under these circumstances. Jake wanted to ask him all kinds of questions, but the first thing out of his mouth was, "What have you done with Sasha?"

Higgins started to laugh. He got a chair and pulled it in front of Jake. He sat down, grabbed a cigarette out of his pocket and lit it. He inhaled it and blew the smoke in Jake's direction. Jake was his best pupil and in some aspect, he was happy to see him. He looked at Jake and said, "Aren't you happy to see me?"

Jake became agitated and again asked where Sasha was, but threw in a couple of non flattering words of what he thought of Higgins.

Higgins smiled and replied, "Where's the love? Anyway after ten years, the first thing that comes out of your mouth is where some chick is. Come on Mustang, you got to have something more to say to me than that."

Jake did not like that Higgins was in front of him, but wanted to make sure that Sasha was fine. "Listen, you low life piece of crap, I do not have much to say to you anymore. I am over what you did to me ten years ago," even though he was not, he continued "All I want to know is where Sasha is and if she is o.k."

Higgins knew that Jake was upset, so he answered, "Calm down. No one is hurt. Everything is fine."

Higgins saw something in Jake he had never seen before, caring for someone else. He said, "Is there something that you want to tell me, Mustang. It seems to me that you care for this girl."

Jake did not answer him. Higgins continued to bate him with questions. "Do you care for her? You are not going anywhere. We can sit hear all day. It does not matter to me."

Jake was upset, but tried to hold it in. He hated this man who was sitting in front of him, but he could not do anything about it. He could only look at Higgins and mutter out, "You better not have done anything to here."

Higgins interrupted, "Or what if I did? What are you going to do about it, Mustang?"

Jake was tired of these games Higgins was playing. "First of all, quit calling me Mustang. I have not gone by that name in ten years and can't stand it now because you gave it to me. Second, you better not have done anything to Sasha or the last breath that you take will be the sight of me killing you."

Higgins found it amusing how agitated Jake had become. He wanted to continue the game he was playing and said, "You really have no leg to stand on right now, do you? You are tied up and have no idea what has happened to your girlfriend. I will get to that in due time, but first we need to talk. When you calm down and I finish what I have to say, I will tell you what I have done with the girl. I do have a question for you, do you want to hear what I have to say or do you want to cry a little bit more about the girl. I think that you will find it interesting and it might answer some of your questions about what happened over ten years ago."

What happened to Jake ten years ago had eaten at him for a long time. He looked up and Higgins could see the interest in his eyes. "Yes, that is right Jake. I know everything that happened ten years ago. Do you want to know?"

"Higgins," Jake said, "I know that you told me that Sasha is alive, but how can I trust you."

Higgins answered, "That is something that you have to figure out, but I can tell you that as of right now she is fine. But I cannot promise for how long. She will remain unharmed as long as you and I are talking to me. Do you understand?"

Jake did and he nodded yes. "Higgins," he said, "I have been waiting for ten years. Go ahead and tell me your story."

* * *

Henderson was getting closer to the palace. He was running along the empty streets, but he heard a gunshot. He had no idea where it had come from and decided to hide behind a fruit stand full of melons. He looked up and saw that one of the melons had been cremated by the shot. Henderson knew that bullet was aimed at him and could tell that it had come from the roof of the palace. Henderson did not have his binoculars, but saw a figure on the roof the palace. He knew that it was a sniper and that he could not go anywhere for awhile. He was able to crawl inside a building and hid so that the sniper could not see him and shoot at him. He knew that he would be a sitting duck if he got back on the street and walked back to the palace.

He called Trahan on his radio and said, "I am trying to get back to the palace, but there is a sniper on the roof. He is firing at me. I am hiding out right now. Is there anything that you can do?"

Trahan radioed back to him, "We are still a little bogged down over here. I will see what I can do. Stay put for now."

Henderson felt that his friend was in trouble, but this time he could not get back to help him. Henderson had to let Jake go it alone.

* * *

Higgins had assured Jake that Sasha would be alright as long as Jake played along. Jake knew the rules and agreed. Jake had been Higgins protégé. He had always seen unbelievable potential in him and brought him in to his agency to do all his dirty work. During their ten year run together, he thought of Jake as a son, but something happened along the way and he had to cut all ties to him. He now sat in front of Jake in the palace of the capital city of East Africa, as an enemy rather than a friend.

Jake now sat in front of the man who he once looked up to. He had been the one who taught him everything he knew. He was a father figure to him. Jake felt as if he had given up a normal life to do what Higgins wanted him to do. He always resented Higgins for pulling the plug on him after the Iran incident and for turning his back on him. He wanted revenge on him and now ten years later Higgins was right in front of him. He was Jake's enemy. Jake did not know what to feel, even though there was hatred for him, he still wanted to hear what Higgins had to say. He just hoped that he would tell him the truth.

Higgins started by saying, "I know everything that you have wanted to know for the last ten years. Are you interested in hearing it?"

Jake, who was still tied up to a chair, answered, "Well, it looks that I am not going anywhere for awhile. So go ahead, I would like to know what you have to say."

Higgins continued, "As you know, twenty years ago, we needed to change the look of the CIA. I was in command of that change and sent agents out all over the country, trying to find the new young agent. We made them take tests and those that exceeded in these tests; we brought in to the agency. Those that did not do well, we kicked to the side of the curb. There was one score that was perfect, and that was your test score. I was called in and told what you did, and I knew that I had to have you in my new agency. I let you bring along your friend, Henderson, and he ended up being a better agent that I thought he would be. I watched you climb up the ladder in the first year of the FBI. Even though you did not know, but I was pulling the strings on everything that you did in the FBI. I continued to monitor your progress and you excelled at everything we threw at you. Early on I could tell that you yearned for more. You did not want to be an average field agent. You wanted to be in the action. That was what I was looking for in an agent. I wanted that certain agent to crave for more and I had that in you.

After a year of watching you exceed in everything that we threw at you, I felt that you were ready for something else. That is why I set up the meeting with you and Henderson to join my special agency. Our country was at war, not a conventional war with another country, but one with individuals or terrorist, if you will. I needed people in the area that could tell me the whereabouts of these dangerous people. Before you came with me, I sent many different agents that were trained just like you and Henderson, but all of them were either killed or captured. Unfortunately, my hands were tied and there nothing that I could do to save these people. If the superiors of the agency knew what was going on, they would shut me down and I could not have that. My plan was coming together and I did not need that to happen. I needed two agents who could do what I wanted and not get caught doing it. That is where you and Henderson came in."

Jake interrupted and said, "What was the plan that you are talking about?"

"That was the only problem that I had with you," Higgins responded. "You always interrupt without hearing the whole story. Now shut up and listen to me."

Jake wanted to bull rush him, but sat silently in his chair and let Higgins finish what he was saying.

Henderson continued, "As you know, you and Henderson had a terrific run. I believe that you were in the Middle East stirring up trouble for over eight years. You helped uncover many plots against America, but along the way you did exactly what I wanted you to do."

Jake asked, "What was that?"

Higgins continued, "I will get to that. I knew everything about you. I even knew what you were thinking all the time. I knew that you wanted to come home to a hero's welcome, but remember, Jake, you did not exist. That would never happen and I know that it got to you. I know that you got angry with the United States government; because you thought that it needed you and Henderson. You always wanted some sort of reward, but you never got it. I know that it ate at you. Remember, the United States viewed you just like the terrorist governments you were trying to destroy. You were an end to its means just as you were to me. But the good thing about what you did was that you actually loved it."

Jake listened to every word that Higgins spoke. He was not telling him anything that he did not already know. He felt that Higgins was just buying a little time and it was irritating him.

"Higgins," he said, "Tell me something that I don't know. I know you know what happened in Iran. Tell me why I was captured."

Higgins grinned and nodded his head. He said, "Yes, Iran. Well, I am getting to that. IF you can remember, you and Henderson had been causing all kinds of problems throughout the region. Neither one of you had been home in over eight years. I studied your every move and the two of you were unbelievable in what you did. Before I get to Iran, there is something else that you need to know.

I had gone into the CIA to make a difference. I had spent a lot of my life in the CIA and felt that I gave my life to a greater cause and also to my country. I was able to move up in the agency and when you met me I had risen to second in command. I had many plans that I wanted to put in place and was waiting my turn to take over, but I was told by my superior that I would be over looked as head of the CIA. I could serve out my time as his second in command and when he stepped down, I was going to be forced to retire as well. That just did not sit very well with me. I had put in my time, built a totally different wing of the agency and deserved to be head of the CIA. I had worked harder than anyone else, especially my superior, and I was given no reason as to why I would be over looked. I am a proud man and did not like the fact that I was not good enough for the leadership of one of the most powerful agencies in the world. I knew that someone or something could use what I knew. From the time that I was told that I would not succeed, I decided to come up with a plan so that I could get back at the United States.

I decided to continue to put my efforts elsewhere. I pulled back all my agents in the Middle East to just you and Henderson. I felt that the two of you could handle more of the load and if you can remember you certainly held your own."

Jake did remember that he had more missions in those two years than in the previous six. He actually enjoyed it more, because he never had a break. He did not have time to think about his life and everything that he had done. He was always on the go and he remembered thinking that he never wanted it to end. Unfortunately it did. He was captured and his life almost ended. Jake still wanted to know what happened in Iran. He always felt that if there were more contacts in the area, he could have been warned and he would never had been captured. He was trying to control his emotions. It was more difficult for him to do the more that Higgins talked, but he knew as long as he could keep his cool and listen to Higgins, the longer Sasha would stay alive.

Jake wanted the story to continue so he asked Higgins, "What did you with all the agents, while Henderson and I risked our necks everyday for those two years?

Higgins answered, "I put my other agents in a totally different area of the world, eastern Africa. I had gotten word of some activity, let's just say, something was going to be discovered in Africa, and I knew that I needed to be a part of it. I sent a few of my men to scout it out and sure enough, they told me the news that I needed to hear. We spent many years here and I knew that this discovery would change the world. I knew that my efforts would be better served if I concentrated on eastern Africa than the Middle East."

Jake got irritated with what he was saying and said, "So you just let Henderson and I go it alone. I could tell that at the end we never had the support that we had on our earlier missions."

Higgins interrupted and said, "Not necessarily. I was always there. I could not abandon my prize pupils. I needed you to continue with my dirty work. Again, what you did was for the good of the country, but also it was for the good of me. I had a master plan and I needed you to continue my work."

Jake asked, "What plan was that?"

Henderson ignoring Jake, continued, "Only three people knew of you and Henderson. Myself, my right hand man, and my superior. You might not believe me, but I appreciated what you and Henderson had done for me and at one time earlier in your career, I wanted to reward you and bring the both of you home. Unfortunately, my right hand man and my superior did not. Even though they had no idea what I was up to, they knew that you and Henderson were too valuable to the United States and wanted to keep you in the field. I did have a change of heart and continued to have you do my work. Even though they had no idea, the two of them actually made my plan easier. I knew that I had to have the two of you to make this work. I never thought of bringing you home again."

Jake just shook his head at what Higgins was saying. He could not believe that Higgins ever wanted to bring him home. He just wanted Higgins to continue, but wanted to know one thing before he did. He asked, "Who was your right hand man?"

Higgins answered, "I will get to him in a minute. I want to go back to the discovery in eastern Africa, in the eastern part of Sudan. You probably have heard about it already, but if you haven't the discovery was oil. I knew about this long before it was told to the world or even the country it was founded in. There were some obstacles that were in front of me so that I could get my hands of this wonderful discovery.

First I had to take care of the others who knew about my discovery. That was by far the easiest thing for me to do. Actually, I never did like to kill anyone, but I knew of two terrorist that had no problem with it. Those two were you and Henderson."

Jake started to think back to earlier missions that he went on. Higgins interrupted his train of thought and continued, "Do not worry about what you did in the past. As I always told you, what's done is done. You took care of a situation and you made the world a safer place."

"But whatever I did," "Jake said, "Benefited you, not the world."

"Don't forget that what I wanted not only benefited me, but also everyone around me."

Jake yelled back, "Your just a selfish old man, make that a selfish mad old man!"

"I am not going to continue this argument," Higgins said. "Think of me what you will, but I will end this conversation and leave you to think about what might happen to Sasha. Is that what you want?"

Jake did not want that. He had to keep Higgins blabbering for longer so he could figure a way out of the situation he was in. Every minute longer was another minute that Sasha was alive and a little longer for him to come up with a plan. He nodded to Higgins to continue.

Higgins said, "The second part of my plan was to have a place to escape to. I had to leave the U. S., but I knew that it would take awhile. I knew that I had to come to where the oil was located. As I said, we discovered it in eastern Africa, but the country it was located in was Sudan. Unfortunately, Sudan was ruled by a government that would never work with the United States or me. I needed a way to take over that part of the country.

I knew that they did not get along Ethiopia, who was their neighbors to the north. A few years later, I managed to cause conflict in the region and with my expertise our agency was able to cause a small revolution in the region concerning the ports on the Red Sea. This lead to our military getting involved and then we formed a new country, East Africa. You may not find it in any history book, but I am the founding father of this country."

Jake chuckled in disbelief, but Higgins was completely serious.

He said, "You may laugh, but I am the man that brought revolution to this part of the continent and helped free these people. I always thought of myself as someone who looks out for the needs of others, as long as it benefits me of course. These people never knew what freedom was and I brought it to them. The problem was, I could not come in and become the leader. I needed to find a local hero to take over the new country and that would enable me to send our resources to help develop the country."

"Let me guess," Jake said, "His name is Kier."

"You are right," Higgins said. "Kier was someone who I knew would be a good leader for this country, but also that I could depend on to keep my seat warm. I know that you have met him, but I do not know if you know much about this person."

Jake wanted to know where Higgins was going with this and told him to go on with what he meant.

"I have known Kier for a long time. I met him when he was in college here in the United States. I knew that he was from Sudan and approached him about becoming an agent. I needed someone in that part of the country. He became my liaison. I saw leadership ability in him and I put him in situations that he would only succeed in. He became a very popular figure and I had him lead the revolution. With Kier leading the rebels to victory, he became a perfect fit to lead the new country.

I had the U.S. government handpicked leader that I wanted. I had my leader, now I needed the resources so that I could get to my oil. Naturally I needed the United States and their wealth. They needed an ally and East Africa needed the money and resources that the United States had. It was a win-win situation for both and a friendship was born.

I was at the center of it all. I knew where to direct the funds that the U.S. pumped into the country and how to use all business to grow East Africa's infrastructure. Over a short period of time, East Africa grew to a small giant. I knew that we could not win against anyone with a small to non-existent military, but I wanted to hit them where it hurt the most and that was economically. Gas prices were through the roof, there was no end to the energy crisis in sight, and my small country that I had created, was sitting on a mountain of oil. The only thing I needed to do was to get over there."

Higgins stopped speaking to drink a sip of water. He offered Jake some, but he shook his head. He would rather thirst to death than be given anything from this mad man. However, he did find the story fascinating and asked Higgins to continue.

"Five years past and I knew that I needed to leave the agency and make my way to East Africa. My exit was smooth and sweet. I did, however, have one of my colleague's give me a hard time, but I was able to elude him and I made my way slowly to East Africa. I went through many different countries, trying to leave a trail that I was in South America. When I knew that I was not being followed anymore, I arrived in East Africa and my new life began.

I was greeted by Kier and immediately shared him my plan and vision for the future. Everything was going according to plan the first couple of years. We continued to use the United States and their resources to build up our country, but this turned into a big problem for me. Kier began to have second thoughts about our future and began to feel that we owed the United States for all that they had done. "

"Are you trying to tell me that Kier was having second thoughts, of betraying the United States," Jake said to Higgins.

"Betraying is such a harsh word," Higgins said. "We were not betraying anyone. If anyone got betrayed it was me, by my country. I was helping a small underprivileged country take advantage of a situation."

Jake shook his head. He could not believe he had to sit and listen to a deranged old man. He continued to think of Sasha and had to believe that she was still alive. He remained calm and said, "You can think whatever you want to and I don't care but you were betraying your country."

Higgins just chuckled and continued what he was saying, "Kier was a good foot soldier for me. He was the leader of this country because I wanted him to be, but when he began to question what I thought was best; I knew that we had to cut ties. Unfortunately, he was a very popular leader of this country and he also worked well with the United States. I was not finished with the U.S. and I could not eliminate Kier, because I still needed him to work with the country. I had an alternative and a solution to my problem."

"Let me guess," Jake said, "and his name was Qatar."

"I guess that you have met him," Higgins said. "He is a nice guy, don't you think?"

Jake looked at Higgins with eyes that could kill. "He killed two friends of mine, or should I say, you killed them."

"They just happened to be at the wrong place at the wrong time," Higgins responded. "To have this plan work, many people have been at the wrong place at the wrong time. It is kind of like you girlfriend. If things do not go the way that I want them to go with us, she will have been at the wrong place at the wrong time, if you know what I mean."

Jake knew exactly what he meant. As mad as he was he continued to force himself to hear more of Higgins' long story.

"As you know in this business you always need an ace in the hole and Qatar was mine. He was someone that I had known for as long as Kier. He was someone that I might need, just in case Kier changed his mind, and that is exactly what he did. I was so close to the end. We had about two more years to finish our objective and Kier had to veer away from our plan. Qatar and I decided it was time for plan B to be put into action."

Higgins stopped talking and got up from the table and looked outside the window. It had seemed that the small battle had stopped. He calmly got some water and walked back to the table and sat down. He offered some water to Jake, but he refused. Jake did, however have a few things to say.

He said to Higgins, "So Kier was just your puppet and when he rebelled, you found another."

Higgins answered, "That probably would not be a fair statement. Kier never knew exactly my intentions for the oil, only Qatar knew, but I have yet to tell him my exact plan. I will get to that plan in just a few minutes. I haven't forgotten about Iran either. I will tell you anything that you want to know."

After saying that, Higgins got up from the table and told Jake he would be back in a few minutes. He walked behind a wall and left Jake alone, still tied to the chair in complete and utter silence. Jake could not believe that the man he once called his mentor had changed so drastically into someone who was evil. Jake could see that Higgins had changed. This was a man, who was a patriot to the United States, was now a traitor in his eyes. He knew that Higgins did not care who he hurt or killed in his way.

He knew that there was no hope for Higgins, that he had already crossed the line of no return. He needed Higgins to continue his story so that he would somehow find a way to escape. He needed to help save Sasha, but right now he needed the crazy man to keep talking. He would do anything to keep Higgins talking. All Jake could hope for is that he would return after leaving him all alone.

CHAPTER 33

Henderson was still hiding in the abandoned building. He could not see if the sniper was still on the palace's roof, but did not want to get back on the street to find out. He had seen too many people gunned down before, and did not want to become one of those statistics. He radioed Trahan and asked, "From your vantage point, have you been able to locate the sniper on the roof?"

"Yes," Trahan said on the other end of the radio, as he looked through his binoculars. "He is perched behind something. There is no way that any of us can get a shot at him right now. We are trying to get into position to take him out, but wait there and don't go anywhere. I will contact you when we take care of him."

Henderson did not like that response. He had a feeling that his friend might be in trouble and that he needed him. He knew that he needed to stay put, but he was getting the itch to take a chance and see if he could make it to the palace. If he was ten years younger he would go for it, but he had too much to live for and decided the best thing was to stay put. He wasn't happy about the decision, but he could not help his friend if he got shot and killed. He just prayed that Jake stayed alive.

* * *

Higgins walked back into the room from behind the wall. He had a cigarette in his mouth and sat down. He offered Jake one, but he refused. Jake asked Higgins where he had gone, and Higgins told him not to worry about it. Higgins seemed to have a new wind to him and he lit his cigarette. He asked Jake if he wanted him to continue and Jake nodded.

Higgins looked at Jake and said, "Where were we, I think we were at Plan B, am I right?"

Jake nodded his head. He still did not know what he was going to do, but he wanted Higgins to continue with what he was saying. One reason he wanted him to continue was to keep Sasha alive a little longer, the other was a selfish reason, but Jake wanted to know what the actual story was.

Higgins continued, "I had given Kier everything and he had turned his back on me. He wanted to keep up relations with the U.S., but that was not the plan. We needed the U.S. for ten years and it was running it course and it was time to get rid of them. Kier was in the way, but I had Qatar in the bag. We waited our time and when Kier least expected, we took him captive."

Jake interrupted and said, "What do you mean you, made him a captive?"

Higgins answered, "We needed him to continue to be the leader of our country, but he had to be under our control, mentally and physically. We had certain drugs that could do that for us. We injected him with them and were able to control his mind, and tell him what to think and what to say. While I had Kier under control, I had Qatar running around our country, causing all kind of havoc."

Jake interrupted again and said, "Don't you mean, murder and rape?"

Higgins did not like hearing that and responded by saying, "I did not appreciate what he was doing, but I did tell him to do whatever it took to make Kier look like an incompetent ruler. He was very popular and we had to put a dent into his popularity. I did not like everything that he did, but as I told you a long time ago, everything has a point to what we do. The unfortunate events served a purpose and we were going to prove our point."

Jake sat there. He knew that there was no integrity left in the man. He could not believe that he ever looked up to him, feeling like he was his mentor.

Higgins continued, "Eventually, our plan was coming together. We had Kier going in front of the camera, blasting the United States and I had Qatar causing problems under Keir's eye. Our plan was coming together. We had kicked the U.S. out, we had the United Nations backing us, and we were about to start to distribute our oil. But Sasha came to our country, followed by you and your small militia. You have put a dent in my plan, but after today, our plan will continue and we will be back on course."

Jake did not want Higgins to start focusing on him. He needed him to continue what he was saying so he said, "Tell me more about the oil?"

"It is funny about oil," Higgins said. "A good month is around five hundred barrels a month. A better month is five thousand barrels in the time period. We are on the verge of something unexpected. We have been building oil wells that will pump ten times that amount. There is enough oil in this country to produce enough energy for more than ten thousand years my experts say."

Jake could care less of how much oil was going to be pumped a day, so he asked another question, "Do you mean to say that the whole country has oil in the ground?"

"Yes," Higgins said emphatically, "We are finding activity all over this country. We evacuated a small village, because we found that there was oil there."

Jake finally figured out why the village had been evacuated. Now he had to find out what happened to the people. "What do you mean evacuated a whole village? What did you do with all the people that lived there?"

Higgins continued to brag at what he had done. He said, "No one is going to miss those people. We took care of them."

"Did you kill them all?" Jake wondered in disbelief.

"I am not that bad," Higgins said. "Qatar on the other hand is, but I would not let him do that to those people. We moved them to the other side of the country. It turns out that we need workers for the oil wells that we have built over there. They are very cheap labor."

Jake interrupted, "Slave labor is cheap. Are you going to let those people go back to their village and continue to live their lives?"

"No," Higgins answered. "They are needed where they are. The village that we overtook is going to become our major distribution center for the oil. The village has been destroyed."

"You are a monster to do that to those innocent people," Jake yelled at Higgins.

"What's done is done," he answered.

"I guess you are right," Jake said as he shook his head in disbelief. He felt bad about the village, but knew that he had to have Higgins continue to tell him about his plan. He asked, "I know that oil will give you a multitude of wealth, but you speak of revenge to the United States. Did you just think that if you had enough money that you could just buy your way back in the CIA?"

"No," Higgins answered. "I didn't want any part of the CIA when I left them, and I don't want any part of them now. I had wasted my whole life in the agency and all it got me was a soon to be pink slip. I did not want that. I wanted power and knew I could have it over here. I also wanted the United States to know that they pissed off the wrong guy. I will make sure that they realize that. Enough about me, do you want to know about your capture in Iran?"

Jake had wanted to know about that situation for a very long time. He tried not to act to anxious and calmly said, "Tell me about that. I don't care, but I guess I would like to know."

Higgins laughed knowing that Jake wasn't telling him the truth. He replied, "I bet you have. Do not forget that I am the one who made you who you are. You may think that I am crazy, but I am no fool. I know that this has been on your mind for quite awhile. I'll tell you what you want to know and I hope you have some time on your hands because it might take me awhile." Higgins looked at Jake's hands and feet and laughed again, "Oh, wait a minute; I guess you will sit and stay awhile."

Jake sat quietly, trying not to show his frustration over what he had said. He wanted to yell and scream, but looked at Higgins and said, "You are right. I am here for awhile. I will sit here and listen to what you said. You have my attention."

"Well good then," Higgins said, "As I said earlier, you were the best agent I ever had. Henderson was good, but I knew that you would be the leader and you did not disappoint me. You did things that I did not feel anyone that I knew could ever do. I had a lot of faith in you and you never disappointed me. You may never have known this, I felt as if you were the son that I never had. You meant a lot to me and I did not want you to be caught up in anything that I did, but unfortunately you were getting close and I could not have that."

Jake, wanted to continue to sit quietly, but had a hard time believing what Higgins said. He interrupted and said, "If you felt that way, then why do you have me tied up?"

"That was a long time ago and a lot has changed," Higgins answered a very serious voice. "Just be thankful that you are still breathing."

Jake knew that Higgins had a point. He knew when to pick his battles and this clearly was not the time. He was glad to still be alive and wanted to keep it that way. He decided to continue listening to the story and asked, "What was I getting close to?"

Higgins felt that he had put Jake back into place. He was pleased that had happened and answered, "I want you to understand something; it was a lot deeper than you could comprehend back then."

Jake did not like the fact that Higgins was attacking his intelligence. "Try me," Jake said, "I am pretty smart, you know."

"I know that you are," Higgins said. "That is why I could not let you get any closer to what my plan actually was."

"Go ahead," Jake said, "Tell me what I was getting close to. It is not like it is going to matter now what you say."

Higgins plans did not have Jake in them and he would get rid of him shortly, so he felt that he had nothing to lose if he told Jake what he wanted to know. He continued the story by saying, "For ten years, I knew where you were at all times, but for some reason, and I do not know why, but you had ventured over into Iran. I came into my office one day and someone informed me, that you were there. I did not authorize that and felt that someone in the agency had triggered this move. They had set this up for you to find something that I could not have you find. If you met up with the contact, it would be easy for you to put two and two together and figure out my master plan."

Jake smiled a sarcastic smile and said, "And what kind of master plan was that?"

Higgins looked across at Jake and told him to quit smiling. This was something that he did not want to discuss, but it did not matter now. He said with a very stern voice, "Nuclear weapons."

This kind of took Jake back a little. He leaned forward in his chare not knowing where Higgins was going with what he was saying. He questioned Higgins saying, "What do you mean nuclear weapons?"

"Iran had been secretly making nuclear weapons for years," he answered. "No one could prove it, but being in my line of work for so long, I had made many contacts that assured me of this. They had a contact for me to meet so I made a secret trip to Iran and met with him. He helped me move up the chain of command to someone who could help me get my hands on some of these weapons. This would be my ticket for me to extract my eventual revenge on the United States."

Jake was blown away. Higgins had obviously put a lot of time and planning into his plan. He still wanted to know how he fit it to this plan over ten years ago. "What could I have done in Iran," Jake asked, "No one knew that I existed. Did you believe I was going to come back to the United States and turn you in? No one would have believed me."

Higgins answered, "That was the least of my concerns. I know that you could not have done anything to me back in the U.S. The problem that I had was that your mission was to eliminate my contact. I was in the early stages of negotiation with Iran. I did not need my contact to come up dead. That would not have been good for business. The people that I was working with also needed me to give them something to prove that I was serious in what I wanted.

You and Henderson were my ace in the whole. The two of you were the most wanted men in the region and I knew that if I handed you over to Iran that I would slowly earn their trust. Later I also turned over other agents following your capture. After a couple of years, I finally earned Iran's trust that I was able to leave the agency. I left and made my way over to East Africa. I have been running this country since I got here five years ago, but I have been in control since we imprisoned Kier two years ago."

Jake finally got an answer to question that had bothered him for the last ten years. He was bait, plain and simple. He had let this bother him for ten years, and finally he knew that he and Henderson never did anything wrong to be captured. He was turned over to Iran by the one man he trusted, his mentor. The man he looked up to, who had taught him everything that he knew, turned on him for greed.

Jake sat quietly for a moment to reflect on the last ten years. He then started to laugh when he realized that his obsession of finding the answer to his capture, did not compare with Higgins' obsession of revenge.

There was still one thing that puzzled Jake. He asked Higgins', "What happened to all the other agents that you allowed to be captured by Iran?"

"They were all eliminated, put down, if you will," Higgins answered.

"I do not understand one thing," Jake said with a puzzled look on his face. "I have figured that our lives had no meaning to you, but why did you have Iran spare us?"

Higgins answered, "I was told that you would be killed. I knew the date and the time, but at the last minute your lives were spared. I do not know why and asked, but got nowhere. The only reason that I could come up with was that someone else for some reason, wanted to spare your life."

"One thing I know about you is that you knew everything that went on in the agency. You must have known who that person must be," Jake asked.

Henderson said, "I do know who that is, but I just found out about it a few hours ago."

That last statement shocked Jake. A few hours ago meant nothing to him. He wanted to know who it was and asked Higgins' who had gotten him out of Iran.

"That would be me," another voice said behind the same doorway in which Higgins had come from behind. "I got you out of Iran."

Jake knew exactly whose voice that belonged to. He did not even have to look at the figure that came from behind the wall. Jake laughed at himself, feeling that he had been fooled once again. He shook his head and said, "I should have known that both of you were in on this, Higgins, and you H."

H came up to the table and sat down with Higgins. Jake felt that he should have put it together sooner. He had been told early in his career that no one should be trusted in this business.

He had not forgotten, but he let his guard down. He did start to realize that all the pieces of the puzzle seem to be coming together. He knew that Higgins had to get most of his information from someone in the agency and H was the perfect fit. He was just mad at himself for not seeing it. He kept his cool, though, because other things were in play now, Sasha and Henderson.

Jake said to H, "The two of you played me for a fool. You both suckered me into this situation, but I still want to know one thing. Why did you bring me back to this line of work, if you wanted to eliminate me ten years ago?"

Higgins looked to H and said, "You can finish the story, I think that I have told him enough already."

H tried to reason with Jake and said, "This is not what you think."

Jake interrupted, "Not what I think. What do you mean, not what I think? It looks to me that both of you had a great plan and brought it together. You have me tied up and have Sasha captured. There is not much to think about here."

Jake was very irritated. He knew that he had been used, not only by Higgins, but H as well. "The problem is," he continued. "That this does not surprise me. I just want to know who's all involved. Is Diotrice involved? Or Trahan? How deep is this thing? Can one of you at least be truthful with me with one thing?"

H answered Jake and said, "You may not believe me, but I am sorry that this all happened. You just have to know that Higgins had the better opportunity for me."

Higgins interrupted, and said, "Money and power will change any man. H contacted me a few months ago and told me that he could help me and my efforts even more. He explained to me what he could do and I told him, 'Welcome aboard'."

H looked at Jake and said, "I followed your career from day one. I was amazed at all the things that you were able to accomplish and how you eluded capture at every turn. I was the one who sent you into Iran. I had heard about the nuclear plans and I sent you there to eliminate the contact that was aiding Higgins. I knew this would shut down anything that Higgins wanted to accomplish."

Jake shook his head in disbelief, "Why did you not tell me this when we met? Don't you think that I would have wanted to know about this?"

H continued, "If I would have told you this, you would not have come over to East Africa. I just could not take that chance."

Jake shook his head, knowing that he would have never agreed to do any of this. He was frustrated at H, but wanted to hear what else he had to say.

H continued and said, "When things did not go according to plan, I found out that you had been captured. I figured that Higgins had set you up and had you captured, but I could not prove it. I felt responsible for what happened to you and the one thing I could do was put into motion a plan to free the two of you from the Iranian prison. I leaned heavily on some of my contacts and eventually I got you released. The only problem was that I had to set a few of our captured terrorist free, but in my mind it was worth it. I had the two of you sent home safe and that is all that mattered to me. Higgins did not see it that way, and wanted the two of you eliminated. He felt that the two of you were still a security threat to him and the best way to get rid of you was kicking you out of the agency. He was the real evil one in all this."

Jake knew that his life would have been different if the episode had never happened. He questioned his whole time in the agency and asked, "Why in the world did you bring me into the agency in the first place? Did you just pick me out of a lineup somewhere and just say I think I am going to ruin this guy's life."

"I know it is hard to believe," Higgins said, "But at one time we believed in the United States and thought that we could help our country. It took awhile, but we realized that we were not appreciated and we had to do something to change that."

"For some reason," Jake continued, "You saved my life, H, and Higgins you kicked me out of the agency. That brings me back to the question I asked earlier, why bring me back in?"

"That was just part of the plan," H said.

Higgins never got a reason why H brought him back in. He had wondered for awhile and wanted to know what plan H was talking about. He turned to H and asked, "What plan was that?" He asked.

H stood up out of his chair and said, "This plan." H pulled a gun out of his pocket and held it to Higgins's head. H said, "I know you find it hard to believe, but I think that you are a mad man, Higgins. I never understood you ten years ago and to this day I never will, but I will not allow you to try and destroy Jake's life and also bring your revenge on the United States. I have waited five years for this moment and it is finally here. I will be getting rid of a mad man today and I feel that I will be justified by doing that."

Higgins started to laugh. He knew that he was always one step of head of protégé and said, "H, I thought you always did good work, but you were never that smart. You never knew and still do not know what or who you are up against."

H still had the gun pointed at Higgins head. He did not like that Higgins demeaned him and said, "What do you mean, I do not know what I am up against? If you haven't noticed, you are the one with a gun to his head. It looks as though you are the one in trouble, not me."

All of a sudden the back door opened that led to the roof of the palace. H and Higgins turned around and saw Qatar standing in the doorway with a gun in his hand. He had a perfect aim and shot right at, H hitting him in the middle of the chest. H dropped his gun and fell down to the floor. Higgins walked over and stood over him.

He grabbed H's gun and said to him, "I really never liked you that much."

H was shot pretty bad and had a hard time gasping for air. Blood was flowing out of his chest and he was slowly dying.

Higgins aimed the gun at H's head and said, "I told you that you should never mess with me. Now you will die because you did."

Right before Higgins pulled the trigger to the gun, the door that led down to the first floor of the palace swung open and Diotrice appeared with a gun in her hand. She aimed it at Higgins and was not afraid to pull the trigger. She fired at Higgins, but unfortunately she missed him. It was good enough, though, to have him retreat to the back door. Qatar was still in the doorway and shot back at Diotrice, covering his leader. She was able to duck behind a chair as the bullet missed by her head. By the time she got up from behind the chair, Higgins and Qatar had left, going through the backdoor that led to the roof.

Jake saw Sasha before the backdoor was shut, and that she was tied up. He saw her being rushed up the stairs to the palace's roof. He knew that he had to get to her or that she would be killed. Diotrice put her gun away and rushed over to Jake and untied him. H was still alive a lying on the floor gasping for air. Jake came over to him, bent down and grabbed his hand. Diotrice looked on hoping that H would survive, but she knew that it did not look good.

As blood continued to spurt out of H's body, he whispered to Jake "You may think otherwise, but I have been truthful with you, from the start. I just didn't tell you the whole story. Higgins had come up with a plan and had come to me and told me about it a long time ago. I never thought he was serious."

H quit talking and started to pass out from the loss of blood. Jake yelled to him to wake up. Diotrice saw what was happening and grabbed something to try and stop the blood that was flowing out of H's body. Jake put his head down, thinking that H was dead, but H opened his eyes and continued what he was saying as if he had not lost consciousness at all. "Later, he disappeared and I felt that he was serious about what he had told me. This is why I started code 7. I started it for the one reason and that was to stop Higgins, but I had no idea where he was until the oil discovery in this country. I sent Sasha here to get me proof and she did. I knew that Higgins was in charge and was trying to get his hands on nuclear weapons."

H stopped, again seeming to lose consciousness again, instead started to cough. Jake grabbed his hand and told him to save his strength, but H continued, "I have got to tell you this. Listen to me; I do not have much time. I knew that you were my last hope to save Sasha after she was captured. I had nowhere else to turn. I am truly sorry that I got you involved in all of this, but now need you to save Sasha again. I thought by making a deal with Higgins that he would let her go, but he has other plans for her. You need to leave me and save her and take care of Higgins and Qatar. If they are able to leave this place, well let me say that they are very dangerous and their network goes further than just the two of them."

Jake turned to Diotrice and put H's bloody hand in her hand. He said to her, "You stay with H. Try and take care of him. Give me your gun. I have got to go save my girlfriend."

Diotrice handed over her gun and looked over H's body. She could see that he was still losing a lot of blood and continued to put a cloth over the wound hoping it would stop the bleeding.

Jake looked down at H and said, "If I don't see you again, just know that I will do my best to save her."

H said in a very weak voice, "I always believed in you, Jake. Now go and leave me."

* * *

"Henderson, Henderson, do you read me?" Trahan radioed to him. "I hope you get this, but it looks as if the sniper has left, but we can tell that there is other activity on the roof. It looks like there is a helicopter that has been started and that it is about to take off. Be cautious, and get to the palace as fast as possible."

Henderson did hear what was said and was on the move. He knew that he needed to get to the palace and as fast as he could. Unfortunately, he went at a snail's pace for fear of the sniper's bullet. He continued to hide in back alleys and behind any object he felt was a shield to him, but he did make it to the palace, and he got there in one piece.

* * *

Higgins had gotten to the roof top of the palace. He had Qatar start the helicopter and he was ready to get out of the country. Higgins' plan was not completely compromised and he did have other options in place. He just needed to get out of the country and let things settle down. He had an escape route planned out. He would fly out of the country in a helicopter and head to a safe location that was unknown to Qatar. He would explain on the way what their plan would be, but did not have time to go over it at the present time.

Qatar still had Sasha tied up. He held her by the arm and waited for Higgins to come over to them. When Higgins got over to them, Qatar told him that there was not enough room to take Sasha with them and asked Higgins what he wanted to do with her.

"You bring up a very valid point, Qatar." Higgins yelled to Qatar so that he could hear him over the noise from the helicopter. "I have plans for the girl, but as for you, your importance for me has run its course."

Higgins pulled out the gun he had taken away from H. He aimed it at Qatar and said to him, "You have worn out your welcome, and it is time for me to cut you loose."

Qatar pushed Sasha away and began to beg for his life. It was too late for him as Higgins pulled the trigger and shot him in the chest. Qatar covered his chest with his hands, but it did no good as he fell to the ground, with blood coming out of his body.

Higgins stood over him and yelled at him, saying "You failed me. You led Jake right to me. I spent over ten years on this project and you single handily destroyed my plan. I should have eliminated you a long time ago, but allowed your life to continue to long. Good bye, Qatar."

Higgins put the gun to Qatar's head and put him out of his misery. He then turned around and grabbed Sasha by the back of her hands and picked her up off the roof. He led her to the helicopter. "I never liked that guy anyway and had to deal with him for ten years. But hey, now we have two people that can fit into the helicopter. Are you ready to go?"

Sasha did not have much to say to Higgins. She had been through a whirlwind of problems since she came on the mission. She did not have time to gather herself and did not know what Higgins' plan was for her in the future. She did not want to end up like Qatar. She still had her stubbornness to her and managed to blurt out, "You will never get away with this. It doesn't matter where you go with me, I assure you that Jake will hunt you down and find you."

Higgins started to laugh at her with his deep sullen laugh. He could care less about what she had to say. He just wanted to get off the roof. He yelled back at her and said, "As long as I have you, I think that I will be okay. Now get in."

Higgins opened one of the doors to the helicopter and threw her in. He ran over to the other side and got in. He put on his earphones and was ready to take off, but Sasha had other ideas, and kicked at him in the side of the face. Higgins did not appreciate getting kicked. He turned toward her and reached back and slapped her across the face. He grabbed her by the throat and yelled, "I do not need any more trouble out of you, now sit there and do not move."

Higgins strapped Sasha in so that she could not move and move back over to take off, but suddenly, out of nowhere, Jake jumped onto the one of the legs of the helicopter. He was able to open the door on the side where Sasha was located on. He said to her, "Did you miss me?"

She smiled and said, "Get me out of here and away from this lunatic."

Higgins saw that Jake had entered the helicopter, but it did not stop him from trying to ascend into the air. Jake reached over Sasha and grabbed the stick that controlled the helicopter, trying to keep it grounded. Higgins struggled with Jake to get his hands off the stick, but he held on with all his might. All Jake wanted was a diversion so that he could get Sasha out of the helicopter. They had ascended a few feet off the roof. It was getting out of control and Jake felt that this was his opportunity to get him and Sasha out of the helicopter. Higgins had taken control of the helicopter, allowing Jake to unbuckle Sasha. He grabbed her and threw her down onto the roof. He looked down and saw that she landed safely and that she was fine.

Jake then turned his attention to Higgins. Higgins had gotten the big machine under control. He was about to fly into the sky when he looked over and noticed that Jake was still in the helicopter with him. Jake had some unfinished business with him and he turned his hand into a fist. He had did not waste time as he hit him across the face. Higgins' head flung back and he almost passed out from the hit. He got his wits back quickly and turned toward Jake and head butted him, knocking Jake against the helicopter's door. Higgins tried to get going and had gotten a few more feet off the roof, but it was hard to ascend when he was fighting off Jake.

Jake came back at him and hit him again. Again, Higgins was startled and he almost lost control of the helicopter, but Jake would not allow that and grabbed the wheel and yelled at him, "Where do you think you are going."

Higgins screamed at him to let go and if he did not that they would wreck. Jake yelled, "Never, if it goes down, then it was meant to be."

Higgins could not believe that Jake had said that and yelled back at him, "But you will kill us both."

Jake could care less. He had been through so much that he yelled back, "I will never let you escape. You are a very dangerous man and the world will be better off with you not in it. If it means that I die as well, then so be it."

Higgins was not about to let Jake take the helicopter down and kill them both. He head butted Jake again and sent Jake back against the door. Then Higgins turned with his feet in the air and kicked Jake right in the chest area, sending Jake out of the door of the helicopter. Jake caught himself on one of the legs of the helicopter. He was hanging on with all his might and was lifting himself back into the helicopter. He looked down and saw Sasha on the roof. She yelled to him to let go. He did not want to let go and let Higgins fly away.

Sasha yelled back to him, "Jake we will get him another day. Let him go. Save yourself and let go of the helicopter. I promise that we will get him. Just let go."

Jake continued to hold on not wanting to let go. He could not wait another ten years to get his mentor. It was now or never for him and he knew that the world would not be a safe place as long as Higgins was still in it. He continued to pull himself up, but Sasha did not give up in having Jake let go and saving himself.

She took one more shot at him and yelled, "Jake, if you let go, I will go on that date to the Supper Club. I promise you, but you have to let go."

Higgins had gotten control of the helicopter and began to go higher and higher into the air. Jake knew it was a lost cause if he continued to hold on. He knew that if he did manage to get back into the cab of the helicopter, he would eventually take out Higgins, but the only problem with that scenario is that they would both die. He did not want to die just yet because Sasha had just promised him a date. He wanted to take his chances with her and live another day.

The helicopter had gotten about fifteen feet above the roof. It was now or never for Jake. He decided to let go of the leg and fell to the roof. It was a long fall, but he landed and rolled so that he would not break anything. Sasha ran over to him and made sure that everything was alright with him. Jake was a little sore, but there were no broken bones and he was just fine. He stood up and loosened the rope that tied her hands behind her back. Once she got free from the rope, Sasha embraced him and said to Jake, "Thanks for saving me again. How many times is that, three times?"

Jake responded, "Four, but who's counting anyway. I am just glad that you are safe."

Sasha looked into his eyes and could tell that Jake was upset. She said to him, "You can get Higgins another day. You win some and you lose some. I promise you that we will track him down and get him."

Jake looked at her and answered, "You are right, but I really wanted to get him today."

He looked up and saw that Higgins had finally gotten the helicopter going. He was now ascending higher into the sky.

Jake saw Qatar dead on the ground. He asked Sasha what had happened and she told him everything that Higgins had said and done. Jake started to laugh and was happy that he did not waste a bullet on him. He went over and looked down at Qatar; he then looked back at the sky and could see Higgins getting further and further away. He was about to walk away until he noticed that Qatar had his rocket launcher draped around him.

Jake stopped in his tracks and said, "Wait a minute, I have got an idea. I think that Higgins is still in range."

Sasha responded, "You're not thinking what I think that you are thinking."

Jake nodded and grabbed the rocket launcher off of Qatar's dead body. He looked inside the launcher and saw that he still had one rocket left inside of it. He motioned Sasha to stand back. Jake opened the gun and put the scope into place. He looked through the scope, lining it up to the helicopter. He thought to himself that he only had one chance so he had to make it count.

Higgins was glad to be rid of Jake and was ready to get out of there. He had gotten control of the helicopter and was on his way to meet the remaining people on his team. This was not what he wanted, but he knew that once everything settled down, he could get his team together and finish up his ultimate plan. He knew that he would have to do things differently and had to hope that he would not see Jake again. He wanted to take care of Jake once and for all. He knew that he did not have a chance to do it as long as he was flying away so he decided to go back down toward the roof. He looked down on the roof to look at Jake for a final time, but he had made a mistake. He should not have come back down because he was able to get a good look at Jake holding a rocket launcher aimed at him. He pulled up, hoping to get away, but it was too late. Jake pulled the trigger and a rocker was launched out of the launcher. It headed right at Higgins. It hit the helicopter's tail, blowing it completely off. Higgins fate was sealed and he and the helicopter came crashing down to the ground, exploding on the other side of the palace.

Jake put down the rocket launcher. He felt relieved to get rid of someone who not only had ruined the last ten years of his life, but many other people's lives as well. He looked over at Sasha and smiled. He knew that he had done it. He sat down out of pure exhaustion. Sasha walked over and sat down beside him. She held his hand and said, "You did it."

He nodded and said, "Yes I did. I finally I got him."

Jake turned to her with his eyes looking into her eyes. He put his hands on her cheeks and was about to kiss her when all of a sudden, the door opened and Henderson came running out with a gun in each hand prepared for anything. He was yelling making sure that everyone was alright.

Jake yelled back to him, "You are a little late for the party and you just missed the fireworks."

Henderson smiled and said, "I got held up. What did I miss?" He then looked down and saw Qatar lying dead on the ground. "I see, you got to have all the fun."

Jake started to laugh and said, "Thanks for being here, bro. None of this would have ever happened had you not come back for us. By the way what happened to the battle down there. Is it over, yet?"

"Yeah," Henderson said, "I am pretty sure that it is. Kier and Trahan have gotten control of all the men. They look like that they are going to be friends. Enough about that, I want to explain why I was a little late. I got held up by a sniper, did you get him too?"

Jake looked over at Sasha and then back at Henderson and said, "We haven't seen anyone else. Are you sure that there was a sniper up here?"

Henderson nodded and answered, "For one thing, he shot at me. Trahan also spotted him as well. He then informed me that the sniper disappeared. I just thought that you took care of him, but obviously you didn't. I wouldn't worry about it, because by the looks of things we should be just fine."

Jake looked again at Sasha and asked, "Was Qatar up here? I mean, did he leave you alone and come up here by himself."

"No," she answered emphatically. "He held me by gunpoint and I was with him the whole time until I was forced to come to the roof with him and Higgins."

Henderson said, "Whoever it was, he must be long gone by now. Jake, don't worry about it, we will go after him another time."

Jake knew that Henderson was right. He wanted to relax and take a deep breath. He thought back at all the things that had gone during his time he had been in East Africa. Jake knew he had plenty of time to reflect, but wanted to get back down to check on H. The three of them went back down into the second level of the palace.

Diotrice was there waiting for them. Jake could tell that she did not have good news concerning H. She said to them, "H is dead. He held on as long as he could, but passed out because of the loss blood. He just never woke up."

It was a somber moment for Jake. H had brought him back into the business that he love, that he craved to be in. He allowed Jake a chance to redeem himself and Jake would never forget him for that. He held on to what H had last said to him and hoped that H had told him the truth.

Jake then looked at Sasha and said, "I am sorry that he did not make it. I think in the end he was a good man. I have to believe that he was a patriot. He did try to stop Higgins plot. I really believe that in the end, he made a difference."

"At least," Jake continued, pausing for a moment and then he said, "H brought all of us, you, me, Sasha, and Diotrice together and we all helped eliminate Higgins and Qatar. I think that we can all agree that the world is a safer place and H was responsible for that."

They all walked toward where H's body was supposed to be, but it was no longer located on the floor. They all stood together in complete quiet, giving H a moment of silence. Jake was surprised the body had been moved and broke the silence when he looked over at Diotrice and asked what had happened to the body. She explained that the body was such a mess that she felt that he needed to be moved and called in some of her men to have it remove. She had ordered for them to take the body to a crematorium and the ashes to be scattered under a tree by the palace. Jake had wanted to give his respects, but Diotrice assured him that he could do so by going to the tree that was located outside. Jake felt that it was strange that his body had been removed so quickly and been cremated and wanted to know more, but he was interrupted by Kier's entrance.

Kier walked through the door with his entourage surrounding him. He had a big smile on his face. He finally felt that he could get control of his country again and Jake was the first one he wanted to thank. He ran over to Jake and shook his hand. He told Jake that he was responsible for his freedom and that he was welcomed to come back anytime. He then looked around, wanting to make sure that his two enemies were eliminated.

He said to Jake, "Again, thank you for all that you did. I would not be here if it was not for you. I have to ask, though, I saw the helicopter come down and I am hoping that Higgins went down with it. Is it true that he was on it?"

Jake nodded, with a big smile on his face.

"And what about Qatar?" Kier asked.

"He is on the roof," Sasha answered. "He won't be getting up either."

Kier was pleased. He said to all of them, "Hopefully, things can get back to normal, but before you go, I want you to know how thankful I am. I am going to throw you all a big party. You need to stay one more night before you go. I command you to." Kier smiled at them and gave them a wink.

Jake was not in the mood to party, but could not say no to the leader of East Africa. He looked at Sasha and Henderson and they both shrugged their shoulders meaning that they did not care. Jake looked at Kier and said, "No fireworks, though."

Kier started to laugh and the rest of them joined in.

CHAPTER 34

Jake had finally gotten a good night sleep again. He was able to get a hot plate of food and a long hot shower. He felt refreshed. It had been a long time sense he felt good about what he had accomplished. He reflected over the last couple of months and he felt that his life was back in order. He could finally put what had happened to him ten years ago behind him and he had closure to the awful situation of Iran. He had gotten back his best friend and met someone who he truly liked. Life could not be any better for him.

Jake left his room and arrived back to the palace with some new clothes, he was freshly shaven and he had a big grin on his face. He walked up to the stairs to the palace and could not believe the changes that had taken place over the last twenty-four hours. One could not tell that there had been a battle at the palace a day earlier. Fresh flowers were decorated throughout the palace's hallways that put out a wonderful flagrance for anyone that entered. There were balloons blown up to the ceiling and confetti all over the floor. People had come from all over and were everywhere in the palace. Jake could tell that this would be one big night.

He walked in and someone took his coat.

"Are you Jake," the servant asked him.

"Yes, how did you know?" Jake wondered.

"I was told for you to come with me. I have something to give you."

Jake followed the servant into the kitchen. He walked in and saw a big banner that read in capital letters, THANK YOU! There were over thirty people in the kitchen that began to applaud him when he entered.

"We wanted to thank you for giving us our lives and jobs back," a voice said in the crowd. "We were told by Kier that you are responsible for not only our freedom, but for the freedom of country. You are our hero. Thank you so much for what you did."

Jake was overwhelmed. He knew that many different people throughout the country had gotten their life back, but he was glad to know that he had made an impact on their lives.

"Now go out there and have fun. If you need anything, we will love to serve you."

Jake left the kitchen and walked to the ballroom. He looked around at all the decorations and was amazed at how well the palace cleaned up and looked. He followed the red carpet into the ballroom and when he entered, he was asked his name by a man who was holding the door. He told the man and the man announced it. The crowd in the ballroom stopped what they were doing and turned toward Jake and gave him a huge round of applause. He did not know what to do so he just waved to the crowd, but they got louder and louder. The crowd finally settled down and Jake saw Kier waiting at the bottom of the stairs for him. Jake walked down the stairs and Kier greeted him again with a hug.

"I just want to thank you, again," Kier said, "For all that you have done for me and my country. If not for you and your efforts, our country would have been run by a mad man. Who knows what would have happened to us all."

"I cannot take all the credit," Jake responded. "I had plenty of help."

Kier said, "That is why you will be a great leader, you are very modest."

Jake looked over his left shoulder and saw Diotrice staring at him. He waved to her to come over to him and Kier. She obliged him and walked over.

Jake said to Kier, "This is one of the unsung heroes. She came to my rescue many times. Kier, you will learn a lot from this woman. You need her help. She is a great leader herself."

Kier nodded and agreed. "As you can see I need as much help as I can get."

Jake padded Kier on the back and told him to get to know Diotrice better. Kier and Diotrice continued to talk as Jake walked away to get a drink at the bar.

Jake sat at the bar, sipping on a bourbon and coke, when a man in a dark black suit approached him.

"Are you Jake Tennyson," the man asked.

Jake turned around and saw a man looking and smiling at him. He thought he had me the man before, but if he had, it was a long time ago. The man came over to him and reached out his, wanting to shake Jake's hand.

"Can I help you," Jake asked him.

"Yes you can," the man answered. "My name is John Claiborne. I received a call from Kier this morning and was told to come to this party. He told me that I might want to meet you, again."

Jake interrupted him and said, "I remember meeting you. I believe that I you are the head of the CIA."

"I guess I do not need to reintroduce myself," he said. "I got briefed on your file on my flight over and I have to tell you that I am very impressed by what you did in your past and what you just accomplished here in this country."

Jake said back to him, "I thought my file was destroyed ten years ago."

"Remember, Jake," Claiborne interrupted, "I am the head of the CIA. We have abilities to find things that seem lost. I also was hoping that you might want to give us a second chance."

Jake started to laugh a little. He finally had his chance to get back into the life he had craved for. This was his chance, but it just did not seem to matter to him anymore. He knew he still had the desire, but there was more to life than chasing after the bad guy. He appreciated that Claiborne had come all this way, but he felt that he was going to be disappointed by his answer.

He looked Claiborne straight into his eyes and said, "You have a lot on your plate and I feel for you. You need to catch up on with Kier and all the other diplomats that are here. This is your time to shine. I am the least of your worries. Do what you need to do and come back and see me. Right now, all I want to do is dance. After I finish, I will give you a call."

Jake started to walk away and Claiborne said to him, "Jake, I expect a call from you and soon."

Jake was walking away, but turned around and came back. He wanted to tell Claiborne one more thing. "I would make sure that you watch Kier. I have a hard time trusting that guy, and I do not know if you guys want to put a lot of faith him. Just giving you a heads up."

Claiborne answered, "I will keep that in mind. Thanks."

Jake left Claiborne and walked over to Henderson who was sitting down at a table sipping on a drink. Jake sat down beside him and said, "Some party."

"Yea, this is some shindig," Henderson responded as he continued to sip on his drink.

"It is amazing how quickly they cleaned this place up. They must have worked all night, by the way what time is your flight."

Henderson took one more sip and said, "I will leave in an hour. By the way, this was a lot more fun than that a science fair I told my wife about."

Jake began to laugh.

Henderson continued, "It probably was not as dangerous, though. You never want to be around fifth graders and chemicals. It can get out of control. Anyway, I cannot believe that this adventure is over. I had such a great time."

Jake continued to laugh at what he said. "That is why I love you man, you can always make me laugh. There are not many people that can, but you can."

"Hey," Henderson said, "I almost forgot, I got you this."

He reached into his pocket and pulled out a cigar. He handed it to Jake and said, "To a job well done."

"Amen, brother," Jake said. "It sure has been fun."

Henderson wanted to know if there were any plans for Jake in the future and asked, "What are your plans? Where do you go from here?"

Jake had lightened his cigar and took a big puff from it. He blew out some smoke and said, "I don't know. I hadn't thought that far ahead. But right now, I will probably relax a little, smoke this cigar, and sit here for awhile."

"That seems like a plan. Good for you," Henderson said as he blew some smoke from his cigar.

"What about you?" Jake asked.

Henderson leaned back in his chair with his cigar in his hand and said, "You know, I have not had one of these in about five years. It sure is good. Anyway, to answer your question, I will go back home and continue to teach. It's not as exciting as this, but it has its moments. By the way, I do miss my wife and kids and can't wait to see them."

Jake thought that was a modest idea and said to him, "Make sure you tell them that I said hello."

"I am supposed to be at science fair. Now how do I explain to them that I saw you again," Henderson asked.

"Just tell them you ran into me at the science fair. Isn't it a fun place to hang out? Maybe I'll go to one sometime."

Henderson grinned, "I will let you know when the next one comes around."

"Jake," Henderson continued, "I want to make sure that you do not become a stranger again. You know where I live and I expect you to come by more often than every ten years."

Jake looked Henderson straight in eyes and said, "You helped me more that you can ever imagine. Not only with this mission, but also helped me realize my potential again. You can expect a lot more visits from me. You are truly my brother."

They got up from the table and put their cigars down. They reached over and hugged each other. Henderson said, "What are you going to do about Sasha. You still think you have a shot with her."

Jake answered, "She is very special. I will tell you if you are a betting man, then put your money on me. She will be mine."

"Is that right," Henderson asked, "Well, this is your chance to prove yourself."

Henderson pointed over toward the stairs and Jake turned around to look. He saw Sasha at the top of the stairs and she was decked out in a beautiful red dress. She had cleaned herself up and was absolutely gorgeous.

Jake looked at Henderson and said, "You know that I love you, man, but I need to leave you for a little while."

Henderson started to laugh and said, "Go get her and don't become a stranger. I expect you to come and see me in the next few weeks. I need to go so I am heading out. I have got to catch a flight."

They shook hands and Henderson headed out of the palace. Jake looked at the stairs and saw as Sasha came down them. She was absolutely stunning. Jake began to smile and walked over to them so that he could meet her. She made it to the bottom of the stairs and Jake held out his hand. She reached for it and he pulled her close to him.

"Can I have this dance," he asked her in a very sweet voice.

"Yes you may," she answered as he led her out to the dance floor.

* * *

The music started playing and they began to slow dance together. While on the dance floor, Claiborne came over and interrupted their dance to introduce himself to Sasha and told Jake that he was expecting a call from him when he got back to the States. Jake nodded and blew him off and then turned back his attention to Sasha.

"What was that all about," she asked.

"He just wants me to come back to the CIA and work with them," Jake answered.

"Well," Sasha said, "what did you tell him?"

Jake grinned and said, "I told him that I had a date at the Supper Club with a pretty girl and that I would let him know at a later date."

"Have I met this pretty girl that you have a date with," Sasha kidded him as she laughed.

"Very funny, very funny," Jake grinned, "You know you owe me a date."

"Why do you say that I owe you a date," she asked.

"Because if you don't," Jake said, "Then you will be missing out on a sure thing."

"Is that right?" Sasha asked.

"You know I am right. Can you see all the girls at this shindig checking me out? I am a hot commodity." Jake said with a grin.

"I will tell you one thing," Sasha whispered in his ear. "You are a very hot commodity to me."

She pulled back looked him in his eyes and closed her eyes ready to kiss him. He moved in then he pulled back.

"You know," he said, "I have been thinking. We never did catch the sniper on the roof that shot at Henderson. I wonder who he was or where he went. There are other things that have been going through my mind, too."

Sasha responded to him, "Like, what?"

"We never did find out who the mole was. Was H on our side or Higgins side the whole time? I still haven't seen his body. Can we really trust Diotrice? There just so much that hasn't been answered."

Sasha could not believe Jake. She looked at Jake and said, "Relax, enough with all the questions. You just finished not only saving me, but also saving this country. You probably single handily just solved the energy crisis for the United States. You are a hero to so many people. Take a deep breath and slow down. We can leave that for another day."

"I want argue with you," Jake said as he looked into her eyes.

She looked back at him and said, "Since you are the hero, you can now kiss the girl."

Sasha grabbed Jake by the back of the head and they kissed. Jake had done it all; he had saved the day and gotten the girl. He could not ask for anything better.

THE END.

"Higgins and H are dead," the voice said as the plane flew in the air. "Are you sure that we will be safe in this country"

"Yes I am," the other person said. "Higgins assured me to go this country if anything ever happened to him. He told me that Iran was a safe haven for us."

"Thanks again for getting me out of that country. I really thought I was left for dead."

"No need to thank me, I was told by Higgins to go and get you. I just wished you would have taken out one of those Americans when you were on the roof," the other guy said.

"Well, we do not need to point fingers, but if we are, you should have done a better job at telling Qatar where they were. You had Jake and Henderson on GPS."

"Qatar was an idiot. He could not follow my simple directions."

"Fifteen minutes until we land in Iran," the pilot told the two passengers.

"I think I can take them out when I get another chance," the voice said again.

"You should get another chance, but let's just get some much needed rest and regroup. By the way how is your chest?"

Chafari, who had been H's contact in Morocco, asked. Simeon, who had been shot and presumed dead and buried, obviously survived, answered "My chest is fine, I will live."

The phone rang. Simeon answered and then hung up. "We have a surprise for us when we land," he told Chafari. "We have unexpected survivor waiting on us when we land."

The plane landed and Simeon and Chafari got off to their new world. They saw their unexpected surprise waiting on them and knew that they other plan would be put into place. They would go after Jake, Sasha, and Henderson another day.

THE END